DESPISE NOT THY MOTHER

A widow's quest for truth

Judy Ford

Bernie Fazakerley Publications

DESPISE NOT THY MOTHER.

Published by Bernie Fazakerley Publications

This book is a work of fiction. Any references to real people, events, establishments, organisations or locales are intended only to provide a sense of authenticity and are used fictitiously.

All of the characters and events are entirely invented by the author. Any resemblances to persons living or dead are purely coincidental. No part of this book may be used, transmitted, stored or reproduced in any manner whatsoever without the author's written permission.

DEDICATION

To the Salvation Army, in recognition of its work to re-unite families with loved ones who have disappeared.

Hearken unto thy father that begat thee, and despise not thy mother when she is old.
Proverbs 23:22

CONTENTS

ACKNOWLEDGMENTS

I would like to thank the authors of a wide range of internet resources, which have been invaluable for researching the background to this book. These include (among others):
- Wikipedia (https://en.wikipedia.org/)
- Google Maps (https://www.google.co.uk/maps)
- The University of Oxford (http://www.ox.ac.uk/)

The story of Olga da Polga and the cat's tail, which is described by Peter in Chapter 19, features in *The Tales of Olga da Polga* by Michael Bond, first published in 1971 by Puffin books.

This, this is the God we adore: a hymn by Joseph Hart (1712 - 1768) is published in a large number of hymn books, including Hymns & Psalms (Methodist Publishing House 1983) which is the source used by the congregation at Angela Johns' funeral in Chapter 16.

Every effort has been made to trace copyright holders. The publishers will be glad to rectify in future editions any errors or omissions brought to their attention.

1 ACCIDENTAL DEATH

'Stop! You can't get out that way!' Detective Superintendent Paige shouted across the rooftop as he stumbled over the sloping leads in pursuit of his quarry. The words left him breathless after the exertion of climbing the steep stairs to reach the roof. He paused for a few moments, panting and trying not to look down over the low parapet to the street below, where two police cars had just arrived.

The man he was chasing continued to run on, intent on reaching the small door at the far end of the roof, which led to a spiral staircase and potential freedom. Then he stopped abruptly and turned to face Paige. Another man had emerged from that very door and was heading towards him. The fugitive threw himself at Paige in an attempt to push past him to get back down the way he had come. Paige was sixty years old and had a poor head for heights. The other man was desperate. In the tussle that ensued, Paige found himself forced against the parapet; for a moment his body balanced on the edge; then came a sickening realisation that he was tipping over; and then the rush of air as he fell.

Detective Inspector Johns gazed up in dismay as his friend and colleague came hurtling to the ground. Within seconds, there was a dull thump as his body hit the flagstones only a few feet from where Johns stood. For a moment, he was unable to move; then he strode across and knelt down by his friend's head. Paige's body was twisted into a shape that no human form ought to take but he dared not move it into a more natural position lest doing so caused more damage. He noted with relief that Paige was still breathing.

'Richard!' he called softly with his face close to Paige's head.

Paige's eyelids fluttered briefly.

'Just lie still, an ambulance will be here soon,' Johns said, aware of a young police constable's voice behind him as she made the emergency call. This was probably the first time she had seen an officer killed in the line of duty – no, not killed, he told himself severely, just seriously injured – but either way, she would need careful handling.

He focussed his attention once more on the man lying in front of him. Paige opened his eyes and gazed up at him. He seemed to be trying to speak. Johns shook his head and placed his hand gently on Paige's shoulder.

'Try to relax. It won't be long now.'

'No – not long now.' Paige's voice was almost inaudible, but Johns immediately comprehended the sinister interpretation that his friend had put on his ambiguous statement. He hastened to reassure him.

'I mean, the paramedics will soon have you off to A and E.' Johns took off his jacket and slid it carefully under Paige's head. 'Just lie back and wait for them to come.'

Paige gave a weak smile, but continued to speak huskily. Johns leaned close and listened hard to catch the words.

'Tell Bernie – tell Bernie, I'm sorry.'

Bernie! Paige's wife. Johns would have to be the one to break the news. He must get to her right away, as soon as Paige was safely on his way to hospital. She must not hear it on the news or via the bush telegraph. Plenty of people had seen the accident; it would be spreading like wildfire within the university by now. How would she take this? Our Bernie was tough, but …

Johns pulled himself together and forced himself to speak naturally.

'You just hang on in there and you'll be able to tell her yourself – if there's anything to be sorry about, which I doubt.'

'Just tell her.' Paige closed his eyes and Johns checked anxiously that he was still breathing. A siren wailed and an ambulance entered the narrow street. Johns stepped back to allow the paramedics to take over.

As soon as he saw Paige being loaded into the back of the ambulance, he turned to PC Tracy Burton, who was standing next to the car that had brought them both to the scene.

'Get in!' he commanded. 'Drive me to St Luke's College.'

White-faced and with her hand trembling on the door handle, she did as she was told. Johns muttered under his breath as the car crawled through streets congested with pedestrians. It would probably have been quicker to walk, but he needed the car to take Bernie on to the hospital. At last they arrived and Johns jumped out, instructing his young companion to wait in the car for his return.

He ran through the entrance, past the porters' lodge, across the patch of grass in the centre of the first quadrangle, through the stone archway leading to Old Quad and up to the door at the foot of staircase 2. He fumbled with the coded lock, managing to get the combination right on the third attempt. He raced upstairs and stood, panting, outside a door bearing the legend 'Dr Bernadette Fazakerley, Fellow in Applied Mathematics'.

He hammered on the door. A voice from within called to him to 'come in and stop trying to beat the door down!'

'Peter!' Bernie swivelled her computer chair round to face him as he entered. Her short, mousey brown hair stuck up on top of her head where she had ruffled it with her hands as she was in the habit of doing when she was concentrating hard. 'What's up?' Her greyish blue eyes looked at him anxiously through metal-framed glasses as he struggled to get his breath in order to answer her. 'It's Richard, isn't it? What's happened to him?'

Peter Johns nodded, still unable to speak after his recent exertions. Bernie got to her feet and picked up the jacket that was draped over the back of her chair.

'Come on! Let's go. You can tell me all about it on the way. Just take me to him.'

Peter caught hold of her as she made for the door and held her to him.

'There's been an accident,' he managed to get out at last. 'Richard fell off the roof. He's on the way to A and E now. There's a car waiting for us outside.'

Bernie looked up at him and gave him a brief hug.

'Thank you for being the one to tell me. Now let's go.'

They hurried down the stairs, back across the quad and out to the waiting car. Peter ushered Bernie into the back seat and got in beside her.

'Take us to the hospital – as quick as you can,' he ordered.

Saying nothing, Tracy put the car into gear and set off.

For a few moments no one spoke; then Peter made the introductions: 'Bernie, this is PC Tracy Burton; Tracy, meet Dr Bernadette Fazakerley – Superintendent Paige's wife. She's the applied mathematics tutor at St Luke's College.'

'Pleased to meet you.'

They stopped at a junction and Tracy half turned in her seat to look at Bernie. She noticed with surprise that Bernie and Peter were holding hands. That, together with the desperation that she had seen in his face as he headed off to find Bernie to break the bad news, convinced her that there was more to their relationship than simply that of a man and his colleague's wife.

On arrival at the hospital, Peter and Bernie hurried into the emergency department while Tracy locked the car and followed behind. They were greeted by an anxious-faced uniformed officer, whom Peter recognised as Sergeant

Michael Harrison.

'I'm afraid he was dead on arrival, sir.'

Peter heard Bernie give a sharp intake of breath and he instinctively put his arm around her shoulders to steady her. He felt her trembling and, looking down, saw that she had turned very white. He guided her to a seat before answering.

'Mike, this is Superintendent Paige's wife. Now make yourself useful and find her a cup of tea.'

'Yes, sir.' Mike Harrison looked aghast, realising how insensitive he must have appeared. 'Mrs Paige: may I say how sorry I am? How do you like your tea? Can I get you anything else?'

'Strong. Milk. No sugar,' Bernie replied in a lifeless staccato, as if she were answering automatically. Then she looked up and gave Mike a weak smile, aware of his discomfort. 'Thank you. And no – there's nothing else. Except – is there anyone here I can talk to? I mean the people who treated him. I'd like to know …'

Tracy became aware that Bernie spoke with a strong Liverpool accent, which she had not noticed up until then. It seemed to her to be incongruous: not at all what she expected from an Oxford don.

Mike nodded eagerly. 'Just wait there and I'll ask the doctor to come and see you,' he promised.

'Why does every man in my life eventually throw himself off a tall building?' Bernie muttered to Peter, who had sat down next to her.

'They don't,' Peter replied in an undertone, taking her hand in his and leaning towards her to speak into her ear. 'It's just your paranoia: you know that.'

'Yes, I know that,' Bernie admitted, still speaking very low, for Peter's ears alone. 'But it still *feels* odd – as if it must be something to do with me.'

A few minutes later, a harassed-looking woman in her mid-forties approached the little group. They recognised her as a doctor by the stethoscope round her neck.

'Mrs Paige?' she asked, addressing Bernie in a soft

brogue. 'My name is Shelagh O'Connor. I examined your husband when he was brought in.'

Bernie stood up and shook hands, 'Bernie Fazakerley,' she said. 'I kept my maiden name, because it's easier for work.' She swayed slightly and then sat down again abruptly.

At that moment, Mike returned with a cardboard cup containing tea. Peter took it from him and put it into Bernie's hands. She sat holding it in her lap, head bowed, concentrating hard on *not* fainting. Dr O'Connor waited patiently while Bernie took a few sips of the tea. The colour started to return to her face and she looked up expectantly.

'I'm sorry we couldn't do anything for your husband. His injuries were too extensive, but at least it may be some comfort that I doubt if he felt any pain – at least not after the initial impact – because the fall broke his neck.'

'Was that what killed him?'

'Either that, or more probably, bleeding in the brain from his head injury. We can't say for certain yet.'

'Presumably there'll be a post-mortem?'

'Yes, I'm afraid so.'

'No need to apologise,' Bernie seemed to brighten up a little at the thought. 'Richard specialised in murders. He was never happier than when discussing cause of death with the pathology team. I'm sure he'd be delighted to be keeping them in employment!'

'Peter!' They were interrupted by the appearance of a black nurse in a sister's uniform, who spoke with a lilting Jamaican accent. 'Thank goodness you're safe. Someone said they'd seen you here and someone else said that a policeman had been hurt; so I raced over as soon as I came off shift-'

She broke off suddenly, catching sight of Bernie. Her face took on a look of horror as the true situation dawned on her. She looked to Peter for confirmation of her surmise.

'It's Richard,' he told her, getting up. 'He was chasing a suspect and he fell off a roof.'

'He's dead,' Bernie added dully.

'Oh Bernie! I'm so sorry.'

'My wife, Angela,' Peter said to Tracy, who was looking rather bemused. 'She works here.'

Tracy looked at them standing together, telling herself severely that she should not be thinking what an odd couple they made: he with his greying, once-red hair and pale skin; she with her Afro-Caribbean features and black fuzzy hair, braided in tight plaits on her head culminating in a tidy coil at the nape of her neck.

'And now, Bernie,' Angela said, taking charge, 'I think it would be best if we get you home.'

Bernie nodded, getting up and taking the arm that Angela offered to her.

'Yes,' she agreed, 'but first, can I see him – just to convince myself that it's really true?'

'Doctor?' Angela looked enquiringly at Dr O'Connor.

'Yes. No problem. He's through here. We're waiting for a porter to take him to the mortuary.'

She led the way into a small cubicle surrounded by curtains, where they saw a trolley covered by a sheet. Angela went forward and carefully pulled back the sheet just enough to reveal the face of DS Richard Paige. Bernie went over and looked down at the dead body of her husband. His face was remarkably undamaged, but the white hair that fell over his forehead was matted with drying blood and one ear was grazed and swollen. She could see that there was more substantial damage to the back of his skull. She stared for perhaps half a minute then stepped back and nodded at Angela to replace the sheet.

'Thank you,' she said, turning to the doctor. 'Now, I know you're very busy; so we won't take up any more of your time.'

Tracy drove them the short distance from the hospital to Bernie's home in Headington, on the outskirts of Oxford.

'Wait here,' Peter instructed her, 'I'll just see Bernie inside and then I'll be back.'

7

Angela started to protest that it was unnecessary for him to come in with them, but fell silent when she saw by the look on his face that he wanted to talk to them out of the hearing of the young police constable.

As soon as they were inside the house, Peter addressed Bernie.

'Richard spoke to me while we were waiting for the ambulance. He asked me to give you a message.'

'Go on,' Bernie urged, as Peter hesitated.

'He said to tell you he was sorry.'

'Sorry? Sorry for what?'

'I thought *you* might know.'

Bernie shook her head.

'I can't think of anything he would need to be sorry about,' she said thoughtfully. 'Apart from being completely impossible to live with in every way!' she went on, after a short pause, becoming almost her usual animated self for a moment as she slipped into a familiar ritual of complaint about her late husband, which Peter and Angela were well used to and knew was not to be taken seriously.

'I thought perhaps he was sorry to have got himself killed,' Peter suggested. 'I'm pretty sure he realised he wasn't going to survive. I told him that I didn't believe he had anything to apologise to you for, but he was very insistent.'

'Thank you, Peter. I'm glad you were with him. You were always the one he'd choose to go with him into difficult situations.'

'Yes, well,' Peter mumbled, uneasy at being praised, 'I'd better get off now.'

Tracy drove Peter back to his office to complete the paperwork about the incident. On the way, she tried to satisfy her curiosity about the relationship between the two families.

'Your wife seems very friendly with Superintendent Paige's widow,' she suggested.

'Oh yes, they've known each other for years. Bernie often used to babysit for us when the kids were young.'

'So *you* must know her very well too.'

'Yes.'

'She looks a lot younger than Superintendent Paige.'

'Getting on for twenty years,' Peter agreed. 'Paige left it rather late in life to get married. We all thought he was a confirmed bachelor.'

'And do they have any kids?'

'Good God, no! Bernie was nearly thirty-nine when they got married, and Richard was fifty-seven. They'd left it way too late for that.' Peter thought for a moment before continuing, 'Bernie will be quite alone in the world again now.'

'So they'd only been married a couple of years?'

'That's right.'

'And he was due to retire next month. It's really sad, isn't it?'

'Yes. Why couldn't he have waited for the backup to arrive and then sent up a couple of fit young PCs, instead of chasing around on the rooftop at his age?'

'I always admired him for getting involved – not like most supers, who stay in the office and expect other people to do the work.'

'Yes, you're right: he always wanted to be in the thick of it. He wasn't looking forward to retirement; I do know that. He wouldn't have known what to do with himself all day.'

About two hours later Peter let himself into his house in East Oxford. Immediately he was inside the door, his son, Edward, burst from the front room and accosted him.

'Where's Mum?' he demanded. 'And what's all this on the news about a police officer being killed in Oxford?'

'Oh Eddie, I'm sorry!' suddenly Peter felt very weary. 'I thought Mum was going to ring you. It's Richard Paige: he got himself killed falling from a roof. Your mum is over at our Bernie's taking care of her. Come and sit down in the kitchen and I'll tell you about it.'

Over coffee and biscuits, Peter related to his son the events of that afternoon. As soon as he had finished, Eddie jumped up.

'We've got to go over there,' he declared. 'Bernie must be devastated. We ought to be there for her.'

'Hang on a minute,' Peter urged. 'Let's take our time. Your mum's there with her, and you know how close they are. Bernie may not want us wading in in our size twelves.'

He thought quickly, unsure how to deal with his son's evident anxiety. He knew that Eddie was very fond of Bernie: as he should be, Peter mused. Bernie had intervened at a time when Eddie looked as if he might well be about to drop out of education and go seriously off the rails generally. She had encouraged his interest in computers – something that neither of his parents understood much about – and managed to convince him that a computer science degree could be the route for him in to a career that he would enjoy. Now he was in the sixth form and expecting to be heading off to university in less than two years' time.

'Tell you what,' he suggested, 'why don't I ring your mum and ask her if she thinks it would be a good idea for us to go over?'

Some twenty minutes later, they were being welcomed into the large house in Headington that Richard Paige had inherited from his father. Angela led them through into the huge farmhouse-style kitchen where they saw Bernie standing by the gas cooker stirring a pan of custard. Peter suddenly realised how hungry he was, having not eaten since noon.

Bernie invited them to sit down.

'We decided it was best to try to carry on as normal,' she explained. 'And it's better to have something to do.'

She moved the pan off the stove and started to serve sausages, mashed potatoes and peas to her guests.

'I'm really sorry about Richard,' Eddie began tentatively,

determined to show his concern, but unsure how to begin.

'Thanks Eddie.'

'You must have been looking forward to seeing more of him,' Eddie persisted, trying to think of something to say, 'with his retirement coming up.'

'Oh, I don't know about that!' Bernie tried to speak lightly, 'Richard hated the idea of retirement, he would probably have been even more impossible to live with without his work to keep his mind occupied.'

'Will you stay here?' Eddie tried again.

'I should think so.'

'It's a mistake to make that sort of decision too soon,' Angela interjected. 'Bereaved people often do things they regret, like moving house or getting rid of their loved-one's possessions. It's better to wait and see how you feel in a year or two.'

'I just thought you might find this place rather big for just you. I wondered if you might move back to your old house, over near us.'

'Of course I'd like to be nearer to you,' Bernie said diplomatically, feeling sorry for Eddie who was so clearly trying to help. 'But this is my home now, and,' she paused and took a deep breath before continuing, 'actually I won't be on my own here, as it happens.'

She had everyone's full attention now.

'I'm pregnant.'

For a few moments, there was a stunned silence.

'Congratulations!' Eddie said at last. Then, seeing his parents' faces, he went on defensively, 'that *is* what you're supposed to say when someone tells you they're going to have a baby, isn't it?'

'Of course you're right,' Angela was the first to recover. 'Yes. Congratulations, Bernie. It's just such a pity that Richard won't be around to see his child.'

'It makes it all the more incredible that he didn't take more care of himself,' Peter muttered, still feeling unreasonably angry with his friend for taking unnecessary risks. 'Three weeks from retirement and with the prospect of becoming a father and he still insists on chasing around on rooftops instead of directing operations from a place of safety!'

'But he didn't know!' Bernie groaned. 'I hadn't told him. I was waiting for the right moment. He was so depressed about this business of being forced to retire that I didn't want to give him anything else to worry about.' She sighed.

'Of course, in all probability it would have been the very thing to give him something to live for after retirement,' she went on, 'but I just wasn't sure. I had no idea how he'd take it at all. You see, we'd never talked about it – I mean about whether we would have liked to have a family – we just sort of assumed that I was too old. At least, that's what I thought – insofar as I thought at all – and I suppose Richard assumed that too. We never took any precautions. I feel so foolish – we were like silly teenagers who think it'll never happen to them!'

Angela put her hand on Bernie's shoulder.

'Try not to dwell on all that,' she advised. 'You're bound to have mixed feelings about it at the moment, but once the baby's born you'll be glad about it, believe me.'

'And when is the happy event?' Peter asked.

'It's due the first week in May.'

'So that makes you-' Angela did some quick mental arithmetic, '- twelve or thirteen weeks, is that right?'

'Thirteen, yes,' Bernie nodded.

'Now Bernie, you're lucky,' Angie continued, 'getting it all over before the summer gets going. My two were both born in September, and July and August were just overpoweringly hot both years. I was exhausted, I can tell you!'

'I know,' Bernie smiled, 'I remember you complaining. The fuss you made when you were expecting Hannah, I was flabbergasted when I discovered Eddie was on the way – I thought you'd have found what caused it and taken steps to avoid a repeat occurrence!'

'Ah but,' Angela said, leaning close to Bernie, 'you weren't taking into account how good it is afterwards when they hand over that little bundle and you've got your own new little human being to bring up! Trust me: this time next year you'll be up to your ears in dirty nappies, but completely happy!'

Bernie laughed.

'That's better!' Angela smiled, 'And now you've got to promise me something.'

'What's that?'

'You've got to promise you'll let me help with the baby. It's years since I've had a little one around the place, and Hannah doesn't seem in any hurry to make me a grandmother, so I'd be very grateful if you'd let me have a turn with your youngster when he or she arrives!'

'OK. You're on! I'm sure you'll make a much better go of it than I will.'

'Now we've got loads of things we can give you for the baby,' Angela continued. 'High chair, cot, baby bath – all sorts. They're all up in our loft. I'll send Peter up to look them all out for you.'

'That's right,' Peter said, pretending to grumble, 'lay it all on me! I might have known it wouldn't be long before your plans started making work for me to do!'

He sat back in his chair and relaxed for the first time that day. He felt very proud of his wife. Angie really knew how to make people feel better. He had no doubt that she would manage to keep talking babies for hours now, making it impossible for Bernie to dwell on her husband's untimely death or her own failure to make him aware that he was to become a father.

2 DUST TO DUST

The funeral – or perhaps it would have been more accurate to say, the memorial service – was to be held at the church in East Oxford, which Bernie and Angela both attended, and afterwards everyone would be invited into the church hall for refreshments. It being Methodist premises, alcohol was not permitted, which Bernie saw as an advantage, since it would prevent any of Richard's police colleagues from over-indulging as they attempted to drown their sorrows. She and Angela surveyed the trays of sandwiches and sausage rolls and checked that there was an adequate supply of paper plates and serviettes

'I've organised a car to bring Richard's mother over from Henley,' Bernie said, looking down anxiously at her 'to do' list. 'She says that she can't stay for long, but I want us to make a particular effort to make her feel welcome while she *is* here. Richard was always very keen to look after her, so I feel obliged to do as much as I can for her. She lives in sheltered housing over in Henley. Richard used to visit her every week without fail.'

'Just leave it to me,' Angela said calmly. 'If you just introduce me to her at the start then I'll make a point of seeing that she's well looked after, while you circulate among the other guests. People will want to have a chance to talk to you.'

'Thanks. I just don't want to be letting Richard down. Unless there are some long lost cousins that I don't know about, I think she'll be the only one of Richard's family here. He's an only child, his father's been dead since before I knew him, and his two uncles were both killed in the war.'

'And what about your side?'

'No one. I was an "only" too and so was my mam, and my parents both died young. My dad was the youngest of thirteen, so there must be plenty of uncles and aunts and cousins in Liverpool, but I've lost contact with most of them over the years, and none of them knew Richard, so I'd be amazed if any of them came down. I dropped a line to my Aunty Dot and she sent a card, but said she couldn't travel so far. I don't blame her: she must be in her eighties.'

She looked around the laden tables and smiled. 'Maybe we've over-catered!'

'Don't you believe it! Richard was killed on duty so you'll get a good turnout from the police – they always love a good funeral anyhow – and I know that there are lots of people from church who are planning to come: and not just the ones who've volunteered to serve the drinks and do the washing up afterwards either. It'll be standing room only, you'll see.'

'You don't think,' Bernie asked anxiously, 'that they'll feel they've been short-changed when they find out there's no coffin or anything? There were a few of them offered to carry it and I turned them down without explaining.'

She had taken the unconventional step of having the burial first and the funeral service afterwards and she was now wondering whether it had been the right decision. She had wanted to see Richard off quietly in the company only of her closest friends. She had invited Richard's mother but, much to Bernie's relief, she had declined to come. Peter and Angie had come with her to the short committal service at Headington Cemetery that morning and then they had all gone back to the Johns family home to eat lunch and to prepare for the public ordeal ahead.

'I'm sure everyone will understand completely,' Angie assured her. 'Apart from anything else, it's much more practical the way you've done it. If the traffic was bad, it could have taken us nearly an hour to do the round trip to the cemetery, between the end of the service and meeting people over refreshments. This way, anyone who wants to can talk to you without having to hang about for hours.'

In the event, it was not quite 'standing room only' but the church was full and it was even necessary to open the balcony. Bernie reflected, as she watched people arriving, that it was a pity that there were always so many fewer attending the Sunday morning services. Indeed, it looked as if the whole Sunday morning congregation was here today. Who would have thought that they would have turned out in such numbers, considering that Richard had never gone to church? She was surprised to see how many staff from her college and university department had come too: almost enough to balance the large cluster of blue police uniforms, which extended from the back to about halfway down the church on the left-hand side of the central aisle. Peter's and Angela's daughter, Hannah, had made the journey back from her nursing studies in Leeds to be there and Eddie had taken the afternoon off school. Richard must have been considerably more popular than Bernie had imagined!

Richard's mother, Eleanor, was a tall, angular woman with permed white hair and thick glasses, which obscured her eyes. She used a walking frame and her poor sight made her peer round in a way that was rather off-putting until you got used to it. Angela assumed that she must be in her eighties but, from her appearance, she could easily have been older: her face looked like crumpled parchment, the lines and creases making it difficult to discern its underlying shape. It was so difficult to estimate people's age these days.

Seventy used to be old, but now some people managed to look merely middle-aged well into their eighties. Bernie introduced them.

'Eleanor, this is Angela Johns – Peter's wife – I think Richard will have mentioned her to you. She's a good friend of mine. And Angie, meet Richard's mother, Eleanor.'

Ignoring Eleanor's undisguised surprise at discovering that she was not the hired help, Angela showed Eleanor courteously to a seat and moved a small table to within her easy reach. Whatever Richard may have told his mother about his colleague's wife, he clearly had not seen fit to mention her racial origins.

'Can I get you a cup of tea or coffee?' she enquired attentively, 'and something to eat?'

'Thank you. Black coffee, please, but nothing to eat.'

Angela hurried off on her mission, smiling to herself at the way that Richard's mother appeared so much more at ease now that this unexpected black woman had slipped into a more familiar subservient role. She found a tray and loaded it with the coffee for Eleanor, a cup of tea for herself, a basin of sugar, two paper plates, another plate containing a selection of eatables and some plastic cutlery.

'Here's your coffee – and sugar if you'd like it – and I brought some food in case you get peckish later.'

She sat down and soon her kind personality and nursing experience broke through Eleanor's reserve and they were chatting like old friends, although Angela had to bite her tongue on several occasions when Eleanor became overtly critical of her daughter-in-law.

'Has Bernadette told you that she's expecting?'

'Yes. It's such a pity that Richard won't be around to see the baby.'

'I don't mind telling you that it came as a complete surprise to me. Fancy even contemplating it at her age! And Richard would have been sixty next week.'

'I should think you must be very excited at the thought of being a grandmother,' Angela suggested, trying to strike a more optimistic note.

'Oh, I don't imagine *I'll* see much of the child. You can't expect Bernadette to want to bother with me now that she hasn't got Richard to bring her over to visit.'

'I'm sure you're wrong about that. Bernie's very keen that the baby knows as much as possible about its father. I'm sure she'll want you to be involved. But, of course,' she went on, seeing by Eleanor's sceptical expression that she was not convinced, 'Richard's death must have been a terrible blow to you. I gather you were very close.'

'I don't know why you should think that.' For no reason that Angela could see, Eleanor appeared to have taken offence. 'He was very *dutiful*, but I wouldn't say we were close. And of course, now I see why Bernadette married him: she was obviously desperate to find someone who was willing to father a child with her before it was too late.'

'Now, Mrs Paige, I know that's not true,' Angela chided gently. 'They were in love. I can vouch for that.'

'With a man old enough to be her father?' Eleanor repeated the cliché in a tone of deep contempt. 'I very much doubt that.'

'Ah, but your Richard was a very special man,' Angela reasoned, trying to placate the older woman. 'And, as you've said yourself, Bernie was no spring chicken herself. At their age, twenty years' difference is nothing.'

'At *her* age,' Eleanor snorted, 'she should know better than to get herself pregnant. The child will probably be deformed and then where will she be?'

'Please, Mrs Paige,' Angela protested, keeping her temper with some difficulty and recalling a conversation on the same subject that she had had with Bernie only the day before. 'While the incidence rate of Downs syndrome and some other congenital abnormalities does increase with maternal age, the vast majority of babies born to women in their forties are perfectly normal. I do hope you haven't suggested to Bernie that she's at risk.'

'I haven't, as it happens, but I've a good mind to warn

her. She ought to be aware of what she may be letting herself in for.'

'But she *is*,' Angela insisted, 'and encouraging her to worry about it won't help anyone. Now, let's talk about something else,' she continued, searching her mind for a safe topic of conversation, 'tell me about your flat in Henley. Whereabouts is it?'

Meanwhile, at the other side of the hall, Peter had been persuaded by one of Richard's old work colleagues to make him known to Bernie.

'Bernie, let me introduce Chief Inspector Jonah Porter. He used to work with me and Richard.'

Bernie looked the man up and down. He was dressed in a smart dark-grey suit, which somehow seemed to fit him better than was usual in plain-clothes policemen. His brown hair was greying at the temples and his blue eyes were looking intently at her.

'Pleased to meet you.' She said politely. 'It's amazing how many of Richard's colleagues have come to see him off. I had no idea he was so popular.'

'I owe him a lot. He took me on when I first joined the CID. He taught me all I know.'

'I doubt that,' Bernie gave a wry smile. 'Aren't you the officer who was responsible for clearing up that big fraud case: the one that was in the newspapers last week? Richard would never have been any good with something like that – his command of even simple arithmetic was absolutely dire. A bent banker would easily have been able to run rings around him. I gather it was quite a coup to get a conviction. You will obviously go far.'

'Oh, I don't know about that,' Porter gave the self-deprecating laugh that Peter had disliked so much when they were working together. 'It wasn't all down to me. Anyway, I didn't come here to talk about my achievements. I wanted to tell you how sorry I was to hear about Richard's death and to say how much I owe to him.'

'And to see what sort of woman would marry him after all these years?' Bernie suggested astutely.

'Since you mention it – I confess I *was* curious to meet you. Richard had been such a very confirmed bachelor – very much married to the job – and we were all rather taken aback to hear that he'd taken the plunge into matrimony at what you have to admit was a fairly advanced age. I mean – it would have to be someone rather special.'

'Or maybe he was just desperate to ensure that he would be cared for in his declining years.'

'I'm quite sure that was not even a part of his considerations.'

'You're probably right. He was generally quite a good judge of character, and if that had been his aim, I'm sure that he could have found someone more suited to the role. I make no pretence of having a caring or sympathetic nature. So, if you're wondering why he married me, join the club – *I* certainly wouldn't have been foolish enough to sign up to living with me on a permanent basis!'

Peter smiled to himself, seeing that even the self-assured Porter was uncertain how to follow this.

'Someone told me you were a don,' Porter said at last, obviously struggling to keep the conversation going.

'That's right. I'm the Applied Mathematics tutor at St Luke's College.'

'It must be the busiest time of the year for you, with all the new students starting. I hope you're allowed some time off, under the circumstances.'

'Well done!' Bernie looked Porter in the eyes and smiled up at him. 'You didn't say it. I'm impressed.'

'Say what?'

'Usually at this point in the conversation, people give a little laugh and say, "I was never any good at Maths at school." And then they start looking for an opportunity to get away and talk to someone more interesting.'

'Ah! But *I* was always *very good* at Maths at school.'

'And at everything else, I'm sure,' put in Peter, with just

the slightest touch of resentment in his voice, 'and doesn't he know it!'

'I must say,' Porter went on, ignoring Peter's interjection, 'you aren't my idea of a typical Oxford don.'

'You mean,' grinned Bernie, 'I don't sound as if I went to Roedean or Cheltenham Ladies College, and you're wondering how I ever came to be allowed into the Oxbridge establishment. Richard always used to say-' Bernie stopped speaking and looked distractedly over Porter's shoulder towards the door.

'Look, I'm sorry,' she went on, 'Richard's mother is just leaving. I must see her off. Thank you for coming. Maybe we can speak again later.'

'Richard always used to say,' continued Peter, who had heard this story many times before, 'that when she was interviewed for her fellowship, the panel asked at the end, "and now, do you have any questions for us?" and she said,' he paused before resuming in an exaggerated Liverpool accent, '"Are youse giving me this job or what?" and none of them had the courage to say "no"!'

Porter turned back from watching Bernie's journey across the room. 'How is she, d'you think?' he asked Peter. 'No tears. Putting a brave face on it d'you reckon?'

'Our Bernie doesn't show her emotions, but don't think for a moment she doesn't feel Richard's death very much.' Peter spoke vehemently, resenting the implied suggestion that his friend's wife could have been anything other than totally loyal to her husband. 'She and Angela are very close – I think that's what's keeping her going at the moment, and of course she's been keeping busy with the funeral and everything.'

'Angela?' Porter queried not recognising the name.

'My wife.'

'Of course! I remember now. And what about the children – you had two, didn't you – a boy and a girl?'

'Hannah's at university studying to be a nurse and Edward's in lower sixth. We were afraid that he was going off the rails, but Bernie took an interest in him and persuaded him that he could indulge in his obsession with computers by doing a computer science degree. He finally knuckled down and actually did quite well in his GCSEs after all, which is a great relief to us all. I must say I don't envy Bernie having it all still to come – and on her own too.'

'What do you mean? She and Richard don't have any kids, do they?'

'Not yet. But … look, I don't think I ought to be telling you this.' Peter lowered his voice. 'Yes, Bernie's expecting – and racked with guilt that she didn't tell Richard before he died. She didn't know how he would take it. I don't think either of them had thought about the possibility, what with her just turned forty-one and him, well...'

'Getting on for sixty, I suppose.' Porter looked thoughtful. Then he took Peter's arm and moved closer. 'Let me know when the baby's born – I'd like to … send a card or something.'

Peter had mixed feelings at the idea that Porter wanted to get involved in some way in Bernie's life. He liked the man well enough and they had worked together quite harmoniously in the past, but the younger man had always tended to outshine him and had overtaken him in the race for promotion. Peter worked methodically and carefully, while Porter was able to make intuitive leaps that often paid off and won him acclaim from his superiors. Peter could not pretend that he had been particularly sorry when Porter had been transferred to another division.

'Yes, of course I will,' he promised.

Why did he feel resentment that Porter wanted to keep in touch with Bernie? He supposed that it must be because of the way they seemed to have hit it off in the brief conversation that had taken place. Their minds were somehow on the same wavelength. But then again, why should he care? It was not as if Bernie were *his* wife – she was not even as much his friend as Angie's. Porter was not in any way threatening to displace him.

When Bernie returned to the hall after seeing Eleanor safely into her taxi, she was met by an unfamiliar woman who looked about the same age as her late husband.

'Excuse me,' the woman said diffidently, 'I wonder if you'd mind coming over and having a word with my father? He knew your husband as a boy and he'd really like to pay his respects.'

'Of course. I'd be delighted.'

'I'm Brenda Jones,' the woman said as she led the way to where an elderly man was seated, very upright with sharp blue eyes which darted round the room taking it all in. 'Brenda Walker-that-was,' she went on, 'We lived near the Paiges and my dad was the local bobby.'

As they approached, the man rose to his feet and held out his hand towards Bernie.

'I'm Ernest Walker,' he said, 'I knew young Richard when he was knee high to a grasshopper!'

'I'm very pleased to meet you,' Bernie said earnestly. 'It's very good of you to come. I never expected so many people to turn out to see Richard off.'

'He was well liked in the force,' Ernest said, 'I used to be a policeman myself you know, and I still have contacts who keep me informed. Sit down, if you can spare a few minutes to talk to an old codger, and tell me about yourself. I'd like to know all about the young lady who managed to sweep Richard off his feet and into matrimony!'

Bernie and Brenda sat down on either side of him.

'Mind you,' Ernest went on, 'there was a time when we thought he'd be escorting Brenda here down the aisle!' He winked at his daughter and gave a little laugh. Brenda smiled.

'Give over Dad! We were only kids then.'

'Anyway,' her father went on, 'it came to nothing and she married a good fella, so no harm done. And now I've got five grandchildren and three great grandchildren.'

'Not all through me,' Brenda added hastily. 'My brother

George has two kids.'

'Richard went to the same school as Brenda and George. That is, until Richard went on to the grammar school. Brenda went to the girls' grammar and George failed the eleven plus and went to the secondary modern; but Richard still used to come round to see Brenda, and then they started going out together.'

'Da-ad!' Brenda protested.

'Alright, alright, I'll say no more. I doubt that Mrs Paige is interested in hearing about all Richard's old flames anyhow.'

'On the contrary,' Bernie said, catching his eye and exchanging a conspiratorial look, 'there's nothing that would interest me more.' She was starting to enjoy Ernest's banter, but seeing that Brenda was genuinely uncomfortable, she went on, 'however, this isn't perhaps the time and place.'

'No, maybe not,' Ernest conceded, 'so now, tell me young lady, who are you? What do you do? And how did you manage to persuade Richard to give up his independence and get hitched?'

'My name's Bernadette Fazakerley, but everyone calls me Bernie; I teach mathematics at the university and I have no idea what got into Richard's head to make him decide to marry me! But I'm really not very interesting, I'd far rather you told me about what Richard was like when he was a boy. I've tried asking his mother, but she never seems to want to talk about it.'

'Hmmph!' Ernest snorted. 'I'm not surprised, the way she behaved. I hope she *is* ashamed to talk about it.'

'Why? What did she do?'

'She just disappeared, that's what. Poor Richard must have been all of eight years old. Not a word to him, not even a note; he just came home from school one afternoon and she was gone. That's how we first met him: he came into the station one day and said he wanted to report a missing person. Of course, there was nothing I could do. She was a grown woman and she'd obviously gone off of her own volition. But it was a cruel thing to do to a little boy.'

'I knew his parents had split up, but I hadn't realised it was so dramatic.'

'So, how come you've been speaking to her?' Ernest asked. 'The last I heard, nobody knew where she was.'

'She came back when Richard's father died. I don't know the details, but apparently she turned up at his funeral.'

'And Richard welcomed her back with open arms, I suppose?'

'As far as I can tell.'

'If this was a film,' Brenda observed, 'it would turn out that she wasn't his mother at all. Did he do any checks to make sure she wasn't an imposter out to steal his inheritance?'

'I don't know. By the time I came on the scene, she was already settled in sheltered accommodation in Henley, with Richard visiting every Saturday. However, you don't need to worry about the inheritance. Richard's father left everything to him – including the family home, which *he'd* inherited from *his* father – and Richard's will leaves everything to me. I was surprised that he hadn't left his mother anything and I was thinking that I ought to give her something. Now you've put me in a quandary in case he deliberately wanted to exclude her.'

'Does she need the money?' Ernest asked sharply.

'Not as far as I can tell. She appears to be quite comfortably off.'

'Then, if Richard didn't see fit to leave her anything, I don't see why you should feel any obligation towards her.'

'But Richard was always so concerned to do the right thing by her,' Bernie argued. 'He never missed his weekly visit – not even once. Even if he was working at the weekend, he always made a point of going over one evening in the week instead.'

'Don't let that influence you,' Ernest said forcefully, 'He was just afraid that, if he didn't do everything she wanted, she'd run off again and he'd lose her. That's what he was like when he was a boy. He was convinced that it must have been because he was naughty that she ran away.' He shook his head angrily. 'That woman has a lot to answer for.'

'But it's all a long time ago,' Brenda said, trying to pour oil on troubled waters. 'There's no point bringing all that up again now.'

'I know, I know,' Ernest muttered testily, 'but I'm just saying that Bernie here shouldn't feel under any obligation towards her, that's all.'

'Now Bernie, we've come to take you home.'

All of a sudden, Bernie found herself surrounded by the Johns family, dressed in their outdoor clothes, ready to depart. The Home Office pathologist with whom she had been talking the moment before tactfully noticed someone he wanted to speak to on the other side of the room and wandered off. Bernie saw that Peter was carrying her coat, which he proceeded to hold out ready for her to put on.

'Come along,' Angela continued. 'You look all-in. It's high time you got a proper rest.'

'I can't come yet,' Bernie protested, 'I'm the host. I can't be the first to leave.'

'Number one,' Peter put in, 'you won't be the first, because Richard's mother has already gone – as you well know.'

'And number two,' added Hannah, 'you've got to look after yourself in your condition.'

'Shhh Hannah!' hissed Eddie angrily, digging her in the ribs. 'Don't broadcast it. Bernie probably doesn't want the world and his wife knowing yet.'

'Never mind, you two,' Angela intervened, 'The point is, Bernie, nobody is going to think badly of you for needing some rest after all you've been through. There's an army of volunteers in the kitchen, all eager to do the dishes and clear everything up, and as soon as you go, everyone else will start looking at their watches and realising how late it's become.

Now – no more arguments!'

'All right, all right, I'll come quietly,' Bernie grumbled, putting on the proffered coat and following Peter past the milling clusters of guests to the door.

Half an hour later, they arrived at the home that Bernie had shared with Richard for the two years of their married life. Peter looked back and saw that she had fallen asleep on the back seat. He got out and, with Angela's help, managed to lift her out of the car without waking her.

Angela had a key to the house and she led the way upstairs to the bedroom. Peter laid Bernie gently down on the double bed. The wardrobe door was open and he noticed the two suits that Richard used to wear for work still hanging there. His shoes were still under the bed. His battered brief case lay on the floor in a corner of the room. A feeling of inexpressible sadness came over Peter: he was going to miss his friend, but how much worse it must be for Richard's wife.

Bernie stirred and opened her eyes. It took her a moment or two to work out where she was, but then she immediately sat up and swung her legs over the edge of the bed. Angela put her hand on Bernie's shoulder.

'Now don't you be in such a hurry to go rushing about again. You've had a hard day. Time for some rest. If I were you I'd go to bed for a couple of hours.'

'But it's only half past four in the afternoon,' Bernie protested.

'So, after a couple of hours' sleep you'll still have the whole evening ahead of you,' reasoned Angela. 'Now, I'm not going to listen to any more arguments.'

She ushered Peter out of the room, instructing him to fetch a drink of hot chocolate, and started to help Bernie to undress. She found two pairs of pyjamas under the pillows.

'I'll put Richard's pyjamas to be washed,' she said, handing the other pair to Bernie. 'Then you can put them away with the rest of his things until you're ready to start thinking about what to do with them.'

'Thanks. I'd forgotten they were there. I've been sleeping on my side of the bed as usual and I just didn't notice.'

Bernie climbed into bed.

'I still feel ridiculous going to bed at this time of day!'

'Now just remember: you owe it to Richard to take care of yourself – for his baby's sake as well as anything else.'

'I know,' Bernie sighed, 'I'll have to try to start acting responsibly now. It won't come easy, you know, after forty years of recklessness.'

There was a knock at the door and Peter entered with the hot chocolate.

Angela plumped up the pillows and arranged them expertly behind Bernie's back, deliberately taking them from both sides of the bed and propping Bernie in a sitting position in the middle. She handed her the chocolate.

'Drink this and then get some sleep.' She ordered.

'Very good, nurse,' Bernie said meekly, taking the mug in both hands. 'I had an idea this afternoon, while I was talking to an old gentleman who knew Richard when he was a little boy. Did you meet him? His name was Ernest Walker.'

'Old Sergeant Walker!' exclaimed Peter. 'Was he there? I didn't notice him or I'd have said *hello*. He retired not long after I joined the force, but he was a real character and he often used to pop in to have his lunch in the canteen and catch up with the gossip, even after he'd left.'

'Anyway,' Bernie went on, 'I'd been thinking about what it would be like for the baby, never knowing its father, and I decided that I'd make a scrapbook of memories about him: photos and mementos of occasions in his life and maybe ask people who knew him to write about what they remember about him.'

'I think that's a splendid idea,' Angela said enthusiastically. 'We could get you started with some pictures from our wedding: he was Peter's best man.'

'And I'll have a word with Eileen, the Chief Super's

secretary,' Peter joined in. 'She's been around for donkey's years and she's got a file of pictures of events – the staff Christmas party, awards ceremonies, that sort of thing – going back to the year dot. Richard's bound to be in some of those.'

'But now,' Angela said sternly, taking the empty mug from Bernie and rearranging the pillows to put her into a lying position, 'we're going to leave to you get some sleep.'

3 RELUCTANT WITNESS

'This is the clock that they were planning to give to Richard to mark his retirement.'

It was some four weeks later and Bernie was paying her regular Saturday afternoon visit to Eleanor in her flat in Henley. She held up a carriage clock of the sort traditionally given to employees on their retirement. It was engraved with the words, 'Detective Superintendent Richard Paige 1956 – 1999.'

'He was in the police for forty-three years,' Bernie observed. 'He started out in the cadets as soon as he was old enough to apply. I don't think he ever wanted to do anything else.'

Eleanor looked unimpressed, so Bernie turned the clock round to show her the warm farewell message engraved on the back.

'The chief super was very apologetic about the wording,' she said, pointing to the wishes from all his friends in the police service for *a long and happy retirement*. 'They'd already arranged for it to be done, before Richard had his accident and nobody thought to contact the engraver until it was too late.'

'I can't think why they bothered at all,' Eleanor said

scathingly, not troubling to look at the inscription. 'It's ridiculous to have a retirement party for someone who's already dead.'

Bernie decided to give her the benefit of the doubt and assume that Eleanor's poor eyesight meant that she could not read the small writing and did not want Bernie to see her struggling. She tried to coax her into taking more interest in her son's send-off.

'You can't blame them for not wanting to cancel the party,' she reasoned. 'They'd made all the arrangements and not everyone could make it to the funeral. Besides, they wanted something special to mark all those years he'd spent with them. You should have come. It would have made you proud to hear all the nice things everyone said about him.'

****

Chief Superintendent Adrian Fuller finished his speech, in which he had summarised Richard's forty-three years in the police service and expressed warm feelings towards him and condolences to his widow, and called upon the Deputy Chief Constable to present the gift, which had been purchased to mark his retirement and would now become a memorial to his passing. Bernie watched with apprehension from where she was sitting with Peter Johns and Tracy Burton. Richard had considered Rodney Meredith, the Deputy Chief Constable, to be a pompous social climber with more interest in generating good publicity than in supporting his officers. She hoped that he was not going to make a long speech. She wished that Angela was there, but this was very much an internal police affair and Bernie was the only one present who was not a serving or former police officer.

To her relief, Meredith restricted himself to a sentence or two endorsing Fuller's eulogy and then invited Bernie to come up to receive the gift. As she walked self-consciously up to the dais at the front of the room she was aware that the waistband of the black trouser suit, which she always wore for formal occasions, felt tight and she told herself severely that it was only in her imagination that everyone in the room was staring at her stomach. She forced herself to smile as she took the clock from Meredith's hands and turned to face the crowded room.

'Well!' she said, 'what can I say? Apart from *thank you all very much*. I'm pleased to see that you allowed your imagination full rein in choosing a novel gift to mark the end of Richard's career!'

She paused to allow a titter of laughter to go round the room.

'And a particular *thank you* to you, Mr Fuller, for so many kind words about Richard. Standing before you all today, I feel that I ought also to make an apology to you all. Over the last few weeks, so many people have told me how surprised they were when Richard got married, because up until then he had always been married to his job, that I feel that I'm the scarlet woman who has seduced him away from his first love!'

More laughter, a little uncertain this time.

'Richard never wanted to do anything other than to be a detective, and retirement was not something that he looked forward to with any relish. In fact, although I am going to miss him terribly, I can't help thinking that in many ways this is how he would have wanted to go: chasing a villain in order to bring him to justice. So now I would like to thank you all again – not just for this splendid clock, but also for giving him the opportunity to do the job that he loved, and for the way in which you have been a family to Richard over many years when he didn't have any other. Thank you.'

There was silence only for a moment before the applause started, led by Peter, who had been primed with the punch line of Bernie's speech and was under orders to make sure that there was no awkward pause at the end. Bernie stepped forward intending to return to her place, but Fuller called her back.

'Just one moment, Dr Fazakerley: there's just one thing more. My secretary, Eileen,' he went on, turning to address the assembly, 'has been neglecting her duties for the last three weeks, because she's been too busy with some project of her own! I'm pleased to say that she assures me that this is now over and that I will soon be able to rely on her once more to type my memos and manage my diary. She has asked to be allowed to show us the fruits of her labours here today. So now I call on Eileen to come up here.'

Bernie watched as a dumpy woman in her sixties with half-moon glasses and short auburn hair made her way to the front, carrying a large cardboard carrier bag. She walked confidently across the dais and addressed Bernie in clear tones that easily reached the back of the room.

'A little bird tells me,' Eileen said, casting a conspiratorial look in Bernie's direction, 'that the scarlet woman's seduction is due to bear fruit in a few months' time.'

Bernie felt her face colouring and glanced rapidly round the room to gauge the effect of this pronouncement on those present. Seeing that it produced no raised eyebrows or looks of puzzlement, she concluded that her pregnancy was by now common knowledge; except, perhaps, to Ernest Walker, whom she spotted for the first time, sitting near the back of the room. She had not sworn Peter to secrecy, but neither had she expected him to disseminate the news quite so far and so fast.

'The little bird also told me,' Eileen went on, looking directly at Peter, who blushed in his turn, 'that you've come up with a wonderful idea for letting the baby know about his or her father so that he or she will be proud of him. And we all wanted to help.'

She put down the carrier bag and took out of it a large, red, loose-leaf folder. On the front in gold lettering were the words *Detective Superintendent Richard Paige 1939 – 1999*. She opened it and beckoned Bernie to look inside it.

'We thought this would give you something to start you off. I managed to track down photos of Richard at all the Christmas parties from nineteen seventy-four onwards,' she said proudly, 'and there's the nineteen eighty-two team-building course in Snowdonia, and I even managed to find the "class of fifty-six" police cadet group photo! And I asked everyone who knew Richard to write a page or two about something that they remembered about him.'

She turned the pages and Bernie saw dozens of handwritten sheets, each signed by one of her husband's colleagues. She broke into a smile and gave Eileen a hug.

'Thank you so much!' she said, turning to face the room. 'Thank you all!'

****

Bernie held out the folder towards Eleanor.

'I brought it to show you. I thought you might like to borrow it – or I can photocopy the pages and let you have a copy to keep.'

Eleanor made no attempt to take it and Bernie eventually returned it to her own lap. She could not understand why Eleanor showed so little interest in her own son. Then it occurred to her that perhaps Eleanor's eyesight was the problem. Maybe she could not see well enough to appreciate the pictures or read the stories.

'Would you like me to read some of the things that people have written?' she asked.

'No thank you. I can't see the point in harping back to the past.'

'It's just that I don't want Richard's child growing up knowing nothing about its father.'

'I don't see why! Richard didn't meet his father until he was nearly six. It didn't do him any harm.'

I'm not so sure about that, Bernie thought, but only said, 'why was that then?'

'Richard was born in November 1939. His father received his call-up papers the April before and they sent him out to France in the September. He got captured at Dunkirk and spent the next five years in POW camps.'

'That must have made it difficult for you.' *But all the more surprising that a few years later you ran off and left the boy that you'd brought up single-handed for so long*, she added to herself.

Eleanor did not answer, so she went on.

'Tell me about what Richard was like when he was little. I mean during those first five years while he was with you. You must have been very close then.'

'I can't remember. What does it matter?'

'Like I said, I want to be able to tell Richard's child as much as I can about-'

'Richard's child, Richard's child,' interrupted Eleanor grumpily, 'you think very highly of yourself for doing that, don't you?'

'What do you mean?'

'Well that's why you married him, isn't it? Your last chance of motherhood.'

'No, it wasn't, actually,' Bernie retorted, finally giving way to annoyance. 'If you must know, it wasn't planned at all. I was as surprised as anyone.'

'Really? And you with your Oxbridge education?' Eleanor taunted her. 'And you're no better at preventing yourself from getting in the club than we were sixty-odd years ago!'

'We were married for two years before it happened,' Bernie pointed out.

'Yes – I'll give you that,' Eleanor conceded, 'but it doesn't make it any less irresponsible to be bringing a child into the world at your age. Now with us it was different,' she went on, unexpectedly volunteering some information about herself for the first time. 'We were young, and there was a war starting, and we thought we had to do everything in a great hurry before it was too late. Edward's father was a bank manager and my father was his head clerk, so of course they insisted on him marrying the girl that he'd "got into trouble" and I was assumed to be grateful to him for doing it. We ought never to have got married but, at the time, it seemed the only thing to do.'

'Hang on a minute: are you telling me that Richard was conceived out of wedlock?' Bernie asked, taken aback by this sudden revelation.

'What a quaint way you do have of putting it! I thought that young people these days thought nothing of that sort of goings on.' For the first time since she had known her, Bernie started to wonder whether Eleanor might not be quite as humourless as she usually appeared.

'As you are constantly at pains to remind me,' she answered, trying to speak in a way that might encourage this lighter side of her mother-in-law's nature, 'I am *not* a young person. Moreover, I had a very strict upbringing, including a convent school education. You can hardly blame me for being surprised to discover that someone whom I hold in such high esteem-'

'All right, all right: you don't need to lay it on so thick,' Eleanor interrupted. She spoke grumpily, but with a twinkle in her eye. 'We both know that you only put up with me for Richard's sake.'

'And is that such a bad thing?'

'No. I suppose not – just so long as you don't expect gratitude.'

'So there you are,' Bernie said to Angela the following day as they sorted and packed Richard's clothes into bags, ready to take to the Oxfam shop. 'I'm still no further forward in finding out why she left Richard and his dad; and I still don't understand why she won't talk about him. I *want* to talk about Richard with people who knew him. It's one of the things that keep him alive for me.'

'Has it occurred to you,' Angela suggested gently, 'that it could be that it's too soon for Eleanor to talk about Richard? People grieve differently. Maybe she needs time before she'll want to talk.'

'I suppose you may be right.' Bernie thought for a few moments. 'Yes, perhaps I ought to lay off badgering her for a while. After all, there isn't really any tearing hurry. The baby isn't even born yet and it'll be years before it starts asking questions about its dad.'

Suddenly she found herself fighting back tears, as she

thought how different her child's early years would be from her own upbringing. She remembered nostalgically sitting astride her father's shoulders to see over the crowds on the football terraces, clutching his hand as she stepped gingerly across on to the ferry for a trip to New Brighton, standing with him on the Pier Head watching the vehicles winding their way off the new Isle of Man car ferry, and squealing with delight as he pushed her higher and higher on the swing in the park.

What would Richard have been like as a father? If he had had children while he was a serving police officer then no doubt they would have complained, as Hannah and Eddie had done, that he was never around. In retirement, would he have devoted himself to his family with the same single-mindedness that he had applied to his vocation?

'Peter said that you were talking to Ernest Walker again at the party.' Angela's voice broke into Bernie's meditation. 'Why don't you ask him to tell you about Richard's early life?'

'Mmm. I thought I probably would. He was very taken with the idea of making a book for the baby. And I think he's probably a bit lonely and would like a chance to talk about the old days.'

'There you are, then. Look him up.'

As things turned out, it was some time before Bernie was able to carry out this plan. She returned to work after the funeral to find a backlog of jobs waiting to be done. She had an undergraduate lecture course to deliver and a full quota of weekly tutorials, and one of her postgraduate students was suffering a crisis of confidence and threatening to give up. The Christmas vacation brought little relief because work commitments gave way to church activities. Christmas itself, she spent, as had been her custom for many years until her marriage, with friends in Newcastle-upon-Tyne. Then, once back in Oxford for the Hilary Term, she had to organise alternative tutorial arrangements for her students during her maternity leave, in addition to her usual term-time duties. So meeting with Ernest Walker had to be put off until the Easter vacation provided a respite from the many other more pressing calls on her time.

Meanwhile she pressed ahead gradually with the task of going through Richard's possessions. It took a long time, because he had lived in this house since he was a child and it became clear that a lot of his father's and grandparent's things had been left undisturbed during the years since they had died, leaving the house to Richard. A bureau in the bedroom that Bernie understood to have been occupied by Richard's father, yielded a pile of old photograph albums containing black and white pictures, each neatly labelled on the back in faint pencil. It looked as if someone in the family must have been interested in photography.

Bernie took them downstairs and carefully cleaned off the dust. She opened them and started leafing through the pages, hoping to find pictures for her scrapbook. She was unlucky. For a long time she only found one picture featuring Richard. It portrayed a baby in a long christening robe in the arms of a clergyman. He was standing on the steps of a church next to a tall man, whom Bernie was able to identify (having seen him in other photographs) as Richard's paternal grandfather. It was clear that there was a woman standing on the other side of the clergyman, because Bernie could see parts of her sleeve and skirt, but part of the picture had been cut off so that the woman was no longer visible.

Bernie turned back to earlier pages. There were gaps where photographs had been removed. With a shock, she realised that the first photographs in the album were Richard's parents' wedding photographs, but all of those featuring the bride were missing. Edward Paige and his best man stood nervously outside the church before the ceremony. There were pictures of various relatives arriving; the groom and best man were each portrayed giving their speeches; but the only glimpse of Eleanor was her hand on the knife as she and Edward cut the cake. Someone had gone through systematically erasing Eleanor from the family album!

4 SUDDEN DISAPPEARANCE

Bernie was grateful that the Oxford terms remained the same regardless of the date of Easter. This meant that, despite Easter being late that year, the undergraduates departed before the middle of March so that, although she would not officially begin her maternity leave until several weeks later, she could work almost exclusively at home from that point onwards. Peter was inclined to be sceptical about the concept of working at home, holding that, as far as he could see, academics did precious little work at any time, wherever they might be.

Be that as it may, Bernie now had the time to carry out her plan of visiting Ernest Walker to pick his brains about her husband's early life. He was delighted with the idea and so, one drizzly afternoon in late March, she set off for the house in North Oxford where he lived with his daughter and son-in-law. His wife suffered from dementia and now lived in a care home a few miles away. Bernie took with her the family albums, which she hoped would jog his memory, and the folder of stories about her late husband.

She was greeted at the door by Brenda, who ushered her into a rather cluttered sitting room where her father sat in a high-backed easy chair. He got to his feet as Bernie entered and shook her warmly by the hand.

'Come and sit down next to me. I've got some things you may be interested to see.'

Bernie sat down and Brenda moved a small table closer to them so that they could both look at a pile of old photographs, which Ernest tipped out of an old manila envelope. He spread out the pile and peered down at them.

'Here you are!' he said triumphantly, pushing one towards Bernie. 'That's the bank where Richard's grandfather worked. And this,' he added, selecting another picture from the pile, 'is the party that they held when his father came back from the war. He was the youngest son and the only one who survived. I knew the family because, in those days, the police were expected to know all the significant members of the community, and of course the Bank Manager was quite an important person then.'

'Do you have any pictures of Richard at about that time?' Bernie asked. 'I've got some from when he was about eight upwards but all the photographs of him before that seem to have been destroyed.'

'And why might that be, do you think?' Ernest asked sharply.

'I think,' Bernie said hesitatingly, 'that it's because someone wanted to get rid of every picture of Eleanor. I think they wanted to erase her from the family records. And the photos of Richard when he was very young probably all had her in them too.'

'Very likely you're right,' agreed Ernest. 'As I say, I knew the family, and I think they felt that it was a disgrace the way she went off like that. I well remember that day when young Richard walked into the station to report her missing. I was in the back, typing up some notes, when I heard the bell ring to let me know that someone had come in. I went out to the front and at first I couldn't see anyone there!'

****

Sergeant Ernest Walker looked around in surprise, wondering what had caused the bell attached to the entrance door to ring. Then he looked down over the counter and saw a small boy looking up at him. He had a mop of fair hair, serious blue eyes and a firm set to his jaw. He wore grey flannel shorts, a white shirt and a green tie, which was coming undone. His socks had fallen round his ankles and his brown lace-up shoes were scuffed.

'What can I do for you?' Ernest asked kindly.

'I've come to report a Missing Person,' the boy said earnestly.

'Have you indeed? Then I'd better take down some particulars. Tell you what: why don't you come round here so that it's easier?'

Ernest lifted a flap in the counter and beckoned Richard through. Soon he was perched on a high stool with his elbows resting on the counter. Ernest took out his notebook and placed it in front of them.

'You'd better start by giving me your name,' he said. 'You're Mr Paige's grandson aren't you?'

'Yes,' Richard nodded eagerly, 'my name's Richard Paige.'

'Right you are,' said Ernest, writing this information down in his notebook. 'And I'm Sergeant Walker. Now, you say you want to report a Missing Person? Who might that be?'

'My mummy,' Richard's voice gave signs of cracking, but he fought back the tears and went on, 'that's Mrs Eleanor Paige.'

Ernest wrote this down.

'And how long has she been missing?'

'Since yesterday: I came home from school and she was gone.'

'I see. And did you ask your daddy if he knew where she was?'

'Yes. He said she'd gone away and wasn't coming back.' Richard's lip trembled. 'He said he didn't know where she'd gone, but she wasn't coming back – ever!'

Ernest wondered if the boy's mother could have died

and this was his father's way of explaining it to him. However, he remembered having seen Mrs Paige only two days earlier, catching the bus into the city. She had looked in the best of health then. Of course, she could have suffered an accident, but it was likely that he would have heard about any sudden death on his beat.

'And what about your grandparents?' he asked gently. 'Do they say the same?'

'Yes. Grandpa said her head was full of ideas and they'd made her run away. Why would ideas make her run away?'

'I suppose it depends what sort of ideas,' Ernest said vaguely, wondering what Richard's grandfather had actually said and what he had meant by it.

'And Grandma said that Daddy should never have married her, and it was probably all for the best.'

'Did your mummy and daddy have an argument at all?' Ernest asked, 'I mean, before she left?'

Richard shook his head solemnly.

'It's just,' Ernest explained, 'sometimes when grown-ups get angry they say that they're going to do things and then afterwards they change their mind.'

'You mean Mummy might change her mind about never coming back?'

'That's right.'

'So, aren't you going to try to find her?'

'I think I'd better have a word with your father first. He might not be very happy about me looking for his wife if she isn't really missing after all. If I walk you home now, will he be there?'

Richard shook his head.

'He doesn't get home until six o'clock.'

'So who will be at home? Your grandma, maybe?'

Richard nodded.

'And does she know where you are right now?'

Getting no answer, Ernest went on, 'I think we'd better get you home right away, before your grandma reports *you* missing!'

A door opened behind them and a dark-haired head appeared round it. Its brown eyes surveyed the room and, seeing that Ernest was alone, apart from a small boy, the head was soon followed by the body of a girl of about five years. She walked up to Ernest and tugged at his tunic. He looked down.

'Now Brenda, let me introduce you to Master Richard Paige. Richard: this is my little girl, Brenda.'

'I'm five,' Brenda announced confidently, 'how old are you?'

'Eight years and seven months.'

'I'm just going to take Master Richard home. Would you like to come along?'

As the three of them walked the short distance to Richard's house, Brenda engaged Richard in conversation while Ernest pondered the situation. He did not like the sound of it at all. Could it be that the boy's mother was dead? If so, his father had handled the business of explaining this to his son extraordinarily badly. If not, why had she run away? And why was her husband so definite that she would never return?

He remembered that there had been some talk, when Richard was born, about how lucky it had been for Eleanor that his father hadn't been called up any earlier. They got married in the May and, almost immediately afterwards, Edward had left to join the army. Richard had arrived the following November. What if Eleanor's husband was not, in fact, Richard's father? If he had recently discovered this, it would give him a motive for banishing her; but surely, in that case she would have been expected to take the child with her?

Alternatively, could Edward Paige have been so enraged at finding that he had been tricked into marrying a woman whom he did not love that he had killed her and hidden the body?

****

'I had a few sleepless nights worrying about that one, I

44

can tell you,' Ernest told Bernie. 'And I couldn't let it rest like that, so I went round one evening to talk to Richard's father.'

'And what did he say about Eleanor's disappearance?'

'His first thought was to chuck me out and tell me to mind my own business; but then he started to realise that, if I was asking questions, soon other people would be asking them as well and he'd better have a story ready for them. He told me that his wife had left him and had given him to understand that she wasn't coming back. He insisted that he didn't know where she was, and I couldn't get the idea out of my head that this was just what he would say if he'd killed her.'

Ernest paused and looked round to see the effect of his dramatic words on his audience. Seeing that he had the full attention of both Bernie and Brenda, he continued with relish.

'I made it clear to him that I needed evidence that she was still alive and had gone off of her own volition. In the end, he showed me the wardrobe in their bedroom, which was full of his things at one side and empty, where he said she'd taken all her clothes, on the other. He said that there were two suitcases missing as well. She'd left her wedding ring and engagement ring on her dressing table – he showed me those as well.

'I pointed out to him that he could have cleared her things from the wardrobe himself; so then he got his mother in to tell me that she'd seen Eleanor leaving with two suitcases the previous Monday morning, shortly after Richard had gone to school. That was the day before Richard came to see me, so it agreed with his story.

'Anyway, to cut a long story short, I kept pressing them to tell me where they thought she might be and eventually they told me that Eleanor had made friends with a group of students from one of the women's colleges and had been meeting them in their rooms. "Filling up her head with a lot of nonsense," as Richard's grandfather described it.

Apparently, the day before she left, Eleanor had told her husband that these women understood her far better than he did and that she intended to go and live with them in London.'

'So, did you look for her in London?' Bernie asked eagerly.

'No,' Ernest shook his head, 'I told the whole story to my superior and he said that we shouldn't get involved – not unless someone reported it to us officially. I pointed out that this was just what Richard had done, but he said that he meant an adult, not an eight-year-old boy. The Paiges were respectable people, you see: Albert – that's Richard's grandfather – was a bank manager and Edward, his father, had a job in the planning office, working on re-building after the war. They were both pillars of the community, as they say, and it wasn't for us to start suggesting that they might have done away with Edward's wife.'

'These students,' Bernie asked, 'did Richard's family give you any names? Did they say which college they were at?'

'No. They just said *one of the women's colleges.*'

'Well, that cuts it down to five, I suppose,' Bernie said, writing this information down in the spiral bound notebook in which she had been jotting down Ernest's story. She underlined it to remind herself to check out the college records, looking for students who might have moved to London together when they went down. 'Do you know how Eleanor met them? Was it some sort of political meeting or philosophical society that gave her those *ideas*?'

'I don't know. I wouldn't have been welcome poking my nose into those sorts of things.'

'No. I suppose not. In any case, presumably they'd all gone down by the time you heard about it. But I can find out if there was a society that women students belonged to in those days, which could have been what influenced Eleanor. Though, of course, she wouldn't have been eligible to belong if it was a university society.'

She jotted down some more notes and made some more

underlining before looking up at Ernest expectantly.

'So was that the end of it all? What did you tell Richard about his mother's disappearance?'

'I made a point of meeting him on his way back from school the next day; and I told him that his father had said that his mother was quite safe and that she was living in London. He wanted to go and see her, so I told him that London was a big place and he wouldn't be able to find her without knowing her address. I could see he didn't really believe me so I invited him to come to tea at our house to talk about it. I was worried that he might run off to London looking for his mum and we'd have a real missing person on our hands!'

'And Eleanor really didn't make any attempt to communicate with Richard after she left? She didn't write to him or ring up?'

'No. Nothing. That's what I found hard to stomach,' Ernest replied. 'Richard was only a few years older than my kids and I couldn't help thinking how bad they would have felt if their mother had gone off and never even written a note to them.'

'But maybe she did,' suggested Brenda, 'and his father or grandparents stopped him getting the messages.'

'Yes,' Bernie agreed, 'I hadn't thought of that. It would be easy for them to intercept letters if they didn't want him to have any more to do with his mother. And of course it would always be one of the adults who would answer the telephone.'

'So anyway, my hands were tied,' Ernest went on, 'but Richard wasn't to be put off so easily, as I discovered a few weeks later. The school summer holidays had begun and it was a warm sunny day. I was walking my beat when a police car pulled up and I saw that young Richard was in the passenger seat. I recognised the constable with him as PC John Langley, whose beat covered Summertown.'

****

'This young man tells me you know him,' PC Langley

greeted Ernest as he held the car door open for Richard to get out. 'He wouldn't tell us his address, but he said that you'd take him home.'

'Certainly I will. What's happened?'

'We found him sitting on a doorstep in Summertown, waiting for the residents to come home. A neighbour saw him and called us, after he'd been hanging around all morning, because she knew that they were away for the week. He claims that it's his grandparents' house.'

'I see. Leave him with me. I'll see he gets home all right.'

The car drove off and Ernest turned to Richard.

'So what's all this then?'

Richard didn't reply, so Ernest took his hand and led him back to the police house. He left him in the capable hands of his wife while he rang Richard's grandmother to let her know that he was safe. To his surprise, she seemed quite unperturbed, Richard having told her that he was spending the day with some school friends.

When Ernest returned to the kitchen, he found Richard, Brenda and three-year-old George busily cutting out biscuits, while his wife, Betty, was engaged in making a pot of tea. He sat down at the table and addressed Richard in what he hoped was a stern but kindly manner.

'Now Richard,' he said, 'tell me what you were doing, going all the way out to Summertown?'

There was no reply, so Ernest tried again.

'Were you looking for your mum?'

Richard nodded.

'And why Summertown?'

'I thought that Grandma and Grandpa Carter would know where she was.'

The penny dropped. Of course! Richard must have been trying to visit Eleanor's parents, in the hope that she would have told them where she was going. That was quite clever thinking for an eight-year-old.

'But they weren't at home?'

'No. A lady came and said they were on holiday, and then

a policeman came and wanted to take me home.'

'I see. Well now, Richard, you can't go wandering off on your own like this: people will get worried about you. How on earth did you get all the way to Summertown anyway?'

'I got the bus. Daddy gives me tuppence pocket money every week, so I was able to pay for it myself.'

Ernest drank his tea in silence. He was thinking about how to help the boy. Surely, something could be done to persuade his mother to come and see him, or at least to write? He resolved to speak to Richard's father again, to try to persuade him to make an effort to contact his wife.

An hour or so later they were on their way to Richard's home. They walked in silence, each deep in his own thoughts, Richard clutching a paper bag, which held his share of the newly-baked biscuits.

'Sergeant Walker?' Richard asked, just as they were turning in at the gate of his house. 'Do you think Mummy went away because I was naughty?'

'Now whatever gave you that idea?' Ernest asked, stopping in his tracks and crouching down so that he could look Richard in the eye.

'I just thought maybe that's why she went without saying goodbye – if she was cross with me.'

'Just put that right out of your mind, young man!' Ernest said firmly. 'I'm quite sure that this is all to do with the grown-ups falling out. It's nothing to do with you at all. It'll all come out all right in the end: you'll see.' He tried to speak with a confidence that he did not feel. He was far from certain that Richard's family would be reunited and convinced that the boy would not be satisfied with anything less.

They were greeted at the door by Richard's paternal grandmother, who shooed him upstairs to his room before inviting Ernest into the spacious living room.

'I'm sorry that my grandson has been causing trouble,' she said, after closing the door behind them. 'I'll make sure that he knows that it mustn't happen again.'

'No trouble, ma'am,' Ernest assured her. 'My little girl loved having him to play with her. I'm just concerned that he may put himself in danger if he goes off on his own again.'

'I will impress upon him the importance of truth-telling,' Mrs Paige said, somewhat ominously. 'He told me that he was going to the Jones boy's house for the day. If he had said that he was intending to go off like that I would have forbidden it.'

Which is probably why he didn't tell you, Ernest thought.

'There's no harm done,' he said aloud. He hesitated and then went on. 'Is there no chance at all that he could see his mother again? He does seem very upset about her going away.'

'If my daughter-in-law is no longer welcome in this house then it is no business of yours,' Mrs Paige said decisively.

'Yes. I'm sorry, ma'am, but,' Ernest screwed up his courage and continued, 'it does seem hard on the little lad. He's only young and he doesn't understand these things. I wonder: could you perhaps ask his mother's family to arrange for him to meet her at their house – if you don't want her to come here?'

'Thank you for your concern,' Mrs Paige said coldly, 'but when we want your advice we'll ask for it. Now, if there's nothing more, I'll show you out.'

****

'I didn't think I'd handled that very well,' Ernest confided to Bernie, 'but something I said must have struck home, because the next time I met Richard he told me that the following week his father had taken him over to visit his mother's parents for the first time since she'd left home.'

'And did they know where she'd gone?'

'They said that they didn't, but I was never sure about that. They surely must have heard *something* from her, or why weren't they worried about her disappearance? But it could be that she only told them the same as she told her husband:

that she was going to live with her friends in London.'

'So she definitely hadn't run home to mother?'

'No.'

'And nobody ever found out where she *had* gone?'

'Well, *I* certainly didn't, and if anyone else did they didn't tell young Richard.'

'And did he carry on trying to find her?'

'Well, he used to ask me sometimes if I'd found out anything, but in the end he seemed to just accept that he wouldn't see her again. The more I saw of the family, the more I came to believe that they were telling the truth when they said they didn't know where she'd gone. And then I got angry with *her* for going off and leaving her little boy without any sort of explanation, because I could see that he still thought that he might have been to blame. And he never stopped thinking about it. I remember, it must have been a few years later, there was a lot of news about Elizabeth Taylor's first divorce and Richard told me that he'd asked his father whether *he* was divorced from his mother.'

'And had they got divorced?' Bernie asked.

'No. And when Richard asked why, his father told him that there was no point, because he didn't want to get married again.'

'And presumably Eleanor didn't want to re-marry either,' Bernie mused, 'or else she was determined not to make contact with her husband, which she would have had to do in order to get a divorce.'

'Of course,' Ernest went on, 'by then Richard's father was very much taken up with looking after his mother. You see, his father – Richard's grandfather – died about a year after Eleanor left, and his mother – Richard's grandmother – took it very hard. Mr Edward Paige – that's Richard's father – completely devoted himself to her.'

'I suppose it must have been hard for her to have lost her husband and two out of three sons,' Bernie suggested, trying to be fair.

'I suppose so,' Ernest agreed, rather reluctantly, 'and I

believe there had been a daughter too, who died in infancy. But I still think Richard's father ought to have made a bit more time for his son as well as his mother.'

'You and Mum were like parents to him,' Brenda said, putting her hand on her father's arm to calm his agitation. 'He was always round at our house joining in whatever we were doing.'

'Yes that's right,' her father agreed. 'I reckon he didn't get such a bad upbringing after all.'

5 HOSTILE WITNESS

Bernie's plan to investigate who the students might be, whom Eleanor had apparently gone off with more than fifty years before, proved to be more difficult than she had anticipated. Although the colleges had been much smaller back in 1948, there were still several hundred names to consider. Moreover, although the colleges all did their best to maintain records of the addresses of alumni for fundraising purposes, they were understandably unwilling to share this information with her. In addition, most female students graduating in those days would have married and changed their names and a significant proportion of them would be dead.

As Bernie sat in her study contemplating the problem, she realised that she had allowed her project of making a collection of memories for the child who was to be born in a month's time to be diverted into an investigation into the reason for Eleanor's disappearance. What right did she have to be seeking this out behind her mother-in-law's back? If she wanted to know the answer to that question, then she would have to tackle Eleanor head-on.

So the following Saturday, she started manoeuvring the conversation round to the subject of Richard's early life.

'I was talking to someone who knew you and your husband when you lived in Headington,' she said conversationally. 'Sergeant Ernest Walker. He was your local bobby.'

'I don't remember him,' Eleanor responded curtly.

'He told me that there were all sorts of rumours flying around after you left home.'

'It doesn't surprise me – people always do talk.'

'Apparently one theory was that you'd run off with some women from the university to set up an all-female commune in London!' Bernie hoped that, this outlandish suggestion might prompt Eleanor to deny it and, in doing so, to reveal what she had actually done. In this, she was disappointed.

'Well, if it amused them to think that, it's of no consequence to me.'

'And there was another theory that your husband had killed you and buried the body in the back garden.'

There was no response, so Bernie decided to give up the attempt to entice Eleanor into a revelation and to revert to direct questioning.

'Eleanor,' she said, 'looking her mother-in-law in the face, 'can't you tell me? I simply can't understand what would make a mother leave her eight-year-old child and go off without even saying goodbye.'

'I told you: I should never have married.'

'So, did Richard's father abuse you? Was he violent?'

'No – not violent. We just ought never to have got married, and that's all there is to it.'

Bernie realised that she was getting nowhere and decided to try another approach.

'I found these albums in your husband's old room,' she ventured, taking the volumes out of her bag and opening the earliest one for Eleanor to see. 'I was looking for pictures of Richard when he was a boy, but there don't seem to be any earlier than this one of him at the Junior School Sports.'

Briefly abandoning her stance of indifference, Eleanor

peered down at the photograph of a boy of eight or nine crossing the line in the sack race. Then she remembered herself, sniffed and looked away.

'I was wondering,' Bernie pressed her advantage, 'if maybe *you* had some photos of him as a baby?'

Eleanor did not reply.

'I thought,' Bernie went on, 'that maybe you'd taken them away with you when you went.'

'Certainly not!' Eleanor retorted angrily. 'I took nothing from that house except my own clothes and the few possessions I'd brought into it.'

'I'm sorry,' Bernie apologised, taken aback by Eleanor's outburst. 'I didn't mean to suggest – I mean, you would have had every right to – that is, I thought you would have wanted to take something to remind you of Richard.'

There was a long silence.

'Tell me, Bernadette,' Eleanor said at last, 'why do you keep coming here? What is it that you want from me?'

'I don't *want* anything,' Bernie answered, annoyed at Eleanor's assumption that she had an ulterior motive. It had been the same when Richard was alive: his mother had always managed to convey the impression that she believed that his attentions were in some way self-serving. It never seemed to occur to her that he might have been genuinely concerned for her welfare.

'I come to see you,' Bernie went on, forcing herself to speak calmly, 'because that is what Richard would have done if he'd still been alive. For reasons that I can't fathom, in view of the way you treated him, he cared for you. You are his mother and he wanted to see you properly looked after; and so I want that too.'

Eleanor opened her mouth to speak, but Bernie ignored her and continued.

'I also hoped that eventually you would feel able to talk with me about Richard and that you might be able to fill in some of the gaps that I don't know about him: not just for my benefit, but for the sake of his child. And I *thought* that you would want to see your grandchild when it's born and that you would want it to know you.'

'I can't think why you would want me involved in bringing up *your* child, when you seem to think I made such a poor job of looking after my own.'

'I never said that,' Bernie argued, managing with difficulty to speak in an even voice. 'Actually, I think you must have been quite a good mother to Richard when he was young; otherwise, why would he be so distressed when you left? I just can't understand how you could bear to leave and not take him with you.'

'Do you really think I didn't want to?' Eleanor demanded, showing more emotion than Bernie could recall her ever having displayed before. 'Of course I wanted to take him with me, but if I'd taken the child they would have come after me. My father was dependent on Edward's father for his job, so he would have had to help them to find me. And I'd have lost Richard in the end anyway. They were the ones with respectable jobs and a big house. Everyone would have been on their side. I had to choose between my son and my freedom, and don't ever think it was an easy choice to make.'

'I'm sorry,' Bernie said humbly. 'I didn't think of that.'

'No, I don't suppose you did.' Eleanor resumed her usual dismissive tone and Bernie realised that there would be no more revelations. Her mother-in-law had put back the barrier with which she was in the habit of protecting herself from the intrusion of others. Clearly, she intended to keep secret whatever it was that had led her to cut herself off from her husband, her son and indeed from her entire family.

'I'd better be going,' Bernie said, getting up. 'Is it alright for me to come again next week?'

'Suit yourself,' Eleanor said dismissively, but Bernie noted that she had not taken the opportunity offered to her to terminate the visits. Perhaps there would be other times when she would let down her guard and reveal something more about her troubled relationship with her husband's family. Meanwhile, Bernie decided to pay another visit to Ernest Walker and his daughter.

6 DOMESTIC VIOLENCE

'It's good of you to come and see me again,' Ernest greeted Bernie as she sat down in his front room again the following week, 'especially when it can't be long before the happy event.'

'Another three weeks,' Bernie confirmed.

'Both of my babies were early,' warned Brenda, smiling, 'so it could be any time now!'

'I've got some more pictures to show you,' Ernest said, opening a large photograph album. 'Brenda here has made copies that you can take away, but I'll show you them here.'

'This is a school photo from when Brenda had just moved up to the juniors. She's there on the front row and Richard's standing behind.'

'So Richard would be, what? Eleven?' Bernie asked, peering at the photograph.

'That's right,' Brenda confirmed. 'He was in the top class and I was one of the youngest. He used to stick up for me when the boys called me names because my teeth stuck out, and he used to hit them when they pulled my plaits.'

'Quite the knight in shining armour, wasn't he?' Ernest chuckled. 'And now, here he is, showing off his new school uniform.' He pointed to a picture of a boy in a school blazer, rather too large for him, and short trousers, with a cap on his head. 'He went to the grammar school. He always was a bright lad. I was half-expecting him to go to university, but he chose the police force instead.'

Ernest turned the pages, leafing past holiday snaps portraying Brenda and George on the beach with buckets and spades, past Brenda in her Girl Guide uniform, past George caked in mud holding aloft a rugby ball. He stopped and pointed.

'Here you are: Brenda and Richard on their first date!'

'Oh Dad!' Brenda protested. 'It was only the school dance. Richard was fifteen and I was only twelve. We both spent the whole evening sitting at the side of the room hoping it would soon be over.'

'Now Brenda, you must admit you did carry a torch for Richard back in those days.'

'That's as maybe, but there's only so long a girl can wait without at least getting some encouragement.'

'How much more encouragement did you want? He took you to the pictures and gave you presents and sat in this very room making sheep's eyes at you while we were watching the telly. What more did you want?'

'But it never seemed to be going anywhere. He never said anything.'

'He probably wanted to wait until he got promotion – so he had something to offer you.'

'That's what I told myself while he was a cadet. And then, when he was made a full constable, I thought: *this is it! He'll propose to me now.* But he didn't. He just carried on exactly the same. We'd go to the pictures every Friday night and go for a walk every Sunday afternoon and he'd be round here doing odd jobs for Mum or helping you in the garden; but he seemed to think it was enough just to carry on like that forever.'

'And then, of course,' Ernest added, 'along came Bobby Jones and turned your head.'

'Your husband?' Bernie asked.

'That's right.' Brenda smiled. 'He asked me out a couple of times and I turned him down because I thought that I was Richard's girl. Then one day Richard and I were planning to go to the pictures but he was called into work at the last minute and Bobby rang while Richard was at our house explaining to me that he couldn't come after all. It was Richard who said that there was no reason why I had to stay in, just because he had to work, so I went out with Bobby. I told him it was *just this once*, but after that he kept asking me, and Richard never seemed to mind, so it got difficult to say *no*.'

'Young Richard was always too nice for his own good,' Ernest observed.

'He was *indecisive*,' Brenda corrected him, 'at least as far as women were concerned. I gave him a whole year after Bobby started paying me his attentions and then Bobby proposed and Richard had still said nothing, so I gave him up as a bad job and plumped for Bobby.'

'And he's been a good husband to you, hasn't he?' Ernest said. 'I won't pretend that I wasn't disappointed that we weren't going to be welcoming Richard into the family, but Bobby has done well for himself and he's been a good dad to your three kids too.'

'You know,' Bernie mused, 'I wouldn't be surprised if it was his mother going off like that when he was small that made it so difficult for Richard to relate to women.'

'He *related* to me OK,' Brenda argued, 'he just couldn't seem to pluck up the courage to pop the question.'

'That's what I mean. What you just described is so familiar it's uncanny, and I don't believe he'd ever got any further than that with anyone before he met me, which you need to remember was at the grand old age of fifty-five. We'd been seeing each other four times a week for two years before he made a move. *I* think that he was convinced that if even his own mother didn't love him, nobody could.'

'That Eleanor has a lot to answer for,' growled Ernest.

'I suppose I ought to be grateful to her,' Bernie observed

with a grin, 'after all, if he'd got up the courage to propose to Brenda then he wouldn't have been free to marry me, would he?'

'But *he* did ask *you* in the end?' Brenda asked, suspecting that the forceful Bernie might have taken the initiative when she realised that Richard was unlikely to make the first move.

'Oh yes, *he* proposed – in the end. To be honest, I was just as bad as he was. I'd had a bad experience while I was still an undergraduate and it had knocked my confidence. So I thought it was completely understandable that nobody would want to commit themselves to a lifetime with me.' She laughed. 'Actually, I think Peter Johns *ordered* Richard to propose to me!'

'And how did that come about?' Ernest asked, intrigued. 'And for that matter, how did you come to know young Peter Johns?'

'*Young Peter Johns* as you call him is seven years older than me,' Bernie pointed out, 'and his wife, Angie, happens to be my best friend. The way it happened was this. I applied for my dream job: a professorship at Newcastle University. I'd been hankering after moving up there for years, because I've got friends there – but that's another story. I never expected to stand a chance. So you could have knocked me down with a feather when they offered me the post. And that was when I realised that I didn't want the job enough to go and live two hundred and fifty miles away from Richard. So in the end I turned it down, but I didn't tell Richard: I just said that I wouldn't be going to Newcastle after all. I didn't want him to think that he was getting in the way of my career.

'But, of course, Angie knew; and she told Peter and, judging by the way Richard suddenly turned up at my college room in the middle of the day, all flustered and talking about marriage, I think Peter must have told him that it was time he stopped leading me up the garden path and decided whether he wanted me or not.'

They all laughed. Then Bernie turned to Ernest and said,

'but that's enough about me. Tell me about how you helped Richard to get into the police force.'

'Ah now, he didn't need much help from me. He had a natural aptitude. Wait a minute! I think I've got a picture of him in his cadet uniform.' Ernest rifled through a box of loose photographs and eventually picked one out triumphantly. 'Here we go. He came round to show himself off to Brenda the day he joined.'

Bernie peered at the rather battered photograph from which an earnest young man in uniform gazed out at her.

'He came to me when he was doing his O' levels and told me he wanted to go into the force. His father wasn't too keen, as far as I remember, but he went along with it. Actually, I think it was more Richard's grandmother, who didn't like the idea. She was getting on a bit by then and very set in her ways. She thought it was a bit of a come down for the grandson of a bank manager to become a policeman.'

'Dad helped him to apply and coached him for his interview,' Brenda recalled. 'I remember them sitting on opposite sides of the table with Dad firing questions at him. He told me afterwards that the real interview was nothing like as bad!'

They all laughed.

'I managed to get him assigned to work alongside me,' Ernest went on. 'He took to it like a duck to water. He always managed to keep calm when there was trouble, rather than wading in as so many of the young ones do. He'd always prefer to send troublemakers back to their homes instead of wanting to arrest them all.'

'But what he always really wanted,' Brenda added, 'was to go into CID. He wanted to investigate and solve crimes, not just to patrol the streets to deter criminals.'

'Prevention is better than cure,' Ernest pointed out.

'Yes, but some crimes you can't prevent and then you need someone who can find out who was responsible and stop them doing it again,' Brenda argued. 'Anyway, that was what really interested Richard. Even before he joined the cadets he was always getting involved in looking for lost cats or lying in wait to catch kids who were scrumping apples from the vicarage garden.'

'He always had a particular interest in missing persons,' Ernest mused, 'especially lost children. Which reminds me – now there's something you might be interested in hearing about.'

'What?' Bernie asked, as he paused dramatically.

'I was just thinking about the time he went off up to London to look for his mother.'

'But that must have been like looking for a needle in a haystack,' Bernie objected. 'Surely he didn't think he could just go to London and expect to find her?'

'Well,' Ernest answered, 'it was a bit like that, but I gather he had some sort of clue to narrow it down.'

'I remember!' Brenda broke in. 'It was when his grandmother died. He told me all about it. A card came through the post and Richard's father read it, then tore it up and threw it straight in the bin. Richard managed to get hold of the envelope and read the postmark. He was convinced it was from his mother and that was why his father had destroyed the card. He collected the bits when his dad wasn't looking and we tried to piece them together. The signature did look rather like *Eleanor* but we were never sure and there was no address, so all Richard had to go on was the postal district where the card was posted.'

'He took a week's leave,' Ernest continued, 'and went and stayed in a hostel. I didn't know anything about it until I was called in to explain what he thought he was doing asking some of the local Bobbies whether they knew of any Eleanor Paige living on their patch. He'd made friends with a couple of the young constables and they'd overstepped the mark a bit in trying to help him. We got it all sorted out in the end. I just had to give him a stern reprimand and he had to write a letter of apology to the senior officer up there.'

He returned to thumbing through the box of photographs, leaving Bernie to her thoughts. The sudden disappearance of his mother had clearly had a profound effect on Richard if he was still so anxious to find her a good ten years later.

'Here you are!' Ernest called her back to the present by brandishing a photograph of Richard in police uniform complete with highly polished tunic buttons and an old-fashioned helmet on his head. 'This is his first day as a full constable.'

Bernie took the picture in her hand and looked at it. It seemed to come from a previous era but, of course, Richard had already embarked on his police career before she was born. In many ways, he did come from before her time.

'How did he make the move into CID?' she asked.

'He just kept applying for every opportunity that came up. I tried to put in a good word for him, but it was just dogged perseverance that got him there in the end.'

'Admit it Dad,' Brenda urged, 'you were sorry to see him go.'

'I was sorry that we weren't going to be working together anymore,' her father conceded, 'but I was pleased that he was getting what he wanted and I always knew he'd do well. Detective Superintendent!' He shook his head in wonder.

'Now, once he was *in* CID,' Ernest went on, after pause, 'it didn't take long for him to start making his mark. I remember the very first case he was involved in, because it happened here on my patch. The investigating officer was DI Hamers, not a man to suffer fools gladly as I recall, but young Richard acquitted himself well and that set him on his way to a high flying career in CID.'

****

Detective Inspector Albert Hamers did not like having new officers to train-up. He had his favoured team of experienced CID men upon whom he could rely. A new recruit would need to be supervised and coached, taking up valuable time that could be devoted to criminal investigation. Worst of all, newcomers, keen to make their mark, often did untold damage by asking the wrong questions or giving away vital information to suspects.

This new man came highly recommended by his sergeant, but what did a uniformed officer from a sleepy little oxford suburb know about what made a good detective? He had joined the Police Cadets straight from school and had an almost unblemished record – apart from a little escapade in London, where he had apparently attempted to do some private detective work of his own. If he tried anything of that sort on Hamers' watch, he need expect no mercy. Hamers liked his officers to toe the line and not draw attention to themselves.

He called the lad in, introduced himself, said a few curt words of welcome and then took him to the briefing room where the other members of his team were gathered to hear the details of a new case that had come in. Trainee Detective Constable Richard Paige sat down in an inconspicuous corner of the room and opened his notebook.

The case was a suspicious death. The victim was one Ronald Arden, an unemployed labourer, who had been found dead by his wife when she returned from her job as a shop assistant. At first, it looked as if he must simply have lost his footing on the stairs and fallen headlong, cracking his skull on the quarry tiles in the hall, but the doctor had found some unexplained injuries on his face and body and there was also a question mark over the time of death. So Hamers had been called in to investigate.

'It was a family of four,' Hamers said. 'Mr Ronald Arden was unemployed, his wife Doris and son Tom are the breadwinners. The daughter Jean is still at school, but it was the half term holiday yesterday, so she was at home until about ten forty-five in the morning, when she says she went to visit a friend. According to her, her father was still alive when she left. Mrs Arden cooked breakfast for the family and then left for work at about quarter past eight. She came back at just before six and found her husband's body. The son does shift work at the motor works. He was on the late shift this week, which meant that he left the house at around quarter past one in the afternoon. He claims that his father was still fit and well then.

'The doctor who examined the body at the scene was surprised to be told that the man was alive after one o'clock, because he thought that death had probably occurred several hours earlier than that. He also drew attention to bruising on the face and torso, which were consistent with the victim having been in some sort of fight prior to falling down the stairs. A post mortem is being done, after which we shall know more about time and cause of death. Meanwhile, we are investigating whether this really was an accident or if Ronald Arden could have been the victim of an assault, which led to his death. Is everyone clear about what I've said so far?'

He looked round the room and was pleased to see heads nodding.

'Good. Now this is what we're going to do. Murdishaw: you take Jones and Clitheroe and check out whether the family really were where they said they were at the times they said they were. What time did the son clock on at work? The same for the wife. And does the daughter's friend agree with the time she said that she got to her house? Oh – and talk to the neighbours. Find out what the family was like: rows, money-troubles, drinking habits and that sort of thing.'

'Right you are, sir.' Sergeant Murdishaw left the room followed by the two constables Jones and Clitheroe.

'And now, Paige,' Hamers said, turning to Richard. 'I want you to accompany me to the mortuary.'

The first thing that struck Paige when he entered the mortuary was the smell, which he took to be some powerful disinfectant. It made him feel queasy, but it was not until the pathologist led them through to show them the corpse of Ronald Arden that the nausea became intense. He felt slightly light-headed and he repeatedly had to swallow the saliva that kept coming in his mouth.

'The lavatory is through that door,' Hamers said, pointing. 'If you must throw up, I'd be grateful if you could do it there.'

Paige nodded, but was at first determined to stay. Then he submitted to the inevitable and ran out, making it to the toilets just in time. As he splashed water on his face and dried it on the roller towel, he reflected that at least he had avoided disgracing himself actually in front of the pathologist. He walked back in and took up his place next to Hamers, trying his best to show an intelligent interest in the proceedings.

'The contents of the stomach,' the pathologist was saying, 'consisted of egg, bacon and bread. Digestion had made very little progress, which suggests that the deceased probably died shortly after consuming breakfast. There was a large amount of alcohol in the blood, but rather little remaining in the stomach, indicating that he probably imbibed copiously the previous night. I've already mentioned the external injuries suggestive of the deceased having been in a fight recently. I now draw your attention to damage to his kidneys and liver consistent with being punched hard and repeatedly in the abdominal region.'

'And was that damage inflicted recently,' Paige asked tentatively, anxious to redeem himself by asking an intelligent question, but unsure whether Hamers would consider it fitting for his trainee to speak at all. 'Can you tell, for example, whether they occurred on the same day as his death?'

'I would say that they almost certainly did. Indeed, I would go further and suggest that the internal injuries are the most likely cause of death, with the major injury to the skull probably being inflicted post mortem.'

'And there's no possibility that the internal injuries were caused by a fall downstairs?' Hamers asked sharply.

'I would not be willing to testify that it was impossible, but in my opinion, it is considerably more likely that the deceased was punched to death and then fell downstairs afterwards.'

'A fight at the top of the stairs,' Paige suggested, 'with

the victim receiving his death blow and then toppling downstairs?'

'That is certainly possible, but the internal damage would not have caused death immediately, so in that case he would probably have still been alive when he fell downstairs. That's not impossible, but I would have expected the head wound to look somewhat different had it been inflicted in that way.'

'So, can I get this straight?' Hamers interjected. 'You're saying that he probably lay dying for some time *after* the fight and *before* falling downstairs?'

'That is my reading of the most likely sequence of events, but the fight at the top of the stairs postulated by your assistant is certainly a possible alternative.'

The policemen turned to go, but the pathologist called after them.

'There's one other thing you might like to know about the deceased.'

They turned and looked at him expectantly.

'His underpants were on back-to-front.'

'Well now, Paige,' Hamers said as they left the mortuary, 'I gather you have worked out a theory for what happened. Would you care to share it with me?'

'Yes, sir,' Paige paused to gather his thoughts. 'Well, sir. I think that the family can't all be telling the truth about seeing Mr Arden alive later in the day, because the medical evidence suggests that he died soon after he had his breakfast – like the doctor who saw him at a scene said.'

'I see. Go on.'

'So the most likely thing to have happened is that one of the family had an argument – well, a fight – with him, somewhere upstairs. He died from his injuries and they got frightened and threw him downstairs to make it look like an accident.'

'Very good. And do you have any theory about which one of the family it was?'

''Well, sir,' Paige said slowly, trying to think it all through logically, 'if the wife did it then both the son and daughter must also be lying to shield her; if either of them did it then she could be telling the truth when she says that he was alive when she left the house.'

'Carry on,' Hamers said neutrally. Paige was unsure whether he accepted the argument and was interested in developing it, or was just offering him more rope with which to hang himself. He pulled himself together and continued.

'In the same way, if the daughter did it, the son would have to be lying to protect her, but if the son did it after the daughter left the house, then both wife and daughter could be telling the truth.'

'I see. But if I were the defending counsel for the son, I might point out that the medical evidence suggests the time of death as being before ten in the morning.'

'And then, if I were prosecuting, I would remind him that medical evidence of time of death is an inexact science and it was possible that death had occurred after the daughter left the house at quarter to eleven. I might also suggest that the severe injuries to the abdomen were more likely to have been inflicted by a nineteen-year-old youth than by his mother or sister.'

'Now, that's more like it! Your original argument is all very well, but if we can establish that neither of the women would have been strong enough to kill the victim by punching him, then it doesn't matter when he died, because the son was there for the whole time. He could have killed him before one or both of the others left the house.'

'But then they would have to be lying to protect him.'

'Believe me, people lie all the time to protect their families. Don't you think your mother would lie to protect you if you were in danger of being accused of murder?'

'I don't know, sir.'

'Right. Now we're going to have another talk with the family. I'll interview them each on their own, so that if they *are* lying to protect each other they may contradict each other's story. You're to listen and take notes – I assume you do know how to take notes – understand? Keep your mouth shut; and whatever you do don't let slip the evidence we have of the time of death. Let them think that we've bought the idea that he died between one and six in the afternoon.'

'Yes, sir.'

When Hamers' team convened again to compare notes at the end of the day, they all felt that they had a good idea what had happened, but it looked depressingly unlikely that they would be able to secure enough evidence to convict. Wife, son and daughter were all sticking stubbornly to their stories. The wife's and son's employers confirmed that they had arrived at work at the times that they said and that they had not been absent for any time during their working hours. The girl's friend was confident that Jean Arden had arrived at her house no later than half past ten and they had been together until she left for home shortly before six.

The neighbours had a low opinion of Mr Arden senior, whom they described as a habitual drunkard and free with his fists at home. They expressed admiration for Mrs Arden whom they saw as having kept the family together, despite her husband's violent behaviour and failure to provide for them. The verdict on son Tom was that he was a 'nice lad' and 'very good to his mother'. The neighbour from one of the adjoining houses remembered hearing shouting and banging coming from the Arden's house that morning, but it was such a common occurrence that she was unable to pinpoint the time or even to be completely sure that it could not have been on an earlier day that week.

Hamers summed up their dilemma.

'I think we can rule out the involvement of anyone outside the victim's immediate family. Almost certainly one of them – or more than one, acting together – had a fight with Arden sometime in the morning. Later, when they discovered that he was dead, they threw the body down the stairs to make it look like an accident. They all claim that he was alive when they left the house, and unless we can persuade one of them to change their story it's going to be very difficult to prove which one of them did the deed and which of them are lying to cover up for one of the others. I had hoped that we could get the doctor to swear that only a man could have inflicted the fatal injuries, but he says that a woman or even a girl could have done it – especially if he was drunk, which he seems to have been most of the time. Whichever one of them we charge, their lawyer will be able to point to the other two as being equally likely, and a jury will most likely acquit on the grounds of reasonable doubt.'

He looked round the room.

'Does anyone have any suggestions for ways of narrowing it down to one or two of the suspects?'

'Sir?' Paige said nervously, after waiting to see if anyone else would speak.

'Yes, Paige?'

'I was wondering, sir: what do you make of the underpants, sir?'

A titter went round the room, which Hamers quelled with a look.

'The pathologist said they were on the wrong way round,' Paige reminded him.

'Too drunk to put them on right,' one of the constables suggested.

Hamers looked at Paige, inviting him to give his own opinion.

'Well,' he started nervously, 'I did think it might have been that he was drunk, but then I thought: what if he wasn't wearing them when he died and whoever killed him dressed him afterwards?'

'And why would they do that?'

'His family might not have liked the idea of him lying naked at the bottom of the stairs. Or they might have thought it would look odd him still not having got dressed by one in the afternoon. Or,' he hesitated and turned rather red, unsure how to express his next idea, 'he might have had his trousers down because he was doing something that they didn't want anyone else to know about.'

Another titter, followed by another glare from Hamers. 'Such as?' he asked coldly.

'I was thinking,' Paige flushed very red at this point and wished that he had not started this discussion, 'perhaps *incest*.'

There was a shocked silence. Then Hamers brought the meeting to an abrupt end.

'Well I don't think we need to talk about that sort of thing,' he said firmly. 'I'm quite sure that some normal family dispute between father and son is quite sufficient explanation for the fight that evidently took place.'

The following Saturday, Paige found Jean Arden sitting on a swing in her local playground. He went over and sat on the next swing. He took out a bag of toffees from his pocket and offered her one.

'I'm sorry about what happened to your dad,' he said tentatively.

She did not reply, so he tried again.

'I'm afraid I don't really believe what you told me about him sitting in the kitchen reading his newspaper when you went out.'

'Why not?' she asked warily.

'Shall I tell you what I think happened?'

She shrugged.

'When I was your age,' Paige began, hoping that he would manage to finish his story without frightening her away. 'I used to like to stay in bed in the morning when there wasn't any school. Sometimes I didn't get up until half past ten or eleven o'clock. I think that maybe that's what you did last Monday.'

He paused to give her an opportunity to confirm or deny the picture that he was painting. She said nothing, so he continued.

'And I think that your dad came in to see you while you

were in bed in your nightie. And you didn't like what he was trying to do to you and you screamed out and your brother came in and got angry with your dad and hit him. And I think that afterwards you found that he'd stopped breathing and you were both afraid that your brother would be accused of killing him and so you tried to hide what had happened by putting his clothes back on him and pushing him down the stairs.'

'So, are you going to arrest Tom?'

'No, you can't go arresting people just because a junior police constable like me thinks he knows what might have happened. We won't be able to do anything unless we find some more evidence to show that it was Tom who killed your father – or unless you or Tom decide to change the statements you made about what happened.'

'And if you got your evidence – what would happen to Tom and me then?'

'I don't know. If you both told the truth without waiting for us to get proof, then I hope that Tom would get away with saying that he was defending you and that he didn't mean to kill your dad, only to stop him doing what he was doing.'

'And they wouldn't put him in prison?'

'I don't think so.' Richard was unsure of his ground here. He was quite clear in his own mind that to punish the girl's brother would be unjust, but he was not confident that the legal system would not nevertheless convict him of manslaughter if not of murder.

'And if you don't get any more evidence, what happens then?'

'We keep looking. And people will always suspect that Tom or you or your mother were responsible for your dad's death.'

'Mum too? Why would they think she did it? She'd gone out before-,' she broke off, realising that she had given herself away.

'Before your dad came into your room?'

'Yes. How did you know about that?'

'I didn't, but there were two things that made me suspect it.'

'What were they?'

'Number one: you got your dad's pants on the wrong way when you dressed him. That made me think that he hadn't been wearing them when he died and that someone didn't want people to know about that.'

'He always said that I must never ever tell anyone about what we did together,' Jean said in a strangely dreamy way as if she were recollecting something from a long time ago. 'He said I was a bad girl leading him on, but I was lucky because he wouldn't ever tell anyone about it so long as I was nice to him. He said if I told Mum about the things we did, she'd be disgusted and wouldn't like me anymore.'

'D'you mean he'd done this to you before?' Richard was shocked. It had not occurred to him that such a thing could have been more than an isolated aberration brought on by too much drink.

'Oh yes. It happened a lot when Mum and Tom were at work. I suppose he must have forgotten that Tom was on "lates" last week. But what was the other thing that made you guess what had happened?'

'It was the way your brother kept repeating that he'd seen your dad alive after you'd gone out. He was so absolutely determined to make us believe that you had nothing to do with his "accident" that I was sure that he must be protecting you from something.'

'Tom was wonderful. He pulled Dad off me and hit him until he fell down on the floor. When he passed out, we thought it was just because he was drunk. He often went unconscious when he'd had a few. So I got up and got dressed. He was still lying there and I thought, what will Mum think if he's still asleep when she comes – with no trousers or pants on? So I got them and put them on him. It was very difficult because his legs wouldn't bend the right way. Then Tom came back and he said it would be better if we put Dad in his own bed to sleep it off, and we started hauling him out of my room on to the landing. But then we noticed his face looked a funny colour and we realised that he wasn't breathing. We thought that if we pushed him downstairs everyone would think that he'd just slipped and fallen. Tom said we mustn't let anyone know I was there when he died in case they asked questions and it all came out. So I went off to Sharon's and stayed there until tea time.'

Richard patted her knee gently. Then he got up to go.

'Thank you for talking to me, Jean,' he said. 'As I told you, there's no point me telling anyone about what you've said to me just now because they'd just think I was making it all up, but if you and Tom were to come into the station and change your statements it might make it a lot easier for lots of people in the long run.'

He walked away across the grass, hoping that what he had just said was true and that he had not just encouraged her to get her brother sent down for murder.

'Well now Paige,' Hamers greeted him the following afternoon. 'It seems that you're not as green as you're cabbage-looking after all.'

'Sir?' Paige looked up from his typewriter with a puzzled expression on his face.

'It appears that we have you to thank for the fact that Tom and Jean Arden are downstairs re-writing their statements. Apparently, after speaking to you, the girl decided to make a clean breast of things. The mother's there too. She's still got bruises from where her brute of a husband kept beating her. She admitted that she'd been uneasy about leaving the girl alone with him and she'd asked Tom to arrange to be on the late shift over the half term holiday as some form of protection for her.'

'What will happen to them now, sir?'

'That very much depends on the outcome of the inquest. If it comes in as murder then it will be difficult not to prosecute the lad, but with luck they'll go for justifiable homicide or even accidental death and we can probably drop any charges.'

'I hope so, sir.'

'Don't you worry. Even if it goes to court, there's not a jury in the land is going to find him guilty of murder when he was only protecting his little sister from a fate worse than death.' Hamers shook his head in disbelief. 'It makes you wonder what sort of animal that Ronald Arden could have been – violating his own daughter!'

'And what about *her*?' Page asked. 'Will she get any help?'

'Help?'

'I mean, it's been very upsetting for her.'

'Don't you worry. She'll get over it. She's young. In a few years' time she'll have forgotten all about it.'

****

'And that's the way we used to think in those days,' Ernest said. 'We never thought about offering people counselling and all that. You just had to get over things for yourself.'

'Oh yes, it was still like that when I was young. I'm sure the nuns at my school would have had no truck with us trying to blame our problems on traumatic incidents on our early life! I suppose we understand the subconscious a bit better now.'

'Like, why Richard could never quite get round to asking me to marry him.' Brenda murmured to herself.

'I wonder,' Bernie said tentatively to Ernest, 'Would you be willing to write this story down – for the baby's book.'

'I'm not sure about that,' he said dubiously.

'Or how about if I type it up and you sign it?' suggested Bernie. 'To make it more personal.'

'Alright,' Ernest conceded. 'You write it all down and I'll put my name to it. I'd like Richard's little one to know its father was a good police officer.'

7 FAMILY ALBUM

'Hi Eleanor! I thought you might be interested to know that you have a granddaughter.' Elated following the birth of her daughter and buoyed up by the assurances from the hospital staff that (in spite of the risks associated with her advanced age) there was nothing detectably wrong with the baby, Bernie was in a mood to be amiable with anyone – including Eleanor.

'I suppose I should congratulate you,' Eleanor answered coolly.

'It's not compulsory,' Bernie replied affably, ignoring her mother-in-law's determination not to get excited about this world-shattering news.

'And mother and baby are both doing well, I assume?'

'Yes, thank you. The parole board meets in a few hours and we're hoping that, with time off for good behaviour, we'll be allowed home this evening.'

'I'm sorry, you've lost me.'

'The doctor will be doing his rounds later today and, providing he's happy with us, we'll be discharged,' Bernie translated. 'Then we'll be on probation with the community midwife service until I've been passed off as a fit person to be left in charge of an infant.'

'I see.'

'I was thinking,' Bernie went on, 'of bringing Lucy round to your place on Saturday at the usual time, if that's OK with you?'

'Lucy?'

'The baby: I'm calling her Lucy.'

'If you like,' Eleanor said levelly, clearly determined not to display any enthusiasm. 'I'll be in, but don't feel under any obligation.'

'OK. See you on Saturday.'

Bernie ended the call feeling a little deflated. Why was Eleanor unable to display even a *little* interest in the arrival of her first (and only) grandchild?

'Here she is!' Bernie declared as the door to the flat opened. Eleanor stood back to give her room to carry in the baby seat containing the sleeping infant. 'Meet Lucy Paige.'

Eleanor did not reply, so Bernie followed her into the main room of the flat and sat down, placing the child seat on the floor next to her chair. It had taken some considerable time to make the journey from her car to Eleanor's flat because of all the people who had stopped her on the way, wanting to have a look at the new baby. The warden of the sheltered accommodation saw her arrive and came out to admire the infant and ask after their health. Several of the residents came over and compared Lucy with their own grandchildren and great grandchildren. The only person who seemed completely indifferent to her granddaughter's arrival was Eleanor.

'She should sleep for a couple of hours now: I gave her a feed just before setting out.' Bernie decided to adopt a matter-of-fact and practical approach, as if a new baby in the family were nothing at all to get excited about, but merely a potential cause of inconvenience.

'I suppose you want me to tell you whether she looks like Richard when he was a baby,' Eleanor said, hardly even glancing at her grandchild.

'Not yet,' Bernie replied, determined not to allow Eleanor's attitude to provoke her. She would stay calm and treat her rebuffs lightly. 'At the moment she looks just like all new born babies: dead ugly!'

Unexpectedly, this brought a smile to Eleanor's face.

'That reminds me of when Richard was born,' she said, mentioning her son spontaneously for the first time since his death. 'We had this little Jewish girl billeted with us – an evacuee from the East End – and when she saw him for the first time she just stared at him and said, "Coo! Ain't it ugly!" I imagine that she was right, but at the time I thought her very rude.'

'I never knew you had evacuees living with you,' Bernie commented, pleased that Eleanor was being a little more forthcoming than usual. 'Were they there for the whole war?'

'Not "evacuees",' Eleanor corrected her. 'It was just the one. Her name was Esther Lyons – I remember, because it was the same name as the tea shops – and she was eight when she came, and must have been thirteen when she left.'

'So you really brought her up: you and your in-laws.'

Eleanor got up, without answering, and went into the kitchen, returning a few moments later with a small tissue-wrapped parcel, which she handed to Bernie.

'This is for you,' she said, 'I thought, since it was bound to be expected of me, I had better make a gesture.'

Trying to hide her surprise, Bernie took the package and opened it. It contained an intricate hand-knitted yellow and white matinee jacket.

'Thank you. Did you knit it yourself?'

'No.' Eleanor somehow managed to convey by her tone that this was a ridiculous suggestion. 'There's a coloured woman in the flat two doors down who's always knitting. I bought her the wool and she knitted it for me in exchange for a donation to her church.

'I suppose I'm not allowed to call her coloured these days,' she went on, 'but I'm too old to start changing the way I talk now.'

'I think "black" is the more politically-correct term,' Bernie ventured, 'but if you're not sure how she'd like you to describe her, why not ask her?'

'Is that what that friend of yours that you left me with at the funeral calls herself?'

'You know, I really don't think we've ever discussed it,' Bernie said thoughtfully. 'Her two kids both consider themselves black; I know that – even though actually they're half white.'

'It must be difficult for them, feeling they're different from everyone around them.'

'I don't know,' Bernie was surprised at Eleanor's interest. She had never before appeared willing to engage in conversation except at the most superficial level. 'It's a very mixed community where they live, so I suppose everyone's different in a way.'

'But to feel that you're different even from your own family,' Eleanor persisted.

'They haven't really got any family – or only in the West Indies.' Bernie commented. 'Peter was brought up in a children's home and Angie left all her family behind when she came over here from Jamaica.'

That seemed to be the end of the conversation. They sat in silence for a few minutes. Then Bernie had another go.

'We've arranged for Lucy to be baptised at Pentecost. It seemed appropriate.'

'Pentecost?' Eleanor queried, realising that some sort of response was expected of her.

'Whitsun,' Bernie said, thinking that this might be a more familiar term. 'That's the eleventh of June this year. It's traditional for people to be welcomed into the church on that day. I had my first communion at Whit, back in sixty-five.'

'I didn't know you were a catholic.'

'I'm not. Well, maybe a bit. My dad was a catholic, so he used to take me to mass every week and I used to go to confession and everything when he was alive; but my Mam was Salvation Army. So I'm a crazy mixed up kid.'

'And this baptism you're so keen to tell me about, what sort of church is that going to be in?'

'The Methodist, where Angie and I go. Angie and Peter are going to be her godparents – or, not exactly godparents, the service book says, "sponsors," but it's the same thing.'

'And I suppose you're expecting me to come?'

'I'd *like* you to come – if you'd like to. I can arrange transport for you if that would help.'

'Very well.'

Bernie reflected on how much pleasanter it would be if Eleanor could bring herself to sound as if she were at least a little interested. Why did she have to behave as if attending her granddaughter's christening were an act of great kindness on her part, for which her daughter-in-law should be suitably grateful?

Back at home, Bernie's life settled into a routine around Lucy's needs for feeding, changing and soothing to sleep. Angela made frequent visits – especially during the first week after Lucy's birth when she felt the need to fend off the numerous visitors who dropped by to see the new arrival – but she had her own family to think of as well as her nursing job, so Bernie was alone when one Sunday afternoon the doorbell rang.

'Hello Dr Fazakerley. I don't suppose you remember me: Jonah Porter, we met at Richard's funeral.'

'Yes, of course I remember you,' Bernie said, recognising the smartly dressed detective inspector. 'You're the man who isn't ashamed to admit to having been good at maths at school!'

'You *do* remember me! How very gratifying.'

'Come in,' Bernie stepped back to allow him to step inside. 'And tell me what brings you here? And how did you know where I live?'

'I came to bring this present for the baby,' Jonah replied,

bringing out from behind his back a gift-wrapped parcel. 'And I knew where you live, because it's the same house that your esteemed husband lived in, with his father, in the days when I worked under him.'

'So you knew Richard when his father was still alive?'

'I certainly did. I think that, at the time that Richard and I first met, we were the only two officers on the force who were still living with our parents!'

'Or in Richard's case, *parent*, because his mother didn't come back until after his father's death.'

'Oh yes!' Jonah gave a small laugh. 'I suppose Peter will have told you about the drama at the funeral?'

'He told me that Richard's mother was there even though they'd been separated for years.'

'Oh, but it was much more than just that; but, of course, I'd forgotten: Peter wasn't there. His wife gave birth to their second on the day of the funeral. That's how *I* came to be there: I was just the sub for old Peter.'

'But what happened?'

'Well, to be fair to Richard's mother, I think all she intended to do was to slip in at the back and watch the ceremony. But there was someone from the funeral directors on the door and he insisted on asking everyone for their name, and when she said that she was the deceased's wife, he took her up to the front and sat her down next to Richard, who had no idea at all who she was. Then, when she told him, you could see that he was completely flabbergasted. I'm quite sure he had no idea that she was coming.'

'Not surprising,' Bernie said, 'seeing as she'd walked out without a word when he was only eight!'

'Really? I never knew that. In fact, until she turned up at the funeral, I'd assumed she was dead.'

'I rather suspect that may have been what Richard had started to think too. It knocked him for six, by all accounts, when she left, so he'd probably been trying to push it to the back of his mind all those years. It must have been quite a shock to find her turning up completely unexpectedly. And now,' Bernie said, getting up, 'having come all this way for the sake of the baby, you'd better come and see her.'

'Not that she's much to look at,' she added, leading the way upstairs, 'just a loud noise at one end and no sense of responsibility at the other! But I'm told that babies improve as they get older.'

'It rather depends what you mean by *improve* and *older*,' Jonah said gravely. 'Mine are sixteen and ten and I'm afraid that I can't recommend the teenage years!'

They entered a large bedroom where Lucy lay sleeping in a white cot, which looked rather out of place surrounded by sombre dark wood furniture that had been there since Richard's grandparents had had the house built for them early in the twentieth century. Jonah walked over to the cot and looked down. He had to admit that there was not much to distinguish this child from every other newborn baby. Her face was pink, her head bald, apart from a wisp of fine white fluff; her eyes were closed, but he was confident that they would be blue – like those of both her parents.

'She looks very peaceful,' he commented.

'That's 'cos she's just been fed. You wait 'til she's hungry and then you won't say that!'

'Open the present,' Jonah urged, 'it's something to keep her occupied when she *is* awake – to give you some peace.'

Bernie carefully pulled off the paper to reveal a plastic cot toy.

'You fasten it across the cot,' Jonah explained, 'and then she can lie on her back and play. Our boys had one. It does work – but only for a few minutes at a time!'

'Thank you. You shouldn't have. You hardly know us.'

'I told you before: I owe Richard a lot. And I couldn't help being interested in seeing what his daughter was like.'

'I'm glad you didn't bring another pink teddy,' Bernie commented, waving her arm towards a pile of soft toys lying in a corner of the room. 'As soon as they hear it's a girl, people seem to go all gooey and sentimental.'

'I'll make a note of that,' Jonah promised, 'No pink toys. Out of interest, what toys do you consider suitable for a girl-child? Train set? Scalextric? Meccano? Air gun? Flame-thrower?'

Bernie laughed. 'Anything that's the same as you'd give to a boy, that's all. I just don't want her stereotyped into becoming a "little princess" or something equally nauseating.'

'No princess gear, nothing nauseating,' Jonah repeated solemnly, pretending to write in an imaginary notebook.

Bernie punched him on the arm in a friendly way, laughing at his antics.

'Come down and I'll make a brew,' she said, turning to go.

'Goodbye Miss Paige,' Jonah said solemnly to the baby. Then he stopped. 'But I don't know your Christian name! What've you called her, Bernie?'

'Lucy: from lux, lucis the Latin for light.'

'Because she's the light of your life.' It was a statement, not a question.

'Yes. I thought you'd understand. And the University of Liverpool has *Fiat Lux* on its coat of arms.'

'And the University of Oxford has *Dominus illuminatio mea*, which is also about light,' Jonah observed.

'And you are altogether too clever for the police service! Why aren't you in academia?'

'I could never be bothered with studying for something as trivial as a degree – chasing villains is much more challenging!'

Over tea and cake (one of several supplied by well-meaning members of the congregation of Bernie's church) Bernie showed Jonah the growing collection of memorabilia which she was accumulating for Lucy to help her know her father.

'I found this fallen down the back of a drawer in his desk,' she said, holding up a rather tarnished silver medal with a grubby ribbon attached to it in blue and grey stripes, with thinner red stripes just visible in the grey.

'That's a queen's police medal, isn't it?' Jonah said, turning it over in his hand.

'I was hoping you might be able to tell me what he got it for.'

'Search me. I had no idea he had one. Doesn't old Peter know?'

'No,' Bernie shook her head. 'We can only assume it dates back even to before they worked together – which is a good long time, I know. I've asked around and the only person who remembers anything about it at all is an old copper who used to be the sergeant at the Headington police station. He says that he's pretty sure that it was something to do with rescuing a child from the river when it flooded sometime in the sixties, but he was pretty vague about it all.'

'No. Richard never breathed a word about it to me, I'm afraid.'

Jonah turned the pages of the folder, looking keenly at the photographs and reading the statements from Richard's colleagues.

'It's a tremendously good idea of yours to make this for Lucy,' he said with admiration. 'She'll know more about her father than I do about mine – and he's still alive!'

'Except for knowing what he was like *as* a father,' Bernie pointed out, 'because Richard never got the chance to be one.'

After about half a minute, Bernie broke the awkward silence that followed.

'Would you write something for the book?' she asked. 'Just something you remember about Richard from the time when you worked together.'

'Yes, of course I will. Does it have to be handwritten, like these? It'll be a whole lot easier for Lucy to read if I type it instead of her having to decipher my scrawl.'

'But it makes it a lot more personal being written by hand,' Bernie argued, 'more real, if you like. If you word process it, it'll be like a book – like a story that someone's made up; if you write it then it'll be like – like a witness statement, I suppose.'

'All right, you've convinced me. I'll use my very best handwriting.'

'Thanks. And Jonah, please, tell it as it is. Don't gloss over Richard's faults, which are legion. Reading all those things that people have written, it's occurred to me that maybe they've all been a bit too nice. I'm afraid that the picture that Lucy will get of her father is going to be a bit too perfect. I'd like her to know what Richard was really like, not a sanitised version.'

Jonah said nothing but raised his eyebrows interrogatively.

'I don't want her to have a picture in her mind of some great hero whom it will be impossible to live up to,' Bernie continued, trying to explain. 'And the other thing is that what she'll get from me will be such a contrast! I don't want her to think that everyone else adored this saintly man and I'm the sad old grouch who goes on about how annoying it was that he didn't like me being out alone after dark or the fact that he twice arranged for us to take his mother out on the day of the FA cup final!'

'So you'd prefer it to look as if there were two of us who found Richard a pain in the backside?'

'You've got the idea,' Bernie grinned. 'But seriously: I want Lucy to be proud of her father, but not to worship him.'

'Will you provide for this your child a Christian home of love and faithfulness?' asked the minister, reading from the service book.

'With God's help I will,' Bernie answered, suddenly feeling very alone as she carefully avoided reading out what was written in the book in front of her: *with God's help we will.* Clearly the authors were expecting two parents to be present, two parents to share the responsibility of bringing up this new human being.

'Will you help her by your words, prayers and example to renounce all evil and to put her trust in Jesus Chris her saviour?'

'With God's help I will.'

'Will you encourage her to enter into the full membership of the Church, and to serve Christ in the world?'

'With God's help I will.'

'Well, God,' Bernie thought, 'you've got your work cut out there! Don't you think it might have been easier for you in the long run just to have worked a miracle and stopped Richard being chucked off that roof so that I had a bit of human support instead of it being all down to you and me?'

The minister turned to Peter and Angela. He had taken the precaution of altering the words in his copy of the book, 'Will you, who have come to support this parent, help her with the Christian upbringing of this child?'

As he said it, he wondered whether it would have sounded more natural to have substituted 'mother' for 'parents' under the circumstances.

'With God's help we will,' Peter and Angela answered.

'Well, at least that's something,' Bernie thought. At least she knew that she could rely on Angela and Peter to stand by her, but it wasn't the same, was it? It wouldn't be the same for Lucy as having her own father to care for her.

The service continued. The creed was said, the water poured, the child named. They came to the final prayers. The minister relaxed, he was on the home straight now.

'Bless the home of this child,' he read, 'and give wisdom and affection to her parents that they-'

He stopped in confusion and looked apologetically at Bernie, who was busily swaying Lucy back and forth in her arms to quieten her after the trauma of having had water poured on her head by a strange man. The minister looked round at the congregation standing silently. He cleared his throat and began again.

'Bless the home of this child and give wisdom and affection to her mother that she may lead her in the way of perfect love.'

There was an audible sigh of relief from the congregation as he finished the prayers and ushered the baptismal party back to their seats.

Afterwards, as they relaxed over tea and biscuits in the church hall, it occurred to Bernie that it must have been very much the same for Eleanor when Richard was a baby. She had found his baptism certificate filed away in a drawer with his birth certificate and passport. He had been baptised a few weeks after birth at the local Parish church, as most babies would have been in those days, she surmised, whether or not their parents attended. The words would have been different, but Eleanor too must have stood there feeling very much alone – except that she had her parents and parents-in-law and her husband's two brothers who, it seemed, had managed to get leave from their military duties to act as godparents to their nephew. Did she too feel the weight of responsibility for the child she had brought into the world while her husband was far off in Germany, not knowing when, or if, he would return?

8 MISSING PERSON

A few days later, a large envelope plopped through the letterbox on to the doormat in Bernie's hall. She picked it up and looked at the postmark: Reading. She did not know anyone who lived in Reading. She carried it back to the kitchen and tore it open with a knife. There was a thick sheaf of papers inside. The top one was a covering letter, printed on an inkjet printer.

'Dear Bernie,' she read, 'as I promised you, here is my contribution to your treasure trove of stories for Lucy. I thought a lot about what you told me about Richard and his mother and it helped me to make sense of something that happened a long time ago. I hope that you consider this a suitable story for Lucy to read about her father. I'm afraid that it does paint him in a rather heroic light. However, I have stuck to the truth as per your instructions and I have done my best to emphasise the shameless way in which he took advantage of my youthful eagerness to persuade me to turn out at his beck and call at all hours of the day and night. I hope that this behaviour is sufficiently egregious to ward off any possibility of his imminent canonisation.'

Bernie smiled to herself, remembering that Peter had told her that Jonah lived in South Oxfordshire and his wife worked in Reading. The typewritten letter sounded just as if he were speaking to her.

'I followed your instructions to write this by hand,' she continued to read, 'but, in case you find my writing illegible (my wife is a doctor and claims that my handwriting is worse than hers!), I've enclosed a transcript as well. Give my love to Lucy. Best wishes, Jonah.'

Bernie laid the handwritten pages on the table in front of her. Jonah had certainly gone to a lot of trouble over them. The paper was thicker than standard writing paper and was a sepia colour, presumably intended to give the impression of age. The words were written in black ink using a fountain pen with a wide nib. Each line was level and each letter large and perfectly formed. What nonsense to suggest that she might have difficulty deciphering it! But, of course, Jonah knew that. Whatever his normal everyday handwriting might be like, this was a work of art. She wondered how long it had taken him to complete it. Presumably the word-processed version was the original, which he had then painstakingly copied out in his best calligraphy.

She started to read. Was there anything this man could not do, she wondered. He certainly knew how to tell a story. Within minutes she was transported back to nineteen eighty and the start of Jonah's career in CID.

****

'Now Porter,' Detective Inspector Richard Paige growled as Jonah walked in, five minutes late and looking bleary eyed. 'I put my reputation on the line asking for you to be transferred to CID, so you'd better show everyone you're up to it.'

'Yes sir. I'm sorry I'm late sir. It won't happen again.'

Jonah momentarily considered offering an explanation for his tardiness. He was normally both punctual and punctilious and was stung by the criticism, all the more so because he knew that it was justified. He wisely decided against making excuses. If he had truly believed that they were valid then he ought to have telephoned in advance to apologise, rather than hoping that his late arrival would go unnoticed.

The truth was that Jonah had slept through the alarm – something previously unheard of for him – after having had a disturbed night. His girlfriend, Margaret, was an aspiring trauma surgeon, currently working as a junior doctor in the Accident and Emergency department of the local hospital. She had been on the late shift last night and, as so often happened, they had been so busy that she had not managed to get away until the early hours of the morning.

On this occasion, the underlying cause of the influx of casualties shortly before midnight was an intercollegiate rugby match. This was not in itself a problem, but unfortunately the two teams had both chosen the same pub to retire to afterwards: the winners to celebrate and the losers to drown their sorrows. The resultant bar brawl oozed out into the surrounding streets and threatened to become a full-scale riot, before the police arrived and arranged transport for those involved to hospital or police cells as appropriate.

Jonah had been wakened at around two-thirty by a call from Margaret saying that her motorcycle had a flat tyre, and could he come out and rescue her from the side of Marston Ferry Road where she was stranded? Of course, he could not refuse, with the result that he had returned exhausted to his bed at four a.m. and the alarm had failed to wake him when it was time to get up.

'We've just had a call,' Inspector Paige was continuing, 'from the mother of a ten-year-old girl, reporting that she's gone missing from her bedroom overnight. Her name's Paula Crossland and the family live in Wolvercote. Porter, you're coming with me to take notes while I interview the mother. Listen and learn – and smarten yourself up before we arrive! Haven't you got a comb? Johns, find out if there have been any reports of anything untoward going on in the area. You know the sort of thing: strangers hanging around the school playground, children being approached in the street etcetera. And while you're at it, see if we've got anything on any of the girl's family. In particular, has there ever been any report of domestic violence.

As they drove out to Wolvercote, Jonah wondered to himself whether Peter Johns minded being left with the boring office work while his junior colleague accompanied Paige on the more interesting task of interviewing the family and looking over the house from which she had apparently absconded. If he had been in Johns' place he would have resented being side-lined by this upstart police constable, whom Paige had identified as a promising youngster and decided to train up as a detective; but Johns never seemed to mind the routine jobs, at which he was very good, so perhaps he was content.

The Crossland family home was a large detached house, set in a well-tended garden. They were greeted at the door by an attractive woman in her early forties who introduced herself as Felicity Crossland, the missing girl's mother. She was clearly extremely worried about her daughter's disappearance but, nevertheless, was immaculately dressed and well groomed. She led them into a spacious sitting room and they all sat down. Jonah took notes as Paige questioned Mrs Crossland about her daughter's disappearance.

It was the school holidays and, since Mrs Crossland had a job at the Oxford University Press, she had an arrangement with her parents to look after Paula at their home in Botley during the working day. Mrs Crossland had gone into Paula's room at seven thirty that morning to tell her that it was time to get up. She was not there; nor was she anywhere to be found in the house or garden. The back door was unlocked, which it had not been when Mrs Crossland retired to bed the previous night, shortly after eleven.

Some of Paula's clothes were missing from her bedroom and her anorak had gone from the hook in the hall where it was kept. Mrs Crossland had immediately rung her parents to find out whether Paula had somehow managed to make her own way there, but they had neither seen her nor heard from her. A round of telephone calls to Paula's friends also drew a blank. So it was that her mother came to call the police at eight forty-five that morning to report her missing.

'You haven't mentioned Paula's father,' Paige said to Mrs Crossland. 'Is he still around at all?'

'No. We don't have anything to do with him,' she answered curtly, as if this were something which she preferred not to talk about.

'So you're divorced I take it?'

'We soon will be.'

'And how does Paula feel about that?' Paige asked quietly.

'She knows that it's all for the best.'

'Did she tell you that?'

'We discussed it and she agreed with me that we're better off without him.'

'I'll need his address. I assume you have it?'

'Yes.' Mrs Crossland got out an address book from a drawer and copied out an address on to a piece of paper, which she handed to Paige. 'I suppose he *could* have come and taken her,' she conceded, 'but I really don't think his fancy woman would allow him to. She wants him to herself and he gives her everything she wants. Anyway, Paula wouldn't go with him and he knows he's not welcome here.'

Paige looked down at the address: Kings Sutton was twenty miles or so north of where they were. That was a long way to walk, but there was a rail service from Oxford.

'Did Paula have any money with her, do you know?'

'Perhaps a few pounds: not much.'

'Have you contacted Paula's father to let him know that she's missing?'

'No. He wouldn't be interested. Anyway, what's it got to do with him?'

'Well, she *is* his daughter,' Paige pointed out patiently. 'He has a right to know. And you never know, he might be able to tell us something that would help us find her.'

'*You* can talk to him if you like.' Mrs Crossland said in a tone that made it very clear that she was not prepared to do so.

'Does he still have a key to this house?'

'I changed the locks.'

'You were afraid he might come back?'

'No. I was afraid he might lose the keys and then we would be vulnerable to burglary.' Mrs Crossland said coldly.

'You said that you are getting divorced: has your husband made any attempt to get custody of Paula?'

'Of course not! I told you: the girl he's taken up with wants him all to herself. We agreed that it would be better for Paula to have a clean break and try to forget about her father.'

'So he has no access to her at all?'

'We both agreed that it was better that way.'

'Thank you Mrs Crossland, that's very clear. Now, we'd like to see Paula's room, if you don't mind.'

She took them upstairs to a rather cluttered bedroom, strewn with magazines and Barbie dolls. A papier-mâché crocodile hung dangerously from the central light fitting. The bedclothes were rumpled and a large toy rabbit leaned precariously over one side. Paige wandered round the room opening drawers and cupboards.

'Is this Paula's father?' he asked, showing Mrs Crossland a photograph, which he had found buried deep in one of the drawers of Paula's desk. She looked down at the picture, which was of a girl of eight or nine standing next to a man in his forties. He had his arm round her and they were both smiling triumphantly. Paige recognised the distinctive shape of an ordnance survey triangulation post behind them and concluded that they had just reached the highpoint of some walking expedition.

Paula's mother nodded.

'He took her off to the Peak District last year – camping. Of course we didn't realise then that he was planning to run off with this girl he'd met at the conservation volunteers.'

'May I keep this? And can you give us a recent photograph of Paula, please?'

Mrs Crossland went back downstairs to find a suitable portrait of her daughter. The two police officers continued to look round the room. Paige was purposefully looking in every cupboard, under the bed and beneath the desk. He seemed to be searching for something.

'The rucksack that Paula's wearing in this picture,' he said, when her mother returned. 'Did it belong to Paula?'

'Yes – it's in the wardrobe, I think.'

'No it isn't. It isn't anywhere in this room. Could she have taken it with her?'

'I suppose she must have.' Mrs Crossland looked in the wardrobe to assure herself that the rucksack really was not there. 'Her sleeping bag's missing too – that was in the bottom of the wardrobe with the rucksack.'

'It looks as if she planned to be away overnight. What about food? Have you checked the kitchen?'

They trooped downstairs and established that Paula appeared to have taken half a loaf, some apples, a packet of biscuits and a Mars bar.

'Now, just to satisfy me that we aren't making fools of ourselves,' Paige said, 'I'd like you to take Constable Porter upstairs and give him a ladder to reach that loft access that I saw on the landing, while I check out the garden and the shed. I know that you've looked everywhere, but you'd be surprised how often missing children turn out to have hidden themselves away somewhere at home.'

'So, what do you make of this case?' Paige asked Jonah, as they got into the car to leave, some twenty minutes later, having established beyond doubt that Paula was not on the premises.

'I think we ought to talk to the father,' Jonah said, confident that Paige also believed that the girl's absent parent was key to her disappearance.

'I agree, which is why we are now heading for King's Sutton. But while you drive, I'm going to get on to Johns to see if he's dug up anything about the family. Is Mrs Crossland just sore because her husband has left her for a younger woman or does she have a legitimate reason for wanting to keep him away from the house?'

'Domestic violence you mean?'

Paige did not answer. He was busy calling up his sergeant on the radio. Johns did not have much to report. There were no recorded incidents involving any of the Crossland family. The area around the Crossland residence was devoid of CC-TV coverage and nobody had reported any sinister strangers lurking in the vicinity in recent weeks.

'We're on our way to interview the girl's father,' Paige told him. 'I think she may be trying to find him. Get on to the bus company and the railway station. If she was aiming for his house, she could have got a bus into Oxford and then a train to King's Sutton. It seems that she must have left the house sometime before seven, when her mother got up; so she could have been on an early morning bus into the city. And organise a house-to-house of the neighbourhood around her house: one of the neighbours may have been out early and seen her. She was probably wearing a green anorak and had a rucksack and a sleeping bag with her.'

Half an hour later, they were knocking on the door of a small, unprepossessing semi-detached house on a council estate in rural Northamptonshire. At first, there was no reply, but seeing a net-curtain twitch in the front bedroom, they knocked again and eventually a young woman opened the door. She was clasping a small baby to her chest while a toddler gripped her firmly round one leg. She looked tired. Paige introduced himself.

'I'm Detective Inspector Richard Paige, and this is Detective Constable Jonah Porter. We're looking for a Mr James Crossland.'

'He's at work. What's all this about?'

'It concerns his daughter. Can you tell us how we can contact him, please?'

'You'd better come in, I suppose. I'll ring him.'

The house was dingy and untidy. A faint odour of dirty nappies pervaded the atmosphere. Jonah considered that, given the choice, he would not have exchanged the spacious comfort of the Crossland family home in Wolvercote for this.

'If you could just give us the address of Mr Crossland's work then we can find him there and we won't need to trouble you anymore,' Paige suggested.

'OK.'

Jonah handed over his notebook, open at a clean page, and she wrote down an address.

'Now can you tell us your name, and give us a contact number in case we need to speak to you again?'

'Julie Shaw.'

'And you live here with James Crossland?'

'What if I do?' she was becoming defensive. 'Now, what is this? Is the kid in some sort of trouble?'

'She appears to have run away from home. We think she may try to come here to her father.'

Paige fumbled in his pocket and then handed Ms Shaw a card. 'If she does turn up here, or if you think of anything that might be useful for us to know, ring me on this number.'

She took it, but said defiantly, 'she won't come! Jimmy made it clear to them both that he wasn't having anything more to do with them. This is his family now,' she indicated the baby in her arms and the toddler, who had started crying when she raised her voice, 'not that stuck-up cow and her stupid kid.'

As Jonah drove the few miles to Mr Crossland's office, Paige looked at the two photographs that he had taken away from his wife's house: the school photograph of a brown-eyed ten-year-old with black hair in tight plaits, and the holiday snap of the same girl, a little younger, with her father's arm resting on her shoulder.

'I can't understand,' Jonah said, 'why he would leave his wife and everything he had – for that!'

'She makes him feel young, I expect,' Paige replied, still looking at the photographs. 'What *I* can't understand is how he could leave a daughter with whom he clearly had a very special relationship, and not, apparently, even *try* to maintain contact with her.'

James Crossland owned a small publishing house in Banbury. He was evidently expecting them: presumably, his girlfriend had telephoned to let him know that the police were on their way. He took them into his office and a secretary brought in a tray of tea and biscuits. The building was a converted warehouse and Jonah could see, through the window, the Oxford canal below them.

'How can I help you?' he asked anxiously. Jonah wondered whether this anxiety was on behalf of his daughter or because he was naturally nervous in the presence of the police. Had he perhaps forgotten to renew his road tax, or been less than totally frank in his income tax return? He was an unprepossessing man: short, balding and, judging by appearances, a few years older than his wife. Jonah thought it odd that he had managed to attract such a woman as the handsome and well-turned-out Felicity Crossland, or even the far lesser catch (in Jonah's opinion) scruffy and harassed Julie Shaw.

'Your daughter, Paula, is missing,' Paige told him bluntly. 'Have you heard anything from her?'

'No. Nothing,' Crossland looked around nervously. 'You surely don't think *I* had anything to do with her disappearance?'

'We thought that she might have been trying to come to you.'

'No. Why would she do that?'

'When was the last time you saw your daughter?'

'It must have been,' he paused. 'Last November,' he concluded eventually. 'Yes, that was it. Felicity summoned me to collect the rest of my things, and I went over. Paula had been playing at a friend's house, but she came back just as I was leaving.'

'And you really haven't set eyes on her since?' Paige sounded incredulous. 'You didn't even, for example, visit her at Christmas?'

'We decided – that is, Felicity and I both agreed – that it would be better for Paula to have a clean break. It would only have unsettled her to have me going round all the time: much better to forget all about me. And it suited *us* too – I mean Julie and myself – we wanted to be together, just the two of us and the baby. After Ben was born I realised that I couldn't go on living a lie any more: I had to be with him and Julie.'

'Last summer you took your daughter on holiday,' Paige said, producing the photograph from his pocket. 'It doesn't look to me as if the girl in that photo was expecting her father to walk out on her forever shortly afterwards.'

'It was a sort of *goodbye* holiday,' Crossland explained sheepishly. 'Julie and I had just decided that we wanted to be together permanently. It was one last good time together for me and Paula.'

'So that was then you told her you were leaving?'

'Well, no. I hadn't told Felicity at that stage, so I couldn't say anything to Paula.'

'So you just went ahead: trying to give her the time of her life, being a fantastic dad – and then three months later you made a clean break and never spoke to her again?' Paige asked scathingly.

Crossland did not answer. Jonah stared at his superior, wondering what had provoked this uncharacteristic outburst. Paige was not in the habit of allowing witnesses to know what he thought of them. He was well-known amongst his colleagues for his detached approach.

'So Paula hasn't, as far as you know, tried to get in touch

with you recently – or at any time in the last year and a half?' Paige resumed, speaking calmly now.

'No,' Crossland said confidently.' Then he hesitated. 'Well, there was a period a few months back when she started ringing the office, but I told my secretary to inform her that she couldn't speak to me, and eventually she stopped.'

'Well, if she should ring again, keep her talking and let me know,' Paige said, handing Crossland one of his cards. 'Try and get her to tell you where she is. We have to be going now, but if you think of anything, anything at all, that might help us to find her, ring me on that number.'

As the secretary showed them out, Paige gave her another of his business cards and repeated his instructions as to what to do if Paula were to telephone.

'Has Mr Crossland's daughter ever visited this office?' he asked.

'Yes,' the secretary replied without hesitation. She was brisk and efficient, in contrast to her employer. 'She spent the day here on two occasions when the Crosslands had problems with childcare. The second occasion was just over a year ago and the first must have been two or three years before that. I can look up the dates in the diary if you like.'

'No – thank you – that won't be necessary. I just wanted to check whether she knew where Mr Crossland worked – in case she tries to make her way here.'

They called in at a bakery in Summertown on their way back, to buy sandwiches for a working lunch. By one thirty, Jonah and Paige were sitting round a table with Peter Johns, comparing notes. Enquiries on the buses and at the railway station had been unfruitful. Nobody had seen a ten-year-old girl. The station staff, in particular, were confident that they would have remembered her because it was unusual for children to travel alone. Copies of both photographs were being produced for distribution to the officers who would be carrying out the house-to-house calls. Other officers had been drafted in to search open spaces near Paula's home and police patrols across the county were on the lookout for her.

Paige spread out a map of Oxfordshire and parts of the adjoining counties on the table. Jonah and Johns hastily retrieved their lunch from underneath it, before joining Paige in studying the area between Paula's house and her father's office.

'I'm convinced that she intended to find her father,' Paige said. 'She'd never been to his house: in fact we're not sure that she even knew the address; but she *had* visited the office. So that's probably where she'd try to go. We know she didn't go into Oxford and get the train, but what about the bus? There are buses to Banbury.'

'Yes sir,' Johns agreed, through a mouthful of cheese sandwich. 'We asked the drivers of the buses going north as well as the ones going south. No reports of a ten-year-old girl on any of the early morning buses going up the Banbury road.'

'The buses don't start until about half past seven,' Jonah put in knowledgeably. He had only recently moved out of his parents' home in Kidlington and was familiar with the bus service to the north of Oxford. 'So she would have been hanging around for a while, if you accept what her mother said about having been awake since six-thirty. We reckoned she had to have been out of the house by then, not to have been heard moving about.'

'So, we don't think she went by train or bus,' Paige muttered, 'could she have planned to walk, I wonder?'

'It must be twenty-five miles!' Johns objected.

'But she might not know that,' pointed out Jonah.

'And she goes on walking holidays with her father,' Paige said thoughtfully. 'She might see it as fitting to be walking to find him, carrying the sleeping bag from their camping holiday in the rucksack that she wore the last time they were happy together.'

'Well, if she *is* walking,' Johns said, standing up to brush the crumbs from his trousers, 'she'll be picked up by one of our patrol cars. She'd be pretty noticeable, striding out along the Banbury road.'

'Yes. That's what's worrying me,' Paige admitted. 'Why *hasn't* she been picked up yet? It makes you wonder whether she could have been *picked up* by someone else. She'd be very vulnerable: young girl walking alone in the early morning. Once she cleared Kidlington – assuming she got that far – she'd be out in the country and easy prey to any passing child molester.'

He too got up. He folded the map and turned to his colleagues.

'Right! Let's get back to work. Johns: you take this list of Paula's friends and find a WPC to go round with you interviewing them. You never know, Paula may have confided her plans to one of them. Porter: you come with me. I've got the address of her class teacher. I'd like to know how she thinks Paula took her father's departure.'

Three hours later, they reconvened. Johns handed Paige a sheaf of notes, saying, 'I've written down everything the kids said, but there wasn't much. They all agreed that Paula was upset at her parents splitting up, but none of them knew anything about any plan to run away. Now, if you don't mind …,' he looked up at the clock meaningfully.

'Yes, yes of course,' Paige said, remembering that his sergeant's wife was expecting their first baby in a few weeks and that Johns had been becoming increasingly anxious to get off home promptly after work each day. 'Off you go. See you in the morning.'

'Thank you, sir. Normally I'd stay, but it's just I told Angie I'd be back by half past.'

Paige waved him away and then looked at Jonah.

'What about you? Is anyone anxiously awaiting your return?'

'No.' Jonah shook his head. 'Margaret's on "lates" this week, so I'm footloose and fancy free.'

'Good. I'd like to go through everything with you again. I can't help feeling we're missing something.'

The telephone rang. It brought news that a witness had been found who remembered seeing Paula that morning. He had been walking his dog before going to work and he had passed her as she descended the path from the canal bridge to the towpath.

'The canal!' Paige exclaimed. 'Of course! I'd forgotten about the canal.'

He opened the map again and traced the course of the Oxford canal from Wolvercote to Banbury.

'It's a good long way,' he observed, 'but Paula probably didn't have any real idea of distance: she just knew that her house and her father's work were both on the same canal. And she'd probably been for walks along the towpath and assumed that all she needed to do to get to him was to keep walking.'

The remaining hours of daylight were spent searching the towpath along a ten-mile stretch on either side of Wolvercote. At Paige's insistence, greater resources were focussed to the north, but the possibility that Paula had gone south towards Oxford city centre could not be ruled out. They were now hampered by well-wishers keen to join in, and by the local press who, immediately that the canal was mentioned, smelled a possible drowning and were keen to be in on the discovery of the body.

At half past eight, Paige called off the search until the morning. With the light fading, they could not be sure that they would see any evidence that there might be of Paula's passage along the path, and everyone was becoming tired. They would be more productive returning to the task fresh the following day. It was a good thing that the weather was mild and there was no rain forecast. Even if Paula was sleeping in the open, there was a good chance that her sleeping bag would keep her from suffering from exposure.

Jonah was alone with Paige in his office. The inspector was showing no signs of going home, so Jonah waited patiently. Paige opened the map again and stared down at it.

'How fast do you think a ten-year-old walks?' he asked.

'Dunno. I don't have much experience.'

'An adult would probably average about three miles an hour, which means that in the time since Paula got to the towpath they could have covered up to forty-two miles.'

'Going flat out non-stop,' Jonah commented.

'Agreed, but even allowing for rests and for Paula walking a bit slower, she could have got a good way on the way to Banbury; just so long as she kept at it. And I think she would have kept at it. Remember what her teacher said: her father leaving transformed her from a lively, outgoing girl into a quiet, introspective one. She obviously took it very hard – whatever her mother may think.'

'So what d'you think we should do?'

'Get some sleep.' Paige got up and folded the map. 'Then, if you're game for an early start, I propose to go out at first light and start walking back along the towpath from Banbury towards Oxford.'

The following day was cloudy, but bright. At five thirty, Jonah and Paige got out of their car outside Mr Crossland's office. They spent some time searching around the exterior of the building, in case, by some great feat of perseverance, Paula had managed to complete her journey the evening before and had dossed down for the night to await her father's arrival in the morning. Then they made their way down to the towpath.

It was very quiet in the growing light of the new day. They walked together in silence, looking this way and that, hoping to see some sign of a child asleep in the long grass or eating breakfast on one of the benches provided for travellers.

Then, an hour or more later, they rounded a bend and saw a small figure coming towards them. Jonah quickened his pace, but Paige held him back.

'Don't rush. We don't want to frighten her. Just go on

as if we were on an early morning stroll.'

After what seemed like an age, they were close enough to see that this was indeed the little girl whose picture had been burned into their memories over the past twenty-four hours. She was limping a little, but still manfully striding out, determined to reach her goal. As the men approached, she stood politely aside to let them pass, but Jonah stood in the centre of the path, barring her way, and Paige knelt down to speak to her. He showed her his warrant card.

'It's OK Paula,' he said gently. 'We're police officers. Your Mum and Dad have been worried about you.'

Paula looked up at him with a mixture of alarm and relief on her face.

'What are you going to do with me?' she asked anxiously.

'We'll have to take you to your parents. They'll want to know you're safe.'

'Back to Oxford, you mean?'

'Well, I don't know. Do you have a better suggestion?'

Paula thought for a moment, looking into his eyes, sizing him up.

'I *was* going to see Dad at work,' she suggested in the end.

'Now there's a thought! That's much nearer. Let's all go there, shall we?'

Paige took Paula's rucksack and Jonah hoisted her up on his back to rest her tired and blistered feet, and they made their way back a short distance to a lock where they were able to cross the canal and join a lane, which wound through fields towards the main road. Paige had radioed through to arrange transport, and a car was waiting for them when they arrived.

By eight o'clock, they were waiting outside James Crossland's office building while he fumbled with his keys to let them in. He was unshaven and had clearly dressed in a hurry when he received the call to tell him that his daughter had been found. Then the efficient secretary arrived and she led them inside and set about taking people's coats and brewing tea.

Paige somehow managed to manipulate things so that Paula was left alone with her father in his office while the rest of the company waited in the reception area for Mrs Crossland to arrive. Paige had deliberately delayed informing her of her daughter's whereabouts to prevent her reclaiming the child before she had had a chance to meet her father. He had done his best. Now it was up to Paula to convince the weak James Crossland that what his old and his new partners had told him was wrong. It was *not* better for all concerned for Paula to have a clean break and never see her father again.

****

Bernie smiled as she added Jonah's story to her folder of reminiscences. She felt sure that this was just the sort of story that Lucy would enjoy hearing when she was older. Jonah was right: Richard's behaviour during this investigation must have been influenced by his own experience of losing a parent at a young age. That was how he had managed to get inside the mind of the little girl who had so single-mindedly tried to find her father.

9 LAST WILL AND TESTAMENT

'Is that Mrs Bernadette Paige?' the caller asked anxiously when Bernie answered the telephone one evening, some ten months after Richard's death.

'No – I mean, yes, I suppose it is,' Bernie replied in some confusion, taken aback at being addressed by her married name, which she had never been in the habit of using. What must the person at the other end of the line think of her? Academics were notoriously absent-minded, but it must surely be unusual even in those circles to be unsure of one's own name!

'This is Melanie Wardle,' the voice went on. 'I'm the warden from Riverside Retirement Homes. Your mother-in-law is one of our residents.'

'Oh yes, of course, I remember. We've met a few times when I was visiting Eleanor. What's the matter? Is something wrong?'

'I'm very sorry to have to tell you that we found her collapsed on the floor of her flat about forty minutes ago. We called the ambulance and she's been taken to hospital in Reading.'

'Is it serious?'

'The paramedics said it might be a stroke. I think you

ought to go over to the hospital.'

'Yes,' Bernie said, feeling that she was obliged to do whatever Richard would have done had he been there. 'I'll go. Will they be expecting me? Do I just turn up at A&E?'

'I told the ambulance people that I was going to ring you. They seemed to think it was important to notify the next-of-kin, and you're the only person who ever visits Eleanor, so I assumed that must be you.'

'I suppose so,' Bernie said dubiously. 'Richard never talked about anyone else. I know she didn't have any siblings or any other children, so I suppose there *is* no one else.'

Bernie felt very out of place in the busy Emergency Department. She had Lucy in a baby carrier strapped to her front and she was carrying a large bag containing all the paraphernalia required when taking a young baby outside the home for an unspecified length of time. She reflected that Friday night was the very worst time for Eleanor to have chosen to be taken ill. The waiting room was already full and, as she looked around for where to go, a siren heralded the imminent arrival of another patient.

She located the reception window and explained why she had come. The clerk scanned a computer screen, searching for Eleanor's name.

'She's been taken to the medical assessment unit,' she said at last. 'Take a seat and I'll ring through to see if anyone can talk to you about her.'

It seemed like a long wait. Lucy woke and demanded to be fed. Bernie looked round for somewhere private to go, decided against asking any of the overworked staff for assistance and concluded in the end that nobody had any right to be more offended by witnessing discrete breastfeeding in a corner of the waiting area than at the antics of the many drunks who were by now congregating there.

Of course, it was just as she was in the process of detaching Lucy from one nipple with a view to moving her over to the other side that a young nurse came up to her and invited her to accompany her to the Medical Assessment Unit. Bernie hastily fastened her shirt and pulled her cardigan across in front of it to hide the dark patch where excess milk had sprayed on to the cotton fabric. She gathered her things together and followed the nurse down a long corridor. They reached the unit and the nurse ushered her into a small office. Soon they were joined by a harassed-looking south Asian doctor.

'You are the next-of-kin to Mrs Eleanor Paige?' he enquired.

'I'm her daughter-in-law.'

'I see. And is your husband on his way?'

'My husband is dead. I'm a widow.'

'I'm sorry. I did not know.'

'My husband died in an accident last October,' Bernie explained, seeing the look of confusion on the doctor's face as he glanced from Bernie to her daughter, who was now once more asleep with her head resting on Bernie's chest. 'Our daughter was born posthumously.'

'That's very sad. I'm very sorry to hear it.'

'But, to get back to Eleanor? What can you tell me about how she is?'

'I'm afraid that I have to warn you that it is not good news. Your mother-in-law has suffered a massive stroke. She has severe one-sided weakness and loss of speech. It is quite likely that she will not survive and if she does, she will be left with significant persistent disability.'

'I see. Thank you for being so frank with me.'

'We will be keeping her here overnight. Then, all being well, she will be transferred to the geriatric ward tomorrow.'

'I see.'

'I suggest that you go home now. The nurse will give you a telephone number to ring tomorrow for news.'

Eleanor Paige died during the night. Bernie tried to feel sorry, but she could not help thinking how nice it would be no longer feeling obliged to pay her visits which never appeared to be appreciated. Eleanor, she reflected must have been in her eighties. She had had a good innings – far longer than either of Bernie's own parents – and if the doctor was right in saying that, had she lived, she would have been seriously disabled, perhaps it was all for the best that she had not survived.

There being nobody else, Bernie accepted responsibility for arranging the funeral. Obviously, if Richard had been alive he would have done it, so now it fell to her. It was difficult to know what she would have wanted – except that presumably she would not have welcomed being filed in the grave in Headington cemetery with her estranged spouse. In the end, Bernie decided on cremation, with the ashes being interred in Richard's grave. Who to notify of the death was another conundrum, since Eleanor seemed to have no ties with either friends or family. A notice in the Oxford Times would have to suffice.

Then came the question of Eleanor's estate. She owned the flat in Henley where she lived and, since she had always paid the service charge on time and appeared to be comfortably off as far as could be deduced from her visible spending, she presumably had some savings to supplement her old age pension. Melanie the Warden expected Bernie to know who would inherit, while Bernie felt that it was no business of hers. Fortunately, Melanie was able to find the name of the solicitor who had represented Eleanor when she bought the flat some five years previously and, when they contacted him, he revealed that he was the custodian of her will. She had recently made a new one, to take into account the death of her son, who had previously been the executor and residual legatee. He made an appointment for Bernie to go to his office to read it.

'You could have knocked me down with a feather,' Bernie said to Angie over a pot of tea the day after her visit to the solicitor, 'when he read out that I was the sole legatee

– well, apart from a small trust fund for Lucy, of which I am trustee, together with the solicitor, who is the executor. I feel dreadful about not liking her now.'

'Don't,' Angie advised. 'If you didn't like her then all the more reason why she ought to be grateful for the way you kept going round there every week.'

'Except that she always managed to convey the impression that she would probably have preferred me not to.'

'Well, I'd say that this just goes to show that she did want you to go to see her, but she just didn't want you to feel good about it.'

Bernie thought about this.

'Anyway,' Angie went on, determined not to allow her friend to continue to feel guilty, 'the main thing is that you did what you thought Richard would have wanted, and what you thought was going to be best for Lucy.'

The flat had to be sold as soon as probate was obtained, since there was a restriction on its use, which required residents to be over fifty-five years of age. In any case, Bernie had no use for it. She also had no wish to keep any of Eleanor's furniture, but she decided that all the personal effects ought to be sorted through, rather than disposed of in bulk. So she and Angie went over one afternoon and emptied drawers and cupboards into cardboard boxes and brought them back to Bernie's house.

One of the drawers of the bureau in Eleanor's bedroom was locked. Bernie got out the bag of belongings that the hospital had handed back to her after Eleanor's death. There were the clothes that Eleanor had been wearing when she was admitted, her wristwatch and an eternity ring, which Bernie remembered having seen on the ring finger of her left hand. Eventually she found a bunch of keys, which had hung on a cord round Eleanor's neck. She identified the small key that fitted the lock and opened the drawer. Inside were a photograph album and a cardboard box, which had previously contained writing paper and envelopes. Bernie looked inside and saw that it was crammed full of letters. She placed the box and the album carefully into the crate where she had already packed various official documents, including Eleanor's birth and marriage certificates, her passport (now expired) and her school-leaving certificate.

On the anniversary of Richard's death, Angie invited Bernie to spend the evening with her, but Bernie declined the offer. She had decided that today would be the day when she would look at the contents of Eleanor's locked drawer and perhaps discover the secret of the life that she had led between her sudden disappearance in 1948 and her equally unexpected reappearance in 1982. She put Lucy to bed, came downstairs and took out a cardboard box from one of the kitchen cupboards. She placed it on the table and opened the flaps at the top.

At the top lay Eleanor's birth certificate. Bernie opened it up and looked at it. 'September nineteen twenty,' she read out loud. 'So she was only nineteen when Richard was born.'

Bernie had assumed that her mother-in-law had been older than this. It turned out that she had been only eighteen when she had married Edward Paige. Perhaps it was not therefore surprising that, five years later, when he returned from incarceration in Germany, she came to the conclusion that the marriage had been a mistake. The next document in the box was the marriage certificate, which confirmed that Eleanor Jane Carter and Edward Cuthbert Paige had been married at St Michael and All Angels Church, Summertown on 13th May 1939.

What must it have been like for the young Eleanor to move directly from living with her parents to living with those of her husband? Parents who might well have had quite different plans for their son, and who perhaps resented his having put himself in a position where he was obliged to marry the daughter of his father's head clerk. She must have felt very isolated in this new family, without even the company of her new husband. For the first time, Bernie felt sympathy for Eleanor. She must have been in an impossible position: trying to bring up her baby son under the watchful eye of her parents-in-law and knowing that her own parents would be unlikely to take her side in any disagreement, because of her father's subservient role at the bank.

Next out of the box was Eleanor's passport. It had long ago expired. Presumably, Eleanor had not travelled abroad in recent years. Bernie opened it and was surprised to discover that it was full of visas for countries all over the world. She looked again at the date of issue. Evidently, during the nineteen seventies Eleanor had led a most adventurous life, travelling to Russia, Turkey, Chile, Venezuela and, it seemed, practically every African country you might care to name. What was she doing in all those places?

Bernie laid the intriguing passport aside and picked up the box, which she remembered contained personal letters: presumably, letters from a friend or friends whom Eleanor wanted to remember.

She opened the first letter, which was an aerogram from Washington DC. The writing was very small and cramped up, presumably to fit as much as possible into the limited space.

Dear Lennie, it began. Bernie was puzzled for a moment. Who was Lennie? Then she realise that this must be someone's pet name for Eleanor.

Dear Lennie,

I'm really enjoying it here in Washington, and I think that it was definitely a good move career-wise. I'm starting to make some useful contacts. Of course, it's a pity that we couldn't find a way of you coming too, but it's only for 6 months and then we'll be back into the old routine.

The letter was mostly concerned with meetings that the correspondent had had with people whose names Bernie did not recognise. She read quickly past a description of a visit to the White House and a chance meeting with someone called 'Podge', who appeared to be an old friend of both Eleanor and her correspondent. There was nothing of particular interest to an outsider. She reached the bottom of the page and strained to read the signature. It looked like 'Ally'. She frowned. Perhaps it was short for Alison or Alice or Alexandra?

There were about ten more of these airmail letters from America, all dated during 1953. It looked as if Ally had written once every two weeks or so during her six months in Washington. It became clear that she and Eleanor had been close friends. Indeed Bernie deduced from references to 'the old place' and 'our dear flat' that they shared a flat in London to which she was planning to return when her period abroad was over. Another thought dawned on her: what was there to say that 'Ally' was a woman? Could the name be short for Alistair or Alan? She had been assuming that this was one of the female students that Ernest Walker had talked about, but there was no evidence of that. Could Eleanor have been cohabiting with a new boyfriend? That would certainly explain why neither her parents nor her in-laws wanted anyone to know where she was.

The next item was a postcard with a picture of the Eiffel tower. It was also from Ally and was very brief, consisting mainly of an apology for not having time to write a more substantial letter.

There were only a few letters remaining in the box. They were all from the sixties and were short letters home from trips abroad, which Ally had made. The letters ceased entirely in 1964. Did this mean that they had fallen out? Or was it that they were never separated for long enough to feel the need to write? Or perhaps the telephone had taken over as their preferred means of communication. Bernie put the letters back in the box and went to make herself a fresh cup of tea before continuing her delving into Eleanor's past.

When she returned, she picked up the photograph

album, which had lain beneath the box of letters. She opened it to see, on the first page, a large black-and-white photograph of a group of five young women. They stood smiling towards the camera, each with her arms around her neighbours. Could these be the students whom Ernest had said Eleanor had become friendly with and from whom she had learned 'ideas'?

Looking more closely, Bernie identified the woman on the left-hand end of the line as Eleanor. The woman next to her looked a little younger and very slightly shorter. She had what Bernie assumed were golden curls (it was hard to judge in black-and-white) framing her face, which was conventionally beautiful with pale, smiling eyes, even white teeth and a delicate nose. The other three women were also younger than Eleanor, but not so stunning. Two of them, one short and dumpy the other tall and skinny, wore spectacles and looked rather owlish; the other had a very spotty complexion and crooked teeth.

Bernie turned the pages. There were more pictures of groups of women: at first, all black-and-white but later colour photographs started to predominate. Bernie was able to confirm her assessment that the woman with her arm around Eleanor's shoulder in the first photograph did indeed have golden hair and blue eyes. This same woman seemed to appear in all of the photographs, while the others were in fewer and fewer as the album progressed. Bernie judged that the photographs were in chronological order, so it looked as if this one woman had remained a close friend while the others had drifted away. Who was she? Could this be the mysterious Ally? On balance, Bernie thought that extremely probable, although she could not help thinking that a male Ally was another definite possibility.

The later pictures featured more and more exotic locations. As Eleanor and her companion reached middle-age they could be seen in Red Square, in front of the Taj Mahal, coming out of an African grass hut and sitting in many different bars and cafés in places that Bernie could not identify. Most often, these later pictures were of the other woman alone: presumably, Eleanor herself had taken them.

Bernie carefully extracted two photographs from the album: the first photograph of the group of young women, perhaps taken in Oxford before Eleanor left home, and a picture of the woman whom she thought might be called Ally from the end of the album, when she looked to be in her late forties. She put these in an envelope and placed it in the drawer of her desk. Then she put the album, the letters and the other documents away and started to think of a plan of campaign.

She still did not have any greater understanding of what it could have been that attracted Eleanor away from her husband and young son, but at least she now had some potential starting points for finding people who knew her during her period of absence. She got out a pad of paper and wrote a list.

- *Look for "Ally" on graduation lists circa 1948.*
- *Show group photo to people who may have known the students: retired tutors, alumni …*
- *Gaudies / other alumni events.*
- *Appeal through alumni associations for people who knew Eleanor.*

She sat staring at the list for a few minutes. Now that it was written down, it did not look as if she had much to go on. Then she remembered her conversation with Eleanor when Lucy was newborn and added another bullet point:

- *Find Esther Lyons.*

10 BIRTHDAY GREETINGS

It was one thing to have a plan for finding out where Eleanor had gone when she left home, but quite another to carry it out. It was the start of the Michaelmas term and Bernie was back at work. She now discovered how little time was left after fulfilling (insofar as it was possible to fulfil) the demands of both a full-time job and a six month old baby. The mystery of her mother-in-law's disappearance no longer seemed so intriguing when she finally got Lucy to sleep in the evening, only to realise that she had a pile of marking that had to be completed before her first tutorial the following day. Conscious that there was still a groundswell of opinion amongst her male colleagues that female academics with young children were a liability, she also felt compelled to maintain her rate of production of research papers, upon which her career depended. All in all, twenty-four was a very inadequate quota of hours to fit in the tasks that it was absolutely necessary for her to complete in the course of each day.

Time passed and Lucy's first birthday dawned. Bernie had carefully arranged her tutorial times during Trinity Term so as to be able to be at home with her daughter for the day. Not, she told herself, that Lucy would appreciate the significance, but it was good to have the excuse to force herself to put parenthood before her job sometimes.

She was surprised when the doorbell rang in the middle of the afternoon. It was too early for Peter, Angie and Eddie, who were coming over after work and school to celebrate the occasion with a tea party. She opened the door and saw the smartly dressed figure of Jonah Porter holding a large gift-wrapped parcel in his hands. She noted with approval that the wrapping paper featured ferocious-looking dinosaurs and not 'my little pony' or fluffy bunnies.

'I've come to see the birthday girl,' he announced cheerfully.

'It's very good of you to remember,' Bernie opened the door wide and stood back to let him in. 'But you shouldn't have,' she added, looking meaningfully at the present, 'really. We didn't even expect a card. It's not as if you're family.'

'Not family?' Jonah exclaimed, pretending to be offended. 'Of course I'm family! I will have you know that Richard was my Best Man. Are you casting me off? Sending me out into the wilderness?'

'Alright, alright, I get the message,' Bernie grinned. 'Come along in.'

She led the way into the living room where Lucy was sitting on the floor playing with an assortment of coloured wooden bricks.

'She's studying Newtonian mechanics,' Bernie explained seriously, as the tower that Lucy was building toppled over and came crashing down. 'She hasn't quite got the hang of calculating the position of the centre of gravity to make sure that her edifices stay in stable equilibrium.'

Jonah stepped forward and knelt down in front of Lucy. She looked at him and, for a moment seemed about to burst into tears. She did not take kindly to strangers invading her home. Then she changed her mind and returned to the problem of stacking bricks. Perhaps if she ignored him, he would go away.

'Good afternoon Miss Paige,' Jonah said solemnly. 'I went to the shop to buy something for you for your birthday. I thought to myself "what can I get for a little princess?" I saw some lovely pink teddy bears, and I thought: "That's just the thing!" but then, just as I was getting into the queue to pay for it, I saw this!'

He presented the parcel to Lucy, who banged it hard with her small fist. Jonah helped her to tear off the wrapping to reveal a box containing a plastic train set.

'Shall I help you set it up?' Jonah asked.

He and Bernie unpacked the pieces and fitted them together to make a small figure-of-eight track, while Lucy played happily with the discarded wrapping paper.

'Look at this Lucy!' Bernie called as she pushed the small plastic engine along the track.

'Our two boys had one of these,' Jonah said, and they played with it for hours. Over the years, we collected an enormous amount of track and rolling stock. It's all in the car – I'll go and get it.'

He got up and had left the room before Bernie could answer. A few minutes later, he returned with a huge cardboard box from which protruded more of the plastic track.

'Oh Jonah!' Bernie protested, 'you can't give us all that.'

'Why on earth not? The boys are too old for it now. It was only gathering dust up in our loft.'

'But weren't you keeping it for when your grandchildren come to stay?' Bernie persisted.

'That'll be years off. And who knows if there'll ever even be any grandchildren? Much better to let Lucy get the benefit of it now. Look, if it'll make you feel better, think of it as a loan, and you can give it back the moment the first grandchild appears.'

He put the box down on the floor and started putting together a much more elaborate layout. Bernie gave in and joined him. Soon a large area of the carpet was covered.

'The difficult bit,' Jonah said, as he exchanged a straight piece of track for a curved one, in an attempt to make two ends meet up, 'is to find a way of using up every piece without having to resort to leaving any sidings going to nowhere.'

'I think,' Bernie replied, undoing a section of track which Jonah had just completed, 'that, if we move those points to *here* and extend that line a bit further, those two lines will meet up under the sideboard.'

Lucy returned to her bricks.

'Of course it was always like this,' Jonah observed, taking off his jacket and laying it over the arm of a chair. 'It was always the grown-ups who got the most fun out of it!'

A few minutes later, they sat back and admired their handiwork.

'I think we've done it,' Bernie declared.

'Well, apart from this!' Jonah retrieved a stray piece of track from under the settee.

'Never mind. Come along, Lucy, look at this!'

Bernie picked Lucy up and placed her nearer to the layout. Then she pushed one of the trains up on to a bridge.

'See now,' she said, 'I'm giving this train some potential energy by taking it up to the top of the bridge, and now,' she let go of the engine and it rolled down and along the track, 'as it runs down under the force of gravity, that potential energy is converted into kinetic energy.'

Lucy watched as the train rolled past her. Then she leaned over, picked it up and put the engine in her mouth. Bernie looked at Jonah and they both laughed.

'I'll go and make a brew,' Bernie said, getting to her feet. 'I'll leave you to continue inducting our Lucy into the business of running a railway.'

When she returned, Bernie found Jonah on all fours pushing the train round the track making 'choo-choo' noises, while Lucy had pulled herself up into a standing position and was clinging to his hair to steady herself as she waved with her other hand whenever the train went past. Bernie put down the tray that she was carrying and rescued Jonah from Lucy's clutches. She sat her down on the settee and handed her a two-handled plastic cup with a lid. Lucy started drinking noisily and Jonah got up and joined them on the settee. Bernie poured mugs of tea for them both.

'Now, you must show me how your magnum opus is coming along,' Jonah said.

For a moment, Bernie was puzzled to know what he meant. Surely he could not know about the textbook that she had embarked upon writing during a wildly optimistic period early in her maternity leave, when motherhood had seemed to consist merely of three-hourly feeds with nothing much to do in between? That project had soon had to be abandoned when she realised that babies became more demanding as they grew older and six months' maternity leave passed quicker than one might imagine.

'I mean,' Jonah explained, 'Detective Superintendent Richard Paige: This is your Life!'

Bernie fetched the red ring binder and opened it in front of them.

'Here's your magnificent contribution,' she said, turning to the pages that Jonah had written so beautifully. 'You really didn't need to go to so much trouble.'

'Are you suggesting that I don't write like this all the time as a matter of course?' teased Jonah.

'I'm suggesting that there would have been nothing wrong with a few sheets of A4 back-to-school special offer lined paper and a blue ballpoint.'

'My father always used to say: *If a job's worth doing, it's worth doing well.*'

'*My* dad used to say: *If a job's worth doing, it's worth doing badly!*' responded Bernie.

'By which he meant?'

'That sometimes it's more important *who* does a thing than how well it's done.'

'What sort of thing?'

'Well, for example: making love to your wife, playing with your kids, writing home to your parents. There are lots of things that each person has to do for themselves, because getting someone else to do it for them wouldn't be any good – even if they would have done it better. In this case, you are the only person in the world who could have written that story about Richard.'

Jonah sat pondering.

'I'm doing pretty well,' Bernie resumed, 'with getting a picture of what Richard was like from age eight onwards. There's all the stuff that Eileen got for me – and your manuscript of course – that covers his time in the police. And I met a wonderful old ex-police sergeant at the funeral, who knew him from when he was eight, up until he was transferred into CID, but his early years are still just a blank.'

'What about his mother? Can't she fill you in?'

'Of course!' Bernie exclaimed. 'You won't have heard: she died quite suddenly last August. Not that she was ever willing to talk about Richard when she was alive. It made me mad the way she behaved as if he was of no relevance to her at all – especially when you consider how attentive he always was to her.'

'Is that really what she was *always* like?' Jonah asked with interest. 'That's exactly how she seemed to me: very detached. I only met her twice: that first time at Richard's father's funeral and then a few weeks later at my own wedding. Richard had agreed to be my Best Man – I think I told you that he was my Best Man – long before she came back on the scene and then, after she pitched up at the funeral, he insisted that I invite her to come as well. He seemed to want to involve her in everything that he did, the way a small boy might. I suppose, when she came back, he treated her the same way as before she left. Anyway, she came, but she managed to convey the impression that she had no idea why she was there and that she would much prefer to be somewhere else.'

'That was just how she always behaved to me,' Bernie concurred. 'Whenever I went over, I got the impression that she would rather I hadn't come, but if I asked her if she'd prefer me not to come again, she wouldn't say. It was as if she wanted me to feel grateful to her for allowing me to come. The really weird thing was that, after she died, I discovered that she'd made a will leaving everything to me and Lucy – even though we didn't ever get on.'

'It sounds as if Lucy was probably her only living relative. I suppose she'd rather give it to her than let the state grab it.' Jonah suggested

'Yes, but she never behaved as if she thought Lucy was anything to do with her. It was all very odd. And she could always have left it to charity if she didn't want it to go to the chancellor or the Duchy of Cornwall or whatever.

'I found this in with her things,' Bernie went on, taking a silver locket out of a pouch at the back of the binder. 'There's a lock of hair inside.'

'Richard's do you think, from when he was a baby? Or maybe his father's?'

Jonah opened the locket and looked inside at the small golden curl.

'It could be Richard's, but definitely not his father's. She left her wedding and engagement rings behind when she left, so why would she have taken a lock of her despised husband's hair with her?'

'Have you got a magnifying glass?' Jonah asked, peering more closely at the inside of the locket. 'I think there's something scratched on the inside.'

Bernie rummaged through the drawers of an ancient-looking dresser and eventually found a magnifying glass, which she brought over and handed to Jonah. He peered through it with an expression of intense concentration.

'A.P,' he read, 'no, not P, F. That's it! A. F. 1949.'

'Well, I don't know who A.F. could be. Are you sure it's not A.P? P could stand for Paige, although Richard's father was Edward, not something beginning with A'

'No,' Jonah said firmly, 'it's definitely F.'

'Well, at least that settles it: it's not Richard's hair, because Eleanor had already left home by 1949.'

Bernie re-filled their mugs and handed Lucy a rusk.

'Now, tell me: what made you choose Richard as your Best Man? He was Best Man at Peter's wedding too, you know. Poor Richard! He seems to have made a bit of a habit of it: a variation of "always the bridesmaid, never the bride"!'

'It was the obvious choice. I couldn't risk asking an old school chum who might remember all sorts of disreputable incidents from my past.'

'I can't believe there are any disreputable incidents in your past.'

'That's only because I've been so good at developing this respectable persona that creates the illusion that I have always been pure as the driven snow.'

'OK then; I *dare* you: tell me about some of your wicked past.'

'Well, there was the time I took home the class hamster for the weekend and our cat ate it.'

'Premeditated murder,' Bernie said seriously. 'I can see why you wouldn't want that to get out.'

'And, when I was four, I took one of my sister's dolls and wouldn't give it back until she gave me a gobstopper.'

'Kidnapping and extortion. I'm beginning to think the British public aren't safe with you at large!'

'There you are! You can see why I chose someone who had only known me for three years. At least with old Richard I was limiting the damage to indiscretions committed in the course of my police duty.'

'And did the bride arrive at the church on her motorcycle?' Bernie asked, remembering what Jonah had said about his girlfriend in the story that he had written.

'She did threaten to,' he smiled, 'but I think her mother put her foot down at the idea of her father riding pillion and then escorting her down the aisle with them both in biking leathers. We did, however, go off on the bike afterwards, for a two-week honeymoon touring the West Country. It was a metaphor for our future life together: Margaret in the driving seat and me holding on for grim life behind her!'

They both laughed and Lucy joined in the merriment,

clapping her hands together and crushing her soggy rusk between them.

'And now,' Jonah said, getting up and reaching for his jacket, 'I must love you and leave you I'm afraid.'

He turned to Lucy, who had raised herself up into a standing position against the back of the settee, and held out his hand as if to shake hers in farewell. She launched herself at him, smearing his jacket and shirt with a messy mixture of rusk and saliva. He caught her in his arms and gave her a hug.

'Thank you Lucy, I'm glad that *you* recognise that I'm one of the family!' he said, before handing her over to her mother.

'Oh Jonah!' Bernie apologised. 'I'm sorry about that. Look at your jacket! Come into the kitchen and I'll find a cloth to clean you up.'

Jonah followed her into the kitchen where she fastened Lucy out of harm's way in her high chair, before wiping his clothes down with a dishcloth. He noticed a cake on the table. It was in the shape of a number 1 and had the words 'Happy Birthday Lucy' written in rather shaky icing lettering, beneath a single candle.

'Is that your handiwork?' he asked.

'Yes,' Bernie admitted. 'It's not very good, I'm afraid, but Angie always used to produce magnificent novelty cakes for her kids when they were young, and I feel that I have to try to compete to keep my end up.'

She stood back and looked at Jonah critically.

'I think I've got it all off now.'

'It'll be fine,' Jonah assured her. 'This suit's seen much worse than that. Now I really must be going.'

Bernie had only just finished cleaning Lucy up, after seeing Jonah to the door, when the Johns family arrived. Eddie strode past her as soon as the front door was open, demanding to know where Lucy was. He found her in the kitchen and extracted her from her high chair. Soon she was squealing merrily as he threw her into the air, catching her again and swinging her in his arms before tossing her aloft once more.

'Come along and see what we've brought you,' he said, carrying her into the living room, followed closely by his parents and Bernie. He stopped short when he saw the array of plastic track winding its way around the furniture.

'Wow!' he exclaimed, 'where did all this come from?'

'Jonah Porter turned up out of the blue and brought it,' Bernie explained. 'It used to belong to his two boys.' She felt unaccountably reluctant to admit to her friends that Jonah had spent money on a gift for Lucy.

'Now that is some train set,' Angie said, admiringly.

'But what was Porter doing here?' Peter asked, puzzled and feeling irrationally put out. 'Does he often pay you visits?'

'No: the last time we saw him was when Lucy was born and he brought over a *Congratulations* card. I think he was just de-cluttering his loft, giving us this stuff, but it was kind of him to think of Lucy.'

Eddie put Lucy down on the floor and knelt down to start pushing one of the railway trains round the track.

'Look at this, Lucy,' he called, 'we're pulling out of the station, chuff-chuff, chuff-chuff, chuff-chuff.'

'Choo-choo,' Lucy responded happily as she staggered round the room, steadying herself by holding on to the furniture, before sitting down 'plop!' on top of the track.

Peter put down the two parcels that he was carrying and stepped forward to move Lucy off the line, so that his son could push the train along the track past her. As he picked her up, she gazed up at him and smiled.

'Beter!' she cooed with delight. Peter was her favourite person, after her mother. Indeed, Bernie sometimes wondered whether she still had first place in her daughter's affections considering the amount of attention that Lucy lavished on her godfather whenever he was present.

While Lucy and the boys played with the train set, Bernie

collected together the teapot and dirty mugs on a tray and took them out to the kitchen. When she returned, she found Angie leafing through the red ring binder, which she had left on the coffee table.

'I see you've been adding to your collection of memories of Richard,' Angie remarked. 'Who did this one?'

Bernie looked over her friend's shoulder and saw that she was pointing at Jonah's contribution.

'Jonah Porter. He saw the file when he came last year and he posted this to me to go in it.'

Peter got up from where he had been trying to incorporate the last remaining piece of track into the layout and came over to look.

'Jonah never wrote that himself,' was his verdict, seeing the beautifully formed lettering. 'He must have got someone else to do it for him.'

'He said not.'

'Jonah's one of those left-handers who seem to write upside-down and back-to front,' Peter continued. 'His handwriting always used to look as if a spider got in the inkpot and then crawled across the page!'

'But this isn't handwriting,' Angie intervened, 'this is Art.'

'That's right,' Bernie agreed. 'It must have taken him ages to do – not like scribbling notes while interviewing a witness.'

Peter felt unreasonably irritated by the knowledge that his old colleague had gone to so much trouble for the sake of the little girl who had touched his heart; then he immediately felt annoyed with himself for feeling irritation. He had no business imagining that he had a proprietorial interest in Lucy, as if he were her father and not just her godfather. Nevertheless, he would have preferred not to have to share her with another man – and especially not this man: the officer who had always been just that little bit quicker and cleverer than he when they had worked together under Richard Paige. Thank goodness, Jonah lived far enough away that he and Lucy were unlikely to meet very often.

'You know, Bernie,' Angie said, breaking into Peter's reverie. 'There's one really important story missing from this book.'

'What do you mean?'

'I mean,' Angie said forcefully, '*your* story. You've got everyone else to write about Richard, but you haven't included how you two met and fell in love. And I'd say that was dramatic enough to warrant a whole book to itself!'

'But I'll be there,' Bernie argued, 'so I can tell Lucy myself.'

Her friend continued to look dissatisfied.

'Mum's right, you know,' Eddie said, looking up from his task of joining all the trucks and carriages together to make a single long train. 'You can't leave that out.'

'But it's not suitable material for a child to read,' Bernie protested. 'Think about how it actually was that I first met Richard. The case was all about a couple of my esteemed colleagues committing murder and mayhem in order to prevent anyone finding out that they were using a student house as a brothel. How am I supposed to write about that in a way that's suitable for the under-fives?'

'I'm sure you could gloss over the sordid details,' Angie said complacently.

'Alright,' Bernie conceded, 'but if I write down *my* story, then I think you ought to write yours too. Richard used to claim that he was responsible for bringing you and Peter together, although he would never elaborate.'

'I'm not sure that I agree with him on that,' Peter butted in, 'although I suppose if he hadn't got me promoted to sergeant I might never have had the nerve to propose.'

'All right,' Angie said, shaking Bernie's hand, 'it's a deal. We'll both write our stories, and Peter can judge which one is better.'

'Oh no! Keep me out of it,' Peter protested. 'I know a no-win situation when I see one.'

11 RELUCTANT HEROINE

Bernie sat in front of her computer screen staring with dissatisfaction at the words that she had just typed. She sighed. Writing the story of how she and Richard had come together was proving even more difficult than she had imagined it would be. She sat back and closed her eyes, trying to picture the scene.

But where should she start? That morning in June 1995 when the newly-promoted Detective Superintendent Paige had arrived at St Luke's college to investigate a suspected crime? Or later that day when they were alone together for the first time? For dramatic effect, perhaps the place to start was the fire at Bernie's house and Richard heroically rescuing her from the burning building.

Bernie shook her head. No. All that belonged to a different story: the story of criminal activity at an Oxford college and the unmasking of the perpetrators by our gallant boys in blue. What she somehow needed to explain was how two people from such very different backgrounds, separated in age by nineteen years and having taken an instant dislike to one another, somehow ended up getting married. And that process, she reflected, must have started at the point when she woke up in hospital after the fire.

****

Bernie gradually became aware of sounds around her. There had been sounds before: ambulance sirens, the clatter of hospital trolleys, people speaking to her in deliberately reassuring voices, which somehow were all the more frightening in consequence; but now the sounds seemed more coherent, less of a jumble. Her head ached and breathing was painful. She wondered whether she dared open her eyes or whether it would be better to pretend still to be asleep.

She lifted her eyelids cautiously and looked around. As she had expected, she was propped up in a hospital bed. As far as she could see, she was in a single room, probably because the police would be wanting to question her later, she supposed. She looked round and saw, sitting silently in a chair at the side of the bed, the detective superintendent who had so annoyed her by the way he had been conducting the investigation into the suspicious death of one of her postgraduate students. For a moment, she thought of closing her eyes again and pretending to be unconscious. Perhaps he would get tired of waiting and delegate the task of questioning her to his subordinate, Inspector Peter Johns. However, it was too late: he had seen her eyes open.

'Welcome back,' he said. 'I need a word with you.'

Bernie struggled to remember what had been happening to her. She had been sitting at her computer, studying a document, which she thought held information that would be useful to the police investigation. She had suddenly worked out what the coded message was that was hidden within the bibliography of her student's thesis. She had gone to the telephone to ring the investigating officer…

And now, here she was, in what must be a hospital ward, with a raging headache and a sore throat.

'What happened?' she asked eventually, and was surprised at the sound of her own voice, which was husky and almost inaudible.

The police officer offered her water in a plastic beaker.

She drank and then repeated the question, this time a little louder and clearer.

'Someone hit you over the head and then set the house on fire. Fortunately their main concern was to destroy your computer, so the flames hadn't reached you when we arrived and got you out.'

Bernie was silent for a few minutes, thinking about this statement. She started to piece together the jumble of memories that his mention of a fire had brought back. She had crawled to the front door, but was too weak to stand up and open it. Then there was a crash and broken glass and a large figure in the doorway and someone groping around to find her and then strong arms picking her up and carrying her out. She looked at Superintendent Paige, sizing him up. She was almost certain that he was the man who had rescued her.

'Oh no!' she thought, '*he* must have saved my life.'

Meanwhile he was continuing to speak, reassuring her that she had not been seriously injured and was set to make a full recovery. Bernie felt increasingly annoyed with herself for having allowed herself to be put in a position where she was indebted to this man. Why had she left the back door unlocked? That must be how her assailant had got into the house. Why hadn't she been able to force her limbs to raise her up so that she could have reached the catch and opened the door for herself? Why did the first person on the scene have to be Superintendent Richard Paige? Paige, who thought women needed to be accompanied if they walked the streets at night, Paige who had wanted to offer her a police guard, Paige who thought that people should be protected from unpleasant realities!

But then she realised that he too remembered the bitter exchange of words that they had had a few days earlier.

'You'll be pleased to hear,' he was saying, 'that, apart from a nasty bruise on the back of your skull and some transient damage to your lungs as a result of smoke inhalation, you are in perfect health and likely to live to a ripe old age. Although I'm probably lying about that to protect you from the hideous truth about your real condition.'

Bernie could not help smiling. She knew that she could never, never like this smug, opinionated presumptuous man, but she had to admit that he was at least trying to appear to understand her point of view; and he did seem to have a sense of humour.

'You know, superintendent,' she said, 'given a very, very long time, I think I *might* just possibly almost get to quite like you.'

'Praise indeed!' Paige said, returning the smile. 'I will try not to allow your flattery to go to my head.'

Their eyes met and, for a moment, her resolve wavered and she wondered whether perhaps she might have misjudged him. There really was something curiously attractive about the man, although she could not have said exactly what. Then the moment passed and she realised that he was speaking again.

'But back to business,' he was saying. 'I need you to tell me what it is you found in those computer files.'

The computer files! Of course! Bernie was suddenly alert and back on the case. This was no time for introspection or studying the inner workings of the superintendent's mind: they had business to attend to.

She levered herself up into a sitting position, and immediately regretted not having been more cautious, because the sudden movement made her head hurt even more. She hoped that her expression did not give away to Paige the degree of pain that she felt. She was determined not to appear weak in front of him.

She started to explain how a coded message had been hidden within the DPhil thesis that had been emailed to her a few days ago. As she spoke, she became more animated, while Paige's face became more and more blank. He might be a very clever police officer and a courageous knight in shining armour ready to rescue damsels in distress, but he knew nothing at all about the intricacies of mathematical typesetting. Bernie remembered how, a few days earlier, he had asked for clarification on exactly what an email was. It was no good! She could not explain. She would have to *show* him what she was talking about.

She got out of bed, and then realised that she was dressed in a hospital gown and did not know where her own clothes were. It took quite some time, but eventually a nurse produced the clothes that she had been wearing when she was brought in. They were smeared with blood and smelled strongly of smoke but she put them on anyway. A doctor was summoned to explain to her the potentially dangerous consequences of discharging herself, but Paige managed to persuade them that it was necessary for his investigation that she went with him at once to the police station, and he gave an undertaking to watch out for any signs of delayed effects from the blow to her head. At last, she was free to go and they set off in Paige's car.

Bernie's first thought was to call in at her house on the way so that she could change into some clean clothes but Paige reminded her that her house had been set on fire and broke the news that the damage was sufficient to make it unsafe for her to return. This was a terrible blow to Bernie. Since her father's death, some twelve years previously, her entire life was stored in that house: family photographs, letters, newspaper cuttings (several showing dockers manning picket lines, an obituary of her mother and a listing of scholarships awarded to the University of Oxford with her name circled by a proud parent). Would these things have survived the fire?

Bernie prided herself on being practical and shunning sentimentality, so she immediately put these thoughts to one side and addressed the immediate problem. She would need somewhere to stay overnight and clothes and other things to tide her over until some more permanent arrangements could be made. She needed to retrieve her insurance documents from the fireproof box in her bedroom – and she fervently hoped that it really *was* fireproof. She would have to try to recover files, which would have been lost when her computer was destroyed, from backups stored on a university server.

But first of all, she must go to the police station with Superintendent Paige and show him what she had discovered.

Paige seemed to have been reading her mind.

'When we get to the station,' he said, 'I'll organise for a WPC to go over and see if she can retrieve some of your things: clothes, toothbrush and so on. You can make a list of anything else you'd like her to look for. And then we'll get you settled into a hotel, with a police guard – unless you have friends or family that you could stay with.'

Bernie never like to be beholden to anyone, so she quickly dismissed the idea of staying with friends, although she knew that she would not feel at ease in a hotel. She always felt that she was somehow under public scrutiny and that the staff would be criticising her manners and laughing at her accent behind her back. She was relieved when they arrived at the police station and the question of where she would lay her head that night could be shelved for the time being.

Peter Johns was there, with a copy of Ahmed's thesis open on the screen in front of him. He got up as she entered and greeted her warmly. She also noticed his pleasure at being relieved of the task of searching for the elusive needle in the haystack of a two hundred page mathematical treatise. He expressed delight at seeing her safe and well and delivered a message from his wife to the effect that they would be very happy to put Bernie up at their house for as long as she needed it.

Bernie knew that the Johns house was none too large for the family as it was and could certainly not accommodate a guest, so she declined the offer with more than a little regret. Angie was the one person upon whom she could rely to be sympathetic without being overbearing.

Their business was soon completed. Once she had the text in front of her, Bernie easily explained to Johns and Paige how to locate the information hidden within the entries in the bibliography. It amounted to an accusation that two of the college tutors were conducting illegal activities with students in two of the college houses. This statement was not enough to convict them, but there was every chance that it would now be possible to collect the necessary evidence. Almost certainly some of the students who were being exploited in this way would be willing to testify – especially once they realised that, in order to prevent their misdeeds being uncovered, their abusers had killed the DPhil student, Ahmed, and attempted to kill Bernie. Now that they knew who the perpetrators were, there was a good chance of finding DNA evidence to connect them with the murder scene or the house fire. It was a good afternoon's work.

Once the excitement of conveying her message to the attentive police officers was over, Bernie began to feel very weary. The headache, which she had been managing to ignore, became a throbbing agony. Perhaps Paige noticed her discomfort: he left Johns in charge of transcribing the coded message and organising a team to make the further investigations that would be necessary in order to convict. Then he addressed Bernie.

'Now Dr Fazakerley, we'd better get your accommodation sorted out and then you ought to get some rest.'

Determined not to display weakness, Bernie protested that she was not a bit tired and did not need his help in finding a place for the night. Paige, however, ignored her protests, explaining that a civilian would only hamper the police investigation now that she had told them all she knew. The best thing she could do to help now was to keep out of harm's way until her attackers were charged.

A policewoman met them on the way to his car and presented Bernie with a suitcase and a plastic carrier bag.

These were the essentials that she had retrieved from Bernie's house to see her through the night. Bernie nodded her thanks and stepped, with a feeling of relief to which she would never be prepared to admit, into the car.

Paige got into the driver's seat and turned on the ignition. Bernie waited for him to drive off, but he did not. Eventually she concluded that he must be waiting for her to suggest a destination, but she could not think which hotel to propose.

'Where do you suggest that we go?' she said in the end.

For the first time since she had met him a few days previously, Paige seemed unsure of himself. When he spoke, it was with a hesitancy that was foreign to everything she had seen of him up to now and his face turned red, as if with embarrassment at what he was saying.

'That's just it – I mean, well, I was thinking…' he stopped as if uncertain how to go on. Bernie did nothing to help him out of his difficulty. 'I was wondering … I was wondering if, if you might prefer to stay with me, rather than in a hotel. Just for a few days, I mean – until you can get something more permanent sorted out.'

Bernie could not think what to say; this was so unexpected. She knew that Paige was unmarried: he was famous for it. Eddie Johns had complained about it to her on one occasion when she had been helping him with his homework while his father was working extra hours at Paige's behest. Eddie considered that Paige would have more regard for the needs of other people's families to see their fathers on a regular basis if he had a wife and family of his own. For the briefest instant it crossed her mind that this confirmed bachelor might have remained that way all these years because he preferred variety rather than plumping for one woman. However, she immediately dismissed this idea: she would definitely have heard about it if this pillar of the police establishment had been suspected of improperly taking his work home with him! Moreover, the tentative way in which he approached the matter suggested that this sort of invitation was by no means a regular occurrence.

'With you?' she asked weakly, trying to buy time to think.

'Yes. I've got plenty of space – a big house with just me rattling around in it. You would sleep in the spare room, of course, and …'

He was definitely floundering. Bernie undoubtedly had the upper hand now. Whether this was merely a kindly gesture or something more, she knew that she had it within her power to deal him a humiliating blow. She knew that she must not – could not – do that, but she was still unwilling to appear weak or dependent on him for anything.

'Of course,' she said in a matter-of-fact voice. 'I would never have expected anything else.'

She paused for just long enough for him to come to the conclusion that she was going to turn down his offer, then, just as he opened his mouth to apologise for having made the suggestion, she cut across him.

'Thank you, Superintendent.' She said. 'That's very kind of you – just for a few days.'

They drove up Headington Hill and into the part of Headington situated outside the ring road. When they turned into the drive of Paige's house Bernie was taken aback at its size. What a contrast with the modest terraced home in East Oxford occupied by the Johns family! It was set back from the road, well behind the building line of the newer properties that had been built around it. The front garden was put down to lawn, with a few mature trees and a copper beech hedge. The house was L-shaped, with the front door at the inside corner of the L.

'*Llanwrda*,' Bernie read aloud from the name carved into the stone gatepost. 'That's an unusual name for this part of the world. Where does it come from?'

'It's a village in Wales.'

'I guessed that much. I was wondering why,' Bernie persisted, hoping to learn more about the man with whom she was to be staying for the next few days. 'Did you choose it?'

'Oh no, it's had that name ever since it was built.'

They parked on the drive and Paige got out, ready to escort Bernie inside. He lifted the suitcase out of the boot and Bernie took hold of it, determined not to allow him to carry her luggage for her. He resisted for a second then released his grip. He locked the car and went ahead to open the front door.

'Tell me,' Bernie asked, 'how does a policeman manage to afford a house like this?'

'I couldn't. My grandfather had it built before the First World War. It was out in the country then. He was a bank manager and, as such, considered himself to be someone of importance in the community, so he wanted a house that would reflect his status.'

'And I suppose he will have had a family,' Bernie suggested, 'and servants, even.'

'Oh yes. There were four children: my father and his two older brothers and a sister who died when she was still a child. There's a room for the maid up in the attic and I'm told that a cook-housekeeper came in daily in those days.'

He gave her a quick tour of the house: the dining room, which was never used now; the spacious living room with its large fireplace, decrepit three-piece suite and handsome Welsh dresser; and the huge kitchen with a table in the middle, which reminded Bernie of the benches in her college dining room.

'When I was small,' Paige said in an unexpected burst of loquaciousness, 'this kitchen was the hub from which my grandmother ruled the household. She was very much in charge at home. You asked about the house name: that was her idea. She was from Wales originally and she named the house after the village where she grew up.'

'It's certainly better than the usual sort of name for a house like this: I would have expected *The Laurels* or *Hill Top*!'

'The drawback is that most people don't know how to pronounce it. You coped with the shortage of vowels remarkably well.'

'Contrary to all expectations,' Bernie laughed, 'we turn out to have something in common. I too have a Welsh grandmother and she taught me how.'

They went upstairs and he showed her the bathroom and the guest room where she was to stay. She put her case down and wandered over to look out of the window, while Paige went to fetch sheets and pillowcases from the airing cupboard. The view was of the front garden. Bernie saw a squirrel running across the lawn and scampering up an oak tree.

'Well, Superintendent,' Bernie declared, 'turning to greet him as he returned with the bed linen, 'this is certainly a very nice place you have here.'

'Please, Dr Fazakerley, can we dispense with the formalities while you're staying here? Call me Richard.'

'OK. In that case, I'm Bernie.'

The following morning Bernie wandered into the large living room and looked around. She was alone in the house, Richard having left for work immediately after breakfast. She had promised, reluctantly, not to leave the premises until he gave her the all-clear. He had worked out the correct strategy for obtaining compliance from the recalcitrant don: advising her to follow a course of action for her own safety merely provoked defiance, while putting it to her that the success of a police operation depended on her remaining in a place of safety produced immediate and complete co-operation.

She looked around, wondering how to fill the hours until Richard was expected to return. She was without her computer, her books or even paper and pencil, so work was out of the question.

There were two framed photographs on the mantelpiece, standing on either side of a black marble clock. She went closer to look at them. One was a portrait of a white haired old lady with a rather sour look on her face; the other was a black and white photograph of a man in his forties. Bernie thought she could detect a family resemblance to Richard in the shape of the face and the pale, slightly anxious, eyes. Yes, this was how Richard had looked the day before, in the car, when he had invited her to stay. His expression had been quite different from his usual air of quiet confidence. So, this was his father, perhaps?

She looked again at the other picture. It was clearly a much more recent photograph. Symmetry demanded that this should be Richard's mother, but Bernie could see no resemblance between this stern-looking woman and the calm gentleness of the big policeman. If this was his mother then perhaps he had developed his calm approach to life in response to her demands. She imagined a possible scenario: the father dies young leaving the son living with his irascible mother. If Richard had been sharing this house with his mother until recently then was that the explanation for his prolonged bachelorhood? She could well imagine that he was unable to find time for courtship in between satisfying the demands of a career in the police force and an exacting widowed mother.

Where then, was this mother now? Perhaps she had died recently, making it possible, for the first time, for Richard to invite someone back to the house. Was she the first? He had certainly seemed very ill at ease when making the suggestion, but then, as she was well aware, she did not make it easy for people to offer her any sort of help. Why then had he done it?

It was nearly seven when Richard arrived home that evening. Bernie heard his key in the door and went into the hall to meet him. He looked tired and harassed. Seeing Bernie, he immediately started to apologise for his late return, but she cut him off.

'There's a hotpot in the oven,' she said briskly, 'I hope it's alright: I found some steak in the freezer. I don't know what time you usually eat, so I made something that can wait until you're ready.'

Richard looked at her gratefully. He had been wondering on the way home how he would feed his guest that evening. As host, it was his responsibility but after a long and arduous day neither of the options that occurred to him – cooking, or taking her out for a meal – had any attraction. Now he could relax and allow her to minister to him instead.

'Right away, if that's OK with you. I didn't manage to get any lunch today.'

They ate in silence for several minutes; then Richard, presumably remembering his obligations as host to make conversation, looked up from his plate and addressed Bernie.

'This is good!'

'It's my Dad's recipe. My mam wasn't well, so Dad and I had to learn to fend for ourselves.'

'And are your parents still living in Liverpool?'

'No. Mam died just before I came up to Oxford and Dad lived just about long enough to see me get my doctorate.'

'I'm sorry.'

'It was all a long time ago.'

Richard said nothing more, so Bernie attempted to draw him out.

'I was looking at the photos on the mantelpiece,' she began. 'I thought perhaps they were your parents?'

'That' right,' Richard nodded. 'My father died quite young – like yours. My mother lives in sheltered housing in Henley.'

'It must have been a wrench for her, leaving all this,' Bernie suggested, waving her fork to indicate that she was talking about the house and gardens.

'No. She never liked the place,' Richard replied shortly. He looked for a moment as if he were going to say something more, but then evidently changed his mind and addressed himself once more to eating.

Bernie was disappointed at not having extracted more information about Richard's family, but she recognised that he had every right to keep such things to himself. So she changed the subject to something of more immediate importance to herself.

'Am I allowed out yet?' she asked. 'I'm supposed to be giving a revision class to the final honours students on Friday.'

'I think we'll be in a position to arrest and charge them tomorrow. Then you'll be free to go.'

Two days later, while she might be free to leave Richard's house, it was not clear where exactly she was to stay. The verdict of the insurance company, and the builder who had been called in to make the renovations, was that it would be several months before her house was habitable again. Once term was over she would be able to beg a room in college, but that would mean being surrounded by conference delegates and foreign language students throughout the summer, only to become homeless again at the start of Michaelmas Term. The insurance would pay for her to rent somewhere, but rented accommodation in Oxford was always in short supply.

'Are you *sure* you don't mind me still being here?' Bernie asked Richard about a week after the offending college tutors had been remanded in custody.

'I told you: you're welcome to stay as long as you like. Stay until your house is ready. There's plenty of room, and you're no bother. It's refreshing to be able to share the cooking. I'd got into a rut of rotating around about half a dozen meals over and over again.'

'Well, if you really are sure ...'

'I'm sure.'

A few nights later Bernie was dreaming. It was the same dream that she had had almost every night since the fire. She was in a smoke-filled room. She knew that she had to get to the door, but she could not see where it was. She shouted out for help, but she somehow knew that nobody could hear her. She waved her arms to try to clear the smoke away so that she could see. Her knuckles hit something hard and the pain woke her.

She opened her eyes to see the door of her room ajar. It closed quietly and, for a moment, Bernie wondered whether she could have imagined it. Then she got out of bed and went to investigate. Although the guest room adjoined Richard's bedroom, the layout of the landing meant that anyone walking between the two rooms had to walk some considerable distance in order to get past the head of the stairs. She could see him there, hurrying along on bare feet, obviously hoping that she would not know he had been outside her room.

'I'm sorry, Richard,' she called, 'Did I wake you?'

He turned and came back towards her, looking sheepish. 'I hope you didn't think …'

'I make it a rule never to think,' she assured him. 'I'm just sorry to have disturbed you. Has it happened before? I'd hate to think that you haven't had a good night's sleep since I came'

'It doesn't matter,' Richard said, not answering her question. 'I just wish I could have thought of some way of helping. I didn't like to come into your room in case you thought …'

'Oh Richard! If you wanted to molest me, you've already had ample opportunity. I know I can trust you. Look, if it happens again, just bang on the wall to wake me.'

'Won't that just make things worse?'

'We won't know until we try it.'

Bernie stretched up her arms, put her hands behind Richard's neck and pulled his head down to within reach of hers. Then she kissed him chastely on the cheek.

'Goodnight Richard. Thank you for being concerned.'

Strange to say, that was the last time the dream recurred, so they never had the opportunity to find out what effect rousing Bernie from sleep by knocking on the party wall would have had. Reflecting on the phenomenon a few weeks later, Bernie had mixed feelings: it was a relief to have undisturbed sleep at night, but galling to think that her subconscious fears had somehow been put to rest by the appearance of a man – particularly that man – on the scene.

And so, they had drifted into a routine. She would cook for them on Mondays and Thursdays while Richard made the meals on Tuesdays and Fridays. On Wednesdays, Bernie ate with the college chaplain before attending choir practice and on Saturdays, Richard visited his mother in Henley. When, four months later, Bernie's house was declared fit for habitation again she was surprised to realise she was going to be sorry to have her life to herself once more. It had been pleasant not to have to do everything for herself and, while most evenings she got on with her work and Richard played the piano or read a book, it had been nice to know that there was someone to talk to if she so chose.

'You must stay to supper,' she insisted, as they carried the last of her possessions back into her own house. 'After all, I always cook for us on Mondays.'

Their eyes met, and somehow she knew that Richard had been thinking the exact same things as she had. That evening, as he put his coat on to go home, she made the suggestion, which she was confident had also been in his mind.

'It seems to me,' she said, 'that it would be an awful waste of effort to go back to each of us cooking and washing up separately every night. How would it be if you came over here on Mondays and Thursdays and I came to your place on Tuesdays and Fridays?'

'Suits me.'

When Angie Johns found out about this arrangement, she teased Bernie unmercifully about her 'secret romance', but Bernie was adamant that it was a simple matter of convenience. It saved them both time, and it was so much easier cooking for two than for one. And Bernie genuinely believed that what she said to Angie was true until, a year or more later, Richard failed to turn up one Monday evening.

At first, Bernie thought nothing of it. He was often delayed by his work and was not always able to ring her to let her know. Two hours later, when she had still heard nothing, she rang his mobile number. There was no reply, so she tried his home landline: no answer. Half an hour later, she followed up by ringing the mobile number again. Eventually she gave in and telephoned Angie to find out if she knew what was going on. If Richard was away somewhere on a case then there was a good chance that Peter was with him or at least would have some idea where he was.

'I'm really not sure what I can say, Bernie,' Angie said nervously.

Bernie was surprised at her hesitancy and became convinced that her friend was hiding something.

'What on earth do you mean, Angie? Is something wrong?'

'I think I'd better let Peter talk to you.'

There was a sound of fumbling at the other end of the line as the telephone receiver was handed over.

'Bernie?' Peter's voice sounded anxious.

'Yes. Can you tell me where Richard is? He was supposed to be having tea with me this evening.'

'Ah, yes,' Peter paused. 'I'm afraid I'm not at liberty to tell you exactly what's going on.'

'Peter, please!' Bernie's heart raced as she tried to imagine what sorts of horrors were being concealed from her.

'It's very hush-hush. Special Branch are involved.'

'But is he safe?' pleaded Bernie.

'As far as we know.'

'And what on earth is that supposed to mean?'

'Tell you what – I'll come round. Now, not a word of

this to anyone, do you understand?'

'Yes, yes, but just tell me what's going on.' Bernie shouted down the phone in exasperation.

Ten minutes later, although to Bernie it felt more like a fortnight, Peter arrived at her house and gave what limited explanation he felt able to confide to her. Richard had fallen foul of some terrorist gang and was being held hostage, along with several other people. The safety of them all depended on absolute secrecy. Peter had already broken the rules by imparting this much information to Bernie, so now she must say nothing to anyone and carry on completely as normal. Peter promised to come round and give her a daily update, but she must not speak about Richard on the phone or allow anyone else to know that she was anxious about his welfare.

Behaving normally proved to be more difficult than Bernie had expected, especially when three more days passed without any news. By Friday morning, her nerves were in tatters and she was glad that she had no engagements to make it necessary for her to leave the house. She had just abandoned the research paper that she was writing – having realised that her lack of concentration was causing her to make so many mistakes that it would be quicker in the long run to start again when she was in a better state of mind – when the doorbell rang.

She wiped her eyes, blew her nose and stumbled her way to the door. And there he was! He looked a bit sheepish, perhaps because he had never called on her unannounced before, but obviously completely unscathed. Suddenly the world was right again. He mouth felt dry, but she managed to croak his name.

His face fell.

'What's wrong, Bernie?' he asked anxiously.

'Nothing,' Bernie found her voice and smiled up at him as he stepped into the house. 'There's nothing wrong, I'm fine.'

Then everything seemed to happen very quickly. Bernie

turned away to go into the kitchen to put the kettle on. Richard grabbed her by the arm to detain her, determined to find out what was upsetting her – it clearly not having occurred to him that she had been worried about his own safety. Bernie snatched herself out of his grip and rounded on him angrily, annoyed with herself for having displayed her distress and with him for having caused it. A heated exchange took place, which somehow ended up with Bernie clasped in Richard's arms, with her face pressed up against his chest while he kissed the top of her head.

Most people might have expected that their relationship would progress quite quickly after that, but instead they dropped back into the old routine. The only change between them was that both parties were a little more willing to display affection through physical contact. Hugs and kisses were no longer unheard of. When they sat together after their evening meal (which Richard called 'dinner' and Bernie insisted on terming 'tea' or 'supper', depending on how late is was when Richard's working day ended and he was free eat) they now occupied the settee instead of separate chairs. They even occasionally held hands in public, dropping them instantly if they met anyone they knew.

Things would probably have continued like this forever if Bernie had not been offered promotion to a job at the other end of the country. She had applied, not expecting to be successful, and when the offer came, the only thing she could think about was how much she would miss Richard's company if she were to move away from Oxford. The decision to turn down the offer was easy, although she did feel a little guilty at having wasted the time of the appointment panel, but what to say to Richard was not. He must never know that he had unwittingly got in the way of her career progression, but Bernie knew that she was a very poor liar.

In the end, the form of words that she decided upon was, 'I won't be going to Newcastle after all.' She hoped that he would draw his own conclusions and not ask any supplementary questions.

It seemed to work. Richard was very sympathetic about her supposed disappointment at being unsuccessful in her application, which was a little trying, but at least he had no idea that she cared more for him than for her job prospects. But then, the next thing she knew, he had turned up in her college room demanding to know whether she would agree to be his wife. She found out later that Angie had confided the true situation to Peter, who had taken it upon himself to tell Richard and, moreover, to impress upon him the significance of what Bernie had done.

****

Bernie stopped typing. Her eyes were too misty to see the screen, and she was sure that the tears dropping on the keyboard would do it no good. As she thought back to the occasion of Richard's proposal, she became angry with herself for making it so difficult for him. It must have taken a lot of courage for him to overcome his ingrained belief that he was unworthy to be loved. Why could she, Bernie, not have simply accepted graciously instead of allowing her own insecurities to dominate? Why had she felt obliged to argue her own unsuitability to be Richard's wife? Thank goodness, he had seen through her arguments and forced her to admit that, for herself, a lifelong union with him was what she wanted more than anything.

Of course, she knew why. It all stemmed from what had happened to the only other man who had ever asked her to be his wife, all those years earlier. She could hardly remember now what Stephen had been like. She had photographs and his parents were happy to reminisce about what he had been like as a boy growing up in Newcastle and to share their own family album; but she could not any longer picture his face in her mind or remember what it was that had made him so special to her. They had been so young – she still eighteen and he just turned nineteen – when they had decided to get married. Looking back, so much of what they had said and done together now seemed rather silly but it had all appeared so very significant to them at the time.

She had been so sure of their future then, until the day that the police brought her the news that Stephen had thrown himself to his death from the top of the engineering building. It was just a week after their last finals exam, and two weeks before their wedding day. Everyone agreed that it must have been depression following finals that had made him do it, but Bernie had never been able to rid herself of the notion that it could have been anticipation of what was to come in a fortnight's time that had disturbed the balance of his mind.

And if it was the case that Stephen had taken his own life rather than face a lifetime with her, then there must surely be something about her that made her impossible to live with. How could she allow anyone else to contemplate taking her on? She knew that it was irrational to think this way, but it was easier not to take the risk of getting involved.

Until Richard came along: Richard who believed himself to be unlovable; Richard who buried himself in his work to avoid having to think about how his mother had betrayed him; Richard who had passed his half-century without ever having had an intimate relationship. What an unlikely pairing! It was a wonder that it had taken as little as two and a half years for them to get it together.

Bernie printed out her story and set to work copying it out in her neatest handwriting. It might not be polished prose, but at least in years to come Lucy would know that she had made as much effort as all Richard's other friends to tell her what her father had been like.

12 SUSPICIOUS DEATH

'Here you are, Bernie,' Angie handed over a manila folder. 'I said I'd write it all down and here it is.'

Bernie took the folder and opened it. Inside was a sheaf of A4 sheets, already slipped into transparent pockets ready to be added to the red ring binder. She recognised Angie's neat, rather old-fashioned handwriting.

'Thank you. I know Lucy will love reading it when she's older. Come to that, I'm rather keen to have a shufty myself!'

'Why don't you read mine while I read yours?' Angie suggested.

****

After six months in Britain, Angela Wheeler still did not feel fully at home. It was not, as so many people seemed to imagine, the weather that got her down; neither was it the occasional overt racism, which she generally managed to shrug off. No, it was more that she no longer had anywhere where she belonged. She was no longer part of a community.

She was not exactly lonely, but she felt that she was an outsider. She belonged to the hospital community, but the way it functioned was subtly different from those at her hospital in Jamaica. She lived in the community of the nurses' home, but again, it would take time for her to understand how that society worked.

Back home she had been part of a large extended family and her whole village had known one another from birth. Her church had also been very important to her and, although she had joined a church here, the atmosphere was more austere and restrained. People were not unfriendly, but their friendliness took different forms from back home and Angie felt that she had to be careful not to offend by crossing invisible lines of appropriate conduct.

Take the girls in her block of the nurses' home, for instance. They happily shared a kitchen and bathroom, but were less open about sharing their thoughts and feelings or news about their personal lives. Still, it was early days, she could hardly expect to become as much a part of this new society in six months as she had been in the place where she had been brought up.

She looked at her watch. It was time to go to bed, she decided. She was on the early shift in the morning. She would just go and make herself a bedtime drink of cocoa and bring it back to her room.

As she walked down the corridor towards the kitchen, Jane Bentham, another staff nurse who occupied the room next to hers, came racing up the stairs.

'Have you seen Susan?' she gasped, stopping to get her breath before continuing, 'Sister's calling her all the names under the sun because she hasn't turned up for her shift.'

'No. I haven't seen her all day. She wasn't around when I came off shift. I'll see if she's in her room.'

She walked briskly down the corridor and knocked on the door of Nurse Susan Parry. There was no reply. The two nurses looked at each other, unsure what to do next.

'What's all that noise?' A door opened on the opposite side of the corridor and Sister Catherine Spencer's head looked out at them.

'We're looking for Susan,' Jane explained. . 'She's

supposed to be on nights in male surgical, but she didn't turn up for handover.'

There was a clatter of feet on the stairs as another of their colleagues arrived back in the home after the late shift. A few moments later, Staff Nurse Elaine Gregg came into view.

'Have either of you seen Susan Parry?' Jane asked looking from Catherine to Elaine and back again.

'I haven't seen her since she came in this morning,' Elaine said. 'I was making breakfast when she and Jill came in. Jill came into the kitchen and had a cup of tea, but Susan went straight to bed. As far as I know she was still in bed when I went on shift.'

'It's not like her to be late for her shift,' Angela commented. 'She's usually very conscientious.'

They stood looking at one another, unsure what to do. Then Sister Spencer took charge.

'I'll telephone the ward and check that she still hasn't turned up,' she said briskly, 'and if she hasn't then I'll get the master key from Mrs Fish so that we can get into her room – in case she's been taken ill or something.'

A few minutes later, the four of them were standing around Susan's bed looking down at her body. She lay there, as if asleep, with the bedclothes drawn up to her neck so that only her face was visible. Somehow, they knew she was dead but Sister Spencer checked for a pulse in the carotid artery to be sure, before sending the others back to wait in the kitchen while she summoned help.

Angela made cocoa for them all and they sat drinking it in the kitchen while the doctor, who had come across from the hospital in answer to Sister Spencer's summons, examined the body. He found a narrow incision in her chest. A tiny trickle of blood had dried on her skin just below it and there was a small round stain on the sheet beneath. This was something beyond his previous experience. Stab wounds on patients presenting at A&E were generally much messier than this: it looked as if it had been done with surgical precision. Could such a small wound have killed this young, apparently healthy woman? There was certainly no other obvious reason for her sudden and unexpected death. He turned to Sister Spencer.

'Call the police,' he said decisively.

She stood for a moment, staring down at the chest wound, taking in the implications of his words; then she hurried out of the room to the telephone.

The police arrived in the persons of Detective Inspector Richard Paige and Detective Constable Peter Johns. The former was a big bear of a man, thickset with wavy yellow hair and pale blue eyes. His junior colleague had red hair of a bright orange shade that Angela had never seen before; his eyes were a strange greeny-brown colour; his face was blotchy white and red; the back of the hand that he extended to shake hers as he introduced himself was covered with an array of orangey-brown freckles. She smiled to herself as she reflected that it was she, and not he, who would be described as 'coloured'.

'I'm sorry to have to bother you at a time like this,' Constable Johns said apologetically to Angela, sitting down with her in the small kitchen. 'I'll try to keep it as brief as possible this evening, but we may need to speak to you again later.'

'I understand,' Angela nodded. 'What do you need to know?'

'First, I need your name.'

'Angela Wheeler.'

'And you're a nurse? You live here in the nurses' home?'

'Yes. My room is next to Susan Parry's.'

'I see. And when was the last time you saw Nurse Parry?'

'Very briefly at the handover on the ward this morning. We're both on male surgical. I'm on "earlies" this week, while she's on nights.'

'I see, and before that?'

'That would be yesterday afternoon. She always goes

straight to bed after a night shift and generally gets up sometime in the middle of the afternoon. I met her as I was coming in after my shift. She was on her way out to do some shopping.'

'And over the last few days, did Nurse Parry seem just as normal? She wasn't anxious about anything, as far as you know?'

'Now you ask,' Angela said, screwing up her face to think better, 'she did seem a bit worried these last couple of weeks; but I thought it was just that she was anxious in case she made any mistakes with a patient. She's newly qualified and it *is* rather daunting for a new nurse to think that we're responsible for people's lives. Especially at night, when there's often only one qualified nurse on duty, it's difficult to know sometimes whether a situation warrants getting the on-call doctor out of bed. Susan takes her responsibilities very seriously and I thought she was just nervous about having to make decisions on her own.'

'I see. Now, just for the record, can you describe your own movements from eleven last night to when Sister Spencer called us?'

'Let me see. Well, I was in bed before eleven last night. I got up at six, got dressed, had breakfast and went over to the ward in time for the start of my shift at seven. I was on the ward until half past three, when I came back over here and changed out of my uniform. I nipped out to the shops, then came back and had a cup of tea in the kitchen with Jill Saunders: she's the other nurse who shares this part of the home; you haven't met her because she's on nights. That would be about half past four.'

'Ah yes. Can I check that I've got it straight? There are six of you sharing this part of the home? And it has a door separating it from the other parts, with a lock that only the six of you have keys for?'

'Well, Mrs Fish, the housekeeper, has a master key and so do Security, but apart from that, yes, only the six of us can open the door.'

'And you each have keys to your own rooms? Do you all keep them locked?'

'When we're out and when we're in bed at night, but I don't think any of us bothers during the daytime if we're in.'

'But Nurse Parry's room was locked when you went to look for her just now: Sister Spencer said that she had to get the master key from the housekeeper's room.'

'Yes. I suppose Susan must have locked it so that nobody would disturb her while she was asleep.'

'The key wasn't in the lock. Do you know where she kept it?'

'She used to put it in her purse when she went out, but I don't know what she did if she locked the door when she was in her room.'

'OK. Now, you were, where, when Nurse Bentham came in looking for Nurse Parry?'

'I was in the passage on my way to the kitchen to make myself some cocoa before bed.'

'And when you met Nurse Bentham you went with her to look for Nurse Parry?'

'Yes. I knocked on the door but there was no reply. Then Elaine and Catherine came up the stairs and Catherine went to telephone to see if Susan might have gone over to the ward after all.'

'And when she came back with the master key, who went in first?'

'Catherine. She opened the door and went in and we all followed her. We all saw that Susan was dead. Catherine checked her pulse and told us to go back and wait in the kitchen. She went down to telephone for help from the hall.'

'And did she lock the door, after you all left?'

'Yes. She said we'd better make sure that nobody wandered in and disturbed anything.'

'I see, so none of you were in the room alone at all?'

'No. We all went in together and came out again together.'

'And Sister Spencer was the first in and the last out?'

'Yes.'

Angela wondered why the policeman was so insistent on getting a precise picture of what had happened when they found the body. After all, anyone could see that Susan had been dead for some time, so what did it matter what order they entered the room or whether anyone had been alone with the body?

'Thank you nurse Wheeler,' Constable Johns closed his notebook and indicated to Angela that she could go. 'We may need to ask you some more questions later, but that's all for tonight.'

Although she was tired, Angela found it very difficult to sleep that night. She kept going over in her mind the events of the previous day and trying to work out who could have stabbed Susan Parry to death – if that was what had happened. On the face of it, the only people who could have done it were the group of nurses who lived in that section of the nurses' home or Mrs Fish the housekeeper (or one of the cleaners using her master key) or someone who had been let in by one of the inmates. It was not pleasant to think that she was sharing a house with a murderer.

She thought it through. The cleaners worked during the afternoon, which was the only time when they could be fairly certain that they would not be disturbing any of the nurses in bed. The nurses were each responsible for cleaning their own rooms, but the cleaners came round emptying bins and cleaning the corridor, kitchen and bathroom. If Susan was killed in her sleep, as it seemed by appearances, then it was probably done before the cleaning staff arrived at around three in the afternoon. So it really did look as if it must have been one of the nurses.

She herself was in the clear, Angela reflected, because her shift covered the entire time from before Susan went to bed in her room until after her usual time for getting up. If she were the murderer she would have had to rely on Susan oversleeping, which she knew from her own times on night duty rarely happened when sleeping during the day. Any of the other nurses, however, could have slipped in when nobody was looking. Jill was supposedly asleep, but she could have got up, done the deed and then gone back to bed. Catherine's shift was a daytime one, in charge of the scrub nurses in the operating theatres, so she would still have been in the nurses' home when Susan returned from her night shift. The other two were on the late shift, so were off duty and awake for the entire time that Susan was in her room.

She considered the other nurses from her residential group. Jane Bentham worked on the same ward as Susan, as indeed did Angela. As far as Angela could tell, they had got on well together. Jane was friendly towards staff and very dedicated to the patients, but Angela considered her to be rather careless. She had twice had to draw her attention to the instructions above a patients' bed indicating which foods they were permitted to eat. Angela could not imagine her being sufficiently well-organised to plan and execute such an efficient murder as this one.

Catherine Spencer had also worked on that ward until her recent promotion to a sister's position in Theatres. Susan always appeared to be rather in awe of Catherine who was considerably more experienced and not above showing up junior nurses in front of patients and doctors. Catherine was undoubtedly technically capable of killing Susan, but what possible motive would she have for doing so?

Elaine was a cheerful young nurse from Birmingham. She was always talking away in her strong Black Country accent about her large family of brothers and sisters, of which she was the eldest. Of all the nurses in their group, this was the one with whom Angela felt most at home.

Jill Saunders was rather aloof. Angela did not feel that she knew her at all. Murders were often described as 'loners' weren't they? All the same, Angela could not really picture tiny, baby-faced Jill thrusting a knife into Susan's chest. If she were to commit murder, it was far more likely that she would do so by purloining a lethal dose of painkillers and administering them in Susan's morning coffee.

Angela sighed and turned over in bed in the hope of getting off to sleep. She really could not believe that any of her colleagues had killed Susan. They were all nurses, trained to save life, not to take it away. She went over the list of suspects in her mind again. What possible motive could any of them have for killing Susan?

When Angela arrived, bleary-eyed, at the ward the next morning she discovered that the news had gone ahead of her. The staff were agog to learn from her all about what had happened. Had she really found Nurse Parry dead in bed? What had the police said when they came? Who did Angela think had done it? Could Susan have killed herself? Sister Humphries shooed them to their places with strict instructions not to talk about the incident in front of the patients. She gave the impression that she saw the whole business as a conspiracy to make it more difficult for her to fill the duty rota for her ward.

Angela tried to push the incident to the back of her mind and concentrate on her work, which she succeeded in doing, until, a few hours later, she was in the laundry cupboard collecting fresh sheets for a patient who had wet the bed. The door was ajar, but she was completely hidden from anyone passing. Two of her nursing colleagues must have stopped just outside and she could overhear their conversation.

'I'd lay money it's that coloured nurse did it,' came a voice, which Angela recognised as Nursing Auxiliary Anne Mountfield. 'Those West Indians can't ever be trusted.'

'She's always very nice to me,' was the tentative response. It was Student Nurse Julie French.

'Oh yes! She's pleasant enough when she's on the ward, but you've got to remember that they're different from us. There's a coloured family living down our street and he's always drinking too much and getting into fights. They just don't have the same self-control as we do.'

'Do you really think so?'

The voices became fainter as they moved away from the door. Angela became conscious that her heart was beating fast. Were others of her colleagues thinking that sort of thing about her? Were they watching her in case she flew into a wild West Indian rage and harmed one of the patients? Did they assume that she must indulge in drinking bouts whenever she was away from the ward? She took several deep breaths before venturing out to see to her patient.

'There you are Mr Perkins,' she said as she smoothed down the clean top sheet. 'All nice and fresh now.'

'Thank you nurse. I'm sorry about that. I don't know how it happened.'

'No need to apologise,' she reassured him. 'It's all in a day's work for us. And don't you worry, we'll soon have you back on your feet again and able to get yourself to the toilet.'

'Excuse me nurse,' the man in the next bed called to her as she turned to leave. 'I'm in agony. Can't you give me some more of the painkillers?'

'I'll just check.' Angela looked at the clipboard at the end of the bed. 'Yes, you're due another dose if you need one. I'll go and get it for you.'

She went off and came back with a syringe and a phial of diamorphine.

'Thank you nurse,' the patient said, after she had delivered the dose. 'I must say, I've been pleasantly surprised at the way I've been treated after what one of my friends told me about this ward.'

'Oh? Now what was that then?'

'He was in for his hernia op, same as me, a couple of months ago and he said that several times he asked for painkillers and one of the nurses said she was going to give them to him, but then she never did.'

Angela was unsure what to say to this. She did not like to suggest that the story was untrue, but equally she felt that she ought to stand up for the professionalism of her ward colleagues.

'Perhaps he got confused,' she suggested. 'Sometimes the painkillers do that to you. They make it difficult to tell how much time has passed and you sometimes forget things.'

'But they didn't give him any painkillers,' the patient insisted, 'that's what I'm telling you.'

'I'm sorry your friend wasn't happy about his treatment, Mr Frost,' Angela said, trying to be conciliatory, 'but I'm sure all the nurses will have been trying to do their best for him.'

'He said it was just this one nurse,' Mr Frost persisted. 'He said he thought she ought to be struck off – or whatever it is they do to nurses.'

'Well if he really feels that strongly, he could make a complaint, but it really is up to your friend to decide,' Angela said firmly. 'I really can't discuss it with you. I'm sorry, but it would break patient confidentiality.'

'Alright. I'll tell him what you said about complaining. Thanks, anyway.'

The next few weeks were very uncomfortable for the five remaining nurses in Angela's residential group. They were all aware that they were under suspicion and they were all displaying signs of nervousness around one another, knowing that one of them was almost certainly a murderer. The police had been back on several occasions, questioning them about their relationships with Susan Parry. Angela became aware that her own movements that day had been under scrutiny. True, she had been on duty when Susan was killed, but she had left the ward for her lunch break during that time and the police had been questioning the ward and canteen staff at length to establish whether or not she would have had time to return to the nurses' home.

Susan's parents had come and taken away her things. Perhaps it was her imagination but, although they were outwardly polite towards her, Angela could not help thinking that they looked at her with suspicion. Did they too think that the coloured girl was the most likely one of their daughter's housemates to have been responsible for her death?

To make things worse, there was trouble on the ward as well. Mr Frost's friend did make an official complaint and Sister was on the warpath looking for someone to blame. The patient's records were carefully scrutinised and they showed that diamorphine had been administered as prescribed. During Sister's cross-examination of the whole nursing team, someone suggested that perhaps the records might have been filled in before actually giving the drug and then another call upon the nurse's attention had led to it being forgotten. This led to a careful check on the stocks in the ward drug cabinet, which (to everyone's great relief) showed no discrepancy between the records and the actual stock of diamorphine remaining.

'Nevertheless,' Sister Humphries said sternly, glaring round at her staff, 'a patient has complained of receiving insufficient pain relief while he was on our ward. 'I would like to remind you that it is every nurse's responsibility to take action when a patient tells them that they are in discomfort. If the standard pain relief regimen is not sufficient then the patient should have been referred to the medical staff for reassessment. We are all very lucky that the pain did not turn out to have been caused by some undiagnosed complication.'

Thus, Angela felt that she was under constant scrutiny from her peers. On the ward, they all felt the sister's eye on them checking that they were not neglecting any patient demands. Back in the nurses' home, they had taken to locking their doors even when they were in their rooms during the day. They watched one another with suspicion, and conversation was stilted and superficial.

To get away from the tense atmosphere at work, Angela devoted her time more and more to her church. It was a busy time of year, especially for the Sunday School, because it was the season of the annual National Children's Home collection. Each of the children in her class had been issued with a booklet of 'Sunny Smiles': small photographs of children from the Home, which they were instructed to sell to their families and friends in exchange for a donation to the charity. Angela volunteered to take responsibility for counting and recording the money. Now it was all in and they were preparing for the 'Festival of Queens' ceremony at which Sunday Schools and Brownie packs from all over the county would come together to hand it over.

On the day of the festival, Angela shepherded her flock of children into the Town Hall. Then she left them in the charge of two of the other Sunday School teachers while she took their 'queen' (a pretty little girl of eight years, with fair hair and blue eyes) and her attendants (seven-year-old twins) to the room where they were to prepare for the procession. Looking round the room, she could not help feeling that her girls were among the best turned out. The costumes, which she had helped to make, were certainly more flamboyant than many of the others and her queen wore her crown with a shy confidence that was extremely endearing.

As the long line of queens left the robing room to process down the aisle of the main hall, Angela slipped in at the back and found herself an inconspicuous seat near the door. She watched anxiously as the girls walked slowly towards the front.

'Hello. It's Nurse Wheeler isn't it?'

Angela turned at the sound of her name and saw that the person sitting in the next seat was none other than the red-haired constable who had interviewed her on the night of Susan's death. She racked her brains to remember his name.

'Detective Constable Johns,' she said at last.

'Please, call me Peter: I'm not here in my official capacity.'

'I'm pleased to hear it. And if we're on first name terms, I'm Angela.'

'Are you here with your church?'

'Yes: I helped to dress our queen. There she is – in the green cloak with the fur collar.'

'Very regal.'

'What about you? Have you got a troop of Sunday School kids hiding somewhere?'

'No. I'm on my own. I don't get to church very often, but I was brought up by the National Children's Home, so I always try to support these sorts of events.'

'They must be very proud of the way you've turned out.'

'I don't know about that.'

They watched as the procession reached the front and climbed on to the stage.

'It reminds me a bit,' Angela whispered, 'of carnival back home. Only there it's out of doors and rather less restrained.'

'Well, with the British weather, it's rather risky doing things out of doors,' Peter whispered back. 'And with the British temperament, you would expect restraint!'

'So would you say that West Indians are very different from British people?' Angela asked, a slight sharpness entering her voice as she remembered the conversation that she had overheard on the ward a few weeks before.

'No – at least I don't know. I was just joking about the famous British reserve. What are you getting at?' Peter was confused. His small talk seemed suddenly to have got him into hot water.

'A little while ago,' Angela said, speaking slowly and in an undertone, 'I overheard someone saying that West Indians were the sort of people who might very well stab someone to death while they were in bed asleep.'

'What!' Peter's voice rose involuntarily. Then, seeing that people were turning their heads, he lowered it again and said in Angela's ear, 'come outside for a minute. We can't talk in here, and you've got to tell me about this.'

They crept out of the hall and walked down the steps and out into the street. Peter took Angela's hand and led her to a bench. They sat down together and then he started to interrogate her.

'Who's been talking such nonsense?' he demanded.

'It was just one of the nursing auxiliaries. I expect she didn't mean anything by it.' Angela was starting to wish she had never mentioned the incident, which she had been trying to forget.

'You don't imagine that the police have that attitude, do you? I mean, surely you must realise that you of all people are not under suspicion?'

'Because I was on the ward that morning? I thought there was a theory that I might have come back during my lunch break.'

'No. We had to consider that possibility, but it doesn't work. Look – I shouldn't be telling you this, so you must keep it absolutely to yourself, but the medical evidence shows that she had to have been killed before eleven. And you were on the ward in sight of other staff until half past twelve. So you really are *not* a suspect.'

They sat in silence for a moment or two. Then Peter spoke again.

'Now, I really wish you'd tell me who it was that made that vile accusation against you.'

Angela shook her head. 'No really. I couldn't. I'm sure she didn't mean anything by it. It wouldn't be fair for her to get into trouble over something that probably lots of other people were saying – or at any rate thinking – people who didn't get overheard.'

'What do you mean "other people"? Has this sort of thing happened before?' Peter demanded.

'Oh it's nothing,' Angela said dismissively. 'It's only natural, I suppose, to be nervous of people who are different.'

'But you're not different – not underneath – not in the things that are important! What business have they got saying that you're different?'

'Please Peter,' Angela begged, 'stop worrying about it. It doesn't bother me. It's just one of those things. OK?'

Peter was far from convinced. He had heard the suspicion and fear in Angela's voice when she had remembered the hurtful remarks and surmised that he might have similar views. However, he could see that she did not want to take this any further and he remembered how awkward he had felt as a child when one of his teachers had tried to clamp down on the children who taunted him for his ginger hair, so he decided to drop the matter – for the moment.

'Shall we go back in?' he suggested. 'The programme says we have comedy trampoline artists and hand bell ringers still to come.'

'I think I'd rather get some fresh air.'

'We could go for a walk in Christ Church Meadow, if you like,' Peter suggested optimistically.

'Yes. I'd like that.'

They strolled along side by side in silence both trying to think of a new topic of conversation.

'What made you abandon the tropical sunshine of the Caribbean for England?' Peter asked at last, hoping that this innocent enquiry would not be interpreted as a veiled suggestion that immigration was to be deplored.

'Well I suppose I thought it would be exciting – a bit of an adventure – but really I have to confess it was mainly the money.'

'I hadn't got you down as a mercenary sort of person.'

'Not for myself. It's my family back in Jamaica. I wanted to be able to send some money back to them. The pay's a lot higher here.'

'The cost of living's higher too. I wouldn't have thought a nurse had much to spare.'

'You're right,' Angela sighed. 'I have to admit, I was mightily disappointed at the end of the first month when I worked out how much I was going to be able to send home; but I'm getting better at economising now, so it's not too bad. It's more than I could have given them if I'd stayed in Jamaica, anyway.'

Are you one of a big family?'

'Oh yes – well big by English standards, anyway. I've got three sisters and two brothers.'

'Do you miss them?'

'Oh yes! I miss having my mum and dad there to give me advice – not that I used to like it when they did! And I miss my brothers and sisters – especially my brother Joseph. He's a spastic and can't do much for himself. I used to help my mother to look after him. I suppose that's what made me think of becoming a nurse. Joseph is the main reason I came here. It isn't easy for them to get the best treatment for him. I thought I'd be able to send money so they could afford more and also find out about new ways of helping people like Joseph.'

'Joseph's lucky. Lots of families would have had him put in a home.'

'I'm sorry, Peter, I forgot.' Angela suddenly felt guilty at talking about her close-knit family. 'It must be difficult for you, not having any family.'

'I don't know,' Peter shrugged. 'My houseparents were very kind, but at the back of your mind, you know that for them it's a job at the end of the day.'

'I understand what you mean. It can't be the same as the way I know that, whatever terrible thing I did, my mum and dad would still be there for me – even if, for example, I *had* killed Susan Parry.'

'Don't let's talk about that,' Peter pleaded. 'Tell me more about your family. Are your brothers and sisters older or younger than you? What do your parents do for a living? What sort of house do they have?'

The time past agreeably as they wandered along the path beside the river. Soon it was time for Angela to go back to be there to escort her Sunday School charges home.

As they approached the town hall, Peter plucked up courage to ask tentatively, 'Angela, when all this business with Nurse Parry is over, would you come out with me sometime – to the pictures, maybe?'

'Thank you. I'd like that very much.'

It was about a week later that there were the first signs that the Nurse Parry murder case might be reaching a conclusion. Two uniformed police officers arrived one morning and took Sister Spencer away to the police station for questioning. Naturally, this provoked a lot of speculation among the other nurses as to why she had been singled out for this attention. Up until now, all the police interviews had taken place in the housekeeper's small office in the nurses' home. When Sister Spencer had not returned by evening, rumours were rife that she had been taken up for the murder. Theories abounded as to why she might have wanted the young nurse dead.

Then, the following afternoon, the four remaining nurses from Nurse Parry's residential group were summoned to the housekeeper's office. When they got there, they found Detective Inspector Paige and Constable Johns waiting for them. Paige invited them to sit down before standing up to address the group.

'I wanted to speak to all of you,' he said, looking round at their expectant faces, 'because I know how difficult it has been for you over the past few weeks, knowing that we have had to treat you as potential suspects in the murder of Susan Parry. I wanted you all to know that you are none of you any longer under any kind of suspicion, and I hope that we shall not need to question any of you again.'

He paused to let the news sink in.

'Please, Inspector,' Jill Saunders asked, 'does this mean that you know who killed Susan?'

'Yes Nurse Saunders, it does. I'm prepared to tell you who it is because the press will no doubt soon get hold of the information, but I would like to emphasise that anything I say to you now is to be treated as strictly confidential. I'm sure that, as nurses, you understand what that means. Not a word of what is said here to anyone outside this room – and especially nothing to any newspaper reporters. Do you understand?'

They all nodded eagerly.

'Very well,' he continued, 'I can inform you that Sister Catherine Spencer has been charged with the murder of Nurse Susan Parry. I can also tell you – and this is where you must remember not to repeat what you've heard – that she has signed a confession, which makes it clear that she was acting alone. We are therefore not looking for anyone else in connection with this murder.'

There was a short silence while they all considered this news.

'But why did she do it?' Jane Bentham asked at last, voicing what they had all been thinking. 'What had she got against Susan?'

'Sister Spencer had been stealing diamorphine from the ward stock and she was afraid that Nurse Parry had discovered about it. She killed her to prevent her telling anyone.'

'So is Catherine Spencer a drug addict?' Jane asked in astonishment. 'She didn't behave like one. I'd never have guessed.'

'No. She wasn't stealing for herself. She took the drug to give to her boyfriend.'

'But how did she manage it?' Jill asked. 'Drugs like diamorphine are very carefully monitored. Someone would have noticed that it had gone missing.'

'But it was recorded as having been given to the patients,' Angela broke in. 'She wrote up in the patient notes that she'd administered it, but she just pocketed the phial instead. That's why Mr Frost's friend complained that he hadn't been given any pain killers.'

'That's correct,' Paige agreed. 'She usually only played that trick once with each patient, but she made a mistake with that one and he was left without any pain relief for twelve hours following surgery. When he put in his complaint, it helped us to put two and two together.'

'So let me get this straight,' Elaine said slowly. She had

been thinking through what the inspector had told them. 'Catherine was stealing diamorphine from the ward and Susan got wind of it and threatened to expose her?'

'I don't think it was a strong as that,' Constable Johns answered, speaking for the first time. 'As far as we can tell, she didn't make any threats. It wasn't blackmail, if that's what you're thinking. She thought that Sister Spencer had forgotten to administer the drug to one patient. She talked to her about it and they went and gave it to him. But she was thinking of reporting the incident as a 'near miss' because Spencer shouldn't have written up the notes until after she'd actually given the drug.'

'And Spencer was afraid that, if the incident was investigated, other instances when she'd purloined the drug instead of giving it to a patient might be found out,' Paige finished.

'So then, a few days later, she waited for Susan to come off her night duty and went in and stabbed her to death in her bed, before going on duty herself.' Elaine had been keeping her own careful notes of the investigation and knew exactly how the times of everyone's comings and goings fitted in.

'That's right,' Paige confirmed. 'Working in Theatres, it was easy for her to take away a scalpel from the autoclave one evening and to return it to the hospital the following morning. Her nurse training enabled her to inflict a fatal wound to the heart – something which is not nearly as easy as most people think. She locked the door when she left, using Parry's key, which she replaced on the bedside table when she came in with the rest of you that evening. None of you noticed her putting it there, because you were all too busy looking at the body.'

He looked round at the four faces in front of him.

'Now, that's all I want to say to you. Remember what I said about not passing this on to *anyone* else. I'm sorry it has taken so long, but I hope that you can all now sleep easy again.'

They got up to go, but Paige called Angela back.

'Nurse Wheeler! If you wouldn't mind staying just for a couple of minutes, Constable Johns has one or two loose ends to tie up and he'd like to ask you some questions.'

He left the room, ushering the other nurses ahead of him. Angela looked at Peter enquiringly.

'I wanted to ask you,' he started. Then he faltered and tried again. 'There's a police dance next week. I was wondering if you might be willing to go with me.'

Angela looked at him for a moment and then burst out laughing.

'Is that what the inspector meant when he said you had some questions for me?'

'I don't know, but that's the only question on my mind at the moment.'

'Oh Peter! Of course I'd love to come, but how did Inspector Paige know you wanted to ask me?'

'Oh, nothing much gets past him,' Peter shrugged. It was not until much, much later – years later in fact – that he told Angela how Richard had deduced that Peter had fallen for her.

****

Peter was eating his lunch in the canteen. A small group of young officers joined him. They were discussing the upcoming dance and whom they were planning to take with them.

'What about you, Johns? Who're you taking?'

'I haven't decided yet.' Peter, who was rather inclined not to go at all, tried to sound off-hand in the hope that they would let the question drop.

'Johns won't have any trouble finding someone,' another of them chipped in, 'what with him having been up at the nurses' home practically every day for the last few weeks. He must know lots of lovely young nurses who'd all be delighted to be asked.'

'I hear one of the ones he's been seeing is a coloured girl. I reckon she'd be a good bet. They can't get enough of it,

I'm told.'

'Enough of what?' Peter heard himself saying naïvely, before he realised what the man had meant. He wished fervently he had ignored the remark.

'Poor Johns!' one of them mocked. 'He's led a very sheltered life. It comes of being raised in an orphanage I suppose.'

'What Constable Adams is saying,' another said, adopting the tone of someone explaining to a small child, 'Is that coloured girls are usually up for a bit of "how's your father" – especially with a white man.'

'How dare you!' Peter was unable to stop himself raising his voice. 'You've no right making that sort of suggestion about someone you haven't even met.'

'Ooh! Hark at him,' the mocker began again. 'I reckon Johns is sweet on that coloured nurse!'

Johns flushed a deep red, but said nothing.

'Look at him! He didn't deny it. He fancies her!'

Peter could stand it no longer. He got up, leaving his lunch unfinished, and walked out.

'It was brave of you to stand up to Adams and his cronies,' Paige said to Johns that afternoon, while they were driving to the hospital to interview the Theatre staff in the hope of getting evidence for the suspicions that they were forming about Sister Spencer. 'I was at the next table. I heard it all. You were right to pull them up about assumptions about people based on race. That's part of being a good policeman: never assume you know what a person's like just because of what they look like, or where they live or what job they do.'

'I don't know about brave,' Johns mumbled. 'I just didn't like what they were saying about Angela.'

'It's Angela now is it?'

'Well, that *is* her name,' Johns said defensively, realising that he had given himself away.

'Of course, you do realise that it would be most

inappropriate for a police officer to form a relationship with any of the witnesses in a murder enquiry.'

'Yes sir.'

'However, once the enquiry is over,' Paige went on, 'that would be another thing altogether.'

****

Angela enjoyed the dance. Not that she had many partners: Peter seemed curiously reluctant to allow any of the other policemen to approach her. He did permit her one dance with Paige, who had arrived in the company of a rather overweight and spotty WPC, whom Peter suspected had been unsuccessful in finding any other escort. As the inspector guided her round the dance floor Angela tackled him on a subject that had been intriguing her.

'Why did you want Peter to ask me to the dance? I mean that *was* the loose end that you said he needed to tie up wasn't it?'

'I didn't want to be stuck here all evening making conversation with WPC Jacobs,' Richard answered in a deadpan voice.

'If you didn't want her company, why did you invite her?' Angela enquired innocently.

'Because I didn't want to have to listen to her for months afterwards sighing and saying what a pity it was that she hadn't been able to come.'

'Wouldn't it have been more straightforward to tell Peter that *he* had to invite WPC Jacobs?'

'No, because then I'd have had Johns going round with a long face, which would have been almost as bad as Pam Jacobs and her moaning. Besides, you'll be good for Peter Johns. He could do with a woman to look after him.'

'Do you mean at the dance or in life generally?'

'Oh generally: it's not good for a policeman to go home to an empty house after spending the day looking at mangled corpses and interviewing victims of assault.'

'What about you then? Peter told me that you were still a bachelor yourself.'

172

'But I live with my father and grandmother. Thirty-five and still never left home: what d'you think of that?'

'I think your father is a very lucky man.'

'What a very diplomatic answer. I thought you would probably think I was very unadventurous, considering you've travelled half way round the world to be here.'

'I had good reason for coming here. It sounds to me as if you had equally good reasons for staying at home.'

The music reached a conclusion and Richard, spotting Peter's red head at the other side of the room, led Angela back to where he and WPC Jacobs had just finished the dance together. They were standing close to the bar at which stood a cluster of young men who were engaged in collecting drinks to take back to their partners. One of them turned to go, lurched sideways and collided with Angela, spilling the contents of his glass down the front of her dress. Peter recognised him as Adams, the ringleader of the group from the canteen. He was evidently rather drunk.

'Oh look Johns!' he called out, 'your monkey's spilled my drink.'

For a few moments, there was a stunned silence in that part of the room. Peter stared at Adams in disbelief while Angela took a step back, looking down and brushing ineffectually at her dress with her hand to hide her confusion. Pam Jacobs put her arm round her and offered her a paper serviette, which she had picked up from the bar. Then Peter stepped towards Adams with a look of thunder on his face, but Richard was too quick for him. He calmly placed himself between Peter and his adversary and looked Adams squarely in the face.

'Peter,' he said, without turning his head. 'I think Miss Wheeler would like you to take her outside for a breath of air. The atmosphere in here has suddenly become very unpleasant.'

Peter obediently took Angela's arm and led her from the room. As they went, she looked back from the doorway and saw Richard speaking to her tormentor. His face was stern and he was evidently making full use of his seniority to rebuke Adams. They went outside into the cool night air and stood on the steps of the hall, unsure what to do next.

'I think I'd like to go home now,' Angela said after a while.

'Yes, of course. I'll walk you back to the nurses' home.'

They set off, walking silently arm in arm.

'I don't suppose he meant any harm,' Angela ventured at last. 'I expect it was just the drink talking.'

'There were a couple of coloured girls in my house,' Peter said, as if thinking aloud. 'Sisters. They were five and three when they came. One day, one of the boys made a monkey joke about them. We were all sitting round the table having our tea. I can still see it now. A lot of us laughed at it. Even one of the coloured girls joined in.'

He paused. Angela wondered whether she ought to say something, but she remained silent waiting for him to go on.

'I never saw my housefather so angry, either before or since,' Peter resumed. 'He didn't raise his voice; he just spoke in a sort of calm fury. I must have been about ten at the time. I was terrified. He told the boy that his remark was the sort of thing that had sent millions of Jews to the gas chambers. He told the rest of us that anyone who laughed at the joke was just as bad as the boy who made it. He said that for evil to triumph all that is needed is for good people to stand by and do nothing.'

'I think it was a bit hard on a ten-year-old, comparing you to the Nazis.'

'But he was right,' Peter argued. 'That's where that sort of thing starts. I made up my mind, then and there, never to be a party to making fun of someone because of their appearance – after all, I get enough of it myself because of my hair! Anyway, it wasn't being called a Nazi that struck home; it was feeling that he was disappointed in us. I bet that's how Adams is feeling now, with Richard Paige giving him a dressing down. Richard's very well respected in the force.'

'He must be young for an inspector,' Angela commented.

'Yes, but then he lives and breathes the police, so it's no wonder he's a high flyer. I shouldn't think he's ever had a girlfriend or any sort of social life.'

'Thirty-five isn't too old to start,' Angela teased.

'Oh well, that's it then!' Peter declared, pretending to take her seriously. 'If I'm in competition with old Richard I might as well give up now. Shall I go back and fetch him so that he can take you home?'

'Don't be silly, Peter,' Angela giggled, squeezing his arm. 'I much prefer redheads – didn't I tell you?'

****

Bernie smiled as she finished reading Angie's account and started putting the pages into her ring binder.

'I'm not sure that my story really belongs in your folder,' Angie said. 'It hardly mentions Richard.'

'But he was there in the background. The murder in the nurses' home was one of his cases and he seems to have been a bit of a matchmaker as far as you and Peter were concerned.'

She broke off and flicked back through the pages, as if looking for something.

'So, Richard's grandmother was still alive when you and Peter first knew him?' she asked, pointing at the relevant passage.

'Yes. I never met her, but I do remember her dying about a year after I met Peter. She must have been about ninety, I should think. Apparently she'd been a widow for a long time and Richard's father had devoted his life to looking after her.'

'And then, when Richard's own mother came back, he tried to do the same for her,' Bernie mused.

'Maybe,' Angie agreed. 'He certainly did always behave as if he had an obligation to her – even after all those years apart.'

Bernie sat thinking for a while, then shook herself and

returned to the task of putting Angie's story into the binder.

'Anyway,' she went on, 'I'm sure Lucy will love to read about her godparents as well as about her dad. So I'm very grateful to you for writing this for us, even if it doesn't really fit. And at least it shows that some people still manage to behave rationally when they're in love – unlike me and Richard!'

Angie handed the pages of Bernie's narrative back to her friend.

'You know, Bernie,' she said, 'in the couple of years before you and Richard got married, Peter and I really used to wonder about the pair of you. I remember saying to Peter you seemed to have become like an old married couple without ever having gone through the starry-eye young lovers stage – and without having actually got married, come to that.'

'Well, you do have to remember that we never were young lovers,' Bernie pointed out. 'Richard was nearly fifty-five when we first met.'

'You know what I mean. You'd settled into a comfortable routine, much the same as most couples do after ten or twenty years of marriage, only it wasn't a case of the passion calming down over time – you never seemed to have been passionate about each other.'

'I'm not sure what you mean by passionate. It would have been ridiculous at my age to have been parading my feelings for all the world to see, like a teenager showing off her first boyfriend.'

'But when you were alone together,' persisted Angie. 'Couldn't you have given him some sort of clue then? Peter and I could never understand how it could be that we could both see full well that you were in love with him, but he didn't seem to have the faintest inkling,'

'I suppose if *I'd* worked out that I was in love with him then he might have stood a better chance.'

Angie laughed.

'No, I'm serious. It really didn't cross my mind that

Richard was anything special to me until I started to think about what it would be like without him. He was like the wallpaper, or an old comfy cardigan that you take for granted. And then when it looked as if I might never see him again, it hurt so much.'

She blew her nose and became very busy putting the loose leaves into the ring binder.

'You and Peter were much more sensible,' she said after a few minutes, 'none of that hiding your feelings from everyone, including ourselves, which made it so difficult for me and Richard to get it together.'

13 MATCH OF THE DAY

'Thanks, Bernie,' Edward Johns said, closing his A' level textbook and putting it away in his school bag. 'It's a lot clearer now.'

'Always happy to help. Now, how's the UCAS form coming along? Have you got your Personal Statement sorted?'

'I think so, but I wouldn't mind you having a look at it. You must know more about what they'll be looking for than the careers teacher.'

'Let's see it then.'

Eddie rummaged in his bag and pulled out a crumpled piece of paper. He passed it across the kitchen table to Bernie. She read it and made some suggestions for improvement, which he scribbled down. He put the paper away and got up to go. Then he hesitated and sat down again.

'Is it true that Mum wrote a story for your book about Richard?' he asked.

'Yes. She did.' Bernie answered evenly, wondering what was coming next.

'About her and Dad and how they met?'

'Well, yes – that did come into it.' Bernie answered

cautiously.

'Can I read it?'

'Did your mum say you could?'

'She didn't say I couldn't.'

'Did you ask her?'

'Well, no, but …'

'What have they told you about it up to now?'

'I know that Richard and Dad were investigating a murder at the nurses' home and that's how they first met. And that they met again at an NCH do, which was how they started going out together. Is that what's in the story? I thought there must be more to it than that.'

'Yes, I think there is. OK, come in the other room and I'll show you.'

They went into the living room and Bernie reached down the red ring binder.

'There you go,' she said, as she and handed it to Eddie. 'The story you want is near the beginning of the "early days in the police" section.'

Eddie sat down on the settee and started leafing through the pages, while Bernie took up a book and sat down in a chair near the window. About half an hour later, she became conscious of Eddie standing over her, holding out the ring binder.

'Thanks,' he said. 'There's a lot there I never knew about my dad.'

'I hope I haven't broken any confidences.'

'No. I don't mean that sort of thing. I mean, I hadn't realised he felt so strongly about racial discrimination and things.'

Bernie raised her eyebrows in an expression of astonishment.

'I mean,' Eddie went on, 'I know *he* isn't a racist, of course; but I always thought he didn't really believe that racism existed. He always seemed to assume that everyone thought the same way he did. Treating everyone the same regardless, I mean.'

'You mean, you didn't think he understood that you might be getting picked on for not being white?'

'I suppose.'

'And does that happen? Do you get picked on, I mean?'

'Sometimes; not so much now I'm in the sixth form.'

'And did you tell your mum or dad?'

'No. I thought they would just say to ignore it. I know that's what Mum does when people say things to her.'

'So is that what you do too?'

'I try to, but it isn't always easy. That's why I started bunking off school in Year Ten.'

'But you didn't tell anyone?'

'No. I thought it'd only have made things worse.'

Bernie sat thinking. She wanted to tell him that, by keeping quiet, he was making it impossible for the perpetrators to be challenged and perhaps prevented from inflicting the same misery on others; but she was afraid of alienating him. It was too late to change what had happened, so what purpose would be served by criticising him?

'And now?' she said at last. 'Do you think you might feel able to tell your dad if that sort of thing happened again?'

'I suppose. Well, maybe. Or maybe it'd be easier if I told you and you told Mum and Dad.'

'I'm very flattered. If that's the way you want it, it's fine by me, but I think they might be a bit disappointed.' She did not like to push things any further, thinking that at least this represented some progress towards persuading him to be more open about bullying in the future.

'Getting back to your book,' Eddie said, changing the subject abruptly. 'How's about I write a chapter for you?'

'How d'you mean?'

'I could write about the great Superintendent Paige and what it was like having him as my dad's boss.'

'You could, could you? What exactly did you have in mind?'

'You wait and see. It'll be good, I guarantee.'

****

It was a Saturday in May 1992 and nine-year-old Eddie was standing in the front room peering out under the net curtain, on tenterhooks waiting for Bernie to arrive. At last he saw her, rounding the corner as she walked from her house a few streets away.

'Dad!' he shouted out, running into the hall to open the front door. 'Bernie's here! Are you ready to go?'

'Won't be a moment!' came a voice from upstairs.

The phone rang just as a smiling Bernie entered the house, clad in a red scarf and with a small rucksack on her back. Eddie's mother emerged from the kitchen to answer it. At the same time, his father appeared at the top of the stairs.

'Peter!' she called up the stairs a few moments later, 'It's DCI Paige for you.'

He hurried downstairs and took the receiver from his wife's hand.

'Richard? What's up? ... But I'm supposed to be going to Wembley ... I understand, but I promised Eddie ... Yes, I do see, but ... Yes, yes, alright I'll be there.'

He turned to his son, an apologetic look on his face. Eddie looked back, knowing all too well what was going to follow.

'I'm sorry, Eddie. I'm going to have to go into work. Something's cropped up and they need all the manpower they can get.'

'But you promised!' Eddie protested, knowing that it would have no effect.

'I know. I'm really sorry, but a kid's been abducted and we need to find her before she gets hurt.' He turned to Bernie. 'Are you OK to take Eddie on your own? I wouldn't ask if it wasn't for-'

'Yes, of course,' Bernie interrupted. 'I'm sure he'll be no trouble – will you, Eddie?'

'Here you are, Eddie. Your packed lunch is in here,' his mum said, putting a bag over his shoulder. 'Now, be good for Bernie. I'll be asking her for a report on your behaviour, so mind your manners!'

'I'm sure we'll get on fine,' Bernie assured them. 'It's a pity to waste the ticket, though. Isn't there anyone else who could come with us: Hannah maybe?'

'No fear!' Hannah butted in, emerging from the front room. 'What would I want to waste my time watching twenty-two idiots chasing a ball around a field for?'

'I'll take that as "no thank you" then,' said Bernie, smiling. 'So Eddie, what about you, do you have a friend you could ask?'

'Not at such short notice,' his mum answered for him. 'Don't you need to get off to catch your train?'

So Eddie and Bernie went to the FA cup final by themselves. He had to admit that they had a good time, despite the disappointment of not having his dad with them. He was a Spurs supporter himself, but happily switched his allegiance temporarily to join with the Liverpool fans cheering their team to victory. It was the first time he had been to Wembley stadium and he stared around, taking it all in, making mental notes to take back to show off to his friends at school on Monday. They would all have had to content themselves with watching the match on the television at home.

He made friends with a boy of his own age, who was there with his father and older brother from the Old Swan district of Liverpool. At half time Dad insisted on buying pies for them all and soon Bernie and he were exchanging reminiscences of nineteen-seventies Merseyside while the boys chattered happily together about the awfulness of their respective schools and the unreasonableness of parents.

When he arrived back home that evening, his dad was out. He was still out when Eddie went reluctantly upstairs to bed a few hours later. The following day, when Eddie wandered into the kitchen in search of breakfast, his father was just getting up from the table, preparing to go out again.

'How was the match?' he asked, as he put on his jacket and felt for his keys in the pocket.

'It was great! Liverpool won two nil. You should have been there.'

'I know. I'm sorry. Another time, eh?'

Eddie looked sceptical. Whatever plans they made seemed to get disrupted by urgent demands from Inspector Paige to drop everything and join him on a case.

About six weeks later, it was Eddie's school sports day. He had been looking forward to it even more than usual, because this year Hannah would not be there making disparaging remarks about his performance to her friends. She had moved on from their Primary School the previous September, something that Eddie viewed with unalloyed joy.

As his class filed out on to the field, he scanned the rows of parents sitting on inconveniently small chairs at the side of the running track. He spotted his mother on the front row, chatting to one of the other mums, but there was no sign of his dad. He had promised faithfully to be there! He had even agreed to run in the fathers' race. The class sat down in neat rows opposite the parents. Eddie kept a close watch on his mother, hoping that she might be joined by her husband at the last minute, but the chairs on either side of her filled up with other people's parents and Eddie's dad did not appear.

Eddie had been practising hard for the sports. He was not very fast, but he had staying power, and so had been chosen to represent his class in the longest race: twice around the school field. He looked towards his mother as he lined up on the starting line with the other boys. She smiled and waved briefly. There was still no sign of his father, still no last minute arrival hurrying towards the front to see his son in action. He ran his hardest and, with a final effort, managed to overtake the boy from the top class who had led the field from the outset, just before they crossed the finishing line. Eddie raised his hands above his head in triumph and looked one final time to see if his dad could have arrived while he was running; but no, his mum was still there on her own, surrounded by other people's parents.

Eddie was in bed before his father got home that evening. He heard voices in the hall and then footsteps coming upstairs. They grew louder as they ascended the second flight to his room in the converted loft. He saw the bedroom door begin to open slowly and closed his eyes, pretending to be asleep. In the silence that followed, he could hear gentle breathing and soft footsteps on the carpet.

'Eddie!'

He ignored his dad's voice and continued to pretend to be asleep.

'I hear you won your race this afternoon. Well done!'

Eddie condescended to open his eyes a crack and look at his father's face through the slit.

'I'm sorry I couldn't be there. Inspector Paige needed me to help him.'

'Why does he always get what *he* wants?' Eddie demanded, sitting bolt upright and banging his fists down on the bed. 'Why don't you ever stand up to him?'

'He's my boss,' his dad said patiently. 'It's my job. I have to do what he says.'

'But you *promised*!'

'I know. I'm sorry.'

Eddie flung himself back down on the bed, turned away and pulled the sheet up over his head. He closed his eyes and waited until he heard steps going back down the stairs.

A few days later, Eddie was surprised to find Inspector Paige waiting for him at the school gate when he came out.

'Hello Edward,' the tall policeman greeted him. 'Do you remember me?'

'You're Detective Chief Inspector Paige.'

'That's right. I work with your dad. Is it alright for me to walk home with you?'

Eddie shrugged his shoulders and stared down at his feet. Then he thrust his hands into his pockets and set off down the street. Inspector Paige walked at his side, stooping slightly in order to speak to him.

'I think I owe you an apology,' he said. 'I gather I was responsible for your dad not being there to see you win your race the other day.'

Eddie said nothing.

'You mustn't blame him: he has to do what I say.'

'He told me you'd given him the afternoon off!' Eddie blurted out indignantly.

'Yes, I did. And then I asked him to stay after all. I didn't realise it was so important. But I should have done. So I'm sorry.'

They walked on in silence.

'You see, Eddie,' Paige began again, 'your dad is my best sergeant, so whenever I have a really difficult job to do I think of him.'

Eddie continued to maintain a sulky silence.

'I hear I also interfered with your enjoyment of the cup final a few weeks back,' Paige persevered. 'I'm sorry about that too, but it really was important to have your dad there. You see a little girl had gone missing and we needed all the manpower we could get to try to find her. And your dad was one person I knew I could rely on.'

'But you didn't, did you? I saw it on the news. You didn't find her and then ages afterwards someone found her body in the woods.'

'No, we didn't find her, but we had to try. You ought to be proud of your dad, Eddie. He's a good policeman. If anyone could have made a difference to that girl, it would have been him. That's why I keep asking him to do things for me instead of letting him go home to his family. It's selfish of me, I know. I'll try to do better in future. No hard feelings?'

Paige held out his hand towards Eddie as they turned into the street where his house stood. Eddie hesitated then shook hands briefly before running off in the direction of home.

****

Bernie looked up from the page and met Eddie's gaze. It had taken him just two days to produce his contribution to Lucy's book. He had come over on his bike to deliver it and was now waiting anxiously for her verdict.

'Thank you. That's very good. And it throws new light on Richard's relationship with your dad. I have to admit, I always thought that Richard took him rather for granted.'

'I never believed all that stuff he said about Dad being his best sergeant and all that. I thought that was all just to make me feel better.'

'I dare say it was, but that doesn't mean there wasn't any truth in it. Your dad was the one person Richard kept by him all through his police service. I'm sure he did really value him. And he's right: you should be proud of your dad.'

Eddie looked uncomfortable.

'Anyway, will it do?' he asked. 'The story, I mean.'

'Yes, thank you Eddie; it will do very nicely.'

14 MOTHERS AND DAUGHTERS

'Hello! I hope I'm not intruding.'

Bernie looked up from the sandpit in the back garden where she was helping Lucy to make sand pies. The face that looked down on her was vaguely familiar, but it was a few moments before she remembered to whom it belonged. It was, after all, a year since they had last met.

'There was no answer when I rang the bell,' Jonah went on, 'so I tried the side gate. I hope you don't mind.'

'No, of course not,' Bernie assured him, scrambling to her feet. Seeing the large parcel that he was carrying, she was about to protest that he should not keep bringing gifts, but then changed her mind. If it amused him to give an annual present to the daughter of his old friend Richard, what business had she to complain? His inspector's salary, together with that of his wife, who was a senior surgeon, meant that he could easily afford such trifles.

'It's very good of you to remember Lucy's birthday.'

Bernie turned to her daughter, who had looked up at the sound of her name, pausing in her task of demolishing the line of sand pies by hitting them with a small plastic spade. 'Lucy, do you remember Jonah? He gave you your train set.'

'Choo-choo!' Lucy said seriously, 'Drain set.'

She got laboriously to her feet and toddled towards Jonah. He sat down on the edge of the sandpit so that his face was level with hers. She tripped on the uneven surface of the sand and fell forwards on to his knees, which she gripped with both arms to keep herself upright.

'Well now, Miss Paige,' he said, showing her a large rectangular parcel, which he had put down on the ground. 'I must congratulate you on reaching the age of two. Please accept this gift in honour of the occasion.'

Lucy took hold of the parcel and started ripping the wrapping paper off it. A brightly coloured cardboard box emerged. Jonah helped her to open it and take out the large plastic digger contained within.

'I'm pleased to see that you are continuing to prepare yourself for a glittering career in the engineering industry,' he went on, 'and I hope you will find this helpful in your endeavours.'

'Thank you, Jonah,' Bernie exclaimed. 'That's just the thing for Lucy's new sand pit. How did you know?'

'Just my natural brilliance and psychic powers.'

'Not to mention your inherent modesty,' Bernie finished for him with a smile.

'Dank oo!' Lucy cried, remembering the coaching that Bernie had given her that morning regarding the proper etiquette when receiving birthday presents. She flung herself at Jonah and deposited a wet kiss on his cheek.

'I'll go and make us a brew,' Bernie said, seeing that Lucy seemed happy with her new companion. 'Will you two be alright for a few minutes?'

'Of course,' Jonah assured her. 'Now Lucy, let me demonstrate this machine's earth-moving capabilities.'

'Sand,' Lucy said, sitting down with a bump and patting the sand with her hands. 'Not earf,' she added emphatically.

'I beg your pardon,' Jonah agreed, 'of course I meant to say "sand-moving capabilities". Now, just watch this …'

When Bernie returned a few minutes later, Jonah and

Lucy were on their hands and knees in the sandpit, busily moving piles of sand around with the digger to create an elaborate network of roads, hills and tunnels. Jonah's jacket lay abandoned on the patio and his shirtsleeves were rolled up. She called out to them to come over to a wooden picnic table for refreshments.

Jonah stood up and Bernie gave a little gasp as she saw the patches of damp sand adhering to his clothes.

'Oh Jonah! Look at the state of your trousers! That's the second suit that we've ruined for you. I can see I need to get some overalls for you to put on whenever you come here.'

'Oh it'll brush off when it dries. No harm done.'

He helped Lucy out of the sandpit and she led him over to the outside tap to rinse the sand off their hands before eating. Within a few minutes, they were all sitting around the rustic wooden table on the patio. Bernie poured milk into a plastic cup, topped it up with tea and put on the lid.

'I see you're starting Lucy off early on the tea drinking habit,' Jonah commented.

'In my family tea was the universal panacea for all ills. Whether it was your heart or your leg or your favourite toy that was broken, the answer was always to make a brew.'

She poured a mugful for Jonah and another for herself, then rescued the plate of biscuits from Lucy who had started picking them up one by one, testing them with her mouth and then replacing them. Bernie removed Lucy's rejects and handed one of them to her, before offering the plate to Jonah. He took one and Bernie put the plate down well out of her daughter's reach.

'Now, tell me,' Jonah urged, 'How're you getting on regarding tracking down old Richard's past and finding out about the mysterious disappearance of his mother?'

'Not that well, to be honest,' Bernie admitted. 'At least – well, it's been a bit mixed really.'

'Would you care to elaborate on that?'

'Well, I now feel that I know Richard a whole lot better than I ever did when he was alive, thanks to all of the things that his friends have told me. However, there's still a big hole as far as his early life is concerned, and I've made practically no headway in finding out why his mother left home, where she went or why she came back. I suppose it's daft to expect to find out those things, really, but having started I'd like to tie up all the loose ends – and there seem to be more of those than ever!'

'Oh?'

'Well, I did the round of the college gaudies last summer, hoping to find out who the elusive "A.F." might be. You remember "A.F." from the locket I showed you?'

'Yes. Go on.'

'And the picture of a group of women, one of whom might possibly be A.F. and/or someone called Ally, who wrote letters to Eleanor?'

'Yes.'

'Well, I met an old tutor who recognised the group in the photo, although she wasn't sure who was who. She must have been nearly a hundred, so it's a wonder she remembers them at all. She said they were a group of four friends who went round together all the time. Two of them are potential A.F.s: Abigail Fossett and Alicia Fortescue née Lowton. I've been trying to track them down, but with absolutely no success. I don't think I'm much of a detective, to be honest.

'Oh! And then there's also another contender for "Ally": one Alexander Fokin, born in London of Russian parents who had come over before the revolution and never went back. I haven't managed to find him either. He was a philosophy tutor at one of the Oxford colleges in the forties and apparently taught two of the girls in the picture: Abigail and another called … let me see … oh yes! Claudia Browne (with an "e"). He disappears off the Oxford radar in 1947 and it seems likely that he got a job at London University, but I don't know which college. That timing could fit in with Eleanor going to London to be with him. Apparently his friends all called him Sasha, which slightly knocks the Ally theory on its head, but if he and Eleanor were lovers then she might well have had her own pet name for him which nobody else used.'

'Did you and Richard have pet names?' Jonah asked irrelevantly.

'Goodness no! We were far too serious for that sort of nonsense. I called him Richard and he called me Our Bernie, like everyone else.'

'Yes – that's what Peter Johns called you. Why is that?'

Bernie laughed. 'It's a way of warning people that I'm a mad scouser who doesn't know how to speak proper. It's not at all fair! I don't make fun of the way you lot mispronounce "grass" and "bath"!'

'No, but I have to admit, when you say something's "not fur" I get this picture of fluffy bunnies in my head and it takes a while before the penny drops that you're talking about equitable treatment of an ethnic minority.'

Bernie gave him a withering look. 'I'm sure you understood *pairfectly*,' she retorted.

'Well, setting that to one side,' Jonah resumed, 'what about that Jewish evacuee you told me about? The one who knew Richard when he was a baby? You were going to look for her too.'

'I did,' Bernie replied ruefully, 'with equal lack of success. I just don't seem to be able to find the right places to look.'

'Maybe I could help. I've just started an eighteen-month secondment to the Metropolitan Police. I could do a bit of digging around in the East End. What was her name again?'

'Esther Lyons, but do you really think you ought to? I mean, Richard got himself in trouble trying to use the police to find his mother.'

'He was only a junior constable at the time. Nobody will question what I'm doing. Besides, I don't intend to use up any police resources, just a bit of my own time and my extraordinary detective prowess.'

'Not that you're given to boasting, of course.'

'Absolutely not. Modesty is my middle name.'

'OK then, but do be careful – and not too much of your

time either: I can't help thinking that we've taken up far more of it than we deserve already. Today, for example: if you're working for the Met now, how come you can find the time to come to Oxford to see us?'

'I've taken some leave – and before you say anything – it's in aid of decorating the dining room. You and Lucy have the pleasure of my company while I'm waiting for the paint to dry. And I'm very much afraid,' he added, getting up and putting on his jacket, 'that it is probably ready for the next coat by now. So I must take my leave.

He bowed to each of them in the manner of an eighteenth century gentleman.

'Miss Paige. Dr Fazakerley.'

'Inspector,' said Bernie, giving a slight inclination of her head in return, while Lucy waved enthusiastically, as Jonah set off round the corner of the house.

Thus it was, that, some seven months later, Bernie found herself ushering into her home a small, white-haired woman by the name of Esther Kaplin (née Lyons). A few weeks earlier a letter had arrived from Jonah, containing the married name and telephone number of the evacuee who had been billeted with the Paige family during the war, and the statement: 'she's expecting you to ring.'

Esther had been delighted to be offered the chance of coming back to the place where she had spent five years of her childhood, and was intrigued to hear about what had happened to the little boy whom she had known when she was there. She immediately suggested coming down to Oxford, from her home in Manchester, to meet Bernie and share her reminiscences. Now she was standing in the hall, gazing round at the familiar and yet unfamiliar surroundings.

'It's a lot brighter than I remember,' she commented. 'The doors were all dark varnished wood and there was horrid dark red flock wallpaper all over the walls. It's a lot more cheerful now.'

She went over and looked at a group of black and white photographs, which Bernie had hung on the wall.

'Is this Richard?' she asked, pointing at a copy of the photograph that Ernest Walker had given to Bernie of Richard in his police constable's uniform.

'Yes. That was when he was first made constable.'

'It seems so strange to think of him as grown up,' Esther said, shaking her head. 'I'll always think of him as a little boy, scared of the dark, or in disgrace after falling in the pond or crying when his puppy was run over. It's hard to imagine him being a policeman and getting married and having his own family.'

'It's quite the opposite for me,' Bernie commented. 'When I look at that photograph I find it hard to believe that someone so young could be the same man I married five years ago. He was fifty-five when I met him and I can't really imagine him being anything other than middle-aged.'

'Had he been married before?'

'Oh no. He never got round to it. I suppose I represented his last chance, what with I also having left things a bit on the late side as far as matrimony was concerned. Everyone said it was because he was too busy with his job, but I think it was to do with feeling insecure after his mother left him. And that's one of the things I was hoping you might be able to tell me. What sort of relationship did he have with his mother?'

'Your friend said that you were making a dossier of pictures and stories about him.'

'That's right. I'll show you what I've got so far. I want Lucy to know what her father was like, even though she'll never meet him.'

Bernie took Esther's coat and hung it up. Then she shepherded her into the living room. Esther stood looking around.

'This room's been brightened up too,' she commented. 'And it's a lot cosier with the carpet on the floor. In my day, it was all quarry tiles and just a couple of rugs. I see you've still got the dresser. That was Mrs Paige senior's pride and joy.'

She walked over to the large oak Welsh dresser, which stood against the wall opposite the door, and peered down at the cupboard doors on the front.

'And here's where I chipped a bit out of it when I fell over carrying the dustpan.' She straightened herself up again. 'I didn't half catch it from Mrs Paige! It was in the kitchen in those days. It must have taken some shifting to get it in here.'

'I suppose Richard, or his father, must have moved it when the kitchen was fitted,' Bernie suggested. 'I always thought it was a bit out of place in here, but it comes in handy now for storing Lucy's toys.'

'And these plates?' Esther pointed at the rows of Wedgewood calendar plates displayed on the shelves. The dates ran from 1958 to 1976.

'Those were my mam's. My dad bought her one for Christmas every year. I never had anywhere to put them up until I came here. Now sit down and I'll make a brew, then afterwards I'll show you round the place, if you like.'

Esther sat down on the settee and Bernie gave her the red ring binder and box of memorabilia to look at, while she and Lucy went off to the kitchen to prepare the inevitable pot of tea. When they returned they found her reading the accounts that Richard's colleagues had written about his time in the police service. She looked up.

'He seems to have been very well respected,' she said. 'That's what your friend said too. He said that he'd worked with Richard.'

'Yes – a long time ago. Jonah Porter isn't exactly my friend. I've only met him a few times. How did he find you? I tried to track down the Lyons family in London and drew a complete blank.'

'Well, the way I heard about him was that one of my sons rang me to say that there was a police officer from London asking for news of an Esther Lyons who had married a

Bernard Kaplin from Manchester in 1955. Of course, that could only be me, so I asked him to find out what it was all about. Our Daniel spoke to him on the phone and decided that he was genuine and arranged for him to come up and meet me.'

'Jonah went to Manchester?'

'Oh yes. He said he didn't want to tell you until he'd checked that he'd got it right. He'd found the records of my marriage, from the registrar's office I suppose, and that told him that my husband was from Manchester. So then he phoned round to all the Manchester synagogues-'

'Which must have taken some doing in itself,' Bernie muttered, aware that Manchester had a large and diverse Jewish community with many synagogues.

'And that's how my son Daniel heard about it. Of course, I was absolutely delighted to hear about Richard after all that time and to come down here to see the place again. And I'm very interested in this book you're making for your little girl.'

'But it must have taken Jonah hours of work to find you,' Bernie said, shaking her head. 'And then to spend a day going to see you in Manchester. I don't understand why he would do that for me.'

'I think perhaps he was doing it for Richard,' Esther said gently. 'He told me that Richard was killed in the course of duty. It sounded as if he was a bit of a hero.'

'I don't know about that. Because he died, he was being brave and heroic; if he'd lived he would have been foolhardy and probably received a reprimand for taking unnecessary risks.'

'Do you blame him for that?'

'No,' Bernie shook her head. 'He was just doing his job the way he always did. It wasn't in his nature to think about his own safety.'

'But you wish he hadn't.'

'Yes. No. I can't wish that he wasn't the way he was. I wish that those circumstances hadn't arisen just then. I wish

…'

'That he was here to be a father to his daughter?'

'That's right.'

'Your friend told me that Richard didn't know there was a baby on the way. I can see why you would find that upsetting.'

'Yes, well, if you've finished your tea,' Bernie said, getting up. 'Would you like to take a tour of the estate? See how things have changed since you lived here?'

They walked round the house, looking in each room in turn. In the kitchen Esther commented on how much more modern it looked now.

'I remember there was a big solid-fuel stove over there, which I had to get coke in from the coal-house for each morning before I went to school. It was a nasty dirty job and I was frightened of all the spiders out there. And that door over there used to lead into the washhouse where Mrs Paige and Aunty Eleanor did the washing every Monday.'

'Aunty Eleanor? Is that what you called Richard's mother?'

'That's right: she thought that "Mrs Paige" was too formal, but it wasn't done in those days for children to call adults by their first names.'

'I suppose not. I had lots of Aunties, when I was a child, who were no relation at all really.'

'Looking back now, she was hardly more than a child herself then, although to me she seemed very grown up.'

'She was only nineteen when Richard was born,' Bernie confirmed. 'And did you know that she'd been married less than six months at the time?'

'No, I didn't. Not that I would have known enough about the facts of life to realise that it was significant. I knew that she hadn't been married long and that her husband had been captured in France, but she never spoke about him at all.'

'You said you had to get coke in from the coal-house,' Bernie said, going back to Esther's earlier remark. 'Were you expected to do a lot of jobs around the house?'

'Oh yes! I gather that they'd had a cook and a maid before the war, so Mrs Paige tended to see me as helping to fill that gap. But I was used to that, because back home my mum used to go out to work so I had to help her with the house. Come to think of it, in many ways Mrs Paige treated Aunty Eleanor more like a servant than a member of the family too.'

'Do you think Eleanor resented that?'

'I don't know whether that's the right word. I think she was scared stiff of Mrs Paige. Like I said, looking back, she was rather like a child who had been taken away from her parents and made to live with other people. Not that I thought about it that way at the time.'

As they climbed the stairs, Esther pointed at the three porcelain ducks arranged on the wall as if flying up towards the first floor.

'These are new. Are they from your home?'

'No. I found them in a charity shop and put them up there to annoy Richard. He used to think I was vulgar, and it amused me to play along with that sometimes. I suppose it was rather childish really.'

They reached the first floor and Esther commented on the modern fittings in the bathroom, which had replaced the old enamel bath with eagle talons on its feet and the large porcelain washbasin.

'I was terrified of the geyser that heated the water for the bath,' she confessed. 'I always thought it sounded as if it was going to explode.'

She did not recognise any of the bedrooms, which had been out of bounds to her.

'My room was up in the attic,' she said, pointing to the flight of stairs that led upwards from the landing. 'It had been the maid's room, so the furniture was very basic. I had a chamber pot under my bed, because I wasn't allowed down the stairs after my bed time until the breakfast gong went.'

They ascended the steep stairs to the attic and Esther led the way to the room where she had slept. It had bare boards on the floor, which was strewn with dusty boxes and old trunks and suitcases. There was an old iron bedstead in the corner, which Esther recognised as the same one that she had slept in all those years before.

'I'm afraid it's just a lumber room now,' Bernie apologised. 'We really don't use the attic except as a dumping ground for things we don't need but don't like to throw away.'

Esther walked over to the window and looked out.

'I used to be able to see right down into the city from here,' she said. 'This house was quite isolated in those days.'

'You sound like my gran,' Bernie commented. '*I can remember when it was all fields round here!* But you're quite right: most of the houses in the road are a good deal more recent than this one. Richard said they got lots of offers from people wanting to buy bits of the garden to build on, but he and his father always refused.'

They returned to the ground floor and went out into the garden.

'It's rather neglected, I'm afraid,' Bernie apologised as they walked down the path, past the overgrown borders. 'I'd never had more than a small yard until I came here, so I've been having to learn gardening from first principles.'

'The Paiges had a gardener when I was here: an old chap – or at least he seemed very old to me – came in twice a week. He did all the heavy stuff and took care of the vegetables. Mrs Paige used to prune the roses and plant out the bedding plants and that sort of thing. She used to get me and Aunty Eleanor to weed them for her.'

They walked on down a path that led alongside an old wall with fruit trees trained against it.

'Is that the pond?' Esther asked, pointed across the lawn to where an outcrop of rock and a clump of pampas grass could be seen behind a fence of palings, painted in bright colours.

'Yes. I put up the fence to keep Lucy out. She's only allowed in under strict supervision. Come and have a look.'

'It was different in those days,' Esther observed. 'We didn't have all this "health and safety". Children were expected to do as they were told. Of course, it didn't work. I well remember the day Richard fell in the pond. What a to-do that caused!'

'Tell me about it.'

'It was a washing day, so we were all busy: that's me, Aunty Eleanor and Mrs. Paige. Richard must have been about the same age as your little girl is now, and he was running around getting into everything. The back door was open because we were carrying out washing to hang up and we were going back and forth from the washhouse to the line. We didn't notice that he'd wandered off. Then all of a sudden, we heard the gardener shouting and we saw him running towards the pond. For an old man he ran pretty fast. And the next thing I knew there he was, standing among the water lilies holding Richard up by his legs to get the water out of him.

'Eleanor was distraught and Mrs Paige was beside herself with anger. I found it terrifying. I think children always do get frightened when adults get angry with one another. Mrs Paige told Eleanor that she wasn't fit to be the mother of her grandchild; that she was ungrateful to them for taking her into their home; that they didn't ask much of her but at least surely she could take proper care of the child, and so on and so on. I tried to run away and hide, but Mrs Paige called me back to help take Richard upstairs and give him a hot bath.'

'It must have been tremendously frightening for Richard too,' Bernie said. 'Hearing all that would have been much worse than the trauma of falling in the pond.'

She undid the padlock, which fastened the gate leading into the area around the pond. Then, taking Lucy's hand firmly in her own, she led the way inside. Esther gazed round and smiled at the scene. Around the edge of the pond were arranged a large family of pottery frogs, each about nine inches tall. They were painted bright green and wore a variety of gaily-coloured clothes. Three of them were seated at the very edge of the pond holding fishing lines that dangled in the water.

'Are these more of your handiwork?'

'That's right. More refugees from the charity shop. Not exactly tasteful, but Lucy likes them. I'm wondering about getting some gnomes for the front garden: what d'you think?'

'I think Mrs Paige would turn in her grave, but it's your house now, not hers.'

'I get the impression you didn't like her very much.'

'I don't know,' Esther sighed. 'Things were different in those days. I was in awe of her – maybe frightened of her – but children were expected to see adults that way then. I don't think I considered the possibility of *liking* her.'

They walked back to the house and sat down in the living room. Esther pointed at the piano, which stood against one wall.

'That was Mrs Paige's piano. And Sidney played it too, when he came home on leave.'

'Sidney?'

'One of the other Paige boys: Richard's uncle. I think he was Mrs Paige's favourite. He was killed in the war. He was the oldest. Then there was Charles: he was killed too. Edward – that's Richard's father – was the youngest and the only one who survived the war. I liked Charles – he treated me like a little sister and played with me – but he was killed quite early in the war, so I only saw him the once.'

'So most of the time you were there,' Bernie said thoughtfully, 'the family was living with one son dead, one in a POW camp and one off fighting. I suppose it's not that surprising if Eleanor's mother-in-law wasn't desperately sympathetic.'

They sat down and Esther took out a small photograph album from her bag.

'I brought these for you,' she said, handing it to Bernie. 'My grandchildren have been studying the Second World War at school and they came to me asking for stories about what it was like to be an evacuee. I sorted out some stuff for them to take to school: my old identity card, some photos, a ration book – I discovered I'd even kept the label that was tied on to my coat when I was put on the train so I wouldn't get lost! My mother had a Box Brownie camera, which she used to bring with her when she came to visit me. These pictures all have Richard in them as well.'

Bernie opened the album and slowly turned the pages. Esther gave a commentary.

'That's Richard in his pram. I loved pushing him around: it was like having a real, live doll. That's in the garden when he was just starting to walk. This is the time we went up Shotover Hill. That's the puppy that Richard's great uncle gave him. It was a dear little thing, but it got out of the garden and was run over by the coal lorry.'

Bernie looked down at the picture of a small liver-and-white springer spaniel. It sat looking towards the camera with its tongue hanging out.

'How old was Richard then?'

'He must have been four. It was the summer just before I went home. They buried the puppy in the garden and I remember putting flowers on the grave the day my parents came to take me back to London. Richard really loved that puppy. Mind you, it caused no end of trouble. Mrs Paige was dead against having it from the start, but when Eleanor's uncle gave it to Richard, there wasn't much she could do about it. He was a gamekeeper, I think, over Witney way. He bred gun dogs. Eleanor took Richard and me over there for a visit and we brought that little fellow back with us. I think Mrs Paige gave Eleanor quite a hard time over it after we children were in bed.'

'Richard never seemed to like the idea of pets when I knew him.'

'Probably didn't trust himself to take care of them. He

was most tremendously upset about the business: you see he thought it was his fault.'

'Why's that?'

'He'd been given strict instructions never to let it out the front. He was playing with it in the back garden, but what nobody realised was that it was small enough to squeeze under the gate into the front. For some reason it ran away from him and got under the gate and ran out into the road. I remember Richard crying and Eleanor trying to comfort him and Mrs Paige standing there looking grim. The coal man carried the body round into the back garden and I think it was my idea to have a sort of funeral for it.'

Bernie closed the album and offered it back to Esther.

'Thank you for showing me these. Would you let me take photocopies for Lucy's book?'

'No, no. I brought them for you to keep.'

'Don't you want them for your grandchildren?'

'I've got plenty of others. I'd like you to have the ones of Richard. To my family he'd only be some stranger boy that I happened to be billeted with.'

'OK, thanks. Thank you very much. That fills the gap I had in Richard's early life. And thank you so much for coming and talking about what it was like living here. I think I can start to understand why Eleanor wanted to get away.'

'I can't,' Esther said bluntly. 'I could never, ever have gone off and left my boys behind, however dreadfully I was being treated by my in-laws. Think about it: would *you* ever consider leaving your little one?'

Bernie looked down at Lucy, building with her Lego bricks on the floor, and shook her head.

'No. I see what you mean,' she said, 'but Eleanor *said* that she had to leave Richard behind because otherwise his family would have come after her and taken him back anyway. She said she had to choose between Richard and freedom.'

'Well, I know which I'd have chosen.' Esther was still unconvinced.

'Maybe her husband was abusive,' Bernie suggested.

'All the more reason for not leaving her little boy,' Esther retorted uncompromisingly. 'You'd think she would have wanted to keep him safe.'

'*Did* she seem a caring mother – when you knew her?'

Esther considered for a moment.

'Yes. She seemed very fond of Richard – and he worshipped her. Mrs Paige senior was very strict and formal, very "children must be seen and not heard". Aunty Eleanor used to play with us and give us treats.'

'So, I wonder what made her change,' Bernie mused.

'There'll be a man at the bottom of it, you mark my words.'

'Perhaps you're right. Perhaps it's not so much what she was running away from as where she was running to. Was there any sign of her seeing anyone when you were there?'

'No,' Esther shook her head. 'They kept her on far too short a rein for that. As far as I could tell she hardly left the house.'

Soon it was time for Esther to set off on the journey home. As Bernie drove back with Lucy, after dropping her off at the station, she pondered on what she had learnt about Eleanor's relationship with her husband's family.

Was antipathy towards her mother-in-law what had driven Eleanor to leave? It certainly sounded as if life had not been much fun for Eleanor, living with such a domineering woman in charge. And Mrs Paige senior did appear to have been very much in charge: her husband – Richard's grandfather – had hardly been mentioned. But perhaps that was because Esther was giving a child's eye view of the household. Perhaps Mr Paige simply left all the domestic arrangements to his wife. Or was it her own husband that had driven Eleanor away? When he returned from the war, was he a different person from the man she had married?

A few weeks later, a large envelope arrived through the

post. It was from Esther. Bernie read the covering letter, which accompanied several handwritten A4 sheets:

'After seeing your collection of memories about Richard, I decided to write something for you to put in Lucy's book. I thought that she might enjoy reading this when she's a little older. Sam, my youngest, drew the pictures.'

Bernie looked at the manuscript and saw that Esther had written a light-hearted account of the pond incident. It was illustrated with cartoon drawings: a small boy toppling head first into the water, an ancient man with a beard holding him upside down with water gushing from every aperture, a red-faced matron who appeared on the verge of apoplexy with a speech bubble filled with stars and exclamation marks emanating from her mouth, a small dark-haired girl hiding in the bulrushes, …

She smiled as she added the pages to the red ring binder. People really were most incredibly kind.

15 BIRTHDAY GIRL

Lucy's third birthday dawned bright and sunny. As befits a healthy three-year-old, Lucy was up and on the go at first light and by five-thirty a.m. was sitting naked on Bernie's bed struggling to put on her tee-shirt. By six, they were both up and dressed and contemplating breakfast. Shortly before eight, they were in the living room experimenting with a plastic construction kit, which was one of Lucy's presents from her mother.

To their surprise, there was a ring at the doorbell. Lucy ran across to the window and peered under the net curtain.

'It's a man,' she reported.

'The postman?'

'No. He's got a grey jacket on.'

'Well, only one way to find out,' Bernie said as she got up. 'I wonder who it can be at this time in the morning.'

She opened the door and there on the step stood Jonah Porter, looking immaculate as usual in a light grey suit with a blue shirt and navy tie.

'I hope it's not too early for you,' he apologised, 'but I have to rush off.'

'No, of course not,' Bernie reassured him. 'You know what it's like with kids: it's the middle of the morning as far

205

as we're concerned. It's good to see you,' she added, smiling. 'I haven't thanked you properly for finding Esther Kaplin for me.'

'On the contrary, you wrote a positively effusive letter of thanks. I was worried that my wife might think that there must be more to our relationship than I was telling her! But enough of us, it was Lucy I came to see. I couldn't let her birthday pass without calling in to see how she getting on.'

'Well, as you can see, she's doing very nicely,' looking down at her daughter who was standing behind her holding a plastic spanner and staring pointedly at the gift-wrapped parcel in Jonah's hands.

He crouched down and addressed her solemnly.

'Good morning Miss Paige,' he said seriously. 'Last time I had the pleasure of visiting you I observed the extensive gardens adjoining your residence and I thought that your mother must need some help with maintaining in them; so I hope you will find these useful.'

He held out the parcel and Lucy immediately dropped the spanner and took hold of it in both hands.

'Come in,' Bernie urged. 'Don't hang about on the doorstep.'

They walked together into the living room where Lucy rapidly tore off the wrapping paper to reveal a trowel, a small fork and several packets of seeds.

'I was hoping to be able to help you sow them,' Jonah told Lucy, sitting down on the floor and picking up the seed packets which had slipped through her fingers, 'but I'm afraid I do have to get off in a few minutes.'

'Why not come again another time?' Bernie suggested. 'We'll always be pleased to see you.'

Jonah ignored her invitation and continued to show the packets to Lucy one by one, talking to her about what each contained and what growing conditions were needed. Lucy settled happily on his crossed legs listening intently and looking at the pictures of flowers and vegetables.

'Do you have time for a brew?' Bernie asked, not

knowing whether to be pleased or annoyed at the way that she appeared to have become superfluous.

'No thanks. I really can't stop,' Jonah replied without looking up. Then he seemed to remember something and relented. 'Well, just a very quick one, if you'll show me the latest on the biography of Inspector Paige.'

When Bernie returned a few minutes later with mugs of tea for each of them, Jonah sat down on the settee with Lucy next to him. Bernie reached down the red folder from the high shelf where it was kept out of the way of small sticky fingers.

'I'm afraid you've been toppled from your position, as number one for artistic merit, by Esther Kaplin and her Samuel,' she joked, showing Jonah the story of Richard and the garden pond.

'Indeed,' he agreed, 'I shall have to find a way of upping my game! Now tell me, did Mrs Kaplin throw any light on the mysterious disappearance of Eleanor Paige?'

'Not really. Clearly, Eleanor didn't get on with her mother-in-law, who seems to have ruled the roost in a rather domineering fashion. That probably explains the campaign to expunge Eleanor from the family record after she left, but it doesn't really make sense of her going off and leaving her son behind. Esther seemed to think she was genuinely fond of Richard.'

'Has it occurred to you to consider not so much what she was running away from as what, or who, she was running *to*?' Jonah asked. 'What about that group of women you were talking about last time? Did you make any headway with tracking them down?'

'No – nor Alexander Fokin, either. I had great hopes that he might have been Eleanor's lover, but apart from getting a definite date for when he left Oxford I've made no progress on that front at all.'

'Tell you what,' Jonah said, draining his mug and getting up to go. 'If you give me the list of names, I'll see what I can do about tracing them.'

'OK.' Bernie had been about to protest at taking up yet more of Jonah's time, but realised that argument would be futile. 'I've been keeping a record of everything I've found out on the computer. I'll print you a copy of everything I know about them. She went upstairs to her study, returning a few minutes later with a page of printout.

She found Jonah in the hall with Lucy in his arms giving him a goodbye hug. He took the paper, thrust it into his jacket pocket and was gone.

16 VIOLENT DEATH

A few weeks later, an event occurred that drove all thoughts of Eleanor Paige's disappearance from Bernie's mind. She had agreed to drive Angela Johns over to Abingdon on a shopping expedition. She was late, having been delayed by the arrival of the postman with a recorded delivery parcel. She glanced at her watch as they drew up outside the terraced house in East Oxford: twenty to ten. She turned in her seat to address Lucy, who was sitting in the back.

'You stay here. I won't be long.'

She got out and locked the car. Then she hurried up the short path to the door and rang the bell, expecting her friend to appear immediately. There was no answer. She stood listening intently, waiting to hear Angela's footsteps in the hall. She heard a loud crash and male voices shouting. What was going on?

Bernie reached into her trouser pocket and took out a large bunch of keys. She selected one and inserted it into the lock on the front door. As she entered, she heard more shouting. It seemed to be coming from behind the closed kitchen door. Then a door slammed and the voices became fainter and then stopped. She hurried down the hall and opened the kitchen door.

The scene that greeted her was horrific.

The first thing she saw was a word scrawled in red on the wall opposite: 'SCUM'. That wall was bare, because the wall cupboards that used to hang there had been wrenched off and lay on the floor, their glass fronts shattered and the contents scattered. Bernie stepped into the room and found herself walking on broken china where crockery had smashed on the tiled floor. She looked down and gasped in horror as she saw Angie lying there motionless. Her pretty, floral print dress was stained red with what Bernie realised must be blood. It looked as if she must have been stabbed several times.

Bernie kneeled down by her friend's head and felt beneath her collar for a pulse in her neck. It felt warm and wet and slightly sticky. Looking down, she realised that the carotid artery had been severed. Surely that must mean that there was no hope? Or did it? Should she do something to stop further loss of blood? But there were so many wounds: how could one person staunch the flow from them all?

Bernie felt nauseated and light-headed, but she knew that she had to act fast. She got up and went back into the hall to the telephone, wiping her hands on her trousers as she went. She picked up the receiver and dialled 999 to call for an ambulance and the police.

After making the emergency call, Bernie went and sat down on the stairs and fished out her mobile phone from her pocket. She found the number of the Kidlington police headquarters where Peter Johns was based and made another call. The secretary who answered was reluctant to put her through, but she was insistent.

'Bernie!' Chief Superintendent Adrian Fuller greeted her, in a tone that made it quite clear that he did not approve of being interrupted in his work by the widow of an ex-colleague. 'What can I do for you?'

'I've just reported a murder,' Bernie began. 'You must tell Peter Johns right away, before he hears about it.'

'What do you mean? What are you talking about?'

'It's Peter's wife,' Bernie said earnestly. 'Peter's wife, Angie, has been stabbed to death. You mustn't let him find out by accident.'

'No, of course not,' Fuller agreed, sympathetic now that he understood. 'He's in his office now; I'll go and break it to him. What else can you tell me about it?'

'Nothing much: she was just lying there in the kitchen when I called round.'

'OK. Don't worry. I'll go and see him right away. Now, are you alright?'

'Yes. I'll be fine. I'll go and wait in the car for the ambulance to arrive.'

Bernie ended the call and hastened outside to join Lucy, who was waiting impatiently.

'Where's Angie?' she demanded, as Bernie got into the back of the car and sat down next to her.

'Angie won't be coming out today after all,' Bernie replied, struggling to know how to explain the situation to her young daughter. 'There's been an accident. I've rung for an ambulance. It'll be here soon.'

'Can't I go and see her?'

'No. There's nothing we can do to help. We just need to wait for the ambulance to come.'

Within minutes, they heard a siren and an ambulance approached, its blue lights flashing. Bernie got out to meet the crew. They had just disappeared inside the house when a police car drove up and two uniformed officers got out. Bernie turned to greet them and realised that Lucy was now standing at her side, having released herself from her safety seat and got out of the unlocked car. Bernie took her firmly by the hand.

'We had a call from a Dr Fazakerley,' one of the policemen said, 'reporting an incident. Do you know where he is?'

'That's me. I rang 999. That's the house,' Bernie pointed. 'She's in the kitchen. It's at the end of the hall, you can't miss it. I'd show you, only …' She looked down at Lucy, who was watching and listening intently, taking it all in.

'No, no, of course not. Leave it to us. We'll need a statement from you in due course, but for the moment, just leave it all to us.'

He turned to his colleague.

'Constable Mowlam, I'd like you to stay out here with Dr Fazakerley while I go inside and see what's been going on here.'

Bernie stood there, holding Lucy's hand firmly, as more people arrived and got down to the business of dealing with the crime scene. Blue and white tape was put across the gate, which those arriving variously stepped over or crept under. She recognised a pathologist, whom, she knew, was a particular friend of Peter Johns and had worked with him on a number of cases. Some of the other faces looked vaguely familiar and she assumed that she had probably met them through Richard at some point.

Then Bernie got a shock to see Peter approaching, followed closely by a woman in police uniform. They had evidently parked a little way down the road, the space in front of the house already being full. His face was white and had a dazed expression. He did not appear to see her as he brushed past towards the front door. Lucy cried out and pulled away from Bernie, trying to go to him, but Bernie kept hold of her hand and pulled her back.

'Not now, Lucy. We'll talk to Peter later.'

They stood waiting, watching the door for Peter to emerge.

'Detective Chief Inspector Gordon MacBride,' said a voice unexpectedly, breaking into Bernie's thoughts. She looked up to see a burly man in his fifties with a bald patch on the top of his head and bushy grey sideburns. He spoke in a strong Glaswegian accent.

'And this is Detective Inspector Alison Brown,' he added, indicating a tall woman in a pinstriped trouser suit, whom Bernie judged to be a little younger than her superior. 'They tell me that it was you who found Mrs Johns and reported the crime.'

'Yes. That's right,' Bernie shook his hand. 'Bernie Fazakerley.'

'And you're Richard Paige's widow, I gather. Chief Superintendent Fuller told me that you rang him as well as dialling 999.'

'I wanted someone to break the news carefully to Peter. It would have been awful if he'd got to hear about it as just another crime.'

'Yes, indeed. Well you can rest assured we will be giving our full attention to bringing whoever did this to justice. Now, I will need to ask you some questions later, but for the time being I suggest we get one of the constables to drive you home. Is there anyone you could ask to come and sit with you?'

'No. I can't go yet,' Bernie objected. 'I'm waiting for Peter. He'd better come home with us.'

At that moment, Peter came out. He saw Bernie and hurried over to her.

'Bernie! I'm so sorry you had to be the one to find her.' Then he noticed Lucy, who had finally pulled her hand out of her mother's grasp and flung herself at Peter, gripping him round the legs, which was all that she could reach. He gave a gasp of horror.

'It's alright,' Bernie reassured him, realising immediately what was worrying him. 'Lucy didn't see anything. I left her in the car.'

'Thank God for that.'

Peter bent down and picked up Lucy. She immediately buried her face in his shoulder and hugged him tight. She did not understand what was going on, but she realised that the adults around her were all very upset about something.

'Alison,' DCI MacBride's voice seemed to come from far away and Bernie struggled to concentrate on what he was saying, 'I want you to drive Dr Fazakerley's car and take them back to her home. Constable Mowlam will follow in another car and bring you back here afterwards.'

Bernie prised Lucy away from Peter and strapped her into her child seat.

'Do you mind going in the back with Lucy,' she asked him. 'I think it will make for a more peaceful journey.'

Peter said nothing but got in the back of the car and strapped himself in next to Lucy. She put out her hand and stroked his face. Bernie got in the front and Alison Brown drove them away from the house, which Peter had shared with Angie all their married life and which now had become the scene of a horrible and incomprehensible crime.

'Is Angie dead?' Lucy asked suddenly.

'Yes, Lucy, she is,' Bernie answered impassively, breaking the silence that followed the unexpected question.

'Like my dad?' Lucy persisted, wanting to be sure.

'Yes Lucy. Like your dad.'

'How did she get dead?'

Bernie took a deep breath and thought hard.

'Some bad people killed her,' she said at last.

'Why?'

'I don't know. It doesn't make sense, but Inspector MacBride and his team are going to try to find out.'

'How?'

'Inspector Brown, please could you give my daughter a brief résumé of the investigation methods you intend to employ, to satisfy her insatiable curiosity?'

'Er well, we'll be asking a lot of questions, to find out whether anyone saw anything suspicious. And taking photographs and samples in case the people who did it left any clues behind which would help us to know who they were: fingerprints, for instance.'

They turned into the drive and pulled up outside Bernie's front door. They all got out. Bernie pressed her keys into Peter's hand.

'Take Lucy inside, will you? While I get our things out of the boot.'

Obediently Peter took Lucy by the hand and led her indoors. Alison Brown stood by the car as Bernie unpacked a pushchair and various bags.

'I gather you don't believe in shielding children from the grim realities of life,' she said.

'That's right. The most important thing is that Lucy knows she can trust me always to tell her the truth. If we lose that, she'll never be able to feel secure again.'

'You don't think violent death might be a bit much for her to cope with at her age?'

'Maybe, but the alternative is knowing that people are lying to her. In my experience, the reality is never as bad as the things you imagine when you know you're not being told the truth.'

A police car drew up and Alison Brown got in. Bernie picked up her bags and carried them indoors. She found Peter and Lucy in the kitchen. The kettle was on and Lucy was carefully spooning tea into the pot.

'Lucy insisted that we made a brew,' Peter explained.

'Well done Lucy! That is absolutely the right thing to do in the circumstances. The cup which cheers but does not inebriate, as my mam used to say.'

The hours passed very slowly that morning. All three found it difficult to settle to doing anything. By lunchtime, the living room floor was strewn with abandoned toys, which Lucy had got out and then discarded. Two half-finished jigsaw puzzles covered the surface of the coffee table. The plastic train set, still a favourite with Lucy and her adult friends alike, wound its way round the furniture, but the train lay on its side in a manner suggestive of a major railway accident.

Bernie heated pizzas for lunch, which both Peter and Lucy generally enjoyed, but somehow none of them felt hungry. It was a relief when the doorbell rang, signifying that Gordon MacBride had arrived, accompanied by Alison Brown.

They came inside and followed Bernie into the living room.

'Do you think your daughter would be willing to let

Inspector Brown take her out in the garden for a while?' he asked Bernie. 'Some of the things I need to ask you are a bit, well …'

'Lucy,' Bernie called, 'this is Detective Inspector Alison Brown. She would like to see the garden. Take her out and show her round it please.'

For a moment, Lucy looked defiant. She looked from Bernie to Peter and back again, then seeing the serious expressions on their faces she decided to co-operate. She nodded and led the way out through the open French windows. Bernie and Peter sat down on the settee and MacBride took an easy chair opposite them.

'Thank you,' he said, taking out his notebook and a pen. 'Now, first: please could you tell me in your own words exactly what happened this morning, starting from when you set out from here?'

'We started out shortly after nine, I think,' Bernie said confidently. She had been going over the events in her mind all morning and was prepared for questions. 'We'd intended to pick Angie up at nine, but Lucy spilled her cereal down her front and we had to change her clothes and then the postman came with a parcel that needed signing for. I put Lucy in the back and strapped her in. Then I put the pushchair in the boot. We went through Headington Quarry and down Divinity Road. There was still a lot of school traffic about, so it took quite a while to get through. I looked at my watch when we got to Angie's because I knew we were late. It was twenty to ten. I was expecting her to be ready to go and watching out of the window for us. I left Lucy locked in the car, because I only expected to be a moment or two. I rang the bell, but nobody came. Then I heard noises from inside, so I got out my key and let myself in.'

'You have a key to the Johns' house?'

'Yes. And Angie has one to this house. Peter and Angie have been very good at helping with Lucy, since Richard died.' Bernie could see that the inspector was surprised and curious about her relationship with the Johns family, but he did not comment on it further.

'I see,' he said, 'and you say you heard noises. What sort of noises?'

'A loud crash and shouting and then a door banging.'

'Was it Mrs Johns shouting?'

'No, definitely not. It sounded like men's voices to me, but it was quite muffled because the door was shut,'

'I see. Go on. What happened next?'

'I went in and went along the hall to the kitchen door, because the sounds came from there. I opened it and saw … well you know what I saw.'

'Was there anyone there? Did you see the people whose voices you heard?

'No. I assume they went out of the back door and that was the door I heard slamming.

'You didn't go and look out of the door to see?'

'No. I was more concerned with Angie.'

'Did you touch anything?'

'Only Angie. I went to see if there was anything I could do for her. I put my hand on her neck.' Bernie looked down at the smears of blood still evident on her trousers. 'When I saw how much blood there was I realised that I couldn't help her, so I went back in to the hall and rang 999.'

'Using the hall phone?'

'Yes.'

'And then you rang Chief Superintendent Fuller to tell him personally?'

'Yes. I thought he would be the best person to tell Peter. I thought it ought to be done face to face, not over the phone.'

'Did you go back into the kitchen at all?'

'No. I came straight out after that, because Lucy was in the car and I didn't want to leave her on her own any longer.'

'So, when the police arrived the kitchen was exactly as you found it?'

'Unless the ambulance crew moved anything. They got there first.'

'Thank you Dr Fazakerley. Now I'd like you to let me take away the clothes that you were wearing when you went into the house this morning, so we can run tests on them. You never know, you may have picked up something on them when you knelt down to see to Mrs Johns.'

'Of course. I ought to have thought of that. I'll change into something else before you go, and let you have them.'

'Thank you. Now, Dr Fazakerley, can you describe to me what your relationship was with Mrs Johns? Would you say you were close?'

'She was my best friend. We'd known each other since shortly after I graduated, which was,' Bernie thought for a moment, 'twenty-four years ago. And she was my chief mentor for motherhood and child-rearing.'

'So, if she'd been worried about anything, you would expect to know?'

'Yes.'

'And *was* there anything worrying her, do you think?'

'No.'

'She hadn't mentioned to you that anyone had been threatening her at all?'

'No.'

'But you think she would have told you if she *had* received any threats?'

'Yes, I'm sure she would have told me.'

MacBride turned to Peter. 'And now Peter, tell me about your morning. Did your wife seem her usual self? Not anxious about anything?'

'No. she seemed just the same as always.'

'Did she say anything about what she was planning to do today?'

'No.' Peter sounded puzzled. 'She said she had a bit of shopping to do, that's all. She never mentioned going to Abingdon. What did she want in Abingdon?'

He turned and looked at Bernie questioningly.

'I can explain,' Bernie sighed. She spoke to MacBride, avoiding meeting Peter's eye. 'In a few weeks' time, Peter and Angie would have celebrated their silver wedding anniversary. Angie wanted to get him something special for it. She asked me to take her to Abingdon to the jewellers where they got their engagement and wedding rings. It was going to be a surprise. That's why she didn't tell Peter.'

She put out her hand and took hold of Peter's. He responded by squeezing hers gently. MacBride watched, but did not comment. Then he resumed his questioning.

'And you left at what time?'

'Twenty past eight, or thereabouts: same as usual.'

'I see. Now, can you think of anyone who might bear your wife a grudge?'

'No. No one.'

'She was very popular,' Bernie put in emphatically. 'Everyone liked Angie.'

'So there hadn't been any disputes with the neighbours, for example?' MacBride persisted.

Peter shook his head.

'Now, you have two children, is that right? How old are they?'

'Hannah's twenty-two: she's nursing in Leeds; and Edward's in his second year at Manchester University.' Peter broke off suddenly. 'I hadn't thought. I suppose I'd better tell them what's happened.'

'We could contact the local police and get them to do it.'

'Or hospitals and universities both have chaplains,' Bernie suggested.

'I think they ought to hear it from me,' Peter argued.

'Yes, but it might be better if you could make sure they have someone with them when they get your call,' Bernie persisted. 'Anyway Eddie's in an exam this afternoon, so you can't contact him until that's over.'

'Is he?' Peter asked, 'How do you know that? I don't remember him telling us.'

'He emailed me earlier in the week, asking for help with his revision.'

Seeing MacBride looking at them interrogatively, Bernie

explained.

'I have a long history of helping Eddie with his homework. He's reading Computer Science and there's a lot of overlap with the sort of maths that I do.'

'I see. Now, perhaps it will be best if we leave off contacting the children until I've finished here.'

Peter looked dissatisfied but waved at MacBride to continue with his questions.

'What about work? Did your wife have a job?'

'She's a nurse at the John Radcliffe.'

'Has she had any trouble there at all? No disgruntled patients making complaints? No bullying or harassment?'

'No. Nothing. She loved her work.'

'Now this may be difficult for you. But I have to ask: has there been any racial abuse directed towards your family at all?'

'No. At least, only the sort of silly name-calling that everyone gets. I mean: nothing worse than I used to get for being ginger.'

'It's a very ethnically mixed population round there,' Bernie put in. 'Everyone gets on very well.'

'So you really can't think of any reason why someone would attack your wife with a knife and then use her blood to write "SCUM" on the wall above her?'

'No. No I can't!' Peter shouted angrily, holding tighter to Bernie's hand. Then he saw MacBride looking at them sitting together on the settee and let go abruptly and clasped his hands together in his lap.

'No,' he repeated more calmly. 'I have no idea why anyone would want to do that.'

'OK. We'll leave it there for now, but if either of you think of anything else that could help, let me know right away. And we may need to speak to you again, so can you tell me where you will be? It'll be a few days before we've finished with your house.'

'Peter's staying here,' Bernie said firmly. 'That's what Angie would have wanted,' she added, looking at Peter to quell any possible objections from him. 'You can have the room I stayed in when my house was burnt out.'

'Right. I think that's all then,' MacBride closed his notebook. 'Now, we'll need your fingerprints for comparison purposes.'

'If you're taking fingerprints from the house,' Bernie put in, 'you'll need Lucy's as well.'

'I thought you said she stayed outside the whole time?'

'*Today* she did, but she's round there two or three times a week. Unless Angie did the most thorough spring-clean imaginable, Lucy's prints will be all over every surface below about three feet from the ground. Go on! She'd love to have her fingerprints taken: it'll make her think she's doing something to help.'

'Very well,' MacBride conceded. 'I suppose we'd better include her too.'

He went to the French windows and called Alison and Lucy back in.

'Do you think we're under suspicion?' Bernie asked Peter as they watched MacBride drive away later that afternoon, complete with Bernie's clothes and a set of fingerprints from each of them. 'I get this feeling that he's got you down as a potential adulterer and me as the Other Woman.'

'No, that's just MacBride's way,' Peter answered rather absently. 'He likes to make all his witnesses feel guilty, in the hope that they'll let out more than they intended in order to allay his suspicions. Personally, I think it's just as likely to make them clam up.'

The remainder of the afternoon was taken up with telephone calls. Peter rang Angie's family in Jamaica and spoke to one of her sisters, who undertook to pass the word on to her parents and other siblings. Then he contacted the ward where Hannah worked and broke the news, leaving her in the capable hands of the ward clerk. Bernie telephoned the Methodist chaplain at the university and he met Eddie when he came out of his examination with a message to ring his father urgently. Peter informed Angela's manager that she would not be coming into work again, which reminded Bernie that Angela also had other commitments.

'I'll have to let the church know about Angie: she's on the rota to help with the Sunday School this week,' she told Peter. 'In any case, a lot of the congregation live sufficiently locally that they'll have seen all the activity this morning and know that something's up. I thought I'd ring Denise, the minister, and she can spread the word. She's bound to want to come and see you. It's her job to give pastoral care to the bereaved, although I suspect this may be rather out of her league. Is that OK with you, or would you like me to find some excuse to put her off?'

'No, no, that's fine: might as well get it over with. I'll have to talk to her about the funeral eventually anyway.'

Peter's mobile phone rang.

'Hello Eddie. How did the exam go? ... No, that wasn't why I wanted you to ring. I've got some rather dreadful news. Where are you? ... Good. It's your mum: she's dead. ... A knife attack ... no, we don't know why yet ... Yes, Bernie told him, but I wanted to tell you myself ... in the kitchen ... Bernie found her this morning ...'

Bernie was on tenterhooks as she listened to Peter's end of the conversation. She was very fond of Eddie and anxious about the effect that his mother's sudden death might have on him. She had seen too many students going to pieces after incidents in their lives far less traumatic than this. Then Peter's tone changed subtly and Bernie guessed that the chaplain had asked to speak to him.

'Thank you for taking care of Eddie ... that's very good of you ... we'll pick him up from the station ... it hasn't really sunk in yet ... thanks again.'

Peter turned to Bernie.

'The chaplain's taking Eddie back to his house for

tonight. He's going to put him on a train to Oxford in the morning. I said we'd pick him up at the station.'

The phone rang again. It was Hannah. She and her boyfriend, Laurence, were going to drive down from Leeds that evening. No, she could not be persuaded to wait until the morning or to consider coming by train. They would be quite all right driving. They just wanted to get down there as soon as they could.

'I'll make up beds for them,' Bernie said when Peter relayed this information. 'Or should that be "a bed"?'

'I'm not sure. We haven't gone into that with her. I think they've still got their own separate places in Leeds, but …'

'I'll put them up in the loft bedrooms. Then they can sleep separately or in the same one and we'll be none the wiser. Come along Lucy, you can help me make the beds.'

The following day was Saturday. Eddie arrived, looking shell-shocked, but calm. He had one more exam before his term ended the following week. Bernie persuaded Peter that he should be allowed to go back and take it.

'He's done all the preparation,' she argued. 'He won't be in any better state to take it in the resits in August, and if he doesn't pass then, he may have to repeat the year. Assuming that the exams he's already done have gone OK, which we think they have, the mitigating circumstances committee are likely to give him a pass if he gets somewhere close in this one.'

Hannah initially planned to stay on to support her father, 'for as long as it takes,' but Peter persuaded her that she would do better going home after the weekend so as to be able to take time off to attend the funeral and the inquest.

Thus it was, that on Monday afternoon Bernie, Peter and Lucy found themselves once more alone together and wondering what to do to fill the time. The doorbell rang and Lucy ran to look out of the window to see who it was. Bernie opened the door to admit MacBride, this time accompanied by a young Asian officer whom he introduced as Detective Sergeant Arshad Khan. Khan was, apparently, a specialist in relations with minority communities. They asked to speak to Peter. Bernie led them into the living room. A look from MacBride prompted her to take Lucy off to the kitchen, leaving the three police officers alone.

MacBride had little progress to report. They had collected a large amount of forensic evidence, but the fingerprints and DNA samples did not match any on the police database. None of the neighbours remembered seeing anyone arriving at or leaving the house that morning. Footprints in the back garden and marks on the wall separating it from the lane that ran down the backs of the houses, suggested that two or three people had climbed over the wall and entered by the back door. Presumably, they had left the same way when Bernie interrupted their activities. The police were continuing to conduct enquiries in the hope that someone might have seen them in the lane either before or after the attack. That was as much as he was able to divulge to Peter at this stage.

He showed Peter some pictures of white youths with a history of racial violence. Had Peter seen any of these hanging around the neighbourhood in the last few weeks? No? Well then, what about these two? Was he aware that they lived only a few streets away from him? And this one? He had been in the same class at school as Peter's son Edward and had been disciplined for his behaviour towards him. Did Peter know about that?

Khan took over. He began with general questions about relations between the different ethnic groups in the Cowley Road area of Oxford. Then gradually the questions became more personal. Most of their immediate neighbours were white: did Peter think that they resented having a mixed race family in their midst? Did Angela associate much with her fellow West Indians? Or did Peter encourage her to see herself as part of the white community? Had he ever considered that Angela might feel isolated, as a black woman in a white society? What about the children? Did they see themselves as black or white? Why did Peter think his son had been afraid to tell him about being racially abused by a white boy in his class? What had motivated Peter to choose to marry a black woman? Did he ever regret having done so?

Peter sat in silence, unable to take it all in. His bewilderment changed gradually to incredulity and finally to anger.

'Stop!' he roared at last, just as Lucy crept in to the room carrying a plate of home-made biscuits. At the sound of his angry voice, she dropped the plate and burst into tears. Peter leapt to his feet, picked her up in his arms and held her to him. Then he returned to his seat with Lucy on his lap. She buried her head in his chest and continued to cry quietly. Peter addressed Khan quietly with exaggerated calm.

'I did *not* choose to marry a black woman: I chose to marry Angela. It made no difference to me whether she was black, white, brown or purple with green spots. That was the best thing I ever did in my life and you have no right to suggest that I ever, even for a moment, thought otherwise.'

'I think perhaps it's time for you to go,' Bernie said from the doorway where she had been listening.

MacBride nodded and stood up to go. Khan followed his lead, continuing to watch Peter closely as he carried on comforting his golden haired goddaughter. They picked their way past the scattered biscuits and out into the hall.

'That was uncalled for,' Bernie said in a low voice, speaking both earnestly and angrily as she let them out of the front door. 'If you had ever seen Peter and Angie together you'd know that they were the most united couple you could imagine. Colour simply did not come into it. It really didn't.'

The police investigation seemed to make painfully little progress. Days passed with no news for Peter to report to Hannah during her daily telephone calls. The day after Eddie returned for the summer holidays, Peter was pacing uneasily around the room like a caged lion, when MacBride arrived. This time he was alone. Peter and Eddie looked to him eagerly, hoping that there had been a breakthrough in the investigation, but MacBride shook his head.

'I've only come to let you know that you're free to go back into your house now,' he said, handing the keys back to Peter. 'I'm sorry it's taken so long.'

Peter hesitated as he put the key in the door, preparing to enter his home for the first time since he had been taken there to see his wife's body amongst the debris of the shattered kitchen. Then he turned the key and pushed open the door. The hall looked clean and tidy. At least the SOCOs had cleaned up after themselves. He walked down the hall to the kitchen door, followed by Eddie, with Bernie and Lucy, holding hands, bringing up the rear.

When he opened the kitchen door, Peter stared round in amazement. The broken furniture and china was all gone. New wall units hung on the wall opposite the door where the message in blood has been scrawled. Behind the glass doors, Peter could see new crockery and glassware to replace those that had been smashed. Looking down he saw that the blood-stained vinyl floor tiles had not merely been cleaned but replaced. The walls and door were newly painted. A vase of flowers stood on the working surface. Peter strode across the room and picked up an envelope, which lay beside the vase. He turned to look at Bernie.

'This is your doing, isn't it?' he said accusingly, 'although I can't think how.'

'It was easy. I persuaded MacBride to tell Denise when he was finished with the house and she organised a working party to clean up the place before he let on to you.'

'But this must have cost a fortune,' Peter protested, gesturing towards the new wall cupboards. 'All these new things.'

'Not when you divide it between a couple of dozen people. Anyway, I told them to keep the receipts, so you'll

probably be able claim on the insurance and pay them back.'
Bernie omitted to mention the large cheque, which she had
handed over to the minister to cover the cost of the work,
so that none of the volunteers would be out of pocket.

Peter opened the envelope and took out a card. It was
signed by about thirty members of the congregation at
Angela's church. He fought back the tears as he read the
names and the words of sympathy. Then he handed the card
to Eddie without speaking.

'People always want to help,' Bernie said. 'It's just usually
they don't know what to do.'

Peter noticed a cake tin lying on the working surface. He
opened it to reveal a homemade Victoria sponge.

'That'll be Betty's,' Bernie informed him. 'That's her
pièce de résistance. Put the kettle on and let's make a brew.'

Peter did as he was told, and Eddie opened the fridge to
see if there was any milk. He whistled with surprise when he
saw what was inside. It was crammed with homemade
goodies: samosas, a quiche, onion bhajis, Jamaican patties,
and a trifle. It seemed that everyone had wanted to
contribute something to welcome Peter back to this house,
which no longer felt like home.

The days passed drearily on. The inquest was opened
and adjourned. Angela's body was released for burial and
Peter started to make plans for the funeral. He spent many
hours, and pounds, in telephone calls with Angela's siblings
discussing the arrangements for members of her family to
be present. Her parents considered themselves too elderly
to make the journey to England, so one of Angela's brothers
would represent them. Joseph was keen to take on that role,
but his cerebral palsy posed difficulties. Would Peter be able
to cope, if his sister Phoebe and her two boys, Paul and Joel,
came with him to help?

Peter, of course, assured them that they must not worry
about anything. He would see that everything was alright.
He had a friend with a big house who had offered to

accommodate any of his family who needed to stay in Oxford. She was a widow who would be glad of the company. Probably Angie had talked about her in her many letters home. Yes, that was right: the professor with the little girl. At least, she wasn't technically a professor, but it amounted to the same thing. She would be delighted to put up Joseph, Phoebe and the boys for a few nights.

Bernie was indeed pleased to entertain members of Angie's extended family in her home. Knowing that Joseph was in a wheelchair, she had arranged for him to sleep in the dining room downstairs, but the irrepressible Paul and Joel insisted that they could carry him upstairs with ease: a feat which they demonstrated within a few minutes of their arrival. They soon had the furniture in one of the spare bedrooms rearranged to suit their uncle's needs and were arguing over which of them would sleep in his room in case he needed anything in the night. Joseph told them patiently that there was no need for that: if he needed assistance, he was quite capable of calling out for help. In the end, the two young men were banished to the loft bedrooms, with Joseph and his sister each occupying a room on the first floor with Lucy and Bernie.

Sitting in church two days later, Bernie reflected on how different this was from Richard's funeral. Once again the church was full, but this time there were only a few police uniforms: Chief Superintendent Fuller was there, and two or three of Peter's particular friends, but not the solid mass of navy blue which had been such a dominant presence nearly four years earlier. The rest of the congregation looked different too: hardly any were dressed in black; instead there was a cheerful array of bright colours. Bernie looked across the aisle from where she and Lucy sat near the front between Phoebe and Eddie and saw two rows of children from Angela's Sunday School class sitting unusually quiet and sombre, rather over-awed by the occasion. They had been practising a gospel song, which they were to perform as their tribute to their teacher.

Joseph, both as the official representative of Angela's parents and on his own behalf, had insisted on speaking. Peter had been anxious about how people who did not know him would react to seeing his involuntary arm movements and hearing his laboured speech, but he was not to be denied. Paul wheeled him to the front while the congregation sang the hymn that Joseph had chosen to represent his sister's life back home:

This, this is the God we adore,
Our faithful, unchangeable Friend;
Whose love is as great as His power,
And neither knows measure nor end.

Joel positioned a microphone in front of him and adjusted it to the correct height as they began the second verse:

'Tis Jesus, the First and the Last,
Whose Spirit shall guide us safe home.

Then the brothers stepped down, leaving Joseph alone on the low dais, just in time for him to join in singing the last two lines:

We'll praise Him for all that is past,
And trust Him for all that's to come.

There was a clatter of feet and a rustling of papers as everyone sat down again, then silence. Joseph paused for a moment to collect his thoughts and then began.

'That hymn,' he said, making a great effort to pronounce the words as clearly as he was able, 'was one of our favourites when we were children. I remember Angela singing it while she helped our mother with the washing – and there was a lot of washing in our family! And she used to sing it to me sometimes at night when I could not sleep. I am sure that she is still singing it in heaven and that she was singing it here with us just now.'

He went on to speak about when he and Angela had been children: how she had been his favourite sister, always willing to give up activities with her friends to stay at home with him, always there to help when he was frustrated at not being able to make his limbs do what he wanted, patient with him when he could not make himself understood. Then he told about her going away to train as a nurse and how much he had missed having her there constantly at his side. He told how, later, he had cried when he heard that she was leaving for England and how he had wished that he were able to argue with her and persuade her to stay. Then he told about how she had sent back money, which had paid for him to have speech therapy, and how, at long last, he had found his voice and that was how he was able to come and tell his story today.

The assembly listened in rapt silence until he finished speaking. Then, after a moment or two, it exploded into applause. As the clapping died away, Paul and Joel got up and added their own tributes to their aunt. After that, to Bernie's surprise, everyone seemed to want to have their say. People, whom Bernie knew for a fact had always declined so much as to read the lesson in church, got up and gave extempore testimony to Angela's influence on their lives. Even Eddie, normally one of the most reluctant of public speakers, stood up and said a few words in praise of his mother.

Bernie was about to get to her feet to make her own contribution when she looked across at Peter, sitting at the other end of the row of chairs, looking rather bewildered at the spontaneous outpourings. She knew that he would never, never bare his soul in that way; but if he were the only person who had been close to Angie who did *not* pay tribute to her, he might feel that he had somehow let her down. Bernie quashed the natural inclination to speak out and remained in her seat, determined that nobody would be able to point the finger at Peter and suggest that he had been uniquely unwilling to express appreciation for his wife.

She was glad afterwards that she made that decision, when Eddie commented on her uncharacteristic reticence over the buffet in the church Hall, which followed the service.

'It's not like you to keep quiet when everyone else is speaking up,' Eddie said to Bernie through a mouthful of chicken vol-au-vent.

'Whatever I could have said would have been inadequate to express what I owe to your mum,' Bernie said, 'and I'm sure I'm not the only one to feel like that.'

She glanced across the room to where Peter was engaged in making conversation with Fuller, before looking Eddie squarely in the eyes. He held eye contact for a moment then looked down.

'Yes,' he mumbled, 'I see what you mean.'

Once the funeral was over and Angela's family had returned to Jamaica, Peter went back to work, feeling that he needed something to give his life a structure and to get him out of the house, which seemed so empty without Angie there. Bernie and Lucy were, of course, frequent visitors and Hannah came to stay for most weekends when she was not on duty at the hospital. At first, MacBride gave them frequent updates on the investigation, but these became more and more sparse as time went on and there was still no progress to report.

Soon it was time for Eddie to return to Manchester to start his final year at university. Peter drove him up, returning in the evening to a meal that Bernie had prepared for him.

'Peter,' she said afterwards, as he was leaving, 'I always keep the bed made up in the spare room. If ever it gets too difficult in the house on your own, you'll be very welcome to stay. Just come over, any time.'

The following weekend, Peter came to Sunday lunch with Bernie and Lucy. Since the funeral, he had taken to going with them to church. This was largely out of gratitude to the church members who had been so kind to him and because it was there that he felt closest to his wife, for whom Christian faith and the church had been so important. As he remarked to Bernie as she drove them back to Headington after the service, 'I'm not sure that God exists, but I like the effect he has on the people who are sure.'

'I don't think anyone is really sure,' Bernie countered. 'It's just that people have different ways of expressing their doubts.'

'Not even the likes of Joseph?' Peter asked. 'Don't you think he was sincere when he said, "we'll praise Him for all that is past, and trust him for all that's to come"?'

'Oh I'm sure he's sincere. He reminded me a bit of my Mam. She had all sorts of troubles and came through smiling: just like Joseph. But you talked about being *sure*. You can't prove the existence of God beyond reasonable doubt: the decision will always have to be on the balance of probabilities.'

'And you think the balance is in his favour?'

'Most of the time I do.'

'Despite what happened to Richard? … and Angie?'

'It was people who did that to them, not God'

'But God didn't stop it.'

'He couldn't: not without overriding their freewill. It would be a logical impossibility. It's like when you told Eddie he could paint his room any colour he liked and he decided on red walls and a black ceiling. You could have stopped him, but then you would have gone back on your promise to let him choose for himself.'

'But what I was getting at,' Bernie resumed after a short silence, while Peter pondered on what she had said, 'was that you shouldn't worry about being hypocritical going to church, because most of us are being hypocritical, to a greater or lesser extent most of the time. If it makes you feel closer to Angie, then that's as good a reason for going as any.'

'I thought it was all supposed to be about worshipping God?'

'Yes, but it's also about fellowship: fellowship with the Church Militant (which is all those people you were just saying you were so grateful to) and the Church Triumphant, which now includes Angie.'

After lunch, Peter played with Lucy in the garden while Bernie worked on finalising a research grant application, which had to be submitted the next day. So he stayed to tea, and then Lucy asked him to read her bedtime story, which if course he agreed to do. It was not until Lucy was tucked up in bed that they realised that Peter's car was standing outside his house in East Oxford and Bernie could not leave Lucy alone while she took him home. The obvious solution was for him to stay the night.

They passed an early morning jogger as they turned into Peter's road the following morning.

'It's dreadful,' Peter confided to Bernie in a low voice. 'Every time I see a white face in this neighbourhood I can't help thinking: "Does he have Angie's blood on his hands?" I can't walk to the corner shop without seeing suspects everywhere.'

'Maybe you should get away from here for a while,' Bernie suggested. 'You know the offer's always open for you to stay with us.'

17 IN PURSUIT

While no definite arrangement was ever agreed, Peter gradually spent more and more time sleeping in the spare room at Bernie's house and less and less living in the house in East Oxford, which increasingly brought back painful memories. Peter moved back home whenever Hannah or Eddie came for the weekend, but in between visits, he was more often in Headington than Cowley Road.

'I'm surprised the post office managed to work out where to send this one,' Peter observed, as he handed Bernie a letter, which he had picked up in the hall when he went to get the milk in off the step one morning in December. 'Talk about illegible handwriting!'

'It's a Reading postmark,' Bernie observed, studying the envelope before tearing it open. 'I have a feeling I may know who it's from.'

As Bernie had suspected, it was a note from Jonah: just a few typewritten lines, giving the following information.

The philosophy tutor, Alexander Fokin, had taken up a post at King's College London in 1947 and had emigrated to the United States in 1953, where he died in 1981.

Edna Knowles, one of the students in the group photograph, had gone on to become a schoolteacher in

Rochester. She had remained single and had died in 2001, leaving her modest savings to a charity supporting girls' education.

Abigail Fossett had become a journalist. She had been based in London for most of her career, but had travelled extensively, reporting from all over the world, with a particular interest in Africa. She had died of throat cancer in 1979 at the age of fifty-three.

Claudia Browne had gone on to do further study and eventually became a classics don at Cambridge, where she still lived. Like Edna and Abigail, she had remained single.

Alicia Lowton had married Rupert Fortescue immediately after graduating in French and Italian. Rupert, later Sir Rupert, was in the diplomatic service and they had travelled extensively until retiring to Dorset some twenty years ago. She was now a widow living alone.

The note also gave the current addresses of the two survivors: Alicia and Claudia. It concluded with the words 'Good hunting!' There was no signature or covering letter.

'What is it?' Peter asked, seeing Bernie's smile as she read the note.

'It's from Jonah Porter. I was trying to find some people in connection with Richard's mother and wasn't having much luck. He offered to have a go. This is a list of who they were and where they've got to.' She handed the paper to Peter.

'I didn't know you were seeing Jonah,' he commented grumpily. He was irrationally irritated to hear that his ex-colleague was still in contact with Bernie, and also annoyed with himself for feeling that way.

'I don't know what you mean by that,' Bernie said archly. 'I've only *seen* him five times in my life: once at Richard's funeral, once just after Lucy was born and then on each of Lucy's three birthdays.'

'But you evidently correspond,' Peter muttered, forcing himself to remember that it was none of his business. He read the note and handed it back. 'Are you planning to follow these up?'

'Yes: although it looks as if I'll have to be quick to catch them before they all die off. Would you like to help?' Bernie suggested, thinking that it would do Peter good to have something to keep his mind occupied outside of working hours.

'If you like,' Peter said casually. He was delighted to have the opportunity to demonstrate that he was just as capable as Jonah Porter, but did not want to appear too eager. 'But you'll have to brief me a bit. Not now: I need to get off to work. Make it this evening, after Lucy's in bed.'

That evening they sat down together at the kitchen table. Bernie had her laptop in front of her to refer to the notes she had made on it. The red ring binder of Richard's life lay on the table alongside the box of memorabilia. Peter picked up the note that had arrived that morning.

'Who are these people?' he asked.

'According to Ernest Walker, Eleanor – Richard's mother – went off without a word to anyone after meeting with a group of students at one of the women's colleges. I think that these – well, apart from Fokin, who was a tutor – are some of those students. This is a photograph of them with Eleanor.'

'And what exactly are you hoping to achieve?'

'I want to know why a mother would go off, leaving her eight-year-old son and have no communication with him for over thirty years.'

'Why?' Peter asked baldly.

'We-ell,' Bernie considered the question. 'At first I was trying to find out about Richard and get photos and things for Lucy's book. But now, I suppose it's partly the intellectual challenge and partly …' she hesitated. 'I suppose it's to do with getting rid of the anger I've got towards Eleanor for what she did to Richard. She let him go through the whole of his life thinking that he was somehow to blame. And, even when she came back, she never appeared remotely grateful to him for all the trouble he took for her. I think if I could find out what motivated her, I might find it easier to forgive. At the moment I don't really even know what it is that I need to forgive her for.'

'OK. I think I understand. So you think these people may be able to give you some insight into what was going on in Eleanor's mind when she upped and left, back in ...?'

'July, nineteen forty-eight,' Bernie filled in. 'Not long after the end of the Trinity Term when Abigail Fossett, Alicia Lowton, Edna Knowles and Claudia Browne completed their undergraduate studies, and shortly after Alexander Fokin left his post at Oxford and moved to London.'

'And your theory is?'

'That Eleanor went to London to join one or more of them. We also have this,' she added, handing the engraved locket to Peter. 'It has a lock of fair hair in it and purports to be from someone called "AF", which I suspect may be the same person as wrote letters to her, between 1953 and 1964, first from America and then from all over the world. Those were signed "Ally", which could be short for Alicia or Alexander.'

'Or "AF" could be Abigail Fossett,' Peter pointed out. 'You can't be sure that "AF" and "Ally" are the same person.'

'No, but it seems a reasonable working hypothesis.'

'Always keep an open mind. That was one of Richard's maxims. Now let me have a read of those letters.'

Peter spent the rest of the evening painstakingly reading through all the documents in the case: the letters, Bernie's notes and all the stories in the red book, whether directly relevant to Eleanor or not. Bernie started to understand why Richard has described his colleague as 'slow but sure'. She knew that he had valued Sergeant, later Inspector, Johns as someone who could be relied upon never to make mistakes through impetuosity or failure to check the evidence; but right now she felt that she would have preferred someone who did not expect to double-check everything before making a move. Eventually he looked up.

'Well, you haven't really got a lot to go on,' he observed, 'but I suppose if you want to know more about these people, you need to talk to the only ones that are still alive. That is Claudia Browne and Alicia Fortescue. You've got their addresses and telephone numbers, so what are you waiting for?'

'OK. I think I'll tackle Claudia first. I rather fancy I'll have a better chance of bonding with a Cambridge academic than with a diplomat's wife.' She looked at her watch. 'But it's too late to ring tonight. I'll try her tomorrow, perhaps in the afternoon. If she's elderly, she may well get up late and go to bed early.'

Bernie sighed as she replaced the red ring binder on its high shelf. 'You know, Peter,' she said. 'I feel that I understand Richard a whole lot more now than I ever did when he was alive. It's terribly frustrating that it's only four years after his death that I've got to the point where I know him well enough to have a fighting chance of making a good wife for him. If I could go back in time, I'd have a good few severe things to say to myself on the subject of tolerance and understanding!'

Bernie's attempt to make contact with Claudia Browne proved fruitless. When she rang the number that Jonah had given her, she got through to an abrasive woman who described herself as Dr Browne's niece. She informed Bernie that her aunt was very ill and quite unable to take phone calls from anyone. Somehow, her tone managed to convey the message, 'least of all eccentric dons with implausible stories about goings-on dating back to the nineteen forties.'

'Of course, I could try to reach her through her old Cambridge college,' Bernie remarked to Peter that evening, 'but I don't want to persecute the old dear if she really is ill.'

'Did the niece give any indication of how ill she was?'

'No. Well, she made it sound serious, but she sounded like the sort of person who would have made anything sound serious just to get rid of me. So I've no idea whether Claudia is likely to get better or if she'll soon be following Abigail Fossett and Edna Knowles, not to mention Alexander Fokin, up above the bright blue sky to the pearly gates.'

'Well then, what about your other lead? Did you try Alicia Fortescue's number?'

'Yes, but no joy there either: I just keep getting through to an answering machine. I'll keep on trying. Maybe she's just out for the day.'

Bernie had still not managed to make contact with either Claudia or Alicia when term ended and Eddie arrived back in Oxford for the Christmas holiday. Peter moved back to his own house, in order to maintain the fiction that he lived there permanently. This meant that he was not there when Bernie finally got an answer to her calls to the Fortescue home, and she was unable to impart the limited information, which she thus obtained, to him. She spoke to a Mrs Thompson, who had come round to check on the house and collect the post while Lady Fortescue was away. Lady Fortescue was spending the winter touring southern Europe and would not be back until March. Bernie sighed with frustration and decided to put off any further investigation until after Christmas, when Peter would be free to help. It would also be good therapy for him, she thought, to keep his mind occupied when his children had gone back up north.

After Christmas, Peter resumed his habit of living almost full-time at Bernie's house, only returning to his own when one or other of his offspring decided to visit. Bernie wonder idly whether Hannah or Eddie realised that the reason Peter had had the landline to the Cowley Road house disconnected was not so much an economy measure as a way of preventing them from deducing that he was never at home except when they were staying with him. Probably not, she thought; young people these days relied entirely on mobile phones, so in all likelihood they thought that abandoning the landline was a smart move on their father's part.

At Peter's suggestion, she made a trip to King's College in the hope of finding out more about Alexander Fokin. At first, she was surprised when she was informed that she was not the first person to have come making enquiries about the philosophy lecturer; but then she realised that she was following in the footsteps of Jonah Porter. Unlike him, as a fellow academic she was welcomed into the Senior Common Room and introduced to an emeritus professor who had actually been taught by Fokin as an undergraduate.

Like many elderly people, Professor James Colshaw was only too pleased to reminisce about his student days, and Bernie came away with a lot of information, only a very small part of which had any bearing at all upon Alexander Fokin. She showed it to Peter the following evening.

'I don't think I'd ever make it as a detective,' she sighed. 'I now know all sorts of things about undergraduate life in the forties and fifties, but not much more at all about Fokin. Apparently he used to smoke a foul-smelling pipe during lectures, cycled to work and wore patent leather shoes, but as to whether he could have been Eleanor's lover, I've gleaned nothing.'

'What about his handwriting? You were going to try to find out if the letters from "Ally" could have been his?'

'I showed some samples to the Prof. Unsurprisingly he couldn't really remember what Fokin's writing was like, but he thought the letters looked too neat to be his. Oh! And he particularly picked up on the signature. He didn't think the distinctive curly L's in "Ally" looked right.'

'You know,' Peter said,' picking up one of the letters and studying it, 'I did wonder about them myself. The L's in the signatures on these letters aren't the same as the ones in the main body of the letter. See here! The end of "really" looks quite different from "Ally" at the end of the letter.'

'Mmm,' Bernie agreed, looking where he was pointing. 'But people often do write differently in their signature. Often signatures don't bear much resemblance to the name at all.'

'But that's because they want a signature that's hard to forge and because they write it so often,' Peter argued, 'but this isn't exactly his signature, is it? It's his name at the end of a letter to an intimate friend. I'm ready to bet he didn't sign himself "Ally" on his chequebook.'

'So you don't think Fokin is our "Ally" then?'

'To be honest, I've been sceptical about that hypothesis all along. OK so he goes off to America in 1953, which is the date of the first letter from America in Eleanor's collection, but "Ally" appears to come back again. As far as we know Fokin stayed over there until he died.'

'Actually, I think I agree with you,' Bernie admitted. 'There was one other thing I've forgotten to tell you. They showed me an old group photo of university staff from nineteen forty nine, which had Fokin in it. His hair was dark brown, nothing like the hair in Eleanor's locket.'

'Right then: we're making progress,' Peter declared. 'We've eliminated Fokin and now have just two contenders to be "AF": Alicia Fortescue and Abigail Fossett.'

'And only Alicia is likely to also be "Ally",' Bernie agreed, 'But the trouble is, she got married straight from college, so could hardly have been sharing a flat with Eleanor.'

'But *was* Ally sharing with Eleanor?' Peter asked. 'The letters talk about "our flat" but could she have been meaning the flat she shared with her husband? Can we be sure that Eleanor was included in "we"?'

Bernie picked up the bundle of letters and began skimming through them, looking for references to the flat in London. Peter was right; it was possible that the writer was not suggesting that it was shared with Eleanor.'

'That's the trouble with the first person plural,' she commented. 'You can't tell whether "we" and "us" includes the person you're talking to or not. I wonder whether there are any languages where you have two different words, so that you can distinguish. Anyway, it looks as if we are now saying that Alicia is our prime suspect. So I suppose we just have to sit back and wait for her to return from her travels.'

To Bernie's surprise, a few weeks later Peter reported the results of an investigation that he had carried out on his own in relation to the mysterious Eleanor. He had managed to track down the uncle who had given four-year-old Richard a springer spaniel pup. He was long dead, but his son, Eleanor's cousin, was still living in the house near Witney that Richard and Eleanor had visited with Esther Lyons. Peter had been over there and spoken to him.

'So what did you find out?' Bernie demanded eagerly. 'And why didn't you tell me you were going?'

'Not a lot, I'm afraid,' Peter said, ignoring the second question. If the truth be known, his motivation for seeking out Eleanor's family had been to show Bernie that he was just as capable as Jonah Porter at helping her with her quest for knowledge about her mother-in-law, and he had said nothing in case the search had proved fruitless. 'But it may be that the fact that this cousin knew next to nothing about Eleanor is significant in itself.'

'How d'you mean?'

'Well, I got the impression that the cousin – Edgar Carter – had been quite close to Eleanor when they were growing up. He told me all sorts of interesting things about the games they used to play around the farm when she came to visit them there. And that seemed to have continued to a lesser extent after Eleanor got married. But then, all of a sudden, she disappears and that's the end. He said that his parents wouldn't even talk about her after that. He assumed at first that she must be dead, but he couldn't understand why there was no funeral. He now thinks that there must have been some sort of scandal, but he doesn't know what it was.'

'Of course, in those days the mere fact of a married woman leaving her husband and child might have been scandal enough,' Bernie mused, 'but for her own parents to disown her quite so thoroughly does suggest something more. Thank you, Peter: you're much better at interviewing people than I am. I'm surprised you managed to get Cousin Edgar to open up like that, considering that he doesn't know you from Adam and he was having to admit to his family having a skeleton in its closet.'

Time passed with little progress being made towards the identification of "Ally" or "AF". Bernie tried ringing Alicia Fortescue's number again, but her winter tour was still ongoing apparently. In the end, she wrote a letter, which she hoped Alicia would read on her return, introducing herself and asking to meet at Alicia's convenience. After that, all she could do was to wait for a reply. In any case, she did not have much time to devote to the search because she was a university examiner that year and was busy with all the administration associated with ensuring that the papers were ready on time and had no errors in them. Almost before she knew it, it was Lucy's fourth birthday: four and a half years since Richard died and nearly a year since Angie's murder.

The doorbell rang while Bernie and Lucy were doing the washing up after lunch. At the sound, Lucy jumped down from the chair on which she was standing in order to reach the sink, drying her hands on her trousers.

'Peter!' she called out excitedly.

'No Lucy, it's too early to be Peter, but why don't you go and see? I think I can guess who it might be.'

Lucy trotted down the hall to the front door. Next to the door was a sturdy wooden chest. Lucy climbed on it to reach the latch and open the door a crack. She peeped out though the opening and came face to face with Jonah Porter.

'Good afternoon Miss Paige!' he greeted her. 'May I wish

you many happy returns of the day?'

Bernie came up behind Lucy and opened the door wide.

'Come in Jonah,' she invited, 'it's lovely to see you again.'

As usual, Jonah carried a gaily-wrapped parcel, which he presented to Lucy. She immediately tore off the paper to reveal a brown and white wooden dog on wheels, with a long pink tongue hanging out of its mouth and a tail that wagged as she pulled it along the floor by a string. She immediately set off along the hall and into the living room, pulling her new toy behind her. Bernie and Jonah followed.

'Why don't you take Jonah to see your garden?' Bernie suggested. 'Show him what you've been doing with his tools.'

It was a fine day and the French windows were wide open. Lucy led the way, still pulling the dog on its string. Jonah followed eagerly, while Bernie returned to the kitchen to make her customary pot of tea.

Lucy's garden was a plot of ground in the wide border that ran along one side of the garden. At the back was the high redbrick boundary wall. Jonah recognised rows of radishes and lettuces and some early cornflowers, which were already in bud. There was also a small rockery with stonecrop and aubrietia growing on it and a washing up bowl half-buried to form a pond. Jonah admired Lucy's efforts and then kneeled down to show her how to thin out the lettuce seedlings. Bernie found them there a few minutes later when she came out to announce that the tea was ready.

'Another smart suit bites the dust,' she observed, as Lucy helped herself to her feet by holding on to Jonah's jacket with muddy hands.

'Mud's clean dirt, as my mother used to say,' he assured her. 'It'll brush off when it's dry.'

Over tea and scones, Jonah enquired about Bernie's quest for knowledge about her mother-in-law. Had the information that he had sent her been of any use?

'Well, yes and no,' Bernie said. 'We've decided that Alexander Fokin is unlikely to be "Ally" and in fact he probably had nothing to do with Eleanor at all. So we're pinning our hopes on it being Alicia Fortescue, but we're still waiting to get an audience with Lady Rupert, who's been out of the country for the last five months. Claudia Browne is being guarded by a niece, who says that she's too ill to be bothered by strangers asking her about her undergraduate life. So we're a bit stuck at the moment.'

'We?' Jonah asked, picking up on the repeated use of the plural pronoun.

'Peter Johns has been helping me,' Bernie explained. 'I thought it might stop him brooding on Angie's death. You did know about his wife, presumably?'

'Yes, it filtered through to me eventually: not in time to send a card or anything though. I was still with the Met when it happened. I'm back on home turf now.'

'Would you have liked to have stayed there?'

'No. London doesn't appeal to me at all. The secondment seemed like a smart career move, but I couldn't have stuck it out much longer. Reading and South Oxfordshire suit me just fine. Well, well, well: so old Peter's helping you with your investigations, is he? And what has he contributed so far?"

'He found what is probably Eleanor's last living blood relative,' Bernie said, detecting the scepticism in Jonah's voice and feeling that she had to stick up for her friend. 'There's a cousin living on a farm near Witney. He confirmed that Eleanor's own family, as well as her in-laws seemed intent on purging her from history after she left. It definitely looks as if they considered her behaviour to be in some way disreputable, but I don't really know enough about the mores of nineteen forties banking circles to be sure about what sort of thing that might include. It could be something that wouldn't raise an eyebrow these days.'

'So not really any more than you knew already?'

'I suppose not – but it might have been the key to the whole mystery,' Bernie argued, irritated by Jonah's tone, which suggested that he had a low opinion of Peter's abilities. 'What is it you've got against Peter? Richard thought very highly of him.'

'As a general dogsbody who didn't mind doing all the boring routine stuff.'

'No: as his right-hand man.'

'Richard put me forward for promotion to inspector ahead of him.'

'Probably because he wanted to keep Peter as his sergeant, while he didn't mind you going off elsewhere,' Bernie muttered belligerently. 'Anyway, what's all this about? Why does it have to be a competition? Can't you just accept that you and Peter have different approaches, but are equally effective?'

'I'm sorry,' Jonah said contritely. 'I couldn't resist winding you up. You really like him don't you?'

'I don't see how anyone could fail to like him,' Bernie grumbled. 'He's straightforward, honest, kind ...'

'All the things I'm not?' Jonah asked, smiling.

'Well, I'll give you "kind"; and I've no reason to doubt your honesty, but I don't think you could be accused of being straightforward.'

'Surely that's all part of my enigmatic charm? But enough about me: what are you going to do next? Isn't it about time you had another go at getting hold of Claudia Browne? You're surely not going to let an aggressive niece foil your efforts?'

'If her aunt really is ill,' Bernie objected, 'it hardly seems right to pester her.'

'But you said yourself that you don't know how ill she really is; and for all you know talking about the old days might be just the tonic she needs. Why not write her a letter? If she's too ill to read it then you haven't done any harm, and if not, it's up to her to decide whether to talk to you or not.'

'OK. I'll think about it. Anyway, Alicia Fortescue may get back to me soon, and then it may not be necessary to bother Claudia. The trouble is I don't have great hopes in

Alicia, because I can't imagine she'll take to me.'

'Why ever not?'

'I don't think I have much in common with *Lady* Fortescue, diplomatic widow, old girl of Cheltenham Ladies College, Modern Languages scholar, etc. etc. I have this feeling that she'll put the phone down thinking I must be a wicked Scouser trying to fleece her of her life's savings! I could do with a full vowel transplant before speaking to her!' Bernie smiled as she imagined a grey-haired woman in twin-set and pearls dropping the receiver in shock at hearing her accent.

'Your wife's a surgeon,' she joked. 'Couldn't she fix me up with a set of long a's and short u's?'

'I think it would be against her principles,' Jonah laughed. 'She's a lassie from Lancashire herself.'

'Really? How splendid! I knew you had good taste! You must bring her over here sometime, and we can compare reminiscences of "up north"!'

'Now Miss Paige,' Jonah said, getting to his feet and addressing Lucy, who was busily organising a tea party of her own on the floor, with an assortment of soft toys sitting around a dolls' tea service. 'I'm afraid I'm going to have to love you and leave you now. Duty calls!'

Bernie noted that he had, once again, ignored an invitation to make an additional visit in between his annual appearances on Lucy's birthday.

Lucy got up and approached him, holding up her arms. He bent down and picked her up. She hugged him round the neck and kissed his face.

'Good bye,' she said. 'Come again soon'

'I will return next spring, when the May blossom once more adorns the hedgerows and the cuckoo returns to the woods and you attain the great age of five years!' he declared, setting her back down on her feet. 'Until then: adieu!'

The anniversary of Angie's death dawned bright and

sunny. Eddie had returned home a few days earlier, having completed his university studies; and Hannah had come down the day before, to be with her father on the day itself. They sat around the breakfast table in silence. There seemed to be nothing to say.

A year on, the investigation into the killing seemed no further on. MacBride had long since given up on providing weekly updates, since there was never anything to report. A television appeal and a reconstruction of the crime had produced no new witnesses: or rather they had only resulted in time being wasted interviewing a few attention-seekers who had come forward with supposed sightings of potential murderers in the vicinity, which turned out not to fit in with the known facts. Now, while the investigation was still officially ongoing, Peter knew that MacBride had also been doing other things. It was only to be expected: when you came to a dead end like this one, you had to accept that there was only so much resource that it was worth putting into one case, however tragic or personal.

That afternoon they visited Angie's grave, each bringing some flowers to put on it. As they crossed the graveyard, they were surprised to see two figures already there. They bent down and seemed to be doing something to the grave. Then they got up again and the taller took the hand of the smaller. They stood for a moment or two then started to move away. Peter quickened his pace and called them back.

'Bernie! Don't go.'

'I'm sorry. I didn't mean to intrude.' Bernie stopped and turned towards him. 'Lucy wanted to bring some of her flowers to give to Angie. I hope you don't mind.'

They all looked towards the grave and saw a small vase of blue cornflowers.

'She grew them from seed,' Bernie explained.

Lucy looked anxiously from face to face, detecting the uncertainty in her mother's voice and wondering whether she had done something wrong.

'No, of course we don't mind,' Peter said hurriedly.

'What lovely flowers!' Eddie said simultaneously, bending down to talk to Lucy. 'I wish I could grow such nice ones.'

Lucy's face lit up in a broad smile and she hugged Eddie round the neck. Then she remembered that this was a solemn occasion and her face became serious again. She went over to Peter and slipped her hand into his. He squeezed it briefly.

'Thank you Lucy,' he said, before busying himself with removing the old flowers, which he had placed on the grave a week earlier, and arranging his new offering.

'Come along, Lucy,' Bernie said gently. 'Time for us to go now.'

'I'm sorry about gate crashing your memorial at the grave the other day,' Bernie apologised to Peter a few days later when they met by chance in Cornmarket Street. 'Lucy wanted to know why you couldn't come over for Sunday lunch last week, and I told her that Hannah was staying, and why, and then she was determined to do her bit to mark Angie's anniversary. I ought to have insisted that she waited until another day.'

'Don't be silly. Why shouldn't she be there? Angie was her godmother wasn't she?'

'Yes but-'

'Don't argue. Look: let's have a coffee. I could do with a chat. I'd forgotten how draining it is to share a small house with Eddie and Hannah at the same time!'

They made their way to a café in the covered market. As Peter stirred in his sugar, Bernie looked at him anxiously.

'How are you?' she asked at last.

'I'm fine.'

'And the kids? How did they cope with the anniversary?'

'Hannah is directing all her energies towards worrying about me,' Peter replied ruefully, 'which is rather wearing. I have to confess to having been rather relieved when she headed off back to Leeds on Monday. Her ministrations are much less uncomfortable when they're done from afar.'

'And what about Eddie?'

'Oh, Eddie's talking about going to Jamaica to find his roots. Do you remember those two cousins who came over to the funeral?'

'Paul and Joel?'

'Those are the ones. Well, Joel has a job in a computer company over there and he reckons he can get them to take Eddie on too. So now Eddie's all fired up with enthusiasm to go over there.'

'Sounds like a good idea to me: see his family, get some work experience.'

'Well, yes, I'm inclined to agree with you in a way, but it's a big step for him to take and I'm afraid that Joel may have painted a rather rosy picture of what life will be like out there for him.'

'If he doesn't like it, he can always come home,' Bernie pointed out.

'Yes, I know. I know being a parent involves being ready to let them go. It's just …'

'Look at it this way,' Bernie said, leaning forward towards him. 'Can you actually *stop* him, if he really wants to go?'

'No, I suppose not.'

'Well then! Much better to give him your blessing, keep your fingers crossed that it all turns out OK and be ready with the tissues in case it all ends in tears.'

'I suppose you're right.'

'I *know* I'm right. So now we've got the kids sorted, back to my original question: how are *you*?'

'And, going back to my original answer: I'm fine.'

Peter,' Bernie said reproachfully, 'You know as well as I do that "fine" just means that you are refusing to engage with the question. A year on from when your wife was brutally murdered, we are no nearer finding out who did it, or why-'

'I would have thought it was patently obvious why,'

Peter interrupted. 'It was because she was black.'

'That's no reason.'

'It is for some people. She was black in a white world and someone didn't want her there. The worst thing about it is that I'm part of that world. I'm part of the white society that hasn't managed to eradicate that sort of thinking. And I'm part of the police service that hasn't managed to take those sorts of people off the streets.'

'Oh Peter! Don't talk such nonsense! Of course we've none of us done enough to combat racism, but you've done a whole lot more than most. You mustn't go round blaming yourself because you can't change the world single-handed.'

'I could have done more to keep Angie safe. Perhaps Khan is right when he says that we should have made more efforts to integrate into the West Indian community.'

'Why? Angie didn't know any of them – except the ones who happen to go to our church. She came over here on her own. She was ready to integrate into the local society: black, white, sky blue pink, whatever. It was up to her if she wanted to make contact with other Jamaicans.'

'But she might have been safer if she hadn't been seen as a black woman who considered herself to be white.'

'You know, Peter, this reminds me of the people who argue that if a woman wears a short skirt and a low-cut blouse she deserves to be raped. Angie wouldn't have wanted you to "protect" her by turning her into someone different from what she was. You know that, don't you? YOU ARE NOT TO BLAME!'

'Yes, I know that, I suppose, but it just doesn't feel like it sometimes,' Peter muttered, staring down at the table in front of him.

'To change the subject,' Bernie said, trying to talk brightly, 'I've arranged to go and meet Alicia (AKA Lady Rupert Fortescue) on Saturday. Would you like to come along?'

'Won't she think it's a bit odd, the two of us descending on her like that?'

'Why should she? You're a detective. It's only natural that I would enlist your help in tracking down Eleanor's past. I don't imagine that people like the Fortescues would do that sort of thing for themselves. They'd pay a professional.'

'I don't like the idea of being portrayed as a Private Detective. I don't make a living from spying on people's husbands and wives and taking photos of them in compromising positions!'

'I don't intend to suggest that's what you are. You're a police officer helping me out of friendship for my husband, aren't you? How about it? I'm sure you'll be able to think of the right things to ask her better than I will.'

'Alright, since you are so insistent,' Peter agreed. 'Although I would like to point out that you are completely transparent and I *know* that you are only asking me because you think it will be good for me. You're trying to take me out of myself, aren't you?'

'Oh dear!' Bernie exclaimed in mock dismay. 'And I thought I was being so clever. I should have known better than to try to deceive the Master Detective! But seriously, I do think she's more likely to warm to you. I put on my best BBC accent on the phone, but I still got the distinct impression that she considered me to be not quite "people like us".'

'And you think I will come across as "people like us"?'

'At least you can talk proper!'

18 ENIGMA VARIATIONS

'Now this takes me back!' Lady Fortescue exclaimed when Bernie showed her the photograph of Eleanor with her four friends. 'I remember the occasion. We'd been punting together and we were just walking back to college when we met Eleanor and her husband.'

'You met her husband?' Bernie broke in, surprised.

'That's right. I think that was probably the first time we met him. We all thought Eleanor was very lucky: he was ever so dishy and quite the gentleman. Anyway, Abby had her camera with her. She was very keen on photography. She went on to become a journalist. That's Abby, next to Eleanor.' She pointed to the golden-haired woman whose arm was around Eleanor's shoulders. 'So we asked Edward – that's Eleanor's husband – to take a picture of the five of us together. Abby got the film processed and gave us each a copy.'

'So that's Abigail Fossett,' Peter murmured, looking at the picture, 'and then next to her is Eleanor. Can you tell us who the others are?'

'The one next to Abby is Edna Knowles,' Lady Fortescue said, pointing at a tall, thin woman with large glasses. 'She went on to become a teacher at a girls' school down in Kent somewhere.'

'Rochester,' Bernie agreed.

'That's right. I can see you've done your homework! We used to exchange Christmas cards each year until she died. That must have been, what? Two, three years ago?'

'Three,' Bernie confirmed. 'It was March 2001.'

'Yes, I suppose that would be right. I remember the funeral was just before the start of the Easter holiday. I was surprised how many people turned out for it, considering she didn't have any family, but there seemed to be a lot of her ex-pupils who wanted to pay their respects.'

'And the other girls in the photo, Lady Fortescue?' Peter persisted gently.

'Call me Alicia, please. Well that spotty girl next to Edna is me, believe it or not.'

Bernie and Peter stared at the photograph and then at the photographs ranged around the room of Sir Rupert and Lady Fortescue on various occasions. There was some resemblance, but it was hard to believe that the unattractive face in the group photograph was the same person as the elegant woman accompanying her husband to embassy balls and foreign office dinners.

'And then the last one,' Alicia went on, 'is Claudia Browne. I lost touch with her, I'm afraid. She was very earnest and terrifically brainy. I think she rather looked down on me as, well a bit flighty and frivolous.' She laughed. 'Do you happen to know what became of her?'

'She eventually got a fellowship at Cambridge,' Bernie told her. 'She's retired now, of course. She lives with her niece. I've been trying to get to speak to her, but the niece says she's not well enough to have visitors.'

'A Cambridge don! Well, well. I'm glad she got what she wanted. That must have suited dear Claudia down to the ground.'

'Getting back to Eleanor,' Bernie said, 'I'd be interested to hear how she came to be part of your group. How did you meet her in the first place? She wasn't at the university.'

'You know, I'm really not sure. I rather fancy it may have been Edna who introduced her. She was very keen on the idea of bringing together Town and Gown, and educating the wives and mothers of the country. She may well have organised some lectures for non-university women to encourage them to become more educated. Yes – I think that must have been how it was. But, as I remember it, she turned up while I was abroad. I was reading Modern Languages and I spent my third year in France and Italy. By the time I came back, Eleanor was well established as part of our little debating society.'

'And was that society just you, Edna, Claudia and Abigail, or were there any others?' queried Peter.

'Well there were a few others who came and went, but essentially it was just the four of us – plus Eleanor, of course. It was very informal: just a group of friends setting the world to rights over a bottle of cheap wine.'

'How well did you know Eleanor,' Bernie asked. 'Did she talk to you about her home life at all?'

'Not that I remember,' Alicia said, answering the second question first. 'She was more Abby's friend than mine – and, as I said, she seemed quite close to Edna too. I think she found Claudia a bit intimidating, because she was so brainy and knew such a lot more than Eleanor did. She used to quote Latin and Greek and all that, which went right over the top of poor Eleanor's head.'

'So you wouldn't have any idea what made her decide to leave home and go to London in 1948?'

'No idea at all. The first I knew about it was when you telephoned me last week.'

'So these letters aren't from you?' Bernie asked, getting out the box of letters from the elusive 'Ally' and handing them to Alicia. 'They're signed "Ally", which we thought might have been you.'

Alicia looked at the first of the letters then burst out laughing.

'I'm afraid you've got it all wrong! Abby never could

write legibly. These are hers. The signature isn't "Ally" it's "Abby".'

Bernie snatched up one of the letters and she and Peter looked at the signature. Yes, they could see it now. The letters were from Abigail Fossett, who was presumably also the "AF" whose curl of hair Eleanor had kept in her locket.'

'Well, Peter,' Bernie said, turning to her companion, 'that's one up to you. You said there was something funny about the way the letter "L" was different in the signature from in the rest of the letter.'

'I didn't realise that they were B's though. That would have been the really clever thing.'

'It all fits now,' Bernie went on. 'Abigail Fossett was a journalist who went all over the world. First she went on her own and wrote letters back to Eleanor; and then later they went together.'

'Which explains all the visas in Eleanor's passport,' Peter agreed.

'And the photographs of them everywhere from Tasmania to Timbuctoo,' finished Bernie. She turned to Alicia again.

'Did you keep in touch with Abby at all?' she asked.

'No. What with her becoming a foreign correspondent and my marrying into the diplomatic service, we were hardly ever in the country at the same time. I can't have heard from her since the early fifties.'

'So you don't know whether she and Eleanor shared a flat in London?'

'I'm afraid not. They were very close, but I never heard anything about them living together. You ought to ask Claudia Browne. She and Abby were thick as thieves, and Claudia went on to study in London. In fact, I thought she was the one who shared a flat with Abby.'

'Getting back to Eleanor's husband,' Peter said, looking down at his notes. 'I'm still rather confused about that. You said that the day that photograph was taken was the *first* time you met Edward Paige. Does that mean that you saw him several times while you were all in Oxford?'

'That's right. He had his job, so he wasn't able to come to our little gatherings very often, but he must have joined the group four or five times, I should think. He was very interested in our ideas for re-building the country after the war. We were all so young and idealistic and he'd come back from Germany determined to help make things better.'

'And how did relations between Mr and Mrs Paige seem to you?' Peter asked. 'Did they seem a united couple?'

'They weren't particularly affectionate as far as I remember,' Alicia said slowly, 'but I had no reason to believe that there were any real problems in their marriage. He was a lovely man: I'm sure he didn't beat her or anything like that.'

'So why did she leave him?' Bernie asked, puzzled.

'I really can't say. As I told you, I had no idea.'

After that there was little more to be said. Bernie thanked Alicia for seeing them and she and Peter returned home feeling rather confused. They had identified the writer of the letters, but the reason why Richard's mother had so suddenly abandoned him was, if anything, even more obscure.

'Do you think Alicia could have been wrong about Edward Paige?' Bernie hazarded, as they drove home. 'I mean, surely if he was such a wonderful husband as she seemed to think, Eleanor would have stayed with him. It's not as if he had a mistress or anything.'

'Not that we know of. But could he have been having an affair with one of the other women in the group? Was that why he came to the meetings and made himself so pleasant to them all?'

'And afterwards Eleanor couldn't bear to stay with the man who'd been unfaithful to her with one of her own friends? But which one? It can't have been Alicia, because she got married almost immediately afterwards; and Abigail was obviously the person that Eleanor turned to, so was it Edna or Claudia?'

'Why not Alicia?' Peter asked. 'She might have been engaged to Rupert Fortescue and having it off with Edward Paige at the same time. If it was Edna or Claudia, why didn't Edward get a divorce after Eleanor left so he could marry again?'

'Maybe he'd had enough of marriage,' Bernie suggested. 'Maybe he didn't like commitment. And I'm still not convinced he was having an affair, anyway. You've got absolutely no evidence of it. I think that maybe he was one of those controlling men who can't bear the idea of their wife having a life apart from them. Perhaps he went along to the meetings to keep an eye on her. I think he was jealous of the women and afraid that they would take her away from him.'

'Which it seems they did.' Peter pointed out.

'Yes, but my theory is that it was only because of his obsessive possessiveness. You hear a lot about this these days: men who stalk their girlfriends because they can't bear to think of them existing except as an adjunct to themselves. And often it ends up with the men being violent in order to keep the women in a position of subjugation.'

'Well, you could be right,' Peter conceded, 'but you don't have a shred of evidence that he wasn't the perfect gentleman that Alicia says he was.'

For a long time it seemed that Bernie would never discover why her mother-in-law had taken the extraordinary step of leaving her loving husband and young son in order to move to London, apparently to share a flat with journalist Abigail Fossett. The summer passed quickly. Lucy was starting school in September and Bernie discovered that this involved more preparation than she had expected. At the same time, Peter and Eddie were preparing for his departure to Jamaica, which was scheduled to take place the same month. Eleanor's strange behaviour was thrust to the back of both of their minds.

That is, until, one day in October, Bernie received an

email from Claudia Browne. It came though one afternoon while Bernie was working on the computer in her college room. That evening, after Lucy was in bed, she showed it to Peter.

Dear Dr Fazakerley,

I am sorry for the long delay in answering your letters. My niece, Suzanne, is a good girl, but she has the strange idea that talking about the past would be distressing to me. Fortunately, one of my old colleagues came across the copy which you sent to my college address and brought it to me, albeit after a delay of several months. If you are still interested in speaking to me about Eleanor Paige and the others, I would be delighted to entertain you and your little daughter to afternoon tea. Please let me know when would suit you best. I don't get out much these days, so any day will be equally convenient for me. The best way to reply to this is by email, because Suzanne has never mastered electronic communication and so will not intercept it!

  Yours sincerely,
    Dr Claudia Browne.

'Who says computers are only for young people?' she smiled. 'I think I'm going to like Claudia. She's obviously a game old girl.'

'Have you replied yet?'

'No, I wanted to see whether you wanted to come as well. I was rather hoping you might: to help keep Lucy under control if nothing else. There's no knowing what sort of havoc she might wreak in the house of an elderly spinster.

I imagine it being full of occasional tables with knick-knacks on them.'

'Perhaps it would be better not to take her?'

'But she specifically asks her to come,' Bernie pointed out. 'She probably wants to see what Eleanor's granddaughter looks like.'

'Or she might just be being polite. You left Lucy with Eddie when we went down to Alicia Fortescue's. Don't you think it would be better if I stay at home and look after Lucy, while you go over to Cambridge to see Dr Browne?'

'Tell you what: I'll ask her which she'd prefer. She sounds like a pretty straightforward kind of person to me. I expect if I warn her that four-year-olds can't be expected to keep still for five minutes together she'll tell me if she'd rather Lucy didn't come after all.'

I turned out that Bernie and Peter need not have worried that Claudia Browne would not be able to cope with a lively four-year-old in her house. She was evidently used to entertaining youngsters.

When they arrived at the small terraced house, they were greeted by a rather austere woman in her late forties, who introduced herself as Suzanne Browne, the daughter of Claudia's youngest brother. She had moved in with her aunt after Claudia had a fall and broke her hip. She was back on her feet again now, but Suzanne had stayed on to 'keep an eye on her' as she put it.

She led the way into the lounge. Bernie was pleased to see that it was sparsely furnished with no obviously breakable items within Lucy's reach. The walls were lined with bookcases and more books were piled up on the floor. Claudia was sitting in an upright chair in the bay window. She greeted them warmly and sent Suzanne off to the kitchen to prepare the tea. Then she took Lucy by the hand and led her to a low table. On it was a large alarm clock of the sort with two bells on the top. On the floor next to the table was a large cardboard box.

'Now young lady,' Claudia said to Lucy. 'The grownups have got a lot to talk about, so I thought you'd like something to amuse yourself with while we natter. See this clock here?'

Lucy nodded.

'Well now, I'm going to set it so that both the hands are at the top. In this box here, I've hidden some treasures for you to play with, but you're only allowed to get them out one at a time. You can get out the first one when I start the clock going and you can get another one when the big hand gets to the number three – here, do you see? – and then another one when it gets down to the six – at the bottom here – and another when it gets up to the nine, and another when it gets back up to twelve. Do you understand?'

Lucy nodded again.

'Very well. Off you go then.'

Claudia wound up the clock, adjusted the hands and put it down on the table in front of Lucy. Lucy lifted up one of the flaps on the top of the cardboard box and Bernie, looking over her shoulder, could see that it was filled with the expanded polystyrene 'shrimps' which are used as protective packaging. Lucy reached into the box and pulled out a picture book. Peter and Bernie watched as she settled down to look at the pages.

'It never fails,' Claudia observed to them as she resumed her chair. 'It used to keep Suzanne and her brothers happy for hours when they came to visit with their father. Now sit down both of you and tell me how I can help you.'

'Well, as I told you in my letter,' Bernie began, 'I'm researching into my mother-in-law, Mrs Eleanor Paige. I think you knew her when you were an undergraduate in Oxford?'

'Yes,' Claudia nodded. 'So you married Eleanor's boy?'

'Richard, that's right.'

'And after he died you starting trying to find out more about him?'

'That's right. And one of the things I found out was that

his whole life seems to have been affected by the experience of losing his mother when he was only eight. So I wanted to know why she left him.'

'Affected? How?' asked Claudia sharply.

'Well, I think he blamed himself for her leaving. In fact, I know he did when it happened, because he told someone that he thought he must have been naughty and that's what made her go. And so I think he was always trying to make up for it.'

'I see,' Claudia smile and turned to look at Peter. 'And where do you come into all this?'

'I worked with Richard. He was a Detective Superintendent and I was Detective Inspector. I'd been with him for more than twenty years, ever since I joined CID.'

'And Peter's wife, Angie, was my best friend,' put in Bernie. 'Peter and Angie were Lucy's godparents.' She broke off suddenly, unsure how to go on, wishing that she had not mentioned Angie and hoping that Claudia would not ask any questions that would require them to talk about her untimely death.

'Anyway, after Richard died, she resumed, 'I started thinking that Lucy – only of course I didn't know the baby was going to be a girl then – would grow up without ever knowing her father…'

'So now you're making a book about Richard, to help her get to know him?'

'That's right. I brought it with us, in case you'd like to see it.'

She reached into her bag and brought out the large red ring binder. She handed it to Claudia who looked with interest at the photographs of the young Richard with Esther Lyons, which were near the front.

'Yes,' she murmured, 'that's how I remember him. Fair curly hair – like your daughter – and rather a solemn expression on his face.'

'Do you mean that you actually met Richard?' Bernie burst out, in surprise.

'Once or twice. Just incidental meetings – nothing planned. I remember bumping into Eleanor in the High one day, when she was taking Richard to buy clothes; and then there was one occasion when I came across them in the Parks. He always gave the impression of being a bit afraid, but perhaps that was just the effect I had on him!'

'Or could he have been afraid of his father?' Bernie asked quickly. 'I'd been wondering whether it could have been domestic violence that made Eleanor leave.'

'No. You can forget about that,' Claudia said decidedly. 'Edward Paige wasn't that sort of man.'

'That's what Alicia Fortescue said,' Bernie admitted. 'She seemed to like him very much.'

'You've been talking to Alicia, have you? I don't suppose she could tell you much,' Claudia laughed. 'Very conventional was dear Alicia. She really had no idea what was going on.'

Peter and Bernie exchanged glances. Then they both spoke at once.

'And what *was* going on?'

'You really can't work it out?' Claudia asked, looking first at Bernie then at Peter. 'Come along! You're the detective: look at the evidence. You have four young women going around together and only one of them ever gets married. And another young woman *is* married and decides to leave her husband and go and live with one of the single women.'

'So we were right in thinking Eleanor lived with Abigail Fossett?' Bernie asked.

'Oh yes! They lived together alright.' Claudia continued to smile.

'Hang on a minute,' Peter said slowly. 'Are you telling us that Abigail and Eleanor were a Lesbian couple?'

Claudia nodded, her eyes twinkling with amusement at the length of time it had taken for the penny to drop.

'Alicia was oblivious to it all. She had no idea that she was the only one of us with the least interest in men. Edna and I dedicated ourselves to our work, but a career wasn't enough for Abigail. She needed love as well, and Eleanor fell for her. I think they were very happy together.'

'It all starts to make sense now,' Bernie mused. 'Eleanor will have been right when she told me that there was no point her trying to take Richard with her when she left. In those days, there would have been no question of allowing him to live with her and Abigail.'

'And Abby couldn't afford the publicity of a divorce or a custody case,' Claudia agreed. 'They had to keep it as low key as possible. Everyone thought they were just two single women sharing a flat. Eleanor passed herself off as a war widow and people admired Abby for taking her in and letting her keep house for her.'

'And did you keep in touch with them?' Bernie asked, 'after Eleanor moved in with Abigail?'

'Until Abby died. That will have been ...'

'Nineteen seventy-nine,' Bernie prompted her, after checking her notes. 'Three years before Eleanor's sudden reappearance at Edward's funeral.'

'That's right,' agreed Claudia. 'I'd never been close to Eleanor. I think she was a bit afraid of me, because I'd had more education, and getting a fellowship at Cambridge only made things worse. So I didn't hear any more about her after that.'

'In nineteen ninety-two,' Bernie went on, 'Eleanor sold the house that she was living in in Henley and bought a sheltered accommodation flat. She invested the rest of the proceeds of the sale and lived on the income from that and some other investments, together with her old age pension.'

'That's right. They moved to Henley when Abby was promoted to a more senior position at the newspaper. Abby was a very successful journalist, so I imagine she left Eleanor quite a nice little nest egg for her old age.'

'But quite a substantial inheritance tax bill too,' Bernie commented, 'though I suppose if the house was in joint names ...'

'What I don't understand,' Peter said, frowning, 'is why

Richard's father didn't divorce her. *She* deserted *him,* surely he could have got a divorce and been free to re-marry?'

'Ernest Walker told me that he said he didn't want to,' Bernie pointed out. 'And maybe he didn't want the scandal that would be associated with it. Or, more likely, his parents didn't want the scandal for the family.'

'Or perhaps,' Claudia suggested, 'he was just a kind man who didn't want to drag his wife through the courts and ruin her life.'

Bernie sat in silent thought.

'You know,' she said at length, 'I still can't decide what to make of Eleanor. I can sort of see why she felt she had to leave, but I'm pretty sure that if she'd left her husband for another *man* I'd be feeling that she ought to have stayed with Edward for Richard's sake – and because she'd made marriage vows which shouldn't just be cast aside at a whim. It wasn't as if he was beating her up or anything. Everyone who knew him seems to think he was a model husband and all-round good egg! Does it really make any difference that it was a woman that she fell in love with?'

'At the time,' Claudia said drily, 'I'm sure it would have made a great deal of difference in most people's minds.'

'I suppose you're suggesting that Eleanor was taking a bigger risk than she would have done if she'd run off with a male lover?' Bernie screwed up her face in concentration. 'But only if people found out. And why would anyone imagine it was anything more than two women sharing a flat for the sake of economy? And I can't get over the fact that her leaving like that, without even saying Goodbye, scarred Richard for life. Subconsciously he felt that if his own mother didn't love him then neither would anyone else. I think that's why he didn't get married until he was fifty-seven.'

'Or perhaps Miss Right never came along,' Claudia suggested.

'But she did,' Bernie insisted. 'I've met her. She was a policeman's daughter called Brenda Walker. She went out with him for years and then finally got fed up with waiting for him to pop the question and married someone else. Of course, that only confirmed his belief that he was fundamentally unlovable. He'd never have asked *me* if Peter here hadn't given him what for and virtually told him he had to!'

'Really?' Claudia said, looking at Peter. 'And how did that come about?'

'Somebody had to do it,' he muttered gruffly. 'I got fed up with watching the two of them together. They must have been the only people in Oxford who couldn't see that they were in love!'

'Aah!' Claudia murmured, looking hard at Peter then at Bernie and then back at Peter again. 'And tell me, Peter, how long is it now since your wife died?'

'A year and a half,' Peter answered. 'Why do you ask?'

'Oh, I just wondered.' She turned to Bernie. 'And your husband died five years ago?'

'Just coming up to five now,' Bernie confirmed.

'Ah well!' Claudia declared with an air of satisfaction, which Bernie and Peter did not really understand, 'Life goes on! And here comes Suzanne with the tea. Put the tray down there, Suzie. That's right.'

19 MARRIAGE OF CONVENIENCE

Eddie Johns seemed to be having a wonderful time in Jamaica. His weekly phone calls to his father, and equally frequent emails to Bernie, were full of news of his new-found family and his new job. Lucy was delighted with the colourful postcards that dropped on to the mat for her every few weeks. The weather was balmy, the people friendly, the opportunities vast. As Bernie remarked to Peter, he would have made a good spokesman for the Jamaican tourist board.

Peter was glad that his son was happy, but reflected sadly to himself that perhaps it had something to do with being somewhere where Eddie was no longer the odd one out, no longer part of a minority ethnic group. Could he have done more, he wondered, to understand what it was like for his wife and children to be living in what was still predominantly a white society?

As Christmas approached, Eddie started to urge his father to come over for a visit. It would do him good to have a winter holiday in the sun. The whole family was dying to see him again. Peter was torn between a desire to see for himself how Eddie was getting on and a worry that being with Angie's family – and especially with Phoebe who so closely resembled her older sister – would bring memories flooding back which he might not be able to cope with.

Somehow, Superintendent Fuller got wind of the invitation and offered to allow Peter to take a substantial part of his annual leave entitlement together so that he could spend a full two months in Jamaica, catching up with the family over there and having a complete rest from work. Hannah rang to say that she would be working on Christmas Day, so would not be able to visit Peter in Oxford this year. Bernie suggested that Hannah should come down earlier in December instead, leaving Peter free to head off to the sun and the hospitality of his in-laws to spend the festive season with them. Bowing to the inevitable, Peter went.

Bernie wondered what Angie's family must make of Peter's almost daily telephone calls to Lucy while he was away. She was convinced that he must be ringing her far more often that he spoke to his own daughter, Hannah. Of course, Lucy was always ecstatic to hear his voice and never had more important things to do than to talk about the exciting places that he had been. On reflection, Bernie decided, the in-laws probably accepted this behaviour as perfectly natural. After all, Peter *was* Lucy's godfather. They probably assumed that, in England, godfathers were expected to take their responsibilities very seriously.

The dreary winter days dragged on and it was soon time to prepare for Peter's return. It was Lucy's half term holiday, so Bernie took her with her when she went round to Peter's house to make it ready for him. He would be arriving on an early morning flight the next day.

'Why isn't Peter coming back to our house?' Lucy demanded, as Bernie put two pints of milk and some butter, cheese and eggs in the fridge.

'Because this is his home.'

'But I want him to stay with us!'

'It's not a matter of what we want: Peter has to decide for himself.'

'So he doesn't want to live with us anymore?'

'Come and help me put these flowers in water.'

Bernie picked up a bunch of yellow chrysanthemums, which she had laid down on the working surface, and took them over to the sink.

'Did Peter tell you he didn't want to stay with us anymore?' Lucy persisted.

'No. I don't think he's made up his mind exactly what he wants,' Bernie admitted, taking out two vases from under the sink and filling them with water. 'It's difficult for him.'

'Why?'

Bernie sighed. She stuffed the chrysanthemums inexpertly into one of the vases and set it up on the windowsill above the sink.

'Bring those other flowers over here for me, love.'

Lucy obediently picked up another bunch of chrysanthemums – purple and white this time – and handed them to her mother.

'You didn't answer my question,' she pointed out emphatically. 'Why doesn't Peter know what he wants to do?'

'Lucy love, it's hard to answer. Come upstairs and help me make up Peter's bed and I'll do my best.'

Bernie carried the second vase upstairs and set it down on the dressing table in the room that Peter had shared with Angie for nearly twenty-five years. A thin layer of dust lay on the top of the dressing table and on the chest of drawers that stood next to it. Bernie looked in the bag that she had brought with her, brought out a duster and gave it to Lucy with instructions to polish all the surfaces. Then, as she busied herself with putting clean linen on the bed, she tried to explain.

'You see Lucy,' she began, 'this house is where Peter lived with Angie for nearly twenty-five years: that's more than five times as long as you've been alive. So it's got lots of good memories for him of when they first got married and when Hannah and Eddie were growing up, and, of course, he wants to be here to remember Angie and all the good times.'

Lucy looked at her mother, wide-eyed and nodded sagely. Bernie put her bag on the bed and fished out a portrait of Angie in a stainless steel frame. She wiped it quickly with a duster and set it up on one of the matching bedside cabinets, which stood at either side of the bed.

'But,' she went on, opening the chest of drawers and getting out a pair of Peter's pyjamas, which she placed under the pillow at the other side of the bed, 'this house also has one very, very *bad* memory.'

Lucy stopped polishing and came over to her mother, who sat down on the bed and lifted her onto her lap.

'I'm talking about when Peter came home and Angie was there in the kitchen, dead.'

'With blood everywhere,' added Lucy.

'Who told you that?' asked Bernie sharply. Although she did not believe in hiding the truth from children, she had not seen it necessary to fill Lucy in on all the gory details of the attack.

'Ben Evans,' Lucy answered, naming the older brother of a girl of her own age who live near them and was in her class at school. 'He read it in the newspaper.'

'I see. Well he was right: there was a lot of blood about. So you can see why it's not a pleasant thing for Peter to think about every time he goes in the kitchen. It's not surprising if it sometimes all gets a bit much for him and he wants to get away and come to stay with us for a few days. What we've got to do is to make sure he knows that he'll always be welcome if he wants to come.'

'Don't you *want* Peter to live with us always?' Lucy asked, with her characteristic directness.

'It isn't a matter of what *we* want, love. Of course, I'd like Peter to come and live with us, but it isn't up to me – or you. Peter still belongs to Angie, not us.'

'Even though she dead?'

'Yes. And of course, there's Hannah and Eddie as well. Peter has to think of them too.'

'But they live *miles* away!'

'All the more reason why it wouldn't be fair for him to spend lots of time with us. Anyway, who knows? In a few years Peter might retire and decide to go to live with Hannah in Leeds or he might even go over to Jamaica and live with Eddie.'

'I don't want him to go!'

'I'm not saying that's what'll happen,' Bernie said quickly, trying to reassure her daughter who looked distressed at the thought of losing her favourite person. 'I'm just saying that it would be wrong of us to try to stop Peter doing whatever he decides is right for him – and Eddie and Hannah.'

'And Angie?'

'That's right.'

Peter gazed up bleary-eyed at the house as the taxi drove away the following morning, leaving him standing on the pavement with his suitcase beside him. He fished in his pocket for his keys and slotted one into the lock. He experienced a moment of panic when the key refused to turn; then he realised that he had automatically selected the key to Bernie's front door instead of his own. He found the correct key and let himself into the house.

Leaving his case in the hall, he made his way to the kitchen and switched on the light. On the working surface ahead of him, he saw two neat piles of post: one containing circulars and catalogues, the other mainly bills and bank statements. Evidently, Bernie had sorted his mail into important and junk categories. Next to them stood a card depicting the entrance to St Luke's College. Peter picked it up and looked inside.

'You'll find milk and stuff in the fridge – enough to tide you over until Monday,' he read. 'Lucy and I are itching to hear about your travels, but I know you'll be tired so don't feel obliged to call on us today. If you do come, it's steak and kidney pie for tea! We'll call in after church on Sunday if we don't see you before. Bernie.'

He reached down a glass from the wall cabinet above his head and went to the sink to get a drink of water, noting with surprise the vase of flowers on the windowsill. He looked at his watch: nine-fifteen. That would be four-fifteen in Jamaica. He had better wait a few hours before ringing Eddie to tell him he had arrived back safely. Or should he go over to Bernie's house and use her internet connection to send an email? He finished the glass of water and then decided to go to bed. The doze which he had had on the plane had not refreshed him and he was almost falling asleep on his feet. It was a good thing it was Friday and he had the whole weekend to recover from his jet lag before returning to work.

He carried his case upstairs and set it down on the bedroom floor. He immediately spotted the flowers on the dressing table and then saw the photograph, which Bernie had put next to Angie's side of the bed. Peter recognised it as one that Bernie had taken some three years before. She must have had it enlarged and bought a frame for it. He sat down on the bed and picked up the picture. Angie's smiling eyes seemed to gaze back cheerfully. Peter replaced it on the bedside cabinet and reached across the bed to retrieve his pyjamas from under the pillow. How had Bernie known which side he slept? He wondered. But of course, she had probably been able to tell from seeing the state of the bedclothes in her spare room when she came to change them after he had been staying there.

He changed into his nightclothes and got into bed. Suddenly he remembered the scene five years previously when he and Angie had put Bernie to bed after Richard's funeral. Angie had made a point of making Bernie sleep in the middle of the bed, instead of leaving an empty space where Richard would have been. Was it time that Peter began to do the same? He experimented with moving his pillow into the middle and tossing Angie's on to the floor. No, it did not work. It felt completely unnatural. He got out of bed and retrieved the pillow. He settled down again, but still sleep did not come. Finally he picked up the photograph and laid it on Angie's pillow, propped up so that he could see it if he lay on his side. It was not the same as having her there in person, but somehow it was strangely comforting to see her face smiling at him.

Some five hours later, Peter awoke. The photograph had slid down beneath the duvet. He retrieved it and set it up on the bedside cabinet. He consulted his watch. By now, Eddie would be at work. He would get dressed and have something to eat – breakfast he supposed, although it was after lunchtime – and then ring him on his office number. He had better ring Hannah too, but what shifts was she working this week? And then …

Well, after that, obviously he would go over to see Bernie and Lucy, and take them the gifts that he had brought back for them: a pair of brightly coloured maracas for Lucy and a carved wooden fruit bowl for Bernie. He had better wait until the evening: Bernie might be in college, busy with tutorials, in the afternoon.

As he got out of the car, Peter wondered whether he ought to ring the bell or to let himself in with his key. It seemed a bit presumptuous simply to walk in on them unannounced, but on the other hand, Bernie might be busy and not welcome having to come to the door. He was saved having to make a decision, however, because as he approached the door it opened by itself to reveal a beaming Lucy standing proudly on a pair of wooden stilts, which had enabled her to reach the latch. As Peter stepped inside, she wobbled dangerously and he snatched her up in his arms, letting the stilts fall to the floor with a clatter. Lucy laughed and hugged him ecstatically.

'I *knew* you'd come!' she shouted out. 'Mam! Peter's here!'

Bernie appeared on the stairs, smiling broadly.

'Welcome back Peter. Come and sit down and I'll make a brew.'

'Thank you for getting the house ready for me,' Peter said a little later as they sat in the kitchen with their mugs of tea.

'It was no bother. It gave us something to do over half term.'

'Did *you* leave the flowers?'

'Yes. Why?'

'But you don't believe in cut flowers.'

'No, but Angie liked them. I wanted to make you feel that you were coming home.'

'Is that a hint that I ought to live there full-time, instead of being round here all the time?' Peter said jokingly.

'No! No! No!' Lucy burst in, banging her mug on the table and spilling the contents.

'Oh Lucy!' Bernie cried out in exasperation. 'Stop that!'

She got up and went over to the sink to get a dishcloth.

'Peter won't want to come here if this is the way you behave,' she chided, as she wiped up the spilt tea.

Lucy's face fell and she looked anxiously from her mother to Peter and back again.

'Sorry,' she said sheepishly, before picking her mug up in both hands and drinking very carefully.

Lucy was very subdued for the rest of the evening. She did not even brighten up when Peter gave her the maracas he had brought back from Jamaica. Bernie was vaguely aware that there was something wrong with her daughter, but both she and Peter were too absorbed with their own conversations and the pleasure of being back in each other's company to take much notice, until they returned to the living room after doing the washing up and saw Lucy huddled miserably in the corner of one of the arm chairs.

'What's up love?' Bernie asked anxiously, going over and putting her hand on Lucy's shoulder.

Lucy turned away and hid her face in the upholstery.

'Come on, Lucy,' her mother coaxed, putting her arm round her and trying to turn her round to face the room. 'Tell me what's bothering you.'

Peter came over and knelt down by the chair.

'Won't you tell me what's wrong?' he pleaded.

Lucy turned her tear-stained face towards him and looked into his eyes.

'Are you going to go and live in Jamaica?' she asked at last.

'No! Whatever gave you that idea?' Peter asked, astonished.

'Mam said.'

'I only said,' Bernie broke in, 'that Peter *might* think of living in Jamaica after he retires. That'll be years off yet.'

'And the idea had never even crossed my mind,' Peter added, still puzzled.

'I was only warning you,' Bernie went on, realising that she had made a misjudgement and trying to repair the damage that she had done by her words to Lucy the previous day, 'that you shouldn't take it for granted that Peter will always stay here in Oxford when his family are in other places.'

'But don't you worry, Lucy,' Peter insisted. 'I have no plans to move away: not for years and years at least.'

'Even if I bang my mug and spill my tea?' Lucy asked anxiously.

Peter looked bemused. He had completely forgotten the earlier incident in the kitchen.

'Oh Lucy!' Bernie cried remorsefully. 'I was only joking! I didn't mean anything. Honestly! You didn't really believe that Peter would stop coming to see us just because you spilled your tea all over the table, did you?'

Lucy looked at her mother, realised that she had got it wrong and burst into tears of embarrassment. She rolled over and hid her face in the chair again, sobbing quietly.

Peter took charge. He scooped Lucy up in his arms and hugged her close.

'Listen to me, Lucy,' he said firmly. 'You know I'm your godfather, don't you?'

Lucy nodded.

'Well now. When I became your godfather, I *promised* that I would help your mam to look after you while you were growing up. And I don't ever break my promises,' he went on, searching his memory and hoping frantically that there were no broken promises in the past which Lucy would be able to remember and hold against him. 'So you see: I *have* to keep coming round here to see how you're doing, because I promised I would. Do you understand?'

Lucy nodded.

'Good. Now, let me show you how to play those maracas properly.'

Some six or seven months later, Peter came downstairs one evening after putting Lucy to bed. He sat down next to Bernie and spread his arms out wide along the back of the settee.

'Michael Bond has a lot of insight into family life,' he remarked, referring to the story that he had been reading to Lucy. 'Olga da Polga bites the cat's tail; the cat runs up a tree; and it's Dad, of course, who has to get the ladder to get it down!'

'Aren't you glad your two have got beyond the guinea-pig stage,' Bernie laughed. 'If Lucy wants one, I'll make sure I keep cats away. In the absence of Dad, I'd be the one shinning up the ladder.'

She put down the research paper that she had been reading and turned towards Peter.

'Lucy loves having you here. She's really disappointed when you're not around to read her bedtime story.'

'Oh that's just her ploy to make us feel guilty. Children are very good at that: it encourages their parents to give in to them against their better judgement.'

'I'm thinking of giving up my widow's pension,' Bernie said, in an apparently abrupt change of subject.

'Why on earth would you want to do that? Richard paid into the pension scheme for years and never got a penny back. You're entitled to it.'

'The conditions say that widows aren't entitled to a pension if they re-marry or start living with someone "as man and wife" whatever that means.'

'So?'

'Well, I'm concerned that lots of people probably assume that we *are* living together as man and wife, and I'm not keen on being put in a position of having to prove that we're not.'

'Wouldn't it be down to them to prove that we are?'

'I suppose so, but what might that involve? I don't fancy the idea of being spied on to check that we aren't slipping into each other's bedrooms at the dead of night! And people would always still suspect. So, I thought if I voluntarily gave up the pension, at least I'd never be in the position of having to try to prove a negative. I've always felt a bit of a fraud about it anyway, because I was never *dependent* on Richard.'

'I still think you're being over-sensitive,' Peter argued. 'The way I see it, you're just getting what Richard paid for. And you *do* have extra expenses for Lucy.'

'I can still keep her allowance. That's separate.'

'Of course, if, as you say, everyone assumes that we are living as man and wife, one solution would be to *become* man and wife.'

'Is that a proposal of marriage?'

'I suppose it probably is.'

'You're sure about that? And you do realise that I can never be what Angie was to you? I mean, I would hate to feel under pressure to fill her boots.'

'Of course not. That's why I could never marry anyone else. You're the one person that I know will understand about Angie. It would be dreadful to be married to someone who expected to be the most important person in my life!'

'I think a lot of people would get a bit narked at that last remark,' Bernie said, smiling, 'but I know what you mean. So let's agree now: no competition and no comparisons. I'm not going to try to be a better wife than Angie and you're not to compare me with her. And the same goes for you and

Richard.'

'Sounds fair enough to me.'

Peter lowered his arm from the back of the settee so that it rested on Bernie's shoulder. She snuggled down next to him with her head on his shoulder.

'How do you think your kids will take it?' she asked.

'Eddie'll be OK,' Peter said confidently. 'He likes you. I'm sure he'll be pleased. I'm not so sure about Hannah. She may think it's good for me to have someone to look after me, or she may decide that I'm betraying Angie by forming a new relationship so soon.'

They talked on into the night, making plans and imagining the future, oblivious of the passage of time.

'Ma-am!'

Bernie became aware that she was being shaken by small hands holding her upper arm. She opened her eyes and realised that she and Peter were leaning against one another on the settee while Lucy, dressed in pyjamas, was trying to wake them.

'What are you doing down here?' she demanded loudly. Then, getting no immediate answer, she went on, 'if you want to sleep together you'd be more comfy upstairs. Mam's bed is big enough for two people.'

'Thank you for your advice, Lucy,' Bernie said, succeeding with difficulty in keeping a straight face. 'We'll bear your suggestion in mind.'

Peter unwound his arm from Bernie's neck and leaned forward to pick Lucy up. He placed her on his lap and addressed her seriously.

'Tell me Lucy,' he said, 'how would you feel about it if I came to live here permanently? And if your mam and I started sharing her bedroom?'

'Do you mean you're going to get married?'

'Yes. That's what we're thinking of. Would you mind sharing your mam with me?'

'So you'd be my real father instead of just my godfather?'

'Well, sort of.'

'Can I call you Daddy?'

'I'm not sure about that. You'd better ask you mam. She might not like it.'

'Mam?'

'If Peter doesn't mind, I don't have any objection: just so long as you don't forget that you've got another Dad too.'

'I won't,' Lucy promised. She twisted round on Peter's lap and put her arms round his neck. 'Now I'll have a Mam *and* a Daddy just like everyone else.'

Lucy was dispatched to school that morning with strict instructions not to tell *anyone* about the wedding plans. She was not at all pleased at being forbidden to share her momentous news.

'Can't I even tell Mrs Topping?' she pleaded.

'No: not even Mrs Topping,' Bernie said firmly. 'There are other people who have to know first, before you tell people at school.'

'Like who?' Lucy asked sulkily.

'Hannah and Eddie for a start. How do you think they would feel if they knew your teacher knew their dad was getting married again before they did?

'Can't you tell them now? Before I go to school?'

'No. Hannah will be on her way to work and it's still the middle of the night in Jamaica. So you must *promise* me not to say a word to *anyone*.'

Peter discovered that he had completely misjudged his children's reaction to his news. When he telephoned her that evening, Hannah declared herself delighted and immediately demanded to be handed over to Bernie to discuss details of the wedding ceremony. Naturally, she and Lucy would be bridesmaids. What would they wear? Who was going to give Bernie away? Was Bernie sure that she could be married without being given away? Well, now she came to think of it, Hannah could not remember anyone giving Bernie away to Richard; but in that case, why did everyone seem to expect it? When was the wedding going to be, or had they not decided yet? Had they thought about a honeymoon?

Bernie allowed her to run on for some time before pleading a need to telephone other people with the news. Hannah reluctantly relinquished the line and Bernie looked helplessly at Peter.

'I'm glad she's happy for you,' she said, 'but I have an awful suspicion that our idea of a nice quiet wedding won't come up to Hannah's expectations.'

Peter waited some hours before telephoning Eddie, knowing that he often did not get in from work until late in the evening. With the five-hour time difference, this meant that he might not be home until nearly midnight UK time.

'Hi Dad!' he answered cheerily. 'What's new?'

'Bernie and I have some important news for you: we've decided to get married.'

There was a long silence. Peter began to wonder if the connection had been cut off.

'Hello Eddie?' he called. 'Are you still there?'

'Yes. I'm here,' Eddie answered in a strange, tight voice, 'But I think I must have misheard you. It sounded as if you said that you were going to get married.'

'Yes, that's right: to Bernie.' Peter continued to speak cheerfully, hoping that the animosity, which he had detected in his son's voice, was only in his imagination.

'How could you? Mum's only been dead two years. How could you think of getting married again?'

'But it's *Bernie*,' Peter protested, taken aback and unable to think of anything else to say. 'I thought you liked her.'

'I do – at least I *did*, until she did this to you. She was supposed to be Mum's friend!'

'Come on Eddie,' Peter tried to reason with him. 'Let's talk this through sensibly.'

'I might do that if you were being sensible, but you're not. I don't want to talk about it. You're just being ridiculous!'

Peter turned to Bernie with a look of shocked disbelief.

'He put the phone down on me. I don't understand it. I thought he liked you.'

For more than two months the impasse continued. Peter would ring Eddie every day, only to have the phone slammed down after a few sentences. Hannah reported that she had received a phone call from her brother, in which he begged her to try to talk their father out of taking what Eddie clearly saw as a disastrous step. She had remonstrated with him, but to no avail. Peter did not know what to do. He had often had a stormy relationship with his son, but their quarrels had always been quick to flare up and equally quick to evaporate. He had no experience of this cold determination not to be won over.

Bernie watched him anxiously, wondering whether she ought to propose that they abandon their matrimonial plans in the interests of family harmony. Was it selfish of her not at least to offer him that option? How long would it be before Peter suggested it himself? The more she thought about it the more she realised how hard it would be to give up the prospect of sharing her life with Peter on a permanent basis, now that it had been offered to her.

'Peter?' Bernie asked tentatively one morning over breakfast.

'Yes?'

'About Eddie: I know it isn't exactly my business and I don't want to be interfering between father and son, but … well, would you mind if I emailed him to try to explain?'

'What about?'

'You know: about us. I mean, I get the impression that he just isn't prepared to listen to you when you ring him. So I just thought that if he had it in writing he might be more likely to hear us out before jumping to conclusions. That's all.'

'Well, if you think he's more likely to listen to you, go ahead.'

So, after Peter and Lucy had gone out, Bernie sat down at her computer and started composing an email to Eddie.

'It's a good thing,' she reflected to herself, as she highlighted the text with the mouse and pressed the delete key for the hundredth time, 'that this is electronic and not on paper, or I'd have wasted a small forest by now!'

Eventually she was satisfied that she had expressed herself as well as she was capable of doing. She re-read it one final time and then clicked 'Send'.

Dear Eddie,

I realise that I am the last person on earth that you want to hear from at the moment, but please read this right to the end before you delete it, consign it to the spam folder or reply telling me to get lost.

I'm afraid that I'm not going to say the one thing that you most want to hear: that your dad and I have changed our minds about getting married. I like to think that you and I have always been friends and for that reason, I don't like doing anything to hurt you, but now that we have got to that point, he is one thing that I couldn't bear to give up – even for your sake.

When Peter told me about your reaction to our news, I thought back to when I was your age and tried to imagine how I would have felt if my father had announced that he was planning to remarry. I came to the conclusion that I might have had two reasons to oppose the idea:

> (1)   It was disloyal to my mother for him to consider replacing her with someone else;

(2)   It was somehow ridiculous for two people of that age to imagine that they were in love.

Addressing point (2) first, I admit that what Peter and I feel for one another is very different from the experience of young lovers, such as he and Angie were more than a quarter of a century ago; but it is nevertheless real. In many ways, our marriage is one of convenience: Peter gets someone to share the domestic chores and company for the long evenings, and I get a father for my daughter. Perhaps it would be easier for you if I told you that there was nothing else to it. But that wouldn't be true – speaking for myself at any rate. The house feels empty when Peter is away. When he is late home from work, I worry that something has happened to him. Having him around makes Richard's absence easier to bear. I like to think that I am in some small way able to make it easier for him to cope with his far greater loss. If we decided to give up the idea of marriage, we would still find ourselves always wanting to be together. In an earlier age, our present conduct would already have caused a scandal.

With regard to point (1), I can only say that I know that Peter still loves your mother more than anyone else in the world, including me. I am under no illusion that I could ever replace her in his affections and I have no wish to do so. As you know, Angie was my very best friend. I believe that gives me the right to claim that I have a good idea about what she would have wanted for Peter. I'm convinced that she would be pleased to see two of her favourite people coming together for mutual support. I can promise you that I will never do anything to undermine Peter's memory of her.

Richard has been dead now for more years than the time that I knew him. And yet there are still days when the pain of losing him is almost too much to bear. It is like being an amputee with a limb that still aches although it's not there. I can't begin to imagine what it is like for Peter to lose his wife after nearly twenty-five years; but I do hope to go some way towards relieving the intense suffering that he is still going through. We're like two cripples holding together hoping that by leaning on one another somehow we'll both manage to stay upright.

I'm sorry that you aren't yet able to feel happy at the prospect of having me for your stepmother. That is completely understandable, as anyone who knows me will agree! I would like to have you welcoming me into your family, but that's not important compared with the way Peter is feeling at the moment about your reaction. If you can't rejoice, please at least try

to understand, and please, please tell
him that you are not angry with him
anymore. He is truly miserable at the
thought that he is hurting you.

Thank you for reading this. I'm
sorry that it had to be so long. There's
no need for a reply: just please do
ring your dad and have a proper talk
about all this.

Love,

Bernie

Late that night Peter's mobile phone rang. Bernie had just dropped off to sleep and when the sound woke her, she reached automatically for the alarm clock before realising that the ringing came from the guest room. She listened intently, assuming that it was a call for Peter to go out to a crime scene. She could hear Peter's voice, but could not make out the words. After a while, the talking stopped and she heard footsteps coming along the landing. She sat up in bed as Peter's head appeared round the door.

'What is it?' she asked. 'Have you got to go out?'

'No, it wasn't work; it was Eddie. It looks as if he's changed his mind, thank goodness. He says he'll be Best Man and he's even got permission from his boss to take some time off to come over for the wedding. He says we can choose the date and he'll be able to fit in around it.'

'What did I tell you? I knew he'd come round to it in the end: he just needed time to get used to the idea, that's all.'

20 ENLIGHTENMENT

'Why don't you take your things up to your room while I sort us out some breakfast?' Peter said, ushering Eddie through the front door after picking him up from Heathrow airport a few days before the wedding.

Eddie obediently carried his cases upstairs, returning a few minutes later to find his father making tea and toast in the kitchen.

'Don't hover in the doorway,' he called out. 'Come in and sit down.'

'You didn't need to move back in here for my benefit,' Eddie observed, sitting down and taking a piece of toast.

'What do you mean?'

'I do realise that you've been living with Bernie, you know. Not that it's any of my business.'

'Living in Bernie's house,' Peter corrected him. 'For your information, although it *is* none of your business, I am still occupying the guest room until after the ceremony.'

'Is that for Lucy's benefit?'

'No. It's what we both want. So we don't feel as if we're being unfaithful to Richard and your mum. I don't suppose that makes any sense to you.'

'Oh, I think it does.'

Eddie buttered his toast and Peter poured out cups of tea.

'I'm so glad you changed your mind about the wedding,' he said. 'At one stage we had visions of you turning up at the church and declaring that you had a "just cause or impediment"!'

'I'm sorry, Dad,' Eddie laughed. 'I wasn't thinking straight. Fancy me imagining Bernie as some sort of femme fatale who had lured you into her clutches! Once I got her email, of course I had to accept that you were doing the right thing.'

'What d'you mean?' Peter asked, puzzled.

'The email Bernie sent, explaining how you felt for each other. Didn't she show it to you?'

'No. She said she was going to write, but I didn't expect to see what she put. I was just glad that it seemed to have the desired effect on you.'

Eddie put down his toast and started feeling in his pockets.

'You know Dad: I think you ought to see it. Hang on! I'm sure I've got a printout here somewhere.'

He pulled out a crumpled piece of paper and smoothed it out on the table before handing it to his father.

Peter hesitated.

'I'm not sure I ought to. Bernie wrote this to you. She might not want me-'

'Go on: read it!'

Peter picked up the paper and began reading. Eddie watched him closely as his father's eyes moved over the paper.

'He is one thing that I couldn't bear to give up,' Peter read to himself. 'The house feels empty when Peter is away. … I like to think that I am in some small way able to make it easier for him to cope with his far greater loss. … I can't begin to imagine what it is like for Peter to lose his wife after nearly twenty-five years. … We're like two cripples holding together, hoping that by leaning on one another somehow we'll both manage to stay upright. ...'

With a struggle, he managed to read to the end despite the mistiness that started to obscure his vision. Suddenly he got up, pushing the paper across the table towards Eddie as he did so.

'I'm sorry, Eddie,' he said, sounding flustered. 'I have to go out. Will you be OK on your own for a bit? I won't be long.'

'Sure. No problem. I was thinking of going to bed right after I finish eating anyway. It's been a long journey and it's only two-thirty in the morning back home.'

Bernie stepped out of the front door and began to pick up the bottles of milk from the step. The sound of a vehicle approaching made her look up and, to her surprise, she saw Peter's car coming down the drive. It drew up in front of the house and Peter got out. She looked eagerly towards the passenger seat, expecting to see Eddie, but Peter was alone. He strode towards her with a strange expression on his face.

'What's up?' she asked anxiously. 'Didn't Eddie get here OK?'

'Eddie's fine. He's on his way to bed. It's the middle of the night back on Jamaica.'

'So what brings you here in such a hurry?'

'I just suddenly had to see you.' Peter put out his arms to embrace her, but was impeded by the milk bottles, which she was still holding to her chest. 'I've just seen the email you sent to him. I hadn't realised ... I mean, I suddenly knew ... that is ... Oh! For goodness sake put down those bottles!'

Feeling rather dazed, Bernie obediently replaced the bottles on the step. As she straightened up again Peter put his arms round her and pulled her towards him and kissed her.

'Hurry up with that milk!' a voice called from close behind Bernie, sounding like a younger version of Bernie herself. They looked down to see Lucy staring up at them.

'I'll be late for school if I don't get it soon,' she went on virtuously. Then she pushed past and bent down to pick up one of the bottles.

'No you don't!' Bernie intercepted her and gathered up the bottles herself. 'I'll take these. You go back and sit down. We won't be a minute.'

'You'd better come in,' she said to Peter. 'No point hovering on the doorstep.'

'I'm sorry,' he said, rather shamefaced. 'I don't know what came over me. I just suddenly felt I had to be with you.'

'Well now you *are* here, you might as well make yourself useful: go on ahead and open the fridge for me.'

Peter and Eddie came round that evening. Eddie, having slept for six hours, was now feeling very energetic and determined to make their meal a celebration.

'I brought this, so that we could drink to you and Peter,' he said as they entered, holding out a bottle of wine to Bernie.

'You can if you like,' she answered, trying not to sound as disapproving as she felt. 'But I hope you'll forgive me if Lucy and I stick to Vimto. I'm too old to change my drinking habits now.'

'What did I tell you?' Peter said. 'Our Bernie doesn't believe in ceremony. Even the wedding is as low key as she can make it.'

'I gave way on the bridesmaids' dresses, didn't I?' Bernie protested in mock indignation, 'against all my principles too!'

'But not even Lucy could persuade you to wear a proper wedding dress yourself,' Peter argued.

'I remember when you married Richard,' Eddie giggled. 'Did you see the Chief Super's face when you walked down the aisle in trousers?'

'They were *white* trousers,' Peter pointed out, smiling

broadly, as he recalled the occasion.

'That was Richard's doing. He had this quaint idea that not to wear white was somehow letting myself down, although, at my age, nobody was ever going to believe in my virginal purity whatever I wore.'

'And were you?' Eddie asked.

'Was I what?' Bernie gave him a hard stare, daring him to ask the question out loud.

'Were you virginal and pure?'

'Yes: we both were if you must know.'

'You mean Richard as well?' Eddie sounded incredulous. 'But he was old. He must have been having you on.'

'Well that's what he told me, anyway. What do you think, Peter? You knew him from quite an early age: did you ever suspect him of hanky-panky with the WPCs?'

'I have to admit, I was never even aware of him so much as asking a woman out on a date,' Peter acknowledged. 'In fact there was a bit of talk – that will have been when he was in his thirties, I suppose – amongst the lads, suggesting that there might be a reason for that, but I never bought that idea. I'd seen that he carried a woman's picture around in his wallet; so my theory was that he had lost the love of his life and no other woman would do.'

'Wow!' Eddie exclaimed. 'And did you ever find out who this mystery woman was? And, more to the point, is this the first you've told Bernie about it?'

Peter and Bernie both laughed.

'Oh yes!' Peter chortled. 'We found out who it was soon enough. It was his mother! She left home in her twenties, when Richard was eight, and he'd been treasuring that photo ever since.'

'He must have stolen it from the family album soon after she left,' Bernie put in, 'before they expunged her from the record; or else maybe it was one that she'd given him to keep for himself. So, apart from holding hands with Brenda Walker in the cinema back in the fifties, I think I really was Richard's first girlfriend. Now, how about you,' she went on giving Eddie a meaningful look. 'If you've quite finished probing into the private lives of your elders and betters, do you have anything to report on your own love-life? Is there some Caribbean beauty pining for you back in Jamaica?'

'Well,' Eddie said slowly, looking rather flustered, 'there might be. I'm not sure how she feels about me yet.'

'And does she have a name?' Bernie asked, teasingly, 'this love of your life?'

'Crystal Clarke. I met her at church: her Dad's the minister.' Eddie looked round the room, trying to think of something to say to change the subject. 'Where's Lucy,' he said at last.

'Over the road, showing off her bridesmaid's dress to the Evanses,' Bernie answered, pulling a face. 'It's very disheartening, after all the efforts I've made to bring her up with a proper attitude towards outward appearances! I've always told her it's what's underneath that matters, not what you look like, but the first opportunity she gets to dress herself up like some silly little Disney princess and she's delighted.'

'Which brings us back,' Eddie said, 'to what you're going to wear yourself. Should I assume, from what you've just said, that it'll be a boiler suit or old jeans?'

'After lengthy consideration,' Peter answered, 'we agreed that I would come in my police uniform and Bernie would wear a doctoral gown over a trouser suit.'

'And what about you, Eddie?' Bernie asked. 'Have you thought about what you're going to wear?'

'I've brought a suit with me: a new one, especially for the occasion. It's orange, so I hope it won't clash with your red gown.'

The doorbell rang and Bernie went to answer it.

'That'll be Lucy,' she said over her shoulder. Peter and Eddie followed her out into the hall.

'Wow, Lucy!' Eddie exclaimed when he saw her. 'Don't you look pretty? You'll put Hannah completely in the shade!'

'Supper's nearly ready,' Bernie put in quickly, taking hold of her daughter's shoulders as Lucy twirled round to show off her dress from all sides and pointing her in the direction of the stairs. 'Let's get you out of this before it gets messed up. We can't have you following me down the aisle with gravy all down your dress, can we?'

'And while we're getting you changed, these lads can make themselves useful by laying the table,' she added, as they made their way upstairs.

When she got back downstairs, she found Eddie pondering on the difficulty of getting a cork out of a wine bottle without the aid of a corkscrew. Without speaking, she left the kitchen, returning a few minutes later with a gimlet, which she handed to him.

'Try this', she said shortly, before returning to the business of getting the meal ready.

The wine was soon uncorked and Eddie placed the bottle in the centre of the table.

'Don't you have any wine glasses?' he asked, searching through cupboards in the kitchen. 'We can't use these tumblers. This calls for proper glasses.'

'I don't know,' Bernie said, looking up from turning down the gas under a pan of runner beans, which had just come to the boil. 'We never needed any. I don't drink and Richard was strictly a pint-down-the-pub-with-his-mates man. You may find some in the dining room. There are all sorts of things that his parents and grandparents used to have in there. Mind you, my Mam will be turning in her grave at the idea of me presiding over a meal where strong drink is to be consumed!'

'Come on Dad,' Eddie called out as he went off in search of the glasses. 'Help me to look.'

The dining room looked as if it had lain undisturbed for years – as indeed it had. There was a layer of dust over the dark wooden dining table, sideboard and assorted tall cupboards. It felt very gloomy. Eddie switched on the light, but the dusty chandelier in the centre of the ceiling seemed to make very little impact on the dimness.

'It reminds me of Miss Haversham's room in *Great Expectations*,' Peter observed, remembering his O' Level English set text. 'I hope there isn't an old rotting wedding cake hidden away somewhere!'

Eddie started opening cupboards and looking inside, hunting for the desired wine glasses. Peter joined the search and soon the air was thick with dust, which they had disturbed. Suddenly Eddie gave a cry of excitement.

'Look at this Dad!' he called out, holding up an A4 hardback notebook, which he had found in one of the tall cupboards. 'It's old Richard's diary. There are loads of them in here. Come and see.'

Peter went over and inspected the cupboard. Just as Eddie had said, there were several shelves containing an assortment of volumes of different shapes, sizes and colours. Those on the top shelf were all A4 format and labelled on their spines with dates. He read aloud, 'May to October 1991, October 1991 to February 1992, February to July 1992.'

'Listen to this, Dad,' Eddie interrupted. He had selected one of the volumes at random and was reading from it. '11th October 1995: I went round to see how the work on Bernie's house is coming along. The builder says that they should be out by the end of the week. I suppose once she moves back in that will be the last I see of her. It will feel strange not to have her around the place. I'm tempted to go round in the night and sabotage the building work-'

'Hang on there, Eddie,' Peter broke in. 'I don't think we ought to be reading this. It's Richard's private diary.

'Well he's not likely to object now, is he?' Eddie protested.

'But Bernie might not like us-' Peter began.

'And what might Bernie not like?' Bernie interrupted, coming in at that moment and looking round the room. 'And what have you got there?'

'It's Richard's old diaries,' Eddie told her. 'There's a

cupboard full of them.'

'Did you know that Richard kept a diary?' Peter asked.

'I had no idea,' Bernie shook her head. 'I suppose he probably thought I'd laugh at him for doing it – which I probably would have done.'

'Listen to this,' Eddie said excitedly. 'October 15th: Bernie's last day. We moved some of her things back to her house today, but I persuaded her to sleep here for one more night and I shall take her over with the rest of her stuff tomorrow evening. I wish I had the courage to ask her to stay, but it would be absurd for her to carry on living in my spare room when she has her own house again.'

Bernie leapt across the room and climbed on a chair so that her eyes were level with the top shelf of the cupboard containing the diary volumes. She ran her hand along the row, studying the dates on the spines, while Eddie, ignoring his father's gesticulations for him to stop, continued reading aloud.

'Bernie didn't seem as pleased about going back as I'd expected. I suppose she must be apprehensive about sleeping in the place where she was attacked. I hope it doesn't bring on a recurrence of the nightmares. It was odd the way they stopped so suddenly before. I hid one of her computer discs down the back of the sofa while she wasn't looking this afternoon. It will give me an excuse to call round in a few days to see how she is. I know-'

'Got it!' Bernie cried out suddenly, interrupting Eddie's flow. 'April to October 1995. I've always wanted to know what he really thought of me when we first met.'

She thumbed through until she found some entries dated June 1995.

'My main witness,' she read, 'is a dreadful woman called Bernadette Fazakerley. She seems to have taken a personal dislike to me. Johns, who knows her slightly through his wife, tells me that it is because I suggested that her student might have committed suicide. He described her as having "a thing" about suicide due to on old boyfriend having topped himself years ago. She objected to me offering to drive her home after we returned from meeting the victim's parents at Heathrow. She seemed to think that it was an insult for me to suggest that it wasn't a good idea for a lone woman to cycle round the streets at two in the morning. I suppose she must be a feminist. She wears trousers, even in the college chapel, and has her hair cut short and talks in a loud Liverpool accent – very strident. Her only redeeming feature is the very kind way with which she treated the boy's parents. She couldn't do enough for them: arranging for them to stay in a room in the college, putting them in touch with the Muslim chaplain, leaving her phone number for them to call if they needed anything. I only wish she would be as co-operative with my enquiries!'

Bernie snorted in mock indignation. 'The cheek of the man!' she declared. She was about to read some more when she recollected what she had come into the room for.

'Supper's ready,' she said. 'If you haven't found any wine glasses you will either have to put off indulging until tomorrow or put up with using what we've got in the kitchen.'

A few weeks after they were married, Bernie and Peter were in bed. He was about to switch off the light but she stopped him.

'Hang on a minute. There's something I want to show you.'

She reached out to the bedside table and picked up the final volume of her late husband's diary. She opened it at one of the last entries.

'Look at this,' she said, pointing at the page.

'Peter followed her finger with his eye.

'I made the most incredible discovery today,' he read silently. 'I accidentally knocked Bernie's desk diary on the floor and the most surprising thing fell out.'

'Look: are you sure you want me to read this?' he asked

uncertainly. 'It's rather private, between the two of you, isn't it?'

'Go on. I want you to see.'

'It was an appointment letter for the antenatal clinic!' Peter read, sounding the words quietly so that Bernie would know where he was up to. 'I kept reading it over and over and there was no doubt about it – it was in Bernie's name. It said "antenatal booking clinic" and the date was this coming Thursday. My first thought was to go straight off to find Bernie and tell her how pleased I was, but then I thought she might think I was angry with her for not telling me about it. And I suppose I did feel disappointed that she hadn't said anything. So I just put the letter back in the diary and put the diary back on the desk and tried to carry on as if nothing had happened. I know Bernie wouldn't deliberately deceive me about anything. She'll tell me herself when she's ready. It must be difficult for a woman to get used to the idea of having a baby – like having your own body taken over by some external force.'

Peter continued to read to himself, then, getting to the entry for the following day, he read aloud again.

'I nearly gave myself away this evening. Bernie brought her bike inside to mend a puncture and I very nearly took it from her and told her that she shouldn't be carrying things. I stopped myself just in time. She hates me doing that sort of thing for her. Maybe the thought of me getting overprotective is one of the things that are putting her off telling me about the baby.'

Peter stopped reading and looked at his wife.

'You see, Peter?' she said. 'All these years I've thought that Richard didn't know, and now it turns out that he did after all. Mind you,' she went on, 'him taking it so well only makes me feel all the more guilty for not telling him.'

Peter put his arm round her and squeezed her shoulders gently.

'You spend altogether too much of your time feeling guilty about things that are not your fault. You might as well say that Richard was to blame for falling off that roof before you had a chance to tell him all about it.'

'Do you think that was what he meant,' Bernie asked, sitting up straight and turning to look Peter in the eye, 'when he said to tell me he was sorry? Is that what he was sorry about? Was he sorry that we wouldn't be happy about it together?'

'Or sorry that he wouldn't see his baby, maybe?' Peter suggested. 'Or sorry that you would have to bring her up on your own?'

'And he was being so careful not to annoy me, too,' Bernie went on, snuggling back down next to Peter, who replaced his arm around her shoulders. 'It always used to drive me mad the way he seemed to want to be the strong man looking after the little woman, and these diaries show that he was really trying to understand and let me have my way. Oh Peter! I do love him so much.'

She put her right arm round Peter's waist and he drew her closer to him with his left. She settled her head against his chest, just under his chin. The tears rolled slowly down both of their faces.

'What was it that Bernie had said in that email to Eddie?' Peter thought. '*We're like two cripples holding together hoping that by leaning on one another somehow we'll both manage to stay upright.* Yes, that about sums it up,' he thought.

THANK YOU

Thank you for taking the time to read DESPISE NOT THY MOTHER. If you enjoyed it, please consider telling your friends or posting a short review. Word of mouth is an author's best friend and much appreciated. Thank you,

Judy.

MORE ABOUT BERNIE AND HER FRIENDS

Bernie features in four more full-length books.

- Changing Scenes of Life: Jonah Porter's life story, told through the medium of his favourite hymns.
- Awayday: a traditional 'whodunnit' set amongst the dons of an Oxford college.
- Two Little Dickie Birds: a murder mystery for DI Peter Johns and his Sergeant, Paul Godwin.
- Murder of a Martian: DI Peter Johns and DCI Jonah Porter are compelled to work together on solving a double murder.

Read more about Bernie Fazakerley and her friends and family at https://sites.google.com/site/llanwrdafamily/

See her latest news on Facebook here:
https://www.facebook.com/Bernie.Fazakerley.Publications

Follow Bernie on Twitter: https://twitter.com/BernieFaz.

ABOUT THE AUTHOR

Like her main character, Bernie Fazakerley, Judy Ford is an Oxford graduate and a mathematician. Unlike Bernie, Judy grew up in a middle-class family in the South London stockbroker belt. After moving to the North West and working in Liverpool, Judy fell in love with the Scouse people and created Bernie to reflect their unique qualities.

As a Methodist Local Preacher, Judy often tells her congregation, "I see my role as asking the questions and leaving you to think out your own answers." She carries this philosophy forward into her writing and she hopes that readers will find themselves challenged to think as well as being entertained.